Violent Inquiry

"Give us the picture, Professor. We know that much now, it was a picture, a framed picture—"

"A picture?" Chandler croaked.

"A document," the smaller man whined. "Maybe a document—"

"Bill Davis didn't give me anything," Chandler cried, *"nothing.* . . . Now, goddamnit, let me see those credentials or get out. . . ."

The big man's fist moved like a large, brutal piece of machinery, faster than Chandler could quite register. The inside of his upper lip had shredded against his front teeth and he felt blood on his face. His entire body and mind felt incapacitated at the shock of such a blow, such overt violence. He kept his eyes closed, waiting for more. One punch, he reflected with part of his mind, one brief economical punch from a professional and the machine comes apart, the protective ramparts of civilization collapse, the barbarians are within the gates and you're left bleeding and gasping and exhausted. . . .

Porkpie cleared his throat: "Now, Professor, that was just to get your attention, y'know? Let that be an end to it."

Books by Thomas Gifford

The Glendower Legacy
The Man from Lisbon

Published by POCKET BOOKS

THE GLENDOWER LEGACY

A novel by
Thomas Gifford

PUBLISHED BY POCKET BOOKS NEW YORK

*For Rachel
and Tom*

**POCKET BOOKS, a Simon & Schuster division of
GULF & WESTERN CORPORATION
1230 Avenue of the Americas, New York, N.Y. 10020**

Copyright © 1978 by Thomas Gifford

Published by arrangement with G. P. Putnam's Sons
Library of Congress Catalog Card Number: 78-9818

ISBN: 0-671-82678-6

First Pocket Books printing September, 1979

10 9 8 7 6 5 4 3 2 1

Trademarks registered in the United States and other countries.

Printed in the U.S.A.

I am not I;
he is not he;
they are not they.

Glendower
> I can call spirits from the vasty deep.

Hotspur
> Why, so can I, or so can any man;
> But will they come when you do call for them?

Glendower
> Why, I can teach you, cousin, to command
> The devil.

Hotspur
> And I can teach thee, coz, to shame the devil
> By telling the truth; tell truth and shame
>   the devil.
> If thou have power to raise him, bring him
>   hither,
> And I'll be sworn I have power to shame him
>   hence.
> O, while you live, tell truth and shame the
>   devil!

> > > Shakespeare
> > > *Henry IV, Part I*

Prologue

VALLEY FORGE

January 1778

William Davis stood sentry duty ankle-deep in the crusty snow, watching the moon slide out from behind the clouds long enough to give the slopes above the Schuylkill River an eerie, metallic grayness—a bright, unearthly gray he'd never seen before. He shook his head: you couldn't touch a color, he knew that, but this gray was something else, it was alive. But that was crazy. The hunger did bad things, not just to your guts but inside your head, too. He listened to his stomach rattle, empty but for the godawful firecake and rice . . . Firecake, invented in hell and sent by personal messenger to Valley Forge, a little flour, a lot of water, baked brittle and indigestible as a skimming stone on hot flat rocks. A bit of rice flavored with vinegar to keep away the scurvy.

Yet he knew he was one of the lucky ones: he had shoes, his feet were still feet, not bloody lumps dangling from scrawny ankles gone black with frostbite and gangrene, and he had a decent heavy coat, more new than old, sent him by his father back in Cambridge. He sighed and felt the breath crystallize on his moustache, in the hairs of his nostrils. His face felt like glass when he touched it. With the thick coat studded with heavy brass buttons he may well have been the best-dressed common soldier in the encampment, though the garment was already soaking up the thick smoke which hung impenetrably in each of the cabins built since their arrival on the bluffs above the Schuylkill . . .

3

He dug his toenails into the soles of his boots until he was clenching his teeth against the pain.

God, how he hated the smoke and the cold and the firecake!

A thousand cabins had been built with axes the only tools. The thatched roofs leaked, the dirt floors never warmed, the green wood they used for fires was as bad as a smudge pot hurled by redcoats into each cabin . . .

But still he was not so badly off. His friend, Ben Edwards, twenty-two just like himself, had been without shoes, had stood guard with his raw feet in his hat, had fallen ill with the dysentery which had done for him a week ago . . . they had amputated his blackened, frozen legs before he'd died but it had been almost for practice. No way could poor old Ben have made it. The dysentery was so bad, it was everywhere, the cabins reeked of the godawful watery shit of the lads whose lives were draining right damn out of them.

The moon was gone again and the cloud cover looked suddenly thicker, permanent, making it a very dark night with only the wind shrieking against the tree line. He had to take a piss. He looked toward the thick stand of trees. He sure as hell wasn't going to take a piss out here in the wind. He'd heard tell, in fact, of a man with a frozen thing—he'd heard tell it had just plain fallen off. He didn't know if that was a true story but there was no point in finding out by personal test.

No, it could be worse, it was worse all around him. He had developed a case of the scabies, though, and when he scratched at himself he thought of the scabies as his war wounds. The only treatment was to have a friend rub your body with the stinking mixture of sulfur and tallow. Christ! Would he ever lie naked with a girl again? It surely seemed impossible while you were standing out in the cold feeling the sulfur and tallow half freeze on your chest and back. Yet, he smiled and heard his beard crackle, he was better off than most. You had to keep remembering that and it wasn't always easy. Shit, there was a time at Germantown when he'd thought he was a goner for sure . . .

But to serve under General Washington, well, that

4

was worth a lot of agony. That thought had gotten him through many a bad night and many a tough scrape, stories he'd someday tell his grandchildren . . . stories of the days he'd served in Washington's army. What a man old George was! William had first seen him at Cambridge Common, a large, broad-bottomed, muscular figure, looking the way a soldier who would ask you to follow him into battle should look . . . almost a man to hide behind if the going got too tough.

He finally pushed off, sinking through the jagged snow with each step, toward the black mass of trees. The wind moaned the closer he got. He remembered how the dark forest used to frighten him as a boy back in Massachusetts. Now all it meant was shelter from the wind and a place to release himself. He grinned at the recollection of boyhood, heard his beard tinkle like breaking glass.

Oh, hell, he knew what some of his fellows said about Washington, the barbs and insults and rude behind-the-back gestures and unjust criticisms. He'd heard them all and he'd like to see them say it to old George's face! Most of the dumb bastards couldn't even read or write! Let 'em carp, damn fools . . . He'd heard other, wiser men say that no other army on earth could have stuck it out the way Washington and his men had. They'd earned the respect of the world, he'd heard them say. By jiminy, that told you all you needed to know about George Washington.

He did his business, felt his body relax out of the wind's battering. Snow blew across the crust, rattled in the night, sifted among the trees. Nothing else moved along the tree line. He kicked a tree trunk, keeping the blood circulating. It was better sheltering there out of the wind. He felt in his pocket for his pipe, remembered he had run out of tobacco, stared into the darkness of the small forest that seemed so large. His eyes were adjusting to the deeper blue-black. Maybe a brief reconnaissance mission into the inviting shelter was called for: he wasn't quite certain who he was guarding against out here in the cold but whoever, wouldn't they be most likely to gather in the woods?

5

He picked up his musket which he'd rested against a trunk. It was like descending into a cave, the deep blue-blackness smelling only of the cold and snow closing in around him. Thirty yards into it he looked back but there was nothing to see, only darkness. Above him, glimpsed among the treetops, the clouds were only a shade or two toward gray. The fear he felt in his chest took him by surprise. He stopped, wiped clammy sweat from his forehead, and blinked. He'd heard of men getting lost in thickets, running themselves to death, hurtling wildly, breathlessly in circles until they fell and froze . . . But panic wasn't in his nature. He knew he was ten minutes from the tree line and he felt he could calmly feel his way back by following his tracks. He breathed deeply, peered around him.

That was when he first smelled smoke. He was too far from the encampment to smell those fires . . . He sniffed, closing his eyes. The wind that penetrated the woods carried the scent; as he turned, trying to judge the direction from which it came, it grew stronger. It was coming from deeper into the woods, no question of that, and his curiosity bloomed like a night flower. Who the devil could it be? Maybe one of the lads had wandered off, gotten lost, needed help. It was farfetched, but then Valley Forge was farfetched. He moved on toward the smell of smoke, forgetting the fears of a few moments before.

Another ten minutes of slow going and he stopped again. The smell was markedly stronger; William Davis was markedly tireder. He rested for a moment, then looked as determinedly as he could toward the apparent source of the smoke. Through the phalanx of trees he glimpsed for an instant a flickering flame, tiny, almost imperceptible but, yes, he was sure it was there. He was husbanding his strength, saw no reason to cry out. In any case, he was still too far away and the wind had picked up. He pushed on, the musket growing heavier with each step.

Moving closer he picked out shadows moving among the trees as the little gusts caught the fire, pushed it this way and that. Wind swirled around him as he picked his way through the snow which was softer in the woods, finer, not so deep. Next, much to his surprise, he caught snatches of conversation, voices borne on the wind then gone, then back again . . . It obviously wasn't some poor bastard who'd wandered off and gotten lost. There were several voices. He heard laughter, then the wind shifted and he was left in silence. But the glow of the fire was brighter and the trees were thinning. There was a small clearing ahead of him. He pushed closer, moving stealthily though he couldn't have said precisely why.

He stopped at last at the edge of the clearing, still hidden in the darkness. There was three—no, four—men, large and bulky in greatcoats, standing and sitting around a fire in the shelter provided by a large lean-to. Their faces were obscured by shadow. They seemed intent on their discussion. As he watched he was conscious of sweat soaking his long underwear, turning it wet and cold against his flesh, making the damnable scabies itch like bites. He wasn't sure what to do but he was quite sure of two things: he was inexplicably afraid and he wanted very much to find out who these men were . . .

All four were now seated. One of them pitched another log onto the fire. Unexpectedly the wind died. The silence brushed their voices closer, but he was concerned only with the sound of his own breathing which struck him as deafening. He held a glove to his mouth, sunk his teeth into it, half gagging. Words came to him from the men, words he could just distinguish without grasping their meaning.

He could not make out the color or markings on their greatcoats; everything looked uniformly black at this distance, in the shifting, blowing campfire light. But seeing the coats wasn't necessary. He bit down harder on the glove, feeling his heart hammering, afraid. They were English, he'd have bet his life on it. He knew the accents; sure, the colonial gentry had that English sound when they spoke and many of them were as loyal as he was himself but the real English, from England, had a different sound. There was no mistaking

7

it: he'd heard them all his life in Boston and he knew an Englishman's voice. At least three of them were English but the fourth, a large squatting figure, close to the fire with his back to William, might have been anyone. He hadn't spoken so far as William could tell, hadn't moved except to reach forward and poke at the fire. He seemed to be listening, staring intently at the fire, while the others talked.

What in God's name had he stumbled on? Was it the beginning of a surprise winter attack? The men had been told such a thing was impossible, that the winter was as cold for the Redcoats as for themselves . . . but what did a twenty-two-year-old foot soldier know about such things? It was all rumor and made-up stories and outright lies—maybe this was the beginning and, God forbid, maybe he was going to be the first victim . . .

He couldn't hear the question but the squatting figure spoke, still looking at the fire. The other three stood or sat watching him, the firelight flickering on their featureless faces. He was an American.

"And how do *you* think the army is? Cold, starving, dying of dysentery, frightened. *I* am frightened myself, dealing with such as you . . . A knife in the back for my reward . . . That's what frightens me, sir!" He spoke strongly and the words carried across the clearing, frustration and dark anger held only just in check. "You ask for information, you demand particulars—Heaven forfend! Look about you! General Winter, sir . . . An army of untrained citizens, without even the meagerest supplies—"

One of the Englishmen said something while another laughed. There was sympathy in the laughter, as if the man were afraid of further angering the American.

"No, damn you," the squatting man said. "Do you think me mad? Deliver the army! Have I come so low as this, dealing with imbeciles?" He threw the log in his left hand into the fire. Sparks showered, flared. "No, I will not—*cannot*—deliver the Continental army! How can one man deliver an army, even such an army as this? There are great and honest men who will choose to fight to the death—brave men. Men who believe we

8

can outlast you . . . And you, sirs, lead me to think they may be right, after all—"

"And you, my man," one of the Englishmen said sharply, "are in too deep to harbor such a thought! Remember your role in this, if you please."

"Why try to frighten me? I am well past that . . . all that frightens me is your treachery. The knife in the dark . . . I'd almost welcome it, sir, and believe me, I'm hard to kill. I'd get a hand on you, sir, and you'd be dead afore me!"

"Come, come," a peacemaker said. "This is pointless . . ."

"Remember, I'm not a joking man," the American said. "This is serious business." He paused still without even shifting on his haunches. "Whatever you may think, I am trying to save this land—from defeat, from scoundrels and jackals. You understand me not . . . my motives are beyond you. We can use each other and I bear it. Only just."

"You cannot deliver the army," the peacemaker said. "We realize that . . . not even—well, no one can deliver an army."

"The point is, it's not worth delivering, don't you see that? That kind of thing would only increase your problems. We must appear to fight to an honorable peace, not quite a surrender, but a peace on your terms —your *generous* terms. Then old King George can sleep soundly again. Not before . . ."

"Your own sleep will not be exactly troubled . . ." The harshest of the three Englishmen stood over the squatting figure. "You will be rewarded, as you damned well know—"

"It's a dice roll. Your word means nothing to me— my reward is to see the country whole again, at peace with the crown . . . a crown that understands her children . . ."

"I daresay you will not reject our offerings." He stalked away toward the trees where William was standing. He stood stock still, watched as the man stopped and wheeled abruptly back toward the fire. William shook with the enormity of what he was witnessing.

Treason . . . somehow, he had to see the crouching man whose shape blotted out the fire. The army and Washington himself were being sold out by this man, this shape without a face whose voice was distorted by the shifting winds in the snowy clearing. He was torn: to get away from this place—but to see the man, the traitor.

"You must sign these papers," the returning Englishman said. "We must have them as security—"

"Blackmail, that is the word, sir!"

"As you will. You must sign." He spread the sheets on a campaign stool and drew a writing case from the folds of his greatcoat. The warmth of his body must have kept the ink from freezing. "Your code name— this acknowledges your code name. *Glendower* . . . Just put the signature on it. You've done it before." He laughed scornfully, placing the ink and pen on the camp stool.

William willed the American to turn around, to reveal himself, though in the shadowy light he might not have been able to make out the features for future identification. In any case, the man remained hunched over.

At precisely that moment, as the pen was being handed back to the argumentative Englishman, the sound of cracking branches and heavy footfalls reached both William Davis and the four men in the clearing. William turned too quickly to see who it might be, tripped over the musket, and fell with a gasp to his knees. The large American turned at the sound of William's falling and the Englishmen looked off toward his right where the other sounds seemed to be coming from.

A cry came from the new arrivals who crashed and blundered through the trees and underbrush: "Hey! Who is it? Is it you, Harry?" It made no sense to William but the large man, the American, was fumbling in his coat for a pistol which came quickly to view, huge, in his hand. He was pointing it toward William who grabbed his musket, spit out the glove, and struggled to crawl behind a tree. "God damn it! We're surrounded . . ." As the American spoke he fired a ball at William who heard it smash into the tree about a foot from his face, splinters flying. The angry flash from the pistol briefly illuminated the man's face but William was ducking, and saw only the pinkness of the face, none of what it signified. He felt his almost empty bladder let loose in his trousers. The man was reloading, coming toward him, but the cries of the newcomers stopped him. Two men broke into the clearing, one of the Englishmen fired point-blank into a face before him and a godawful screech pierced the heavy quiet. The man staggered back, moaning, hands to what had been his face, and fell dead in the snow, his feet jerking. The Englishmen and the traitor fled back across the clearing, kicking the fire to embers in the snow. The soldiers, encumbered by their muskets which weren't much good at close range, stumbled clumsily after them, shouting. Another pistol shot exploded as the conspirators reached the tree line across the clearing. No one fell and the sounds of several men crashing through the underbrush filled the night. As if by magic the clearing was empty but for the dead Continental.

Reacting instinctively, William darted across the twenty-five feet of open space to the dying campfire and picked up the piece of paper from the stool, felt it catch on a splinter and tear. Afraid to wait he stuffed what he had into his pocket, turned and caught his coat on a sharp edge jutting out from the lean-to. Driven by fear he desperately yanked away, heard his coat rip, and charged back into the covering darkness of the trees. He couldn't find his musket; he must have missed the exact spot—he heard from the darkness another explosion followed by a strangled cry and a shout, "Over here, over here!" Another explosion cut the voice, separated it from life with awesome abruptness. All of the firing had been from pistols: the Continentals were reduced by three and not a musket had been fired. He didn't know how many of them there were but going back to look for Harry, whoever he was, had cost them their lives.

Afraid to move, he leaned against a tree feeling his wet trouserfront freeze stiff. He heard no more skirmishing but the sounds growing faint of what he assumed were his comrades—what was left of them—escaping back through the woods. What must they think, he wondered. Three men dead—Christ, what to do? How had the quiet night turned into this? He shook uncontrollably, like a man with a fever.

Were the men he spied on gone for good? He hardly thought so: they'd taken nothing with them when they'd fled. But where were they? He had to wait. He couldn't face the risk of running into them in the dark; obviously they thought nothing of killing . . . He couldn't fall asleep for fear of freezing to death; he couldn't move for fear of signaling his position. He sat finally, waited. It must have been an hour before he heard them returning from across the clearing. At their first sounds he began his own stealthy departure. He'd vomited on his sleeve. He smelled himself. No musket, a torn coat, a scrap of paper in his pocket, trousers frozen with piss, witness to three murders and high treason . . .

And the fear had just begun.

The next day William Davis was asked nothing about his lost musket. It was a large encampment intent on surviving, not fighting. He heard rumors about three newly missing men but there was no official announcement, just vague rumors nobody cared much about. There had been no bodies found: William surmised that the three dead men were being written off as deserters, which was precisely what their terrified companions had actually done—deserted, gone home, leaving Valley Forge behind them.

William pondered what to do. Could he tell anyone, without proof? Then he remembered the piece of paper which was still in his trouser pocket. Alone, he peeled it loose and looked at the words, smudged and soiled but still legible. All but the top corner of the sheet had survived. He read it, his vision hazy from the constant feeling of dizziness, and felt himself go faint, his legs soften.

He couldn't cope with it. He couldn't show it to anyone. He couldn't go to General Washington's headquarters, he couldn't take it to Captain Whittaker, he dared not show it to anyone—not until he'd thought it through. Surely, it couldn't be true . . . but he'd seen it happen and, by God, now he recognized the shape coming toward him with the drawn pistol. He saw it again and again when he closed his eyes, the featureless face in the flare of the pistol shot.

Befuddled and exhausted, he tied the sheet of paper along with letters from his mother to the back of a framed portrait of her which he kept at the bottom of his small kit bag. He had no place else to hide something. Then he told his bunkmate, John Higgins, to make sure his few personal effects reached his family in Cambridge should he fall victim to the dread dysentery or expire in any other way. Death was everywhere, all around him. He grew depressed as the day wore on, found himself unable to eat. He felt as if a rat were gnawing at his bowels. What was he meant to do with such an unbelievable piece of information?

That night he couldn't sleep. Past midnight, his guts in an unholy uproar, he wrapped his torn coat around his shivering body, pushed his way past his sleeping mates sprawled here and there in the cabin, went outside coughing from the ever-present smoke. He wiped soot from his eyes, felt the tallow and sulphur congealing on his flesh the moment he left the cabin. It was dark as he paced numbly through the alleyways of frozen, rutted mud and snow toward the latrine. A hard wind took his breath away as he leaned forward. At first he didn't see the two men who stepped from the shadows into his path.

"Soldier," one of them said, a soldier he'd noticed walking beside him earlier in the day. "Soldier, stand!" the man said softly. The voice was insistent. The second figure joined him, something fluttering in his outstretched hand.

"What?" William Davis said. "I've got to get to the latrine—"

"Tell us, is this yours, soldier?" The second man held out the torn shred of heavy cloth. The brass button

13

caught the light of a torch across the way. "Take a closer look, soldier. . . ."

"It's mine—I tore my coat. . . ." He was having trouble focusing his eyes. He hated it but he thought he knew what was happening inside his body: fever, unable to eat, the latrine half a dozen times that day. The significance of the torn coat escaped him until it was too late. He felt the hand clamp like a vise on his arm, couldn't resist as he was pulled into the darkness.

William Davis's body wasn't found until spring when the snow in the deep woods melted. By then no one really cared; so many men had died. No one ever noticed the stab wounds in the thawed, bloated, distended corpse.

Only the officers in charge that winter, living in the stone farmhouses, had known the truth: that William Davis had been a proven traitor, that he had consorted with British spies in the woods, and that he had been undone by a scrap of cloth left behind when he fled the scene of his treason. Only the officers in charge knew that his summary execution had been decreed to save the army a blow to morale which might have been the final cause of its disintegration.

And one officer—only one—knew an even greater truth which would forever remain buried with the ghastly remains of young William Davis.

BUCHAREST

December 1975

Nat Underhill had never really expected to see Bucharest again, not after fifty years, but here he was pushing eighty and there was the old city below his hotel window, dusted with a dry snowfall that blew like smoke in the grayness of late afternoon. No, he still couldn't quite believe it, that he'd lived to see Bucharest again. He lit his old black pipe, tasted the Louisburg Square mixture he'd smoked for years, heaved a mighty sigh of relief and satisfaction, snapped his braces, and let his mind wander toward the past, beyond his reflection in the streaked pane of glass.

Night was falling sharply, like a shade being yanked down for privacy, and it could have been the city of half a century before. He'd been a student at the time, researching Transylvanian history, and he'd fallen in love with Bucharest, the night life of the cafés, dining at midnight, the almost Spanish feeling of the city without the implied cruelty he'd found in Spain. But, in fact, it wasn't entirely the city which had smitten him, but a fetching Romanian girl with well-to-do and vaguely aristocratic parents. The war and the Russians had erased them like irrelevant markings on a blackboard, leaving Nat Underhill with something approaching a broken heart, one of life's loose ends which seems so important at the time.

But the war had replaced the girl in his thoughts. He had been stationed in London where there were, however, a good many other Romanians. They'd all made pledges to see one another when it was all over, when—

17

as Vera Lynn sang—the world was free. But, of course, they never did. History had never been kind to the Romanians, and the post-World War II era had been no different from any other. Boston and Bucharest seemed hardly to be points on the same planet.

In time, things changed. In the course of his various historical researches he had discovered the world of books, letters, journals, documents, and diaries. Not so much the reading of them—although he read them, too—but the buying, selling, and collecting of them. Coincidence worked its way with his life, and fifty years later two specific events had conspired to bring him back to Bucharest for a bittersweet farewell.

First, there had been the announcement of the convention of antiquarians set for the Christmas holidays in Bucharest—certainly an example of Romania's reaching out toward the West. But he'd needed an excuse to attend; simply seeing the city again was not enough for his frugal New England soul.

Then the Davis boy had come to see him in his elegant, cluttered little shop, tucked away on Beacon Hill literally within a stone's throw of the State House. Bill Davis was a Harvard student, stringy long hair, gold wire-rimmed spectacles, not at all designed to appeal to Nat Underhill's Brooks Brothers aplomb. However, hideously scruffy appearance notwithstanding, the Davis boy had come bearing so incredible a piece of paper that Nat Underhill had required a chair and an immediate fresh-brewed cup of English Breakfast tea.

Was it genuine, the boy had wanted to know. Was there any way to be sure?

As to the document's age, yes, of course there were ways to authenticate it. As to the validity of the contents —historically speaking—that was something else again, falling within the purview of the trained historian and the handwriting analyst. But there had been a feeling in his stuffy little office that morning, a feeling wholly unlike anything else his profession had ever produced. His heart had beaten oddly. His dry wrinkled hands had shaken when he touched the document itself. His mouth

18

had dried up. In all of the years he'd spent in the company of antique bits of paper he'd never seen anything to match it. Never . . .

Having urged the lad to put the prize in a safe deposit box after showing it to his most trusted professor—and Harvard's Colin Chandler was preeminent in the field— Nat settled back in his creaking swivel chair and watched the late autumn wind whipping at the politicians who seemed to spend their days hurrying back and forth past his office window conducting the affairs of the Commonwealth. As of that moment, Bucharest was a most reasonable destination. Such a document, dating from the winter of 1778, was almost beyond simple monetary value . . . but one would be required to set a figure. But even its very existence would create a storm of interest and debate. And even more than that there was the satisfaction to be derived, the opportunity to place a capstone on his career. That was beyond valuation of any kind. He would now become a footnote in the history books—no, considerably more than that. He smiled. Puffing a pipe, smoke swirling around his head, he arranged for his flight to Basel and the train accommodations thereafter, as well as the reservation at the Athénée-Palace in Bucharest.

Nat had debated when to unveil his spectacular find: he wanted it to be cast in the proper setting, a climax to the week. Europeans were not easy to impress when it came to historical documents, their own histories being so much lengthier and therefore richer than Nat Underhill's. But they were knowledgeable, they knew American history, and the photocopy of the document he had in his possession would astound them, even if it wasn't a thousand years old. It was the sort of thing men in their profession dreamed about, more often than not went a lifetime without ever once finding—the document he was thinking of himself as agent for wasn't simply a nice, bold reinforcement of history . . . this one *changed* history!

The final night of his stay in Bucharest was obviously the time. He arranged for a group of his old friends to dine as his guests at a warm, dark, odiferous cellar

19

restaurant he remembered unchanged from the thirties. There were six of them, as well as a young Romanian called Grigorescu who had ingratiated himself with the older men during the weeks, acting as an informal guide to the new Bucharest. Grigorescu was not yet thirty, full-faced, pale, always seeming somewhat over-heated in his sweater and a suitcoat straining its seams. His complexion tended to pastiness with deep-set, cavernously shadowed eyes: he reminded Nat Underhill of certain blind men. But he was quiet, helpful, nervous, anxious to please and gather in the wisdom of the elderly westerners.

Crowded around a large corner table, shoulder to shoulder and made especially convivial by the heat and the rich Romanian red wines, they smoked and relived the past and ate plates of *mamaliga* and the tiny skewered meatballs called *mititei* and sausage and steak and the sour soup and devastatingly heavy casserole, leaned back exhausted with fruit and cheese and *tzuica*. They toasted Nat Underhill, teasing him about his advanced age though three of them were past seventy themselves. Grigorescu smiled shyly, perspired, wiped his forehead, listened, interpreted specifics with the waiter. Finally they lit their pipes and cigars and Nat Underhill looked around at their faces. Then he withdrew a plain envelope from his pocket and tapped it on the wine-stained tablecloth. The candles had burned low, wax melting in ornate patterns, dripping.

"Gentlemen," Nat Underhill said, "I have a story to tell you . . . An example of the sort of wonders lurking around each corner in our line of work. You never know, Grigorescu, what may happen tomorrow. You are just beginning . . . and I am nearing the end, but Fate can take any one of us by the hand at any time." The fat young man nodded solemnly. "Less than a month ago Fate brought me the most remarkable document of my life . . ." He waved the envelope slowly before him, like a conjurer about to produce a rabbit from someone's ear. "It came out of the blue . . . and it will force a rewriting of the history of the American revolutionary war! Nothing less . . . and you know me,

I have never been given to hyperbole. Let me explain . . ."

When he was done with the story he passed the photocopy around the table. He recognized true admiration in their faces: such men didn't show it often and when they did there wasn't a doubt. He smiled watching them. This was the payoff, the closest any antiquarian could come to a Nobel: the sincere, unspoken praise of his fellows.

They said their farewells in the grand lobby of the Athénée-Palace. Nat was checking out early in the morning. Some of his colleagues he'd be seeing in New York come spring, others—most particularly young Grigorescu—he would surely never see again. He slapped the Romanian on the back, shook his moist hand repeatedly, and tottered off to bed. Nat Underhill had never, all things considered, been happier than that winter night in Bucharest with the wind rattling the windows of his bedchamber and the radiators banging.

MOSCOW
February 1976

Maxim Petrov, director of the Komitet Gossudarstven-
noi Bezopastnosti, arrived for work in a good mood.
The carburetor problem on his black Zil limousine, a
car worth seventy-five thousand dollars which he felt
justified in thinking should work regardless of the
temperature outdoors, had at last been solved. His
chauffeur was for once in a halfway decent mood, and
his wife had been in an excellent frame of mind. She
was going shopping at No. 2 Granovsky, The Bureau
of Passes, where she had promised to pick him up a
case of Courvoisier cognac and a new Louis Vuitton
datebook. They were—all three of them—rested and
fit, having spent a long weekend at the *dacha* forty miles
from Moscow before returning late Sunday evening.

Though Moscow was in the grip of a winter somewhat more ghastly than usual, Petrov's mind was else-
where. It was the same every year at this time and the
Americans were to blame. He whistled "Oh, What a
Beautiful Morning" as he entered his private office with
its snowbound view of Red Square. *The New York
Times* was folded on his desk, alongside *The Sporting
News*. As director of the KGB there were very few
people to whom he had to answer; none of them knew
about *The Sporting News*.

Continuing to whistle he sat down behind his newish,
antiseptic, glass-covered desk, took a sip of hot coffee
from a cardboard cup, and flipped the *Times* open to
the sports section. His mind was far from Moscow . . .
in places like St. Petersburg, Orlando, Vero Beach,

25

Tampa. Spring training was under way, the pitchers and catchers and rookies were in camp already. God, how long since he'd seen a ball game! He could close his eyes and watch the ball soaring against the blue Caribbean sky as the crack of the bat lingered like a gunshot trapped in a canyon.

Baseball. It had all begun in the thirties when he'd been at Harvard and continued in New York when he'd worked toward his doctorate at Columbia. The Red Sox at tiny Fenway Park, later the Yankees, Giants, and Dodgers . . . the Stadium, the Polo Grounds, Ebbets Field. A ball game every day his studies or teaching assignments allowed. Baseball was the real reason he was so fond of Fidel, personally fond; the man had played the game, knew what it was all about.

Petrov had no illusions about himself: he was a relatively lazy bureaucrat whose primary efforts had been aimed all along at preserving his job rather than at carrying off great espionage coups. He had come to intelligence work, both internal and external, during World War II, thereby avoiding as much of the unpleasantness in the West with the Germans as was possible. Beria had liked him, had mistakenly thought he was loyal and uninspired and no threat. In fact, Petrov thought Beria a beast and helped engineer his downfall. On the whole, he found the entire espionage establishment, East and West, a very dim business at the best of times. He had watched with detached amusement as it had grown exponentially, increasing its inefficiency in direct ratio to its size. After all, it was impossible to keep secrets of any kind if the other side really wanted to find out.

In half the countries of the world the spies were falling all over each other. Singularly unimportant and frequently undesirable little men were getting killed in the course of one intelligence agency or another justifying its own existence. Yet the spy himself was outdated; in his place, the technicians and the clerks—the fellows with the high-sensitivity microphones and the long-distance cameras, the scientists who fired the satellites into place overhead, the fellows who read and clipped the newspapers—the boring people with safe, sane, secure jobs were the spies who mattered. The responsibilities of the KGB were so vast that he occasionally wondered how anyone imagined they got it all done, even with the half million employees . . . Which was the more difficult task, he'd asked himself, keeping our citizens inside the borders or keeping an eye peeled on the rest of the world? Maintaining surveillance of the forty-two thousand miles of Soviet borders was, for one example, an absurd responsibility on the face of it. Well, at least they no longer had to keep track of the nuclear warheads . . .

He sighed, glanced out the wide thermal-pane window at the ridiculous line of people, thousands of them, snaking across the Square, half obscured by snow which seemed to hang from the low gray clouds like a curtain. Every day the line was there, the KGB lads keeping them quiet and orderly and frisking them for bombs. He winced at the thought: some nut blowing Lenin and his tomb to pieces . . . Talk about a public relations problem! The unnerving thing was, the friskers found a bomb of one kind or another about once a month. On the other hand, Petrov supposed that a maniac's exploding device might be the only way he'd ever find out for sure if it really was Lenin or a wax figure . . . It *looked* like wax but you never knew. And he'd never had the nerve to come right out and ask anyone who might know.

He finished Red Smith's column and folded the paper back to the entertainment section. He was dying to see *A Chorus Line,* thought for a moment of taking up the possibility of an exchange program with the snotty bastards in Cultural Affairs. He sipped the coffee which was growing cold and beginning to taste of cardboard. It was Monday morning. He frowned at his gold Rolex. Fifteen minutes yet.

It was a boring age and the Monday morning meetings added immeasurably to his boredom. His mind wandered back to spring training. Arden Sanger, director of the Central Intelligence Agency, was a good friend but he could take baseball or leave it, a state of mind Petrov deplored. They did occasionally correspond during the football season since Arden was, predictably, an enthusiastic fan of the Washington Redskins. Like old jocks the world over, they did not shrink from the occasional practical jokes. It fit their natures.

As Petrov walked down the hallway to his meeting, he wondered what new absurdities would come flickering his way like hot smashes to third: that's what he felt like as he approached the large conference room, an old third-sacker whose ultimate responsibility was to get in front of those hot smashes down the line like Red Rolfe at Yankee Stadium so long ago. Well, God help Mother Russia if one ever got past him.

Petrov tried at all times, and usually with considerable success, to keep his sense of history, perspective, and humor intact and on call. But the Monday morning staff meetings were his severest tests. Dull, very serious men each bearing a crumb and the earnest hope of an approving glance or word from Petrov himself. He tried to pass his approval around evenhandedly, tried to present a solid, interested visage upon which they might gaze admiringly for a few hours and from which they might draw some strength. But it was just plain murder as they used to say in Brooklyn, no other word for it.

Midway into the third hour a case officer caught his attention with a report from a fieldman in Bucharest called Grigorescu.

"I search my brain," Petrov said, rolling a very ripe cigar between his broad spatulate fingertips, "and I find nothing about this Grigorescu."

"No, no, Comrade Director, you would have no reason—he's a new man, very junior. Very, very junior, actually."

"God, are things really so slow these days?" He glanced at the severe face of the man scribbling in a shorthand book. "No, secretary, if you'd be so kind as to strike that . . . Thank you. Now, comrade, what has this infant Grigorescu to tell us?"

The bald, portly man in a brown suit pursed his plump lips and waved a forefinger before his face like a metronome. "Allow me, please, to preface my remarks with a comment on this report—the fact is, Comrade Director, it strikes me as exceedingly unlikely that you'll believe a word of it—"

"You find that unusual?" Petrov smiled against his better judgment. "You suppose I believe this kind of thing? Ever?" He was the only man in the room smiling. "No," he said to the secretary, "no, you don't need to record that. Now, Rogoshin, go on with your unlikely tale. And allow me to correct myself. The fact is, I find myself willing to believe almost anything these days. Say on . . ."

"Well, let me begin at the beginning," Rogoshin said, frowning. "The youthful Grigorescu is alarmingly thorough, I'm afraid. It all begins with an American from Boston called Underhill and another American who died two hundred years ago at a place called Valley Forge . . ."

An hour later Maxim Petrov was back in the antiseptic office standing at the window, staring down at the line of people in Red Square. The line never seemed to change but Petrov was aware of his own shift in mood. He was smiling, full of wonder at how unlikely the sources of amusement can occasionally be. He was contemplating Harvard College, Cambridge, Massachusetts, not normally a cause for merriment, but in this instance pure inspiration . . . On his lined yellow pad he had written three words, carefully underlining them twice. He turned back from the window chuckling. He'd get the ball rolling right away. It was just too priceless . . . He buzzed for his private secretary and contemplated the yellow pad.

JOKE ON ARDEN!

His secretary found the great man laughing aloud behind his immaculate desk.

BOSTON

March 1976

Monday

Bill Davis sat at the counter of the Zum Zum restaurant around the corner from Harvard Square, sucked at a Lucky Strike, and pushed the egg-smeared breakfast plate away from the cuff of his red-and-black flannel lumberjack's shirt. He was trying to place the face of the man at the next counter: he'd seen the guy before but he couldn't quite remember where, when. But you couldn't miss a black-and-white houndstooth porkpie hat, not in the 1970s. It had a little green feather sticking out of the band and the houndstooth motif was carried on in the pattern of the gray raincoat. He couldn't remember seeing a costume like that since he'd been a little boy and his father had been similarly gotten up. The man was sipping steaming coffee and writing with a Bic ballpoint in a little brown spiral notebook. Bill focused on him, blurring several dangling sausages which were hanging between them, presumably for decorative effect. As if cued in to Bill's curiosity the man looked up from his notebook and smiled, open and disingenuous like an on-the-go insurance salesman about to undergo a mid-life crisis. There was a vaguely anxious, friendly, not absolutely trustworthy look to the man's face, particularly around the eyes and at the fixed, upturned corners of his mouth. He smiled again at Bill across the fifteen feet, nodded fractionally as strangers do when their eyes happen to meet. Standing closer he'd have commented on the weather.

Bill smiled back, took another hit on the Lucky, and slid off the stool. His corduroy jacket was still damp.

He wrapped the maroon-and-white muffler around his throat. The man still sipped his coffee, staring out at the midday traffic working its way, headlamps on, through the cold rain. Bill decided the guy would have voted for Nixon. He picked up his green baize bookbag and headed for Adams House where he lived on the top floor, with an angled view of *The Lampoon* building.

He sat at his desk beneath the Escher poster with the birds somehow flying in both directions at once and lit another Lucky. In the circular glow from the old goose-necked lamp he carefully cut strips of masking tape, fixed the cardboard backing to an antique framed likeness of one of his ancestors, a woman who had been young and shy-appearing long before the revolutionary war. The contents of the frame bulked thickly and the taping went slowly, punctuated by exhalations of *shit!* and *goddamn it!* He squinted against the smoke, finally ran his thumbs along the backside of the frame, satisfying himself that the tape was secure.

Stubbing out the cigarette, he tore the cellophane from a package of plain brown wrapping paper. Still working with meticulous care he covered the framed picture with several thicknesses of wrapping, taped the folded ends and concluded his operation by trussing up the entire parcel with stout white twine. He held it before him, dropped it flat on the desk to test the padding of paper, and sighed contentedly. He looked at his watch. He had just enough time to get up to the Square, stop at the Coop, and get to Chandler's office in the history department before the office hours ended. He emptied several books and pens out of the bookbag and slid the brown parcel in, cinched the bag tight.

He was leaving the cluttered, frenzied activity of the Coop, standing in the spacious portal across from the newspaper kiosk and subway entrance, watching the rain and tightening his muffler, when he saw the man again. You couldn't miss the silly hat and the matching raincoat. He was leaning against one of the pillars near the sidewalk reading a newspaper. Now there was a second man with him, large, well over six feet, more than two hundred pounds, wearing one of those tan rain hats with the little plaid band, the brim turned down all the way around. Hat freaks . . . Maybe it was some new fag thing, hats, like signet rings on your little finger and keys on your hip pocket. Bookbag over his shoulder Bill pushed through his fellow shelterers, past the two in their funny hats. The big one caught his eye this time, quickly looked away, yawning nervously, covering his cavernous mouth. Bill Davis shrugged and jogged across the rainslick street to the kiosk, heading for the Yard past mounds of discolored snow piled along the curbsides like garbage.

Through the clouded glass on his door, Professor Chandler's office was dark. The office hours on the card were being precisely observed: he'd arrived two minutes late. Crap . . . He stood by the door fuming, considered penciling an obscenity on the thumbtacked card, then walked back down the musty-smelling, overheated hallway to the secretary's office. She was sitting at a wooden desk copy-editing a typewritten manuscript, chewing on a blue pencil.

"Chandler's gone," he said.

"You got it," she said without looking up.

"Will you take a message for him?"

"Why don't you just give him a ring tomorrow?" She glanced at him quizzically. "He might not stop in here for his messages, y'know?"

"Look, it's important. Gimme the pencil, okay?"

She made a face at the extended interruption. He scribbled: *Prof. Chandler—Please call me at KL-5-8786 as soon as possible. Big Deal! Bill Davis.* He handed it back to the girl.

"If he comes in, y'know?" he said.

She read the note: "Big deal to you, not him." She shook her head.

"Don't worry about making value judgments, okay? Just fight fiercely, Harvard."

"You know it." She was already back in the manuscript.

He left shaking his head. It was the tail end of winter

35

and everybody had cabin fever. Next thing he'd be wearing a nifty little porkpie himself.

When he left the building he turned toward the Square, hurried through the slowly diminishing drizzle past Matthews Hall. He beat the light to the subway entrance, failing to notice the man in the porkpie hat and the man with the rain hat who were stopped by traffic on the Yard side of the street. He picked up a *Christian Science Monitor* at the kiosk and dived down the stairway, bookbag banging his back. The train to Park Street was waiting when he burst through the turnstile; he leaped aboard as the doors were closing. Turning, he saw them. The houndstooth hat stood out from the crowd. They were waiting in the line to purchase tokens. Bill Davis felt an unaccountable, unpleasant shiver along his spine.

Porkpie hat turned to rain hat as they stepped back from the token window. Rain hat drew a Tiparillo, cherry flavored, from its pasteboard packet, sniffed it, applied a match struck on his thumbnail. Porkpie hat coughed in the smoke, batted the fumes away.

"Brookline," he said. He was wearing black plastic-rimmed glasses now and they were speckled with rain. He looked up at his companion. "We can wait for the kid in Brookline . . . I know damn well it's in the fuckin' bookbag. That's why he went to the history office, to see his adviser—what's-his-name, Chandler."

"You don't *know* anything . . ." The big man's voice was deeper than Ivan Rubroff's. His face was round and jowly, permanently flushed, and beneath the little hat he looked like any of a million suburban golfers on a cloudy, threatening afternoon. But an edge of worry slid across Thorny's mind as he watched the smoke curl up from the Tiparillo: the big man's lips trembled, his hands shook. Thorny had seen it happen before to men in their line. Nerves going, age creeping up, too much booze, a wife who walked out: Ozzie didn't have much future, but the trick was to get him through one more job . . . keep his temper under control.

36

"I know it's the bookbag. Trust me, Ozzie."

"I'm too hungry to trust you."

"That doesn't make sense."

"Right, that's how hungry I am."

"We'll stop at a McDonald's. On the way to Brookline. He always goes home to see his folks on Tuesday nights. Never misses."

They walked through the drizzle to Brattle Street. Miraculously they'd found a parking place near Design Research. There was a ticket on the windshield, soggy beneath the wiper blade. The smaller man tore it in two, dropped it in the gutter. Ozzie had a tough time cramming himself into the red Pinto.

"Say, Oz, you know what I'm thinking?"

"Yeah, I know."

"What? Smartass—"

"You want me to be sure I've got the pliers."

"Sometimes you amaze me." He wiped his glasses with a Kleenex from a tiny package on the dashboard. "You're a damn good partner . . ." It was a lie, or a memory. Once he had been a good man and in those days their friendship had been forged; now it was a question of getting through the job, one day at a time.

"Then you can buy the Big Mac, Thorny."

Bill Davis was frightened and he didn't know why. They were the same men, but what the hell sense was there in finding anything ominous in them? They were 1950s, harmless, middle-aged. He wouldn't even have noticed them if they hadn't worn the hats. He hadn't seen them more often than he'd seen twenty other people in the Square that day; it was just that these two stuck in his mind. So why should two guys in funny hats spook him? It didn't make any sense.

He ran up the stairs at the Park Street Station, pushed through the customary pigeons who permanently inhabited the corner of Park and Tremont, and went up the hill toward Beacon Street. He took a right just short of the State House and entered a narrow doorway, past a window with discreet gold lettering. A second door, polished wood and a brass plaque, and he was in the

37

coziness of the old man's office and showroom. There were two dark-green leather wingback chairs, a small table, an electric fireplace, and a middle-aged woman in a Rosalind Russell vintage '39 suit and a graying bun. She looked up and paused at her first sight of the long blond hair and the patchy plot of beard. She'd not been in place on his previous visits.

Working up a smile, she managed, "Yes? Is there something?"

"Is Mr. Underhill in?" He smelled the old man's cigar smoke but that didn't mean he was present. He'd been smoking in the same offices for a very long time.

Before she could answer, Nat Underhill appeared in the doorway, thumbs hooked in his vest. He smiled, his watery blue eyes twinkling; he was a small man but erect, fit.

"Bill! How are you?" He motioned Bill through the doorway to his private office, hot, dry, cluttered with memorabilia, bits and pieces of a lifetime spent digging at the past. "You may lock up now, Miss Thompson, and get a head start home. Nasty weather. Be sure to take your bumbershoot, that's the girl. Now, come on, Bill, have a chair. Don't tell me you've made another find . . ." He settled down in the leather swivel chair behind the broad gleaming desk.

"Nope, same find, sir. But to tell you the truth—ah, it makes me a little nervous carrying it around." He swallowed drily. "Y'know what I mean? Say I lost it or something, the glass got broken and cut it up . . . And I don't like to leave it in my room either. No damned security, stuff always disappearing, y'know?" He put the bookbag on the desk, pulled it open, and withdrew the package. "I mean, look, I don't know if it's as valuable as you say—no offense, Mr. Underhill, I'm sure it is—"

"No offense taken, I assure you. Go on."

"But the value, that's your business. My interest is historical, what it means to all of our scholarship if it's true . . ." He shrugged. "Look, can I leave it here with you? You've got a place, a safe, something?"

"Of course, of course." Nat Underhill poured tea

from a china pot and offered it to Bill who shook his head no. Methodically he poured cream, dipped a tiny spoon of sugar. "Did you show it to Professor Chandler?"

"No, I went today but missed him. Anyway, he can come down here and the two of you—both experts, you can look it over together. It makes sense to me . . ."

"That's fine with me, Bill. We'll get together on it. No problem."

They chatted a few minutes while the heavy ormolu clock ticked loudly and the clouds darkened over Beacon Hill. They both knew the documents packed inside the frame, knew them backwards and forwards, and there was nothing left to say. And neither one of them knew just what to do with them. They'd gotten used to their staggering implications but they were at a loss as to the future . . . You couldn't just have a press conference and blurt it out, not something like this . . . The thought was absurd. But what to do? Perhaps Chandler would know.

Back outside in the rain which had become a spitting drizzle and was making the steep sidewalk slippery as night fell, Bill Davis felt relieved. Getting the damned thing off his hands was the best thing he could have done. Now it was Underhill's problem. At the newsstand among the pigeons he bought a *Penthouse, a Playboy, Time, Newsweek,* and *The Village Voice;* he stuffed them into the green bookbag, looking forward to crawling into his old bed at home with the Celtics playoff game on the radio and no class on Wednesday until noon. With luck Chandler would call him at Adams House in the afternoon. Now that the picture was gone he'd forgotten the two men in funny hats.

The smell of Big Macs and fries lingered in the Pinto's interior. Ozzie was making it worse with another cherry-scented Tiparillo, nervously chewing the mouthpiece, working his hands one on the other in his lap. The trees along the Brookline residential street were bare, grasping, streaked with rain, black in the glow from the streetlamp. Thorny had opened his window a couple of inches in an attempt to air out the car. Ozzie coughed: "God, these things really do taste like shit. Well, here he comes." He was sweating.

"Okay." Thorny folded down the corner of the page and put the book in his raincoat pocket. "First, let's just ask him for the fuckin' bookbag. Polite . . ."

"Right." Ozzie opened the door and began the task of levering himself out of the cramped front seat.

It didn't go well.

Right off the bat the kid saw them, recognized them. Ozzie's rain hat caught on the roof of the car as he struggled upward; it rolled onto the sidewalk. Thorny had gotten around the car and was standing on the sidewalk, between the kid and the front lawn of his parents' house.

"Bill Davis?" Thorny inquired politely. "Excuse me, Bill—"

"You guys!" Bill Davis stood still. "Who the hell are you guys? I've been seeing you all day . . ."

Ozzie had retrieved his hat, stood up feeling the weight of the pliers in his coat pocket. Pliers weren't going to be worth a good goddamn tonight. His head ached; he hated the taste of the cherried tobacco. He focused on the boy.

"Look, son," Thorny said, taking a step toward the kid. "Listen to me very carefully, son. We're police officers . . . we've got to have a word with you, Bill."

"About what?" Bill backed off warily.

"About your bookbag," Ozzie said. He was upright, rain hat jammed down on his large round head. Smartass Harvard kid . . . *fairy* . . .

"Goddamn it, I knew it!" Bill peered through the gloom at the two men. "But why? What the hell do the police—"

Thorny moved closer: "We've got to have your bookbag, son . . . we need your cooperation." He reached for the bookbag, calmly, slowly, anything to keep Ozzie from losing his grip. "Be reasonable, son."

"All I've got is some magazines, creepo—"

"Come on, son. Just hand it over—"

40

Bill Davis assumed a karate stance: "Don't fuck with me, asshole! I'll break your goddamned neck!"

"You're not going to give us the bag, right?" Ozzie loomed behind Thorny. "Am I right, Bill?" Ozzie's deep voice was toneless: he stood quietly, one hand jiggling in his raincoat pocket.

"You bet your ass. Buy your own goddamn *Penthouse* . . ." He began to edge onto the lawn, his hands raised like chopping devices. Lunatics on the streets of Brookline, for God's sake.

"Shit," Thorny said. "Don't be stupid, there's no point—"

Ozzie took an automatic equipped with a screw-on silencer from the quivering pocket and shot Bill Davis in the heart. As the boy fell backward the second bullet caught him in the side of the head, blowing him sideways into the grass. He went down on his face, dead. Ozzie wrenched the bookbag from his limp hand. He scowled at Thorny: "Nothing's ever easy . . ." Thorny watched, frozen, too slow to have done anything to stop it. Christ . . . he needed a drink.

The street was still deserted, low ground fog appearing like instant shrubbery. They got back into the Pinto and drove slowly away. The street was still. In the car, Thorny couldn't think of anything to say and Ozzie wore a mask of satisfaction, fingers rhythmically tightening on the pliers in his pocket. Sometimes the pliers took too long . . .

"The fact is, Thorny old pal, you fucked up."

They sat in the all-night cafeteria. An ancient wino was mopping one corner of the long, narrow, white-tiled floor. Above, the fluorescent lights flickered aggravatingly. The floor was covered with tracked-in slush. In the back behind the counter, the man yelled, "Toast the English!" for the twentieth time in ten minutes. Thorny himself stared at his toasted English muffin.

"You killed him," he said disconsolately.

"Harvard fairy bastard . . . You weren't getting anywhere, that's for damned sure."

"Well, I'm still sure it *was* in the bookbag. I'm posi-

41

tive. So he must have gotten rid of it after we lost him . . . but where?" He rubbed his eyes with his knuckles.

"Don't cry, Thorny," Ozzie cautioned. "We'll get it. Just like the old days, we'll kick a little ass, show 'em how it's done."

"My eyes are tired. I'm getting a cold."

"I've got a feeling that people are going to be mad as hell at us." Ozzie's mood darkened too quickly. Thorny saw the signs, wondered what to do: could he use Ozzie's state of mind? God, what a thought. . . .

"I wouldn't be surprised, Oz." He took a swig of coffee. With a glass of ice water he washed down three Excedrin. "Goddamn stroke books," he mused. "He could have mailed it to somebody . . . He could have given it to somebody in Boston, it was the Park Street car—"

"If he got off at Park Street."

"What we've got here, Oz, is a shitload of imponderables."

"He could have left it with Chandler . . . If he had the stroke books in the bag we wouldn't have noticed if the picture was gone."

They sat quietly, staring into the almost empty, discouragingly cold and dirty street beyond the huge naked windows. A truck rumbled by and drenched the Pinto with clinging gray crud.

"You know," Thorny said, tapping his fingers on the stack of magazines, "I sometimes wonder what the hell is so important about the picture . . . what makes them want it."

"Hell, I wonder who's putting up the money for the job—ten grand for a snatch like this." He sighed deep in his vast chest. "And now we got a dead guy and no picture—"

"I don't know about you but I'm scared to tell them." Thorny seemed to be shrinking inside his coat. He blew his nose and stared into the Kleenex.

"What else can we do?" He pleaded with his eyes, like a dog. "I need this payday, Thorny, y'know?"

"Well, let's think of something . . ."

42

"How mad are they gonna be? Really?"

"Mad. But they'll forget it when we find the stuff . . . But, Ozzie, for Chrissakes, we gotta be careful. You dig? *Careful* . . ."

In the upper reaches of the bedeviled John Hancock Building, towering over the genteel antiquity of Copley Square like a frozen shaft of silver-blue ice, three men sat around a stark table which fit perfectly with the spirit of the building. The slab of glass forming the tabletop was an inch thick, fifteen feet long, anchored well off center to a massive, squat cylinder of marble. There were three leather-and-chrome armchairs drawn up, each occupied by a tweedy gentleman who would have looked more at home at the Harvard Club on Commonwealth Avenue. Other than a chrome lamp reflecting the scene in its conical reflector, the room was empty but for some scraps of lumber, a sprinkling of sawdust, and two large sheets of plywood. As it was, there was only one remaining pane of glass, floor to ceiling; as was so common in the sixty-two-story building, the others had been blown out by the wind and replaced with plywood. From the outside it gave the building a visage not unlike that of a gap-toothed village idiot.

The oldest gentleman rubbed his palms on the bowl of his tan Dunhill Bruyère, warming them. It was cold in the naked room. Their breath hung in the air before them.

"Do you have the foggiest idea what's going on?"

"I must, Andrew. I called the meeting."

"Well, what is it? I've got to get back to Washington tonight . . . We do work for our living down there."

"You won't make it tonight. I have plans for you— and Logan's fogged in. Look . . ." He pointed out the single window. The moon shone brightly through a partly cloudy sky. "Up here, clear . . . but on the ground, rain and dense fog. We'll put you up at the Ritz." He puffed, clicking the stem against his teeth. "Liam, you too."

"The Ritz is fine." Liam had once had a full head of

43

red hair, though now it was a rusty-gray fringe of memory riding low over his ears like a dust ruffle.

"So tell us what's up . . ."

"I don't actually *know* what's up, of course, but there are some disturbing alarums going off in odd places . . . most curiously here, Boston. Two mercenaries—that is, no sustained allegiance to anyone—arrived at Logan a couple of days ago. By some miracle one of our airport personnel recognized them, let us know, and we had them followed. They haven't given any indication they've spotted us . . ." He tamped the pipe with a tiny bronze Mr. Pickwick, sucked it moistly.

"Who are they working for? Why are they here, for Christ's sake?" Andrew interrupted himself, making a tiny circle, an O, with his neat little mouth. He blinked behind wire-rimmed spectacles.

"Obviously I have neither answer. The point that concerns me is this, our Masters tell me nothing, neither confirm nor deny employment—which means that these two blokes could be working for *us* this time . . . Now I spent the day on the scrambler talking myself blue in the face, trying to get a simple yes or no, and couldn't get even a soft belch. They aren't telling!" He sighed heavily, yanked his scarf tighter at his throat. He was far from a young man; if the fact were known, he was far from well, but that was something he could handle later on. "Whoever they may be working for, they checked in at the Harvard Motor Hotel—"

Andrew expelled a long groan through the tiny circle: "This sounds like one of those goddamn defections . . . Harvard or MIT." He shook his round head and whistled softly: "Jesus, I hate those . . . the worst one, I'll never get over that—"

"Setting up a fatal car crash on one-twenty-eight," Liam mused, "is a one-time thing." He shuddered at the memory. "What a mess."

"Let's not immediately leap heavy-booted into violence. These men may be working for us, you really mustn't forget that. Somehow we're going to have to find out . . ."

44

" 'Nobel Laureate Defects,' " Andrew said. "I can see it now . . ."

"How do we find out? If our side won't tell us?"

The oldest man, pipe clamped between his teeth, stood up slowly, pushing his gnarled, blue-veined fists into the pockets of his gray herringbone jacket. He went to the one glass window, stared into the night. Below him Boston was a pink and yellow blur through the groundfog.

"We know two things. First, they've been following a Harvard student by the name of Bill Davis. Second, three hours ago they killed him and stole his book-bag . . ."

"Killed him?" There was surprisingly little emotion in Liam's voice.

"Yes, Liam. Now, I no longer am moved to give the slightest fuck in the universe what our Masters are playing at . . . I want to know who these sods are working for and I want to know why they killed Bill Davis. Find out who the boy was close to at Harvard, dig around, and watch these men . . . I want to know everything. Understood?"

Liam and Andrew nodded quietly. Liam knocked a clot of ash from the thickly caked bowl of an old black pipe.

"Andrew, you'll go back to Washington when we're done here."

The old man slipped into his heavy Burberry and picked up his umbrella. "I'll be in touch. Enjoy the Ritz, gentlemen."

Wednesday

Beyond the streaked windows of the overheated class-room Harvard Yard was soggy and dirty with late winter snow and a slanting cold rain that made things even worse. It was Professor Colin Chandler's favorite time of the year: he was an indoors person and this kind of weather offered no lures at all, nothing to pull him away from his fire and his books and the clutter of his own mind. He found also that his students seemed to have less on their own minds than at other, more exuberant seasons.

While he folded his late edition of *The Boston Globe* and placed it carefully next to his gloves and scarf on the plain wooden desk, they shuffled in blowing their noses and stacking rundown backpacks against the walls and stomping wet sludge from their boots. He looked down at them from his six feet four inches; at forty-five he was beginning to feel less a physical presence than his students and the arrival of middle age had taken him rather by surprise. They had more ahead of them than he did and he wasn't overjoyed by the thought.

Waiting for them to get settled he caught sight of himself, reflected in one of the windows, and watched for a moment. In outline he didn't look any different than he had twenty years ago: tall, broad, slightly stooped shoulders, brown Harris tweed jacket that went back to Adlai Stevenson, foulard tie, striped button-down blue shirt, heavy brown horn-rims, dark vaguely wavy hair, a hawk's nose separating dark brown eyes, heavy eyebrows, blah blah blah—he lost interest. There he stood, Tradition in its forties, a stalwart old gun-slinger in the path of change. Gregory Peck in *The Gunfighter* with Skip Homeier lurking, Frisbee behind his back . . . He smiled, squinting a little, took off his glasses. He knew he was a comparatively handsome man and the knowledge made lecturing more fun, made him feel freer. It was all an illusion but you had to go with what you had.

"Good afternoon," he said, nodding. There seemed to be about twenty-five on hand, almost all of the registrees for his favorite upper-class course, history majors only (others by permission of the instructor). "You will note by the hissing radiators and the fact that this place will soon begin smelling like a locker room, you will note that at Harvard there is no energy shortage . . . other, perhaps, than among its servants. For now, I will provide the energy and you can just lie there, soaking it up. Your turn, I need hardly add, will come."

"Did you have that memorized?" Sheila, one of the nine Radcliffe students, was a frank and candid member of the Frisbee and backpack and Earth Shoe generation. "I mean, it sounded like you were leaving little spaces for the laugh track." She seemed troubled.

"No, my dear, I made it up myself as I went along. In real life we often find ourselves doing that, thinking and talking, thinking and talking. You might say that most of us write our own material."

"Well, it sure wasn't funny. Maybe you should hire a writer . . ."

He enjoyed this bunch; he let the conversation banter along. As he listened he noticed a woman sitting at the back of the room, clearly not a student, though her face was strangely familiar. Huge eyes, a thin French mouth, high cheekbones, short hair, a dampened rain-coat. She sat attentively, by the door, hands folded on the desk. She'd taken a tissue from a Vuitton bag, dabbed her nose. He smiled at her when their eyes met, then straightened up and went to stand behind the lectern. He undid the buckle on his Rolex and placed it on the lectern and began to talk about illusion and reality. The grayness outside was being obliterated by the steam edging up the windows.

"We live in an age of easy handles and instant analysis," he said, "the present becomes history in a matter of seconds, the transistorized lightweight, hand-held color television cameras put us right there where it's going down—listen to me, 'where it's going down.' That, my young friends," he grinned sourly, "is television talk . . . that cop show, the short muscle-bound guy with the bird? He always says that and now I'm saying it and I am neither a cop nor a street person. It's instant, subliminal influence, and it doesn't make the slightest difference whether it's street talk on cop shows or John Dean 'at that point in time' or Lockheed payoffs or Nixon going to China . . . We look up from our everyday lives and get a fast half-minute summary of the history of Sino-American relationships, or corruption in government, or the role of the spy throughout Western Civilization—life is becoming an endless, unbroken stream of Bicentennial Minutes, brought to us by Shell Oil, and racing through the years ever more urgently—"

He stopped and watched them. They were a television generation, one of the early ones, and he wondered for the thousandth time if they really understood what he was talking about. They *were* what they'd spent their lives watching. Could you blame them? Could Harvard undo the damage in four quick years?

"Now I'm not saying that's all bad," he went on, shaking his head, "not by any means. But it's not enough—that one view of who we are and how we got here, it's just not enough. Since television time is money, the answers and analyses have got to be quick, strong, and even entertaining. Quick, strong, entertaining . . . not necessarily intelligent or thoughtful or valid. An illusion is being created by TV—it has created the great communal living room where we all sit around the electric sages and soak up the same stuff, each one of us, the same stuff, right or wrong. And the very numbers of us who soak it up have the power to make all this stuff fact—the *truth,* as seen by CBS and NBC and

48

ABC. But it's not the truth . . . it's just a piece of it, a corner of the truth . . .

"So where is the truth? In *The New York Times?* Well, some of it is in *The New York Times*. And some of it is in *Newsweek* and some more of it is in *Rolling Stone* and there are bits and pieces in the volumes of memoirs which are auctioned off to the highest bidding publisher." He leaned forward and tried to fix a few of them with his eyes. "But mainly what we read and see today, about ourselves and people who lived centuries ago, is part of the salable illusion called 'history' . . . and far too little of it has anything to do with reality. It's history cut to order, conveniently fitted into any of the various chic theories which happen to be—to be going down at the moment . . .

"And with the American revolutionary war we're back to illusion and reality. You've got to get yourselves into *their* eighteenth-century shoes, see what they saw, see how much they knew and how much they were missing of what went on around them, what they *thought* was real. . . . The easy labels we pin on men who turn the course of history are seldom very accurate, are more often merely convenient."

He let the flow of his ideas carry him along, ideas he'd carefully worked up over the years, and it was largely automatic. At least it was today. He spoke of great men and cads and why they were what they were and he watched the woman in the back row. Familiar . . . someone he knew? No, not that . . . but familiar . . . when he looked at her she was always watching him closely, but then why not, he was the lecturer.

He strode across to the radiator and kicked it, having learned several weeks before that no rational attempts to control its output had the slightest effect. He put his hands in the pockets of the tweed coat, ran his fingers through the lint, loose shreds of tobacco, movie ticket stubs, and waited. He always liked to give them a chance to get the point of things clear in their minds before he began to get specific. Damn, she was still staring at him. Why did he feel that her name was only just out of reach?

"Okay, then," he said. "We now come to the hub around which this course really turns, the American Revolution. And before we get into the nuts and bolts of it, let me make a point or two about the meaning of two more important words, revolution and treason—because, as commonly used, they are not in fact what they seem.

"For instance, a survey of Americans not long ago indicated that they have almost no valid information relevant to either geography or history, although they *think* they do . . ." Chandler slipped his spectacles off the hooked nose and thrust them at the point he was making. "And they have a greater fund of misinformation about the American Revolution than about any other period of our history . . . presumably, you are all better informed than the populace at large. But, let me get at a couple of basic points . . .

"First, the state of mind that produced the American Revolution—it is misunderstood rather widely. In the summer of 1773 Ben Franklin wrote a letter to John Winthrop here at Harvard, and I quote—" Chandler flipped open his Harvard three-ring notebook but hardly needed to look at it.

" 'As between friends every affront is not worth a duel, between nations every injury not worth a war, so between governed and the government every mistake in government, every encroachment on rights, is not worth a rebellion.' "

Chandler leaned on the lectern, his hands clasped before him, glasses dangling, letting the words sink in: "And so it went, Franklin and Jefferson and John Adams, none of them wanted a *war* . . . or independence. In seventy-five Adams said the idea of independence was universally disavowed on our side of the water . . ." He dogged the point, pressed the idea that both the American Whigs and the Tories looked upon themselves as profoundly loyal to the crown. And when it came to war, he told them, it was a war by Whigs who sought to uphold their rights *as Englishmen.*

"These are crucial points to keep in mind when applying yourself to the study of the American Revo-

50

lution . . . Revolution is a word with many meanings . . ."

He put his glasses back on and thrust his hand back into his pockets, straining the buttons on his jacket. He looked at the blackboard.

"The other word . . . treason. Now, out of this new angle on revolution, it stands to reason that we're going to get a new look at treason. And, incidentally, treason is an almost entirely subjective word—one man's traitor is almost always another man's hero. It's an untrustworthy word, treason, yet the history of the American Revolution is riddled with . . . one righteous accusation of treason after another. But what is the illusion and what is the reality?

"Think—it started as anything but a revolution. Hell, no sane man could conceive of a war against the immeasurable might of England! These men thought of themselves as Englishmen, none more English than themselves—loyal subjects and proud to be. Yet events kept on conspiring as events will, pushing these loyal subjects toward a war . . . a war they didn't want. But even as the spirit of independence was growing, even after July 4, 1776, the populace was far from unanimous in support of this declaration . . . in every corner of the country, in every city, there were thousands, tens of thousands who utterly opposed this precipitate act of insurrection—a suicidal rush to war.

"But get the point—they all saw themselves as patriots . . .

"And as the revolution gathered steam, as war engulfed them all, the differences and similarities grew in intensity. Political controversy had become a shooting war. Political views were reduced to only two, the population was polarized . . . You were either a patriot or a loyalist. The patriots insisted you were either willing to fight for the rights and liberties of Americans or you weren't. And the loyalists said that was all irrelevant crap—the fact was, you were either for or against the lawful government.

"Naturally there were a great many intelligent, circumspect men who looked this way and that, unable

51

to accept this harsh separation, this black-and-white view . . . and these men might be called, ah, realists. They were simply not convinced of the absolute rightness of one view or the other, they could not irrevocably join one side or the other . . . or, finding themselves serving one side or the other, they could not turn off their brains, they could not keep from seeing the other side's point of view . . .

"The fact was, many great and powerful men were capable of shifting loyalties. Did that make them traitors?

"Shifting loyalties. Keep that in mind. You may be quite amazed at some of the fellows who found themselves prey to shifting loyalties . . . Quite amazed." He sighed, picked up the Rolex and snapped it back on his wrist. "You've got the reading list. Keep at it." He smiled, picked up his scarf. "That's it for today."

The woman with the huge eyes and the rakish cheekbones approached at a determined clip while he was struggling into his scruffy Burberry with the frayed cuffs, floppy plaid lining, and the odd spots that clustered to him, it seemed, wherever he went. He watched her coming toward him, trying to place the face with a name: Audrey Hepburn was as close as he could come and unless his life had taken a sudden, dramatic turn for the better, it wasn't going to turn out to be Audrey Hepburn. She spoke his name, held out her hand, which he shook awkwardly, entangled in the voluminous coat.

"I'm Polly Bishop. Channel Three News—"

"Of course," he said, smiting his forehead, "I've seen you a thousand times but I—"

"That's television, we become as familiar as the furniture . . ." She smiled winsomely: "And just as forgettable."

"Like history professors, I suspect." He began strangling himself with the scarf, wondering why he had such difficulty with apparently simple tasks.

"Here, you're caught in the little flap," she said, pulling the scarf loose. "Do you always have this problem?" She was smiling broadly, the corners of her wide mouth curling up.

"Not always, thank God, just usually. What exactly can I do for you, Miss Bishop?"

"You were pretty rough on us television people, Professor," she said, ignoring his question. "Here, don't forget your umbrella . . ."

"No rougher than you deserve, surely. Television has a good deal to answer for, don't you agree?"

"Oh, it's certainly no worse than a draw, the good and the bad." She cocked her head, still smiling, appraising his ensemble. "Maybe we've even done a little better than that—"

He wasn't overjoyed by the smile, the air of amused tolerance. "Look, you justify your existence any way you like—"

"Oho, it's my whole existence that's in question now . . . oh, dear."

"Look, Miss Bishop, I don't know what brings you here but surely it isn't to badger me about my credentials as television critic . . . As I can tell from the look on your face, you've enjoyed watching me fight it out with my coat and scarf. So why don't we get to the point or just leave it at that." He was stuffing papers and books into his briefcase. He picked up his *Boston Globe* and she reached out, tapped it with a neatly manicured nail:

"That's why I'm here." Her smile was gone. "I'm sorry, Professor, I didn't mean to get off to such a lousy start . . ."

"Bill Davis's murder," he said softly. The boyish, long-haired face, a typical class portrait, looked up blankly from the sheet of newsprint. His hand trembled for a moment; then he stuffed it into the bulging briefcase. "Senseless, awful thing . . . You just never know—" He closed the briefcase and looked down at the woman.

"I'm covering the murder . . . it's a big story, 'The Harvard Murder.' That's why I'm here." She looked around the room, back to him, shrugged sheepishly. "You happened to be lecturing. I stayed."

"I don't understand," he said, shook his head. "Why me? I hardly knew him—"

"You were his adviser, Professor. And you say you hardly knew him?"

"He got switched over to me this semester. We'd only met once or twice, he seemed like an independent kid, working on some things that weren't really ready for me to see—his previous adviser had gotten Bill's motor started and there wasn't much for me to do yet . . ." He shook his head again, as if it were the only gesture left. How many ways could you exhibit futility and sorrow? "I don't know anything about . . . this . . . what happened to Bill."

"Well, Professor, you seem to be all we've got, the only lead. The police have already spoken with you and they won't say a word . . . that makes you interesting to us, Professor. You seem to be the only person at Harvard they have talked to, the only link to Harvard and, quite frankly, it's Harvard that makes this murder of more than passing interest. You understand? I don't mean to sound callous—"

"I'm disgusted, Miss Bishop, by that kind of sleazy sensationalism. The invasion of my privacy is bad enough but the connection to Harvard making the kid's life of more than passing—"

"Not his life. It's his death we're discussing and Boston is full of bodies, every day." She was about to flare up, her face coloring.

"The Harvard murder, good God!" He tried to push past her but she wouldn't move. The heat in the room was awful. He was soaking his shirt beneath all the layers of clothing.

Polly Bishop fixed him with a stern eye.

"Your name was found on a piece of notepaper in his pocket, along with your office hours . . . We know the secretary saw him leaving your office the day he was killed, only a few hours before he was killed—"

"Do you think I did it? Do you want me to account for my time? Well, I was at the University Theatre in Harvard Square watching a revival of *Charade* with Cary Grant and . . . Audrey Hepburn." He cleared his

54

throat self-consciously. "No, I wasn't in the company of Cary and Audrey, they were in the movie. Yes, I have a witness called Brennan . . . He didn't kill Bill Davis either. And now, Miss Bishop, I've had about enough of this interrogation—"

"Why did Bill Davis come to see you that last day, Professor?"

"Listen," he said angrily, "what is it with you? You know why my name and hours were on his person—I was his adviser. Yes, he came to see me. No, I didn't see him. He was late! We missed each other!" He felt the muscle flickering along his jaw. Goddamnit, woman . . .

"Just not his lucky day, is that it?"

"That's funny," he said sourly. "Very funny."

"Why was he coming to see you? Why did he stop and tell the secretary to have you call him? What was so important?"

Chandler threw up his hands and looked around the room: "Listen to her! Just listen to her! Miss Bishop, I don't know what he wanted with me. I didn't see him—can you grasp that?"

"I think there's something you know and aren't telling!" She bobbed her head decisively. "You're just the type—"

"Oh, for God's sake!" He stormed past her and charged through the doorway. Why did God make such an attractive woman so bloody irritating? Why? Chauvinism lives . . .

She followed him, her boots pounding along behind him. She drew near and he got a whiff of her perfume. Gardenias or something. There were dainty little crow's-feet at the corners of her eyes, little ridges of determination around the mouth. Thirty-five? Why the hell did he care?

"You may not *know* that you know," she said, vaguely conciliatory. "But I'll bet there's something, some little thing . . ."

"You, lady, are pissing in the wind."

"Smooth," she said, "very smooth. You Harvard men . . ."

He went through the outside door onto the entry stairway and, as if by a bolt of lightning, he was momentarily blinded. Someone had snapped on a high intensity, hand-held lamp, and Chandler realized too late that he'd been had. There was a cameraman, a light man, a guy holding a microphone and some other kind of apparatus. There was a big green numeral three inside a chocolate-brown rectangle painted on each piece of equipment. Someone was holding an umbrella over the camera and the light. Chandler turned, astonished, to Polly Bishop and dropped his umbrella which clattered down the steps. "Talk about lucky days," he muttered.

She grabbed the microphone, struck a pose, took a signal and began talking. Chandler looked into the camera, began edging away, felt a tug on his sleeve and realized she had neatly hooked her arm through his: he was trapped and, short of striking this extraordinary woman a stunning blow, he was about to be interviewed on television. He heard her talking as the rain dripped down from the gray, spongy overcast.

"We're in venerable old Harvard Yard, within the sound of bustling Harvard Square . . . and also within the spreading shadows of the violent death of young Bill Davis, the Harvard student brutally gunned down less than forty-eight hours ago on the lawn of his parents' home in suburban Brookline. We're speaking with Bill Davis's adviser, Harvard's well-known historian and author, Professor Colin Chandler—" She turned to meet his eyes, her face bright and serious, the earnest newshound whose good looks he'd admired so often on the evening news. Sharp features, soft brown eyes, a few flecks of gray artfully arranged in the thick chestnut hair swept back covering her ears. He almost smiled, then he heard the question. He wished her an evening with snakes in her boots.

"Is it true, Professor Chandler, that you were the last person at Harvard to see Bill Davis alive?"

"No, that is patently untrue, Miss Bishop, as I have just taken some pains to tell you. Bill came to my office on the afternoon of the day he was killed—I wasn't there and he went away."

"Do you know why he wanted so desperately to see you? Why he left word with the secretary that you should call him as soon as you came in?"

"The desperation is entirely yours, Miss Bishop. So far as I know there was nothing desperate about the message he left—he simply wanted me to call him. Many people leave messages for me and are not subsequently murdered . . . I surely would have called him had he been alive when I got the message."

A small crowd of students paused to watch, pointing, smirking. Chandler didn't blame them. Two men stood uncomfortably beneath a bare-limbed tree, rain blowing against them. They looked curiously out of place and out of date, particularly the shorter one wearing a checked raincoat and matching porkpie hat.

He barely heard what she was saying: his anger and frustration at her handling of the situation helped blot out her voice. The students lost interest, moved on. The two men stomped their feet, acted embarrassed at being so attentive to the television antics. Chandler's eyes moved across the Yard, dreading the thought of any of his colleagues stumbling across this ridiculous charade. Two more men were standing on the stoop of Matthews Hall where Chandler had lived as a freshman. They weren't watching him, fortunately; inexplicably they seemed to be watching the two men beneath the tree. An image registered in Chandler's mind: a bald man, with a ruffle of gray hair over his ears, wiping his dome with a white handkerchief.

"And so," she was saying, her voice dramatic in the easy way of those who deal with a new horror each day, "the mystery of Bill Davis's murder deepens and the question which lingers and which must eventually be answered is—what was so important about his seeing Professor Chandler? It's not much to go on but right now it's all any of us has got . . ." A weighty pause, Chandler heard his own teeth grinding. "Polly Bishop for Channel Three News in Harvard Yard."

The lights went off. She unhooked her arm from his. She handed the microphone back to the man who'd given it to her and patted away the rain on her face. She smiled at Chandler as if nothing had happened.

"Miss Bishop, in the last two minutes you have made me see what a reasonable act murder can be . . ." He felt his jaw clenching involuntarily.

"Well, that's show business, Professor. Quick, strong, entertaining . . . not necessarily intelligent or thoughtful or valid. You should be very pleased with yourself and your little theory." She picked up her Vuitton bag, slipped tight brown leather gloves over elegant, long-fingered hands devoid of rings, and looked him rather wickedly in the eye. "But the fact of my life is this—we're the number one news station in Boston. We are reporters, not talking heads . . . we go out and find out what's going on. And we don't just report on murders in this town, or corruption, or scandal, or the mob—we try to *do* something about it. In this case we're going to find out who killed Bill Davis!" She was at the bottom of the steps looking up, the softness in her eyes replaced by an angry glitter. "Here, take your stupid umbrella."

He took it, drew even with her: "Well, at least we agree about my television theory. You really are something, Miss Bishop, number one in Boston . . . I don't doubt it for a moment, whatever it's worth." He pulled away, clutching his umbrella and briefcase. There was rain spattering his glasses.

"Thank you for your time, Professor. Really." She had the most remarkable ability to switch her attitude, ignoring the previous instant. He'd never encountered anything like it. "And if you think of anything important about Bill Davis, if anything occurs to you, if anything *happens*—and believe me, things are always happening in murder cases . . ." She was following him again. "Get hold of me, at home or at the station." She handed him her card and reflexively he took it, stood staring at the small white rectangle.

"If I were you, Miss Bishop, I wouldn't count on me as a source."

She smiled, unperturbed: "Well, thanks anyway. And, you know, don't carry a grudge. It'll wreck your stomach and you'll wind up with an ulcer, like me." She waved whimsically, turned back to the crew. Beyond the gates to Mass Avenue he saw a station wagon, green and brown, a 3 on the front door. The motor was running, wiper blades clicking.

Frustrated, he crumpled the small card and dropped it at his feet. Turning abruptly he brushed past the man in the porkpie hat and got out of her range as quickly as possible. God, what an irritating creature! But she was right: everything he'd said about television was proven.

Hugh Brennan hailed him as Chandler was passing alongside the dark-red brick pile that was Matthews Hall. Chandler looked up from the sidewalk which he'd been steadfastly regarding in the hope of passing out of the scene unnoticed. Brennan pulled even, a thickly constructed, rather short man whose physique matched his personality: there was something of the good-natured barnyard animal about him, a readiness to go passively along until the point when he rooted in, stood his ground, and prepared to fight to the death. He was a professor of English, specializing in the nineteenth-century novel, Trollope, in particular. "What ho," he said matter-of-factly, then flashed a quick grin which was very nearly a permanent feature of his round face. His reddish-blond hair, curly, was plastered against his head by the rain.

"You weren't a witness to this television mockery, I hope."

"Ah, but I was . . . There you were, bathed in light, a resolute though peevish look on your face, a veritable budding star—a Galbraith, an Arthur Schlesinger—and the girl! A looker." He saw Chandler's grimace. "So what the hell was it all about?" His chins overhung the heavy cableknit turtleneck, giving the impression that his head rested directly upon his shoulders. They fell into step, skulked out of the Yard into the Square. Drivers were turning headlamps on. The rain continued, steadily drizzling, blowing.

Chandler described the television interview, concluded: "She just disregarded what I'd told her, what she knew to be the truth, so she'd have a good question to start off with—was I the last one to see Bill Davis alive . . . Goddamn show business crap!"

Brennan's grin faded, his eyes went flat, as gray as the sky: "Did you really know the kid?"

"No, not really, you know how it is . . . he struck me as bright, kind of an introvert. I talked to him a couple of times, briefly, but no, I didn't know him."

Brennan nodded: "Well, why did he come around to see you? The day he got killed?"

"Beats me. Said he had something to show me, never said what it was."

"The cops did talk to you, though?"

"Sure, they found my name on him, they followed it up, but it was nothing, ten minutes of routine questions and thanks for my cooperation. Period."

"So, don't let it bother you. It's over."

"It's that Bishop woman. She tricked me, she made it seem as if I'm somehow involved. She's devious and she doesn't give a damn, and tonight everybody in Boston's going to see the goddamn interview and start wondering, why was the kid so desperate—her word—desperate to see me." They crossed the Square, stopped for a moment in the shelter of the University Theatre marquee. Brennan stuck a cigarette in his mouth, lit it, puffed and coughed. "She's a breaker," Chandler went on, "a wrecker, some women just can't avoid it . . . it's their nature."

"Yeah, yeah," Brennan muttered impatiently, survivor of two marriages, one to an English actress, the other to a Charlottesville belle. "Did you see *Robin and Marian?*"

"Audrey Hepburn," Chandler said wearily. "I know, I know . . ."

"Well, I could take a lot of bullshit from that kind of woman—tough, independent, intelligent, beautiful—"

"Who says she's intelligent?"

"It's all over her, for God's sake. She handles herself well—and she makes a good living! As my sainted Irish mother would have said . . . did say, in regard to

60

my immortal first wife, Brenda the Star." He punched Chandler in the arm. "Don't let her get to you. Cheer up!"

Chandler shrugged impatiently.

"Look," said Brennan, "let's go have a drink and a dinner at Chez Dreyfus. Do you good—I'll tell you a new joke!"

"No, I'm worn out. I'm just going to pig out at home, look at a stroke book and go to bed." Chandler sighed, peering into the steady rain that was heavier now, as it grew darker. "As a matter of fact, I've taken to writing for stroke books—"

"Just so you don't pose—"

"No, I've got that *Playboy* piece . . . 'The Real American Revolution,' that's the latest title. Dubious scholarship among the tits and beavers."

"I hate celebrity academics," Brennan allowed. They turned the corner by the church and headed toward the restaurant, jockeying for position beneath the single umbrella.

"You know," Chandler mused slowly, "I wish I had been there when he came to my office. I keep turning it over in my mind, wondering . . . he did say something to me, last week I think, but I can't quite get hold of it —it was no big deal, no clue, but he just came up after the lecture, looking at me through the hippie glasses, said he had something he wanted to show me. He was shy about it, he said something . . . wait, I've got it, he said I wouldn't believe it but I had to authenticate it!" He stopped and pinched his lower lip together: "That's it, something he wanted me to authenticate! Hugh, that's pretty damn strange . . . what the hell would a kid like that have that needed an authentication?"

"Document, maybe? Some kind of historical thing, you mean?"

"Something old or something with a questionable pedigree . . . maybe a possible forgery? God, it's weird, the way it just came back to me."

"So Polly Bishop is no fool, my lad. She said you knew something and she was right—"

"But it couldn't have anything to do with the murder—"

"Well, you never know, do you?"

In front of Chez Dreyfus, Brennan stopped him again.

"Let me lighten your day," he said.

"A joke," Chandler said grimly. "You're going to tell me a joke . . ."

"An English professor is out on the town with three graduate students. Ahead of them they see a gathering of ladies of the night—hookers, to you. The professor sets a problem. If a gathering of geese is a gaggle, lions a pride, sheep a flock, then what is a congregation of hookers? Well, being bright lads and steeped in literary allusions, the answers were snappy. Number One shakes his head, strokes his chin, suggests . . . 'a volume of trollops'! Which is pretty damn good. But Number Two tops him with 'a jam of tarts'! Well, Number Three has his back to the wall and triumphantly comes up with . . . 'a flourish of strumpets'! The professor has to give them credit, they've done well for old Harvard . . . but they're all wrong. The correct answer, and as students of English literature they really should have known—the correct answer is—"

"An anthology of pros," Chandler said, his spirits lifting. He couldn't help laughing. Brennan's face clouded.

"You've heard it . . . I've told you before . . ."

"No, no, it came to me as in a dream."

"Don't bullshit me, somebody told you . . ."

Moving on by himself Chandler came to the market on the corner of Brattle Street, nipped in for some coffee and Brie and fresh crusty bread. But what, he wondered, had Bill Davis wanted him to authenticate?

Even in the aftermath of a lousy day Chandler drew comfort and pleasure from an evening at home amid the clutter of his life, the bric-a-brac that in the end adds up to a life. He had made a fair amount of money from his books, one of which had been a main choice of the Book-of-the-Month Club, and his well-paid labors at Harvard. He had never taught anywhere else: in fact he was one of those rare birds who had entered at eighteen and never left Harvard. In some ways, he was well aware, it had been a sheltered life but it was the life he would have chosen for himself over any other. He had never married, though on a couple of occasions he'd come rather close. He had no views on marriage, rarely thought of it: he'd either get married or he wouldn't. At the moment he had no serious lady friend and that didn't bother him one way or the other. What would happen, would happen.

Feeling he deserved a treat for dinner he'd ordered in a pepperoni-and-mushroom-and-anchovy pizza which now lay in ruins on the coffee table before his deep, overstuffed armchair. The slipcovers were wearing out at the arm but unlikely to be refurbished in the foreseeable future. The book-packed library where he spent most of his time contained a black-and-white television set which dated from the Army-McCarthy hearings, some Boston ferns which had been dying for five years, a brick-fronted fireplace full of blackish ashes, and a large copy of Houdon's bust of George Washington. Despite the clutter it was a clean room, as was the entire twelve-room, two-story house he'd bought fifteen years before.

Stretching mightily, he went to the spotless kitchen where he poured a fresh cup of coffee from his Chemex. When he made coffee, he ground his own beans. He went back to the library and sat down again. He picked up two empty cans of Carling Red Cap Ale and dropped them into a wastebasket. He liked his life: maybe he was a bachelor after all, had become one without really thinking about it.

He sipped the steaming coffee, unfortunately glanced at his watch. Damn! It was time for the late news . . . Having fought off the impulse to watch Polly Bishop at six, he now weakened, got up with a sigh and flicked on the set which knew nothing of transistors and color guns and took forever to warm up.

The blow-combed anchorman faded in, like a broken photograph coming back together, and smiled unctuously: "Next, our Polly Bishop talks with the Harvard historian who may have been the last person to see Bill Davis alive . . . after this word . . ."

A dog food commercial used up a minute, then one for a bank shilling china, then one for a horror movie, then Polly Bishop was there, serious and competent, a very good media personality—he had to admit her effectiveness—going on about venerable old Harvard Yard and the well-known Harvard professor . . .

God help us, he did look angry and insufferably arrogant and stuffy! It irked Chandler to see himself as a snotty prig, scowling and being nasty to this pretty, sincere woman who was not only doing her best but was guaranteed in the station's advertising to be a "crime fighter." Finally, unable to watch, wondering if Bill Davis's murderer was watching and figuring that this wise-ass professor ought to get the big sleep, too . . . he turned to stare out the window into the rain dripping off the porch, dribbling sibilantly through the shrubs beyond the railing.

When she had finished he turned and addressed the set: "Lady, you're the reason male chauvinism just won't die . . ." He turned the set off, packed a pipe, lit it, and went out on his porch to air himself out in the clean moist chill.

Across the street two men were out for a stroll in the rain, hands in raincoat pockets, heads down. The shorter man wore a checked porkpie hat that matched his raincoat. Chandler squinted at them through the rain, smiling to himself. My God, there couldn't be two men in one day with the same taste in haberdashery . . . He shook his head. New neighbors, maybe.

Then he went back inside, locked up for the night, threw a couple of logs onto the grate, lit them, and settled back down to read.

Thursday

He woke up the next day thinking about Bill Davis and Polly Bishop and the cops. She'd been right: he had known something he hadn't been telling her. *Authentication* . . . He sure as hell wasn't going to call Polly Bishop but he'd better tell somebody. Namely, the cops who'd called on him two days before. Brookline cops.

Brennan dropped by Chandler's office just past ten o'clock for coffee. The percolator on top of the bookcase was rattling, about to explode. Chandler leaned back in his swivel chair, put his feet on the desk, and stared out the window at what appeared to be sunshine. There had been a marked springiness in the air as he'd walked to work. It was bound to be a better day.

"Did you use yesterday's grounds?" Brennan made a face at his coffee cup. "Admit it—"

"Don't be ridiculous. This coffee was brewed from very special beans I ground at home this morning. Very expensive stuff—"

"Tastes funny. Special beans . . ."

"Kona Java Supreme, I believe. With a *soupçon* of cinnamon. Connoisseur's delight and, therefore, entirely wasted on you. I've had very good comments, believe me."

"Not from me," Brennan sighed, settling down in the leather easy chair dating from the time of John Harvard himself. "Well, I caught the Polly and Colin show last night." He sipped, frowned, sniffed at the cup like a wary dog.

"I did too—incredibly depressing. Woman's a menace."

"A knockout, she is. You're the menace. What a prick! The kid's just trying to do her job—"

"Kid? Ha! Job? Some job . . ."

"Did you tell her what you'd remembered about Davis?"

"You're kidding, it's none of her business—use your head."

"Well, you can't keep it to yourself. Cinnamon? This stuff tastes like oregano . . . or sage, or something not normally associated with coffee—"

"I'm about to call the Brookline cops, the guys who came down here to question me." He yawned. "I was up until three reading—"

"You need a real live girl—"

"Did you a helluva lot of good." He yawned again.

"Had its moments."

"I'm sure—"

There was a knock at the door. "Come in," Chandler called.

Two men entered, looked inquisitively about: the first blinked nearsightedly behind wire-rimmed spectacles. He had a fiftyish look and a face full of concern. "Professor Chandler," he said. "Have you got a moment?"

"What is it?"

"Police," he said. "Just a couple of questions, Professor." He looked at Brennan: "If you'll excuse us?"

"That's all right, Hugh. Stay put. Look, you're a little late if this is about Bill Davis. I talked to your people the other—"

"Ah, that's it, that's just it, Professor, if you don't mind." Both men were in the small office and the door was closed. It was tight. "We're new people, don't you see? Boston homicide."

The other man sidled along the bookcase. He was chewing on an old black pipe. He was bald but for a fringe of grayish hair over his ears and around the base of his skull. There were freckles spattered over his dome and face. "You know how it is, Professor, the

66

Brookline lads just aren't used to this kind of thing—they asked us to come in, take over, give it our fine touch." He smiled rather like a leprechaun left over from *Finian's Rainbow*. He sucked his pipe, a hollow, damp sound. "You might say they're playing it safe. They can blame us when everything goes wrong . . ." Both of them had a good chuckle over that. "What do they know about homicide, eh? Not damn all!" He leaned back against the bookcase, folded his arms across his chest, smiling benevolently.

"Well, I'd like to see some identification," Chandler said. "No offense . . ."

"Of course not," the first man said, withdrawing a wallet. He flicked it open and held it out.

Chandler leaned forward, inspected the ID. "Fennerty? Andrew Fennerty . . ." He nodded. "And you . . ." The leprechaun offered his wallet. "McGonigle? You guys are kidding—two Boston cops, both Irish? Fennerty and McGonigle?"

"Look at it this way," McGonigle suggested. "It's too bloody absurd to be a fake. You can imagine, we take a lot of ribbing, Fennerty and me." He had another good laugh. Everyone was having a wonderful time. Brennan grinned: "Hey, would you guys like some special cinnamon coffee?"

"Are you satisfied, Professor?" Fennerty pocketed his ID. "Sure, I'm game for some coffee, Mr. . . ."

"Brennan." He blew dust out of two cups and poured.

"Sure, sure, I'm satisfied." Chandler leaned back again, watching. "What can I do for you?"

"Just run through this last visit you had from Bill Davis," McGonigle said, taking his coffee from Brennan. He sniffed it suspiciously and set it down on a bookshelf.

"Oh, God," Chandler moaned and began the recital. Fennerty and McGonigle listened intently, nodding solemnly. Chandler worked his way toward the end: "Contrary to the implications made by that woman on television last night, I did not see Bill Davis that last day. Got it? *Did not* . . . However, I did remember

67

something." He told them about the authentication business, explained the possibilities.

"Well, well, well," Fennerty said, bobbing his head, making a tiny O with his mouth.

"That could be very important," McGonigle said. "Or it might be meaningless . . . Say, would you mind if I filled my pipe?"

Chandler pushed the tobacco tin toward him.

"It's our job to find out," Fennerty said.

"Okay, now are you guys going to keep pestering me? I don't know anything else. Nothing." McGonigle got his pipe going and smoke wreathed his head. "You people, that damnable TV woman, cops from Brookline, cops from Boston . . . I'm not an idiot, y'know, there's got to be an end—"

"Now, now, Professor, nobody said you were an idiot—"

"I saw you guys yesterday, both of you, you were standing over at Matthews watching me make an ass of myself on television . . . spying on me, damn it!" Fennerty suddenly looked into his coffee cup as if he'd discovered a snake. He put it down on Chandler's desk. "It's got to stop!"

"We're only doing our job, sir," McGonigle said soothingly. "We're only asking you a few questions. We're not spying on you."

"We don't want to cause trouble," Fennerty said.

"Well, it looks like hell, cops all over my office. I'm drawing attention to the college and I don't like to do that, not this kind of attention. This institution is one of the good things left and I don't like to drag it in the mud—"

Brennan smiled: "Fight fiercely, Harvard."

"I'd hardly say you were doing anything like that, Professor," Fennerty remarked softly. "Why, no one loves Harvard more than I . . . I went through Harvard myself—"

"You did?" Chandler felt himself drawn up short.

"Sure, every morning on the way to grammar school . . ."

Brennan laughed loudly.

"Brennan likes lousy jokes," Chandler said brusquely.

"Well, a sense of humor is the greatest gift," Fennerty said. "You should develop yours, Professor."

"I have a wonderful sense of humor," Chandler said. McGonigle was filling an oilskin tobacco pouch with Chandler's Balkan Sobranie mixture. "Patience is what I'm short of, dammit." The stubby freckled fingers dug down into the black and brown tobacco. "Help yourself," Chandler muttered.

"Don't mind if I do, lad. Fine tobacco. My wife buys me awful junk at the supermarket, Cherry Blend . . . Now, Professor, one last time—are you sure that Davis never *gave* you whatever it was he wanted authenticated . . . maybe he posted it to you, maybe he left it with your housekeeper—"

"Maybe," Fennerty said heavily, "maybe you don't know you have it . . ."

"Nonsense. He gave me nothing, left nothing, mailed nothing . . . to me."

McGonigle and Fennerty made ready to go.

"Honest to God, you guys are worse than Polly Bishop!" Chandler stood up.

"Please, Professor, we can find our own way out." Fennerty blinked rapidly behind the thick circles of glass, pursed his tiny lips: his hand was on the doorknob.

"By the way, Professor," McGonigle said, puffing on the old black pipe, "you might watch Miss Bishop this evening. We're not at liberty to discuss it but I believe you'll find her report interesting . . . And, if anything pops up in your memory about Bill Davis, be sure to let us know—or better yet, sit tight on it. We'll be in touch. We don't want information about this case floating around—we'll definitely be in touch."

They nodded to Brennan, went through the doorway. Fennerty stuck his head back in: "You be sure to watch the news tonight, Professor." The door was pulled gently to.

Brennan stood up, poured more coffee: "Abbot and Costello live." He fished around in the pocket of his jacket, came up with the stub of a pipe. "Do you mind?

Maybe the tobacco will take the taste of the coffee out of my mouth . . ." He reached for the tobacco jar, a plaster of paris copy of Houdon's Washington, small and gleaming white, which a long-ago girl friend had given him. The top of the skull lifted off.

"What a waste of time that was," Chandler said.

Brennan stopped digging in the tobacco, looked up with a curious expression on his wide, fleshy face, hand still inserted in Washington's head. "What the hell?" he muttered, rummaging. Spraying bits of tobacco across the desk he extricated his hand and held up a small black disk between thumb and forefinger. "This is not," he said, "tobacco!"

"Then why is it in Washington's head?"

Brennan peered closely at it, balancing it on his fingertip. "Plastic." He placed it on a sheet of white paper.

Chandler squinted at it. It was flat, about the size of a dime, even smaller.

"It's a bug," Brennan said at last. "An electronic listening device."

"You're not serious—"

"Indeed I am. I saw a picture of one in a magazine not long ago . . . this exact device. Cost a thousand dollars . . ."

"McGonigle," Chandler said, not quite believing it.

"McGonigle," Brennan slapped his hands together. "Hot damn! Right here in real life, this nut puts a bug in your Washington head! Jeeesus, I don't believe it . . ."

"This is going too goddamn far," Chandler said softly. He picked up the bug and whispered directly into it: "Too far, you stupid clumsy dumb bastards." He frowned at Brennan: "What in the name of God do they think they're doing?"

Brennan shrugged, went to the window, tugged it upwards. He pointed at the window box of dead, weedy debris. The walls of the old building were thick with ample ledges. Chandler leaned across the radiator and burrowed a hole into the dirt which was still damp from melting snow and the recent rains. When he'd reached the middle of the window box he dropped the tiny microphone into the hole and packed the dirt back in on top of it. Brennan eased the window shut.

Chandler whispered: "Do you think that'll keep it from working?"

"Who knows? But it won't do it any good. We could have flushed it . . ."

"But then the evidence would have been gone. And what do I care, I haven't got anything incriminating to say about Bill Davis . . . it's the principle of the thing. God, I feel like I'm going nuts—" He grinned at the window box, then at Brennan. "What are we whispering for? It doesn't make any difference."

"Well, you should be out of it by now. You told them about the authentication thing. Finis . . ." He shrugged the massive, burly shoulders. "Looks to me like you're squeezed dry." He went back to filling his pipe. "Why would they go on spying on you?"

"That's another funny thing. They weren't spying on me yesterday . . . it occurred to me right after I accused them of it. They were spying on, watching, observing, whatever, the other two guys . . . the guy in the funny hat and his big friend . . ."

"What are you talking about?"

Chandler told him about the two men. "Then," he concluded, "last night I saw them, the funny hat guy and company, outside my house. Walking in the rain."

Brennan raised his eyebrows, looking at Chandler across his coffee mug.

The morning's interview jostled around in Chandler's brain through the lunch hour and on into the afternoon. How remarkably clumsy to leave the bug in a depth of tobacco so shallow. How obvious and unconstitutional . . . Yet, he might not have found it at all: the tobacco was dry, he seldom smoked in his office: it had been found by sheerest chance. But more bothersome than the planting of the bug was the question it raised: what could they possibly imagine that he knew and was keeping from them? And was it customary for homicide detectives to have such costly devices for everyday use, the matter of legality aside?

And, further, what kind of Boston cops would use words like *posted* for mailed, *lads* for guys or boys or men, or would be moved to say that the Brookline police didn't know *damn all* about homicide? Chandler couldn't say where an expression like *damn all* could have come from. Acting on a vague hunch, late in the afternoon, he called Boston Homicide and without so much as a flicker of hesitation a central switchboard operator confirmed the existence of Fennerty and McGonigle. Well, McGonigle had said it was too bloody absurd to be a fake . . . and there you had another oddity for a Boston cop . . . *bloody absurd.*

He stopped and picked up shrimp chow mein and egg roll for dinner. The sun was too low for warmth and he shivered as he mounted the porch steps. He pitched the mail onto the rolltop desk, slipped into a heavy cardigan, and began heating water for the Chemex. He lit rolled-up newspapers under a stack of dry logs; slowly the library took on a warm glow. Attending to his various housekeeping chores, he chatted absent-mindedly with the bust of George Washington. George was the perfect companion: he didn't require feeding or long inconvenient constitutionals before bed, he didn't have a box to be shoveled out and deodorized or a filthy newspaper in the bottom of a cage, he made no irritating noises, listened attentively, set a good and prudent example, and was indisputably the greatest figure—all in all—America had produced. What would George have thought of policemen who left bugs in your tobacco jar?

He munched his way through the chow mein, adding some soy sauce. It was time for the early news. There was no point in ignoring McGonigle's suggestion. He popped the remainder of an egg roll into his mouth, got up, turned on the television. It wasn't long before McGonigle's insistence took on a particular, ghastly validity. "Murder," the anchorman intoned, "in the news again tonight. Reporting from Beacon Hill, Channel Three's Polly Bishop . . ."

Feeling a sudden queasiness, Chandler leaned forward in his chair, tension running like a current through

72

his body. The camera panned down from the burnished dome of the State House with a clear, brilliant sky behind it, came to rest on Polly Bishop, tracked along with her as she walked slowly down one of the narrow streets running away from Park Street.

"This afternoon there came a tragic new twist to the murder of Harvard student Bill Davis some seventy-two hours ago." Chandler realized they'd taped it earlier in the day but she was adjusting the time to approximately when it would be aired. Just when had McGonigle and Fennerty learned about it all? They'd visited his office in the morning . . . Her soft doe eyes looked directly into the camera, her voice firm, precise. Shadows lingered across her cheekbones, in the hollows of her pale, elegant face. A thick ribbon held her hair in place as the wind gusted in the twisty street. "The twist? A second brutal murder, this time an antiquarian, a dealer in rare books, seventy-nine-year-old Nat Underhill, a world-respected expert in his field. Mr. Underhill was found shot to death in the back office of his shop on Beacon Street where for thirty years an exclusive clientele has sought both rare books and documents as well as his unparalleled expertise."

Chandler knew the name: if not a world class expert, Underhill had been a respected figure. Chandler had met him once or twice over the years, couldn't have claimed to know him. But what had he to do with Bill Davis? *Authentication* . . . inevitably the word, the idea, dropped into place. Polly Bishop had stopped walking, now turned to face the viewers head-on, her trenchcoat collar turned up, the tight brown gloves wrapped around the microphone.

"Apparently during the night, or perhaps even this morning—we must wait on the coroner's report to set the time more accurately—unknown assailants visited Mr. Underhill in his office and shot him twice, killing him instantly. Lieutenant Anthony Lascalle has informed us that the crime was discovered when Underhill's secretary, Nora Thompson, arrived at noon to open the shop. At the time of his death Underhill was cataloging new acquisitions, Ms. Thompson explained.

The shop normally opened at noon except by appointment, since casual walk-in trade played no part in Underhill's business."

Nora Thompson discovered the crime at noon!

Holy Jesus . . . McGonigle and Fennerty had known before it was discovered . . .

"Channel Three has learned—and this is what's really crucial here—we've learned from a Boston Homicide source that the name of *Bill Davis,* that's right, Bill Davis who was murdered in Brookline, was written in Underhill's hand on a notepad found on his desk." Pause for effect. "Now three names have been raised in this strange case—Bill Davis, his adviser at Harvard, Professor Colin Chandler, and now Nat Underhill . . . What links them all together? Was the gun that killed Davis the same that killed Underhill?" She made eye contact with hundreds of thousands of viewers.: "Those are the questions that the Boston police are asking themselves tonight . . . and as yet there has been no break in the case. This is Polly Bishop, Channel Three News, at the scene of the crime on Beacon Hill . . ."

The camera panned away from her face, slid on toward the discreet lettering on Underhill's office window, lingered there until the cut was made to a commercial.

Chandler's knees were shaking and he felt on the verge of a spasm of hyperventilation. How in the name of God could those two clowns have known about the murder of Underhill and gotten to Harvard to bug his tobacco jar—*before* the body was discovered? One answer leaped to mind and Chandler couldn't ignore it: McGonigle and Fennerty had been the unknown assailants, they had killed him . . .

But there had to be a different, better explanation. Didn't there? The operator had confirmed the existence of McGonigle and Fennerty. Maybe for some reason the police wanted Nora whatever-her-name-was to be the official discoverer of the corpse. But why? And could McGonigle have been referring to something other than the murder when he urged Chandler to watch the television news? Good Lord, that seemed unlikely enough—but still, if you subtracted everything that seemed unlikely, Bill Davis and Nat Underhill would be alive, nobody would have brought up the subject of authentication, Polly Bishop would still be an impersonal adjunct to his television set, and nobody would have put a bug in George Washington's head.

The news was still rattling on but he wasn't hearing it. The question of McGonigle and Fennerty aside, for at least the moment, he was angry and frightened at the continuing use of his name by Polly Bishop. His name included in a threesome with two murder victims—it was unspeakable! Christ, the implications of it . . . And the woman—she couldn't resist dragging his name into it, *could not resist!* No wonder she had an ulcer. It was guilt, sheer guilt. "George," he croaked, forcing himself to his feet, "what the hell are we going to do with this woman? Don't just sit there, George, say something . . ."

He went upstairs and put on his pajamas and robe. He was cinching the belt when the phone rang. Sliding his feet into slippers he hurried downstairs.

The voice on the other end of the line was strained, strung tight, unaccustomed to the tricky position in which it found itself.

"Professor Chandler, my name is Nora Thompson. You don't know me but—"

"I just heard your name, Miss Thompson," he said. "On television. What can I do for you?" He was afraid he heard a giveaway tremor in his voice.

"I have to see you, Professor. I can't talk on the telephone. I'm afraid—all you hear about these days is people listening in on your private conversations. I don't know, anybody could be listening in."

"I see. Anybody special in mind?"

"Somebody killed Mr. Underhill," she said, rushing, hurrying past his question. "I've been with Mr. Underhill for twenty-five years, he was a lovely old man, kind and blameless, and they killed him. They killed the Davis boy. You or I could be next . . ."

"It may be a coincidence, Miss Thompson. You can't go by what you hear on television—"

"Mark my words," she whispered, "it's no coincidence. I *know*. The same killers, believe me. It's all

75

tied together and I've got to see you. As soon as possible. I live in Lexington. Can you come out here? Tomorrow?"

"I suppose I can." He was reacting to the urgency in her voice and the prickling he felt on his own neck. "Give me your address."

"No, no, they're watching my house—"

"Who?"

"How should I know?" she cried impatiently. "The killers . . . the police. I don't know, I feel it . . . It's you I have to see. Meet me at Kennedy's Drugstore. You can't miss it, center of town. I'll get out of the house and meet you, eleven o'clock. Don't be late, Professor. Please."

The line was dead before he could reply. He replaced the telephone, picked up the cold coffee and sipped. What could she have to tell him? Or, God forbid, *give* him . . . Not the whatever-it-was that everyone seemed to want. The item in need of authentication . . . He had to keep the appointment: the woman was terrified. Obviously paranoid. Obviously? What the hell was he saying? People bugging your tobacco and you call Nora Thompson paranoid! Damn, he knew what was happening but he couldn't do anything about it: he was being drawn deeper and deeper into the mire. But how did you step back now? How?

The telephone rang again. It was Brennan.

"I've been thinking, Colin," he said. "Do you think maybe you should tell Prosser about this? He's got some clout around here, chairman of the history department—he's got connections, you know that. He could really raise hell about this bugging thing. The more I think about it, the less I like it. It's not just a bad joke—and I should know." He chuckled nervously.

"Maybe," Chandler said. "But Prosser's so damned far removed from reality. He doesn't live in our world —he's probably in Washington telling Kissinger how to shape up his act."

Brennan said: "Well, keep it in mind. You want to hear a joke?"

"Yes, actually, I do—"

"You're serious?"

"Yes, tell me a joke."

"Okay, there are these two titled Englishmen, they meet at Boodles, reading room full of old duffers dozing behind *The Times* and *The Economist*, trays of sherry, smoke of good cigars. 'I say, Binkie,' says one to the other, 'have you heard the latest about Favisham?' " Brennan laid on a terribly British dialect: it reassured Chandler that the world had not gone entirely to hell. " 'Favisham?' says he. 'By Jove, I can't say as I have.' 'Seems he's gone off to Equatorial Africa—left his wife, he has.' 'You don't say? Silly old blighter, Favisham!' 'Ah, Binkie, that's not the half of it . . . he's living in a tree with a gorilla!' 'Favisham? In a tree? With a gorilla?' 'S'truth, old Favisham in a tree with a gorilla in Equatorial Africa!' 'Well, tell me—this gorilla, is it male or female?' 'Oh, female, of course. Nothing *odd* about Favisham . . .' "

Chandler sought total ordinariness for the remainder of the evening. He did his Chemex routine in the kitchen, brought it to the library, set it on the heating ring, along with cream and sugar, beside his comfy chair. He put *The Magic Flute* on the McIntosh, settled in. He was deep in the music, eyes closed, when the doorbell rang. Pulling his robe tight, he stood stock still for a moment: McGonigle and Fennerty? Would they have realized he'd know their secret by now? Would they come back to finish him off? God, it was all nonsense . . . He went to the door feeling put upon.

The first thing he saw was the checked porkpie hat, then the heavy glasses resting on the prominent nose, then the shape of the big man standing just beyond the light from the hallway. Just for a moment he thought he was going to lose his chow mein: but he thanked God it wasn't the Irish mafia, swallowed hard, clenching his jaw reflexively.

"Professor Chandler?" The short man had a high, nasal voice with a touch of a whine to it.

"Yes," he nodded. He was shivering under the robe: he couldn't stop.

"We're from the district attorney's office, Professor, special investigators assigned to this Bill Davis business." He smelled of a mint breath deodorizer. Behind him the big man breathed adenoidally, through his mouth, a raspy sound.

"The district attorney's office," Chandler said.

"May we come in, Professor? This won't take long but it is important, terribly important."

"You might say time is of the essence." The big man leaned into the light, smiled distantly, an official smile. His mouth jerked in a nervous tic. "We've got a full night ahead of us, Professor—we need just a moment of your time." A gold tooth caught the light, flickered like the last ray of hope.

"Sure," Chandler said tiredly, full of fear, ashamed of himself. "I've noticed you guys, yesterday, last night. Come in, come in." The last thing in the world he wanted was having these two in his house but he was worn down. What could he do?

"Aren't you the observant one," the large one said softly, sucking air. They followed him into the library. "Sit down, Professor," indicating the deep chair.

"Would you like some coffee?" Chandler felt a great hand on his shoulder, pushing him down into the chair, gently. He looked up about to complain but the face, mouth open, staring, stopped him. The large man's pale eyes were uninviting.

"The D.A. is very upset with you, Professor," the small one whined. "He says you're obstructing the investigation. Now there are two stiffs and he figures at least the old man is your fault—"

"How? What does he mean?"

"No point being cute with us—the kid talked before he died."

The other voice came from behind his chair: "That's right—he said, 'Chandler's got it' and kicked the bucket. *Chandler's got it.* That means you, Professor." The man was moving behind him, crossing, coming into his peripheral vision on the left.

78

"I don't believe he said that." Chandler felt a constricting in his forehead, his throat. He had no faith in his ability to end this interview. "In any case, I have nothing—he gave me nothing." *The Magic Flute,* which may well have been the noblest accomplishment of the humanistic spirit, was doing no good, the bad guys weren't listening. George Washington was mute, blind, had nothing to offer, no advice.

"Cut the shit," the large man growled. Chandler heard his breathing, almost a groan. Everything was changing. Civility had just died. "We've been plenty patient. Now where the hell is it? Two men have died, why run the risk of being the third . . . We can't protect you if you don't cooperate with us. Goddamn it, the D.A. wants action! Now!" He glared down at Chandler who felt the fear giving way to anger.

"Tell the D.A. to shove it!" he flared back. "You and the TV reporters and the Boston cops—you can all go straight to hell! Tell me what it is I'm supposed to have . . . I don't know. *I don't know.* Check with your colleagues in homicide—I told them the authentication angle—" He started to get out of the chair but this time the big man, who was by now in front of him, leaned across the table and slammed him backwards, like a child being kept in his high chair. No effort. The face impassive, mouth open for breathing.

Chandler looked up, heard a rushing in his head.

"That's it," he said as calmly as he could. "I want to see your credentials. Right now—hand 'em over." Sweat was breaking from every pore.

"The hell with credentials . . ." The big man whirled, as if possessed, a sudden dervish, did an elephantine pirouette, lifted the bust of George Washington from the pedestal and smashed it on the floor. Plaster chips stung Chandler's face, a cloud of white dust erupted from the exploding head. The big man gagged on the fine particles, coughed. Washington lay in a million pieces. Chandler felt hot tears burning his eyes. His heart throbbed, terror touched him. The big man circled the low table and leaned over him from the left. His breath smelled of French fries and salt. "Give us the picture, Professor. We know that much now, it was a picture, a framed picture—"

"A picture?" Chandler croaked.

"A document," the smaller man whined. "Maybe a document—"

"Bill Davis didn't give me anything," Chandler cried, *"nothing* . . . Now, goddamnit, let me see those credentials or get out . . ." He pointed at the mess on the floor: "And you're sure as hell gonna hear about that!" He pointed at the doorway. His hand was trembling and he knew they wouldn't let him out of the chair. "Now, right now—or get out!"

The big man's fist moved like a large, brutal piece of machinery, faster than Chandler could quite register, and he felt something like a hammerhead smash against his face, pain ricocheting through his nose and sinuses, tears immediately flowing. The inside of his upper lip had shredded against his front teeth and he felt blood on his face, tasted it in his throat as his nose, inside and out, grew wet and sloppy with it, thick, salty. His cheeks were wet with tears, his glasses had been driven into his face, but somehow remained more or less in place. His entire body and mind felt incapacitated at the shock of such a blow, such overt violence. He kept his eyes closed, waiting for more. One punch, he reflected with part of his mind, one brief economical punch from a professional and the machine comes apart, the protective ramparts of civilization collapse, the barbarians are within the gates and you're left bleeding and gasping and exhausted . . .

Porkpie cleared his throat: "Now, Professor, that was just to get your attention, y'know? Let that be an end to it." He was leaning against the big man, getting between them, restraining him.

Chandler moaned quietly, wetly. His lip was split: he swallowed blood and mucus, spit a gob of something onto the floor. Why had the son of a bitch broken George? He flicked a glance at the big man, still standing to the left of him. Why George?

"What was that, Professor?"

"Who are you guys?"

80

"D.A.'s office . . . tactical squad, the tough guys. When the heat's on, they send for us. Licensed to kill—"

"Bullshit!"

Chandler hadn't been paying attention: the big man had gotten further behind him again and he didn't see it coming, a hard slap to his left ear. He heard something crack inside his ear, heard himself shriek in pain, fall sideways in the chair, his face nearly colliding with the Chemex in its heat ring. He touched it with his hand, burned his fingers, yanked back, hung on the chair arm, staring past the Chemex at the remaining fragments of Washington's noble head lying in dust on the hardwood floor. Miserable bastards! He fought for breath.

He prayed his eardrum was all right. The inside of his ear felt as if it were dripping. He had further chewed up the inside of his mouth.

"The picture, Professor," Porkpie said.

"Honest to God," he groaned, cupping a hand over his ear, "I don't know. You think I'd go through this if I could just give you the goddamn thing . . . I don't know, I don't know . . ." He fumbled, straightened his glasses on the painful bridge of his nose.

Porkpie, hat still firmly in place, stared down, shook his head as if in deepest sorrow or trying to sell a used car.

"You're going to regret this attitude, Professor," he said. He looked at the big man. They were both so utterly unruffled. "Get the pliers."

Porkpie went around behind the chair and Chandler felt strong hands on his shoulders, anchoring him against the chair. They knew their man, Chandler thought: weakened, terrified, hurt. The big man took a huge hand out of his pocket, leaned toward him, knelt beside the chair. The gold tooth glinted through the open mouth. Chandler heard the deep, resonant, labored breathing.

Suddenly a great paw clamped down on Chandler's left hand and pressed the fingers flat on the arm of the chair. Chandler strained, fought back the urge to vomit. The big man, expressionless, held a pair of simple pliers and stared into Chandler's eyes. "This is gonna hurt,"

81

the big man said softly. He had laugh lines etched deeply at the corners of his mouth, a friendly face.

The porkpie spoke near his ear, pleading: "You sure you don't remember where it is? Save yourself all sorts of trouble . . ."

Pain was replaced by absolute, unreasoning terror: Chandler's breath came in desperate gasps, he felt Porkpie's arms, like barrel bindings, come around his neck, a hand smelling of Big Mac smothered his mouth too tightly to bite.

"Well," the big man said philosophically, "by the time you've run out of fingernails, we'll either have the goddamn thing or we'll be pretty damned sure you haven't got it . . ."

Chandler watched the pliers move toward his fingertips, the metal shining in the lamplight, cold and icy, more pain in palpable form. This was all impossible, it couldn't be happening . . . He felt the anger and frustration gurgling in his chest, in the brain: he felt the first gentle tug as the pliers were fitted to the nail on the little finger of his left hand. The big man looked up, perspiration on his forehead, a thin smile playing across his wide, pasty face: "Last chance, Professor, it's gonna make you toss your cookies—"

At the last moment, as the pliers clamped tight and he felt the first white-hot pain searing his hand and arm like a lightning flash, as he knew he couldn't stand it or make them stop by giving them the answer they wanted—Chandler grabbed the Chemex with his right hand and threw the hot coffee directly into the big man's face.

Chandler never knew how long it took, maybe a second or five, but it was just long enough to get the job done.

The big man screamed, clawed at his face, the pliers clattering away to the floor. Porkpie's grip loosened in surprise. Chandler lunged forward pushing the big man backwards from his kneeling position, knocking him against the edge of the coffee table. Chandler skirted the table with Porkpie's hands scraping at the back of his bathrobe. With a desperate yank Chandler freed the old television set from its moorings, swung it in a brief, violent arc which ended as it intersected with Porkpie's ridiculous hat. The glass screen broke and the picture tube exploded, sending Porkpie staggering backwards in a shower of broken glass and puffs of whatever resides in an antique picture tube. Porkpie fell across the armchair. The picture tube had exploded like a fireworks bomb, filling the room with a nasty, acrid smell. Chandler grabbed the pedestal which had lately held poor George, wrenched it upward, his feet slipping in the plaster wreckage, and launched it lengthwise across the big man's chest as he struggled to his feet; his face and raincoat were brown, streaming hot coffee. He howled as the pedestal smashed him, fell back clutching his chest. Turning, Chandler rammed the base of the pedestal into the small man's breastbone, thought he felt something give . . .

Chandler wasn't thinking: he was reacting mechanically, a machine working its way through a survival program. It seemed to him that he'd never moved so fast, his slippered feet barely skimming over the floor, his heart a driving, nearly bursting engine, adrenalin overloading, providing a hectic frenzy of energy he'd never dreamed possible.

He was out of the room, through the front door, across the yard past the tree, sprinting to the right on Hawthorn, his bathrobe open, a tall man with a bloody face, running like a son of a bitch in his bathrobe and pajamas . . . He'd covered two blocks when he slowed, a wicked stitch developing in his side, finally came to rest against a mailbox out of the yellow blur of the streetlamps . . . The sidewalk was empty, a car moved slowly past in the opposite direction. He looked at his, Rolex, legs shaking, eyes bleary, his mouth dry but for the taste of blood. He felt it caking on his face. Looking back the way he'd come, he saw nothing, no one in sight.

Trying vainly to get his breath back, he realized they weren't coming after him, *couldn't* come after him. He grinned painfully to himself, satisfied at the damage he must have inflicted. Then he staggered off along Brattle

83

Street past the looming ominous tower of St. John's Chapel, left down Mason Street toward the blurred lamplight of the Radcliffe Courtyard. He mounted the stairway between the white pillars and down into the dark cloister surrounded by college buildings. He tied the belt of the old blue monogrammed robe, summoned up his last patches of dignity, and marched resolutely into the open from among the protective shrubbery.

The night air was cold and wet, held a faint mist in it, and you could see your breath before you. He found a wad of Kleenex in his pocket, gingerly dabbed at his nose, licked his upper lip feeling the blood like a fragile crust beneath his nostrils. He was still operating on the fear-borne adrenalin surge, legs moving mechanically, heart refusing to calm down. It was almost midnight; he was just a man in his bathrobe wandering around the Radcliffe Courtyard. With blood all over his face. And his ear on fire. And a library full of damaged goods at the house in Acacia Street. God . . . he was beginning to shake again, not with fear or pain this time, but with anger. Anger like he'd never thought he could feel. Things are always happening in a murder case, that's what she'd said. Out of her experience with such things, it was almost as if she'd been warning him.

He passed a young couple, he with his arm around her, hugging her in the night, and they didn't even look up at him. Chandler wasn't as young as he used to be: the stitch in his side wouldn't quit and he was having trouble getting his breath. Damn it, no business for a professor . . . He reached the center of the courtyard as he heard the chimes at midnight. He sagged down on a bench, hung his head for a moment between his knees, then leaned back, drawing in the night air, wiping sweat from his forehead with a sleeve. He prayed that no watchman would find him. He needed to rest . . . The miserable shits, he thought, seeing before him the smashed bust of George Washington. *I made them pay, I made them pay . . .*

Somehow he managed to avoid terminal hypothermia sitting there sweating on the little circular bench which hugged itself around the trunk of what he identified

from a plaque as a maple tree honoring the memory of
the mother and father of one Miriam H. Kramer, '23.
He read the inscription in the dim mist-diffused glow of
the courtyard's lamps, clutched the robe tight around
his clammy, rapidly chilling body. Later he couldn't remember dozing but somehow, miraculously, he heard
a bell chiming one o'clock. He couldn't have been sitting
there shivering like an idiot for an hour . . . but, yes,
apparently he had. Perhaps he'd passed out for a bit.
He wasn't accustomed to much exercise, let alone to
stark, unreasoning terror. Awake and aware once again
of his ridiculous situation and appearance, he took stock
and realized he didn't want to leave the safety of the
courtyard. The two monsters who'd attacked him
couldn't be expected to just lie there licking their
wounds until morning: the big one might well need hospital treatment for coffee burns—and the other one
could have a broken rib or two, perhaps even a punc-
tured lung. Chandler was oddly ashamed when he discovered himself smiling at the prospect. But perhaps
they weren't as injured as he hoped, perhaps they had
pulled themselves together and were even now out and
about, prowling the streets with blood in their eyes,
scouring alleyways and darkened porches for a man in
a bathrobe . . .

It was one o'clock, he was toying with pneumonia and
God only knew what else, and he had to do something.

He got up and walked slowly over to Harvard Square.
The lights were brighter there and he didn't know if
that was better or worse. Now he could be seen, if they
were looking for him. But he might be able to summon
help . . . maybe. The Square was dripping and rather
deserted. Light shone from Brigham's ice cream parlor,
people moved inside. Who were they at such an hour?

So, what the hell was he going to do?

Providentially he found a single dime in the lint and
wadded Kleenex in his pocket. He couldn't imagine a
single reason for having a dime in the pocket of his
bathrobe, but there it was, loose change he'd picked up
or change from paying the paper boy. He stopped to
rest under the University Theatre's marquee, leaned

85

against the wall in the shadows. Presumably he should call the police, tell them what happened. There was, however, one problem with that stratagem. He had no idea just whose side the police were on.

Finally he went to the telephone booth midway in the block, deposited his dime, and dialed Hugh Brennan's number.

No answer. Twenty rings, no answer. Obviously Brennan was off in search of amorous adventures, gone for the night. It was one-fifteen. It was cold. He rubbed his hands. Who to call? Damn, he had a flash! Goddamn Polly Bishop! She'd started the whole thing, dragged him into it, and now she could damn well get him out of it. What had she said as they stood at the bottom of the steps while her crew packed up the television gear? *If anything happens—and believe me, things are always happening in murder cases . . . Get hold of me, at home or the station.*

Well, Polly, here goes, your fondest hopes about to come true. Things have been happening all day.

Unfortunately she wasn't listed in the directory, not Polly-the-Star, nor did Information have a listing. He swore, rubbed his nose unthinkingly, felt warm blood trickling back into his throat, down his upper lip. He sniffed. Fuck it . . . He couldn't think of another alternative so he called Channel Three. A youngish man answered, his voice edged with tiredness and too many cigarettes. Chandler went into some detail in an attempt to be convincing, explaining that he was an old friend of Polly's from the coast, stopping over at Logan International, and that he had forgotten her telephone number, wondering if he could get it from the station . . .

"Polly Bishop's telephone number, right? Lemme get this straight. And you're an old pal, right? From Biloxi, the old hometown . . ."

"Well—sure, Biloxi."

Harsh, worn-out laughter: "Look, Big Boy from Biloxi, do you have any idea how many guys call us wanting Polly Bishop's number? Any idea? Hundreds, no kidding, hundreds every month. Half the studs in Boston want that number and they're all old pals . . .

Biloxi! Jesus, that always gets 'em! Sorry, buddy, I don't even have her number. But believe me, if I had it, heh, heh, I'd call her!"

Depressed and angry he slammed his fist into the glass panel of the telephone booth. "Damn, damn, damn," he said aloud. "This woman deserves me, she deserves all the trouble I can give her . . ." It was all her fault, none of it would have happened if it hadn't been for her. Then he had another idea, a long shot but better than nothing. His dime was gone and anything was better than nothing.

Clutching his robe he dashed across the wet street to the Yard, remembering that first godawful encounter with Boston's answer to, to . . . well, Christ, he'd never come across anyone else quite like her. He scuttled along past Matthews Hall to the spot where she'd interviewed him, stationed himself where he'd stood at the bottom of the steps. He looked over his shoulder, hearing footsteps, feeling his heart pound: a student wandered past whistling under his breath, took no notice of the peculiar fellow in the bathrobe.

Alone again, sniffling, Chandler dropped to one knee on the sidewalk and blindly began feeling about at the base of the shrubbery, plunging his fingers in among the roots and the mud and the wet, decomposing leaves of the previous autumn. It had to be here, it had to be . . . but, of course, it didn't *have* to be, it could have been kicked God knows where, or he could be digging around a foot away, or he might even touch it and fail to recognize it for what it was. It would, in fact, be a miracle if he found it. But he did find it, held it up between filthy, mucky fingers.

Wet, crumpled, cruddy. The business card she'd given him and which he'd disgustedly thrown away. He smoothed it out, hands shaking, the night's cold covering him like a shroud.

Polly Bishop.

Her telephone numbers, business and home, and her home address. Beacon Hill, of course, where else?

He nipped back across Mass Avenue and sneaked up on a taxi in front of the bank. He leaped into the back seat before the unsuspecting driver could glimpse his peculiar costume and refuse the fare. What a man could be driven to! In this case, he asked to be driven to Chestnut Street on Beacon Hill.

Chestnut Street. He'd walked it again and again, one of Boston's most historic areas . . . Bullfinch, Jim Curley, John Marquand's country. He huddled in the back seat, wishing more of the heat were working its way toward him. It was two o'clock, he had no money, and he couldn't stop shaking. Too old, absolutely too old for this sort of thing. As if he'd ever been the right age. Streetlamps glistened, reflected in the slick streets. Just like a movie which was of only passing consolation. Turning off Beacon Street the taxi groped its way through fog onto Chestnut, the driver peering at house numbers, finally stopping.

Chandler left the vehicle as nimbly as possible, revealing himself in bathrobe and pajamas.

"Oh, shit," the driver said, doing a nice double take.

"Now, now, no need to be alarmed. Though I myself am temporarily without funds, be of good cheer. Bear with me for just a moment—" He gestured toward the narrow, recessed doorway and above it the glow of a lamp behind draperies in a second-floor bay window.

"Why me?" the driver remarked bitterly. He had a bushy natural and droopy moustache, reminded Chandler of a television comedian. "Shit . . ."

Chandler stumbled on the curb and fetched up in the dark fumbling for the doorbell. *Come on, Polly, baby* . . . He found it, gave it one prolonged stab. He could smell the wet earth of flower boxes, heard a steady drip from an eave somewhere nearby. Something brushed against his ankles and he let out a stifled cry. He heard a cat meow. He kept his finger pressed on the button.

"Hey, man, come on, I can't wait all night—"

"It's your money, you imbecile," Chandler flared angrily, "so leave if you want . . . Christ, no wonder you drive a cab!"

"No point in getting personal, asshole!" He opened the car door: "What are ya, anyway? Wearing a dress? Some kind of faggot? Hunh?"

"Miss Bishop!" Chandler bellowed. "Look, down here, it's me . . ." He stepped back onto the sidewalk where he hoped she would see him. "Down here, it's me, Colin Chandler—from Harvard!"

"I shoulda known," the cabdriver said disconsolately, "Hahvud. Crap."

"Miss Bishop," he screamed, "open the goddamn door!"

As if by magic the narrow door swung open and she stood in the light of the hallway. He assumed it was she, but the light was behind her. She was wearing a robe. Inexplicably she knelt down and seemed to be speaking in some sort of code.

"Ezzard," she cooed, "Ezzard, you poor rapacious little darling . . . Such an undisciplined little devil . . ." The cat hurtled into her arms.

"Ah, Miss Bishop—"

"Yes, Professor Chandler," she said calmly, stroking the cat's thick damp fur. "I've heard your cries . . . why don't you pay this young man and let him go about his business? I can't tell you how glad I am to see Ezzard, he's been missing for almost a week—did you find him?"

"Lady," the cabdriver said, joining Chandler on the sidewalk, "look at this man. He's wearing some kind of housecoat—"

"It's called a bathrobe, soldier," Chandler said.

"This fruit ain't got no bread, lady," the cabdriver said patiently. "I think he's gonna stiff you with the tab, see? Six-eighty. Six-eighty and I'm gone, you can get it on with the guy in the housecoat—"

"I see," she said, straightening up, cradling Ezzard. "I'll be just a moment." She disappeared inside, closed the door, reappeared in less than a minute which time the driver passed whistling "Hello, Dolly" between tight teeth. "Eight dollars," she said, "and you be careful, driving around Boston in the middle of the night picking up men in housecoats . . . Goodnight."

"Hey, you're the TV broad—"

"Goodnight." She smiled, large white teeth flashing. "And thank you."

As the cab pulled away, she beckoned to Chandler with her forefinger.

"Come on, Professor. You obviously need something—"

"Help, Miss Bishop. It's called help."

"Ezzard is named for a former heavyweight champion and I'm a pretty tough customer myself." She steered him toward the doorway. Ezzard yawned from the warm stairway inside, baring small gleaming fangs. "You've come to the right place."

In the light at the foot of the stairs Polly did a gratifying double take, said: "You do need help, don't you?" She stood on tiptoes and inspected his nose. "You're leaking blood . . . you're all muddy, what a mess." She smiled on the verge of a giggle. "But you are alive—"

"Don't laugh," he muttered. "You should see the other guys." His ear was throbbing and felt as if it had a cork in it. His legs were shaking and he felt old and exhausted. He was having trouble feeling the proper anger toward Polly Bishop.

"What *machismo!*" But she took his arm and guided him slowly up the stairs. "But I can see you've had a tough night—it's like *Starsky and Hutch.* Come on upstairs and we'll see if we can get you back together." The cat dashed to the top, stood waiting, curious, as he felt his way up the banister.

"I'm a wee bit wobbly and cold as hell . . ."

She sat him down at the kitchen table and turned on the faucet in the sink. He watched her moving calmly, decisively about the kitchen. She put a soft dish towel, a box of tissues, a metal mixing bowl of water, and a bottle of Courvoisier out on the table.

"Lean your head back, close your eyes, let's find out just what's coming loose here."

He felt her smooth fingertips on the bridge of his nose: "Hurt?"

"No," he croaked. "But my nose feels clogged."

"Blood." He closed his eyes, heard the sound of water being wrung out. "But I don't think your nose is broken, which, believe me, is a godsend. I had my nose broken once at school, girls field hockey team. You get awfully

90

tired of breathing through your mouth, makes it hard to eat, too. I remember that because I'd had my first pizza about a week before and then, with the bashed-in nose, whenever I ate I felt like I was going to suffocate. I wanted pizza so badly . . ." He felt lukewarm water, soft strokes under his nose wiping the blood away. He heard her talking, her voice soft and low and soothing. Jesus, he was going to be all right. He felt the dried blood come away from the corners of his mouth, from the split lip, from his chin. It didn't hurt: she was very gentle.

"Look at my ear," he said. He opened his eyes: her face was very close, he could see the pores of her face, the ridges at the corners of her mouth, the thin line of her lips. She was squinting at him through circular wire-rimmed glasses, intent on drying the water from his chin. There were several tissues on the table, the paper soggy and pink-stained.

"Can you hear me?" she whispered on his bad side. He nodded.

"That's good. The ear's probably okay. I'll wipe the blood away." She probed tentatively with a finger. "Ouch," she sympathized, "your earlobe's got a little tear in it." She went on dabbing.

"You're disturbingly calm," he said. "If most women were confronted with a bloody hulk in the middle of the night—"

"Say no more. You don't know any more about most women than the tedious stereotypes we're supposed to have outgrown. I'll thank you to remember that in future—"

"No lectures, please," he muttered, feeling her finger-tip swabbing out the shell of his ear. Painless. But, God, spare the lectures.

"You're risking a punch in the nose," she went on quietly, "*another* punch in the nose. I hope your dedication to male sexist bullshit is very deep. Otherwise it's not worth the pain. Can you blow your nose?"

"Are you kidding? I'd blow my eyeballs out."

"I'm not a lunatic feminist, I don't read the trashy novels by bad lady poets or the sexual guerrila tactic junk and I've known how to masturbate since I was about fourteen." She stood back, tightened the belt of her Halston robe, surveyed the repaired wreckage before her, and clucked her tongue. "But I don't like men who say generally insulting things about women. Specifically insulting things about specific women, I can handle that. Got it? We want to be friends, so let's give ourselves a chance. Now wash your hands in this bowl, get the mud off . . ." The cat crouched on the corner of the butcher-block table, behind the bowl and the tissue box, watching him.

"Tell Ezzard it's not polite to stare."

While he washed his hands she put coffee on, got snifters for the brandy and poured out generous shots. The cat strained forward, nose crinkling at the Courvoisier.

"How do you feel? Drink up." She brushed her hair back, heaved a trembling sigh, and lit a Pall Mall.

"I'm okay." He downed a slug of brandy, quaked inwardly at the heat of it in his chest. "You are a field medic when it comes to this patchwork. Really, I don't know what to say . . ."

"Legacy of the sixties. Civil rights marches, peace marches, I did all that stuff, I marched in the first wave of them, covered the next wave as a reporter. People were always getting knocked on the head and maced and we all learned how to, you know, repair the damage . . ." She looked him in the eye: "Are you really so unpopular?"

"What the hell is that supposed to mean?"

"Most people—get that, *people*—get beaten up, they stagger off to their best friend . . . a girl friend, a pal, a chum . . . You take a cab you can't pay for to the home of somebody you don't know." She raised a hand. "I'm not complaining—just curious. I love excitement. But it makes my ulcer flare up." She went to the cupboard and took out an economy-size bottle of Maalox and filled a third brandy snifter. She took a sip, watching him over the rim. She had the biggest, brownest eyes he'd ever seen. "Who's staring now?" she said.

"Sorry, I'm a little slow." He shook his head. "You've got Maalox in your moustache."

"See, that's a nice specific insult. I can handle it." She took another drink, made a face. "So, why me?"

"Because, Miss Bishop, all these comforting ministrations aside, you deserve me and all my troubles. It's all a result of your dragging me into Boston's hottest new murder spree. It seemed fitting, somehow." He took another sip of brandy, winced this time as it burned its way into the cut lip.

"Well, well." The thick, rich eyebrows raised, made an arch over the vast eyes.

"Half the studs in Boston," he said.

"Beg pardon?"

"Forgive me, my mind is wandering. Addled."

She crooked a finger at him: "Let's go sit by the fire. Come on, Ezzard."

The cat and the professor followed her.

A green glass-shaded antique student's lamp glowed quietly on a heavy old desk stacked high with books. Another lamp, brown ginger jar, sat on a table by the bay window where she'd arranged a wingback reading chair. The curtains were long, cream-colored, nubby. Flanking the fireplace were two couches in a blue and brown floral print, above the mantel a round mirror in a deep gilt frame, green ferns and vines in the corners, hanging from hooks by the windows. The fire had burned low and an all-night FM station was blowing soft jazz from speakers hidden in the corners. Chandler felt that dying in such a room would not be an altogether unpleasant fate.

She sat down on one couch, curled her feet under her, received a hurtling Ezzard, and pretty well finished the Maalox. She set it down and sucked on the Pall Mall, then flipped it into the fireplace.

"The whole story," she said. "I've got a feeling it's a beaut."

"As I said, it's entirely your fault, Miss Bishop." He sat as close to the fire as possible, across from her. "It was incredible . . . The man in the porkpie hat told the

93

big guy with the deep voice to beat me up, he hit me in the face and ear, and he'd already smashed my George Washington—"

"Your George Washington. I see."

"Then he took pliers and tried to pull my finger-nails out . . ."

"And why didn't he?"

"Well, I was pretty pissed off by then, and scared shitless, of course—"

"Of course. It hardly needs saying."

"—and mad about George . . . then I felt the cold metal of the pliers on my fingers . . ." As he spoke he felt it again, the tug at his fingernails: "So I poured the hot coffee in his face and hit the little one with the George Washington pedestal and ran away—"

"Where? When?"

"Cambridge. My house." He swallowed hard. "Just now, before I came here."

"Who were they? Did you know them? What did they want? Were they burglars?"

"Burglars! Burglars don't do that fingernail thing! Of course they weren't burglars . . . What a reporter!"

"Now run through the part about it all being my fault, Professor. I want to get it all straight." She stroked Ezzard who made cat sounds, presumably exhausted, from his recent amours.

"Let me tell you, Miss Bishop, I was a completely innocent college professor as recently as last Wednesday—insulated from all of life's nasty realities—sure, I was sorry about Bill Davis, but I wasn't really involved, I didn't *know* him—and then you arrive in my class-room and set upon me like the furies and with your white teeth flashing . . . an ambush! You were full of tricks and implications and armed with television cam-eras, all of which you used to connect me to Bill Davis's murder . . . utterly spurious, of course. Lots of people saw that broadcast, including the killer. *What was so important about his seeing Professor Chandler?* Those, I believe, were your words . . . In a matter of a couple of minutes you'd transported me from the safety of Harvard Yard into the middle of a murder case."

"You were the boy's adviser." Ezzard smiled with his eyes as she ran a finger under his collar. "He had come to see you just before he was killed—anyway, I'm not going to argue with you." She bit her free thumbnail, stared pensively into the fire, shadows playing on her face. "I wonder what he did from the time he left your office until he died? Did he actually go to Underhill's shop? His name was on Underhill's notepad—Bill could have been there . . . but why?" She glanced up sharply: "Anyway, the point is, you were—are—part of the case."

Chandler sighed: "My God, there's no reasoning with you—"

"Just tell me what's been happening to you, minus all the editorializing. Remember, you came here—"

"Because you earned me and my problems."

"Go on," she said patiently. Good-humored. Obviously she was more accustomed to violence and danger than he.

"All right, from the beginning. First I remembered something Bill Davis had said to me. He told me that he had something I wouldn't believe but that I had to authenticate for him—but he didn't tell me what the item was. A document? Some kind of artifact? There's nothing else I'm qualified to authenticate. But that would explain why he might have gone to poor old Underhill." He could hear his breath whistling through his blocked nasal passages: it was a nasty sound. His eyes burned from lack of sleep.

"Must be the revolutionary period," she said. "If not, why you?"

"The same night I was watching you on television, interviewing me, Polly Bishop the old crimefighter—God, I've seen those ads, stoop to anything to snare the last bleary-eyed and undecided viewer—anyway, I've watched the blasted interview and I'm fuming to myself—"

"You'll get an ulcer," she interrupted, "worrying about things you cannot control. I did."

"And I went out on my porch to breathe deeply and calm myself. It was raining and I saw these two guys

95

across the street, standing around in the rain—my street, Acacia, is not exactly a thoroughfare, you know, but I didn't attribute any malevolent motive to them. I just thought it was funny, seeing these two characters —one in his silly porkpie hat, the other a great hulking bozo in a little tan rain hat—seeing them twice in one day—"

"Twice?"

"Twice . . . they were in the Yard watching me when you did the TV interview, they were standing in the rain watching me, getting all wet. Those silly hats . . . And here they were again, back out in the rain outside my house—"

"My, but they'd spent an inclement day! And it didn't strike you as ominous? I'd think anyone would find it strange—"

"Nonsense! I've got a normal life. I don't suspect everything of being part of a plot, for God's sake."

She nodded grudgingly, frowning. Ezzard got up, stretched and yawned.

"Which brings us to Thursday morning, Miss Bishop, and things get stranger still." He took a deep breath, leaned forward, rubbed his hands in the glow of the fire. "Two third-rate comics called Fennerty and Mc-Gonigle show up at my office claiming to be from Boston Homicide, Brennan is with me in the office, I've got a solid witness to what I'm about to tell you . . . Fennerty and McGonigle question me, all the while doing this tiresome leprechaun routine, and I tell them about the business of the authentication, and they began to piss me off, see? So I told them I'd seen them the day before, in the Yard—yes, *these* guys had been standing in the doorway of Matthews Hall while you interviewed me—"

"Wait," she said. "Let me get this straight, there were *two* sets of men watching you? Porkpie and Rain hat getting wet and the two leprechauns at Matthews Hall . . . Everybody watching you and me, then turning up later? Incredible . . ."

"Oh, we're just getting started. My revelation cut no ice with the Irish Rovers, but they did tell me to watch the news on the tube in the evening, hinting clumsily that there'll be something to interest me. So what the hell was that supposed to mean? I was ready to forget these two jerks when my pal Brennan goes to fill his pipe to get the taste of my coffee out of his mouth and inside George Washington's head—"

"What are you talking about?"

"I've got a humidor made of Houdon's bust of Washington—"

"Yes, and it got broken."

"No, no, I've got another big one at home—*had,* I should say—"

"Of course."

"So Brennan reaches into Washington's head and finds something other than tobacco! A bug, a tiny microphone, put there when the vile McGonigle was loading his own tobacco pouch with my tobacco—"

"Good Lord," she cried, half amused, "what an obvious place, you'd find it the first time you filled your pipe."

"Listen, you didn't see these guys, they were not the height of spy fiction sophistication . . . it was like a joke. If it wasn't *my* tobacco they were fucking with I'm sure I'd find it awfully funny. But it was my tobacco—"

"I'm afraid your McGonigle is an idiot—"

"Well, anyway, we dug a hole in the dirt in my window box and buried the bug in there."

Polly burst out laughing, covered her mouth.

"Yes, awfully amusing," he said. "But once I'd thought about them I remembered a curious thing. Fennerty and McGonigle hadn't been spying on me in the Yard. They'd been spying on Porkpie and Rain hat . . ."

The logs had burned low. It had begun raining hard again, drumming on the window, and thunder rumbled over Beacon Hill. Somewhere a car backfired and he felt himself flinch. Thank God the rain had held off until he'd gotten inside, safe. Polly got up and laid three more birch logs, the bark peeling away as the flame caught. She left the room and returned a few minutes later with a blanket and fresh coffee.

"You're shivering," she said. "I don't want you to do a man-who-came-to-dinner on me." She spread the blanket across him. "Come on, feet off the floor. Invisible drafts, as my mother used to say . . ." She stood back, smiling indulgently: "Comfy? That can be your bed tonight . . . Are you up to coffee? It'll get you through the rest of the story—"

"Sure, fine, let's get on with it—"

"Calm down, I'm just taking care of you." She poured coffee and handed him the purple Heller cup. "I don't think you know just what a wreck you are . . . You're no spring chicken, not anymore."

"Would you just shut up and sit down? It's three-fifteen and I'm not done with this saga."

"I'm waiting for the rapine and pillage," she said.

"Enough whimsy." He clutched the heavy blanket around his bare feet, sipped the coffee, focused his tired eyes on Polly Bishop's face which was developing a tendency to blur. "Thursday evening I couldn't resist, I watched your broadcast—"

"It's the mongoose and the cobra all over again."

"Apt, very apt. And there you were going on about Nat Underhill's murder. Was that what they wanted me to watch? Well, it must have been . . . so I'm watching and a particularly awful thought occurs to me. McGonigle and Fennerty were in my office telling me to watch you *before* Nora Thompson got to work and found Underhill's body—well, Christ! Now, Miss Bishop, I must say the look on your face is very rewarding."

"But how could they—"

"Indeed. Well, you can imagine my surprise." He worked up his last few drops of irony. "And, of course, I would cheerfully have taken a meat ax to you—you just wouldn't let go of me, linking me with two guys who'd just been murdered . . . honest to God, like you're setting the stage for my murder—"

Ignoring the tone of his remarks, she said: "And this was nine hours ago?"

"Seems like only yesterday," he growled. By telling her everything he was lowering the barriers between them: he realized that, saw his anger with her ebbing.

By talking to her, by watching her face, by accepting her blanket and hospitality, he was beginning to feel a vague closeness, a sense of shared purpose, whatever the hell that meant. His mind was wandering: he yanked it back. "I was still reeling from the news that McGonigle and Fennerty knew things they shouldn't know when the telephone rings—it's Nora Thompson—"

"Too much," she marveled. "Why call you?"

He passed her a dour glance: "She insists she's gotta meet me in Lexington in . . ." He looked at his watch. "A little over seven hours . . . She has something she has to tell me. It won't wait. Don't ask, I don't know what it is but I'm betting it's not her recipe for Apple Brown Betty."

She lit a cigarette: "There can't be much more . . . You're almost up to knocking on my door—"

"All that's left is Porkpie and Rain hat visiting me, passing themselves off as D.A.'s special investigators. The little one smelled like a mint breath deodorizer, the big guy had adenoids and a deep, deep voice . . . and a gold tooth. They told me the D.A. was angry with me, I'm obstructing his investigation and two guys are dead—*because of me!* They said Bill Davis said some damn thing, 'Chandler's got it,' before he died . . . Now they think this thing I've got is a framed picture—I ask you, how the hell do you authenticate a picture? Then they—he, the big bastard, broke George! Just smashed him on the floor. And then the little one told the big one to hit me which he did with passionate efficiency . . . then he started with the pliers and I went off the deep end and threw the Chemex at the one, hit the other with the pedestal, the television set blew up, and I got the hell out . . ."

"And came here." She was watching him from beneath lowered lids. He nodded, shrugged. "Well, I'm glad you did . . . Can you imagine trying to explain it to anybody else?" She smiled gently. "Whatever you think of me, Professor—and I suppose you think you have your reasons for hating me—I must tell you, you

99

did very well tonight. If we weren't enemies, I'd be very proud of you—"

"Look, I'm sure you're a very nice person—"

"Person. See, you're getting the hang of it. But I'm not . . . a very nice person. Single-minded, egomaniacal selfish, headstrong—my husband used to say that. I learned them, like the Boy Scout thing . . . trustworthy, loyal, helpful, friendly, courteous, kind, obedient, cheerful, thrifty, brave, clean, and reverent."

"Amazing!"

"My brother was a Scout. I helped him learn the list. I never forget anything. Want to know the starting lineup of the 1919 Chicago White Sox, known to history as the Black Sox because they threw the World Series? Or how about Academy Award winners?"

"I'm having an awfully hard time believing this." He yawned.

"Poor thing. You do need some sleep." She stood up and began to pace. At the window, she peeled back the curtain and stared out into the rain. Ezzard leaped onto the sill and stuck his head out the opening. The clock ticked. Chandler leaned back, stretched full length on the couch, fitting himself in among the cushions. He had just closed his eyes when she began speaking. He edged an eye open. She was standing over him. Thunder cracked.

"Professor, I think you'd better realize something. You're a marked man, I don't mean to be melodramatic, but I've a little more experience in the real world than you do."

He closed his eyes.

"You're going to have to stay out of sight, away from your home and Harvard—"

"But I've got to go see Nora in the morning."

"That's all right—"

"But I don't have any clothes—"

"We'll take care of that in the morning. But the thing that bothers me is these four guys, let's call them the Buggers and the Goons . . . I can check on Fennerty and McGonigle with Homicide, I'll call Tony Lascalle . . . and I can call the D.A.'s office about the other two,

100

but they're obviously not special investigators. Somebody killed Bill and Underhill, and Porkpie and Pliers are pretty high on the probable list. Wake up, Professor."

"I am awake. And call me Colin, will you? And I'm only resting my eyes."

"You're about to pass out."

"Well, I'm no spring chicken."

"Go to sleep. We'll figure out the details in the morning."

"Thanks for putting me up, Miss Bishop."

"Polly."

Alone, after she'd gone to bed, Chandler lay on the couch listening to the rain and the crackling logs, feeling the soft breeze from the window, trying to remember the list of Boy Scout things. He'd been a Boy Scout once, but he couldn't remember them. He couldn't even come close . . .

At first the old man thought it was a thunderclap that had wakened him. He came to with a spasm of pain in his left side, shook it off with a grim frown, and turned on the bedside lamp. He heard the thunder exploding above him and the rain pounding on the slate roof but it was the telephone, not the storm, which had dragged him from his customary light, restless sleep. He hated to be wakened in the middle of the night: the three or four hours of rest each night were the most his poor heart ever gave him and he guarded them jealously. Unfortunately, in his line of work calls in the night came with relative frequency. He had so many men working for him, off and on. At any given moment a goodly number seemed to face crises in the wee hours and there wasn't much he could do about it.

Tonight the call came in on the green telephone. The color coding—red, green, and white—enabled him to know who was on the other end before he answered. It was four o'clock precisely. He gave the green telephone a dirty look, hooked his spectacles over his ears, and extended a liver-spotted, prominently veined hand, clawlike, from the sleeve of his pima cotton pajamas.

His outward placidity returned in an instant, though he knew for sure there was a problem. Something had gone wrong with the Chandler scenario. The green telephone meant it wasn't Andrew and Liam. It was the other two, the out-of-towners. Pursing his lips, he brushed his white moustache with a parchment knuckle and picked up the jangling green telephone.

By four-thirty his Rolls-Royce was pulling up at the service driveway of the John Hancock Building. The traffic lights in Copley Square blinked on empty, rain-swept streets. He extinguished the lights, ducked out of the car, and let himself in through the metal door. He took the elevator to the sixtieth floor. The two floors of heating and air-conditioning equipment overhead throbbed in the stillness of the night.

Alone, waiting, he sat at the glass slab table, packed his Dunhill and got a good smoke going. The unfinished corner of the observation-deck-to-be where he met his operatives was damp and cold and drafty. Puffing clouds of smoke as if it warmed him, he hugged his muffler and raincoat about himself, wondering if it was all still worth it. He was old, his ticker was failing, his blood was thinning, he couldn't sleep much anymore, and by rights he should be retiring to the arid Arizona desert or a condominium in Florida. But you couldn't change your nature: he still enjoyed the game . . . he'd always enjoyed it, for thirty years, and he'd done so well out of it, been so well repaid for his efforts.

Now, let's see: he forced himself back to the matter at hand. Ozzie and Thorny, he didn't know as much about them as he would have preferred. In any case, he had no choice but to make do with the men he was sent. But they were sloppy. And they were wasteful. And they were not his kind of people at all.

He'd been so convincing with Andrew and Liam because he'd actually felt much of the outrage he'd portrayed. The murder of Bill Davis was not merely wicked but absurd, obscene. Senseless death was wasteful and drew attention to things better left unattended. But he wasn't quite sure what tack to take with these two menials . . . God, the things a gentleman had sometimes to do. Lie down with dogs, get up with fleas . . .

The red light above the elevator door announced their ascent.

Their actual appearance was a shock.

They seemed to have been set upon by a band of maddened dervishes. The big one, Ozzie, was inexplicably tinged with brown stains, and his broad face was partially hidden by white bandages. He smelled of a greasy unguent. Thorny spoke so raspingly that he was almost impossible to understand: his face was contorted with pain when he spoke and his breath came in short wheezing gasps.

Astounded, the old man heard them out. That Chandler could have left them in such a shambles was very nearly beyond comprehension. Ozzie sat in a full-blown sulk, eyes half-closed, the unbandaged side of his face red and swollen. Exhausted from speaking, Thorny leaned back in the chrome-and-leather chair, shifting his weight gingerly, clutching his chest. Both men seemed weighed down by the old man's obvious disapproval.

"And after Chandler beat you both into submission, and escaped . . . into the night—we know not where, of course—what then? What did you do? How wide a trail did you leave, thrashing through the underbrush of Cambridge?" The stem of his pipe clicked against his teeth.

"We went to Mass General's emergency room," Thorny croaked. "We figured it was the busiest, we wouldn't be remembered . . . Used false IDs and insurance cards—"

"Not memorable, eh? A hulking beast drenched in hot coffee isn't memorable, eh?"

"Did you ever see Mass General's emergency room? Believe me, there's nothing to worry about."

The old man packed the ash down in the bowl of the pipe with his tiny bronze Mr. Pickwick. "I'm horrified," he said finally, "at your conduct. Such bungling is really beyond any previous experience of mine. . . . You've killed two innocent human beings

103

and been dealt with rather roughly by a Harvard history professor without any previous inclination toward violence. In the course of your researches you have learned almost nothing . . . Have you any suggestions as to how you might advance our cause?" He looked from one to the other: "Come, come, speak up!"

Through the silence came the sound of thunder and the rain lashing the building.

"I see," the old man said. "Well. We still don't know where the package is, do we? We're not even quite sure when and where it disappeared . . . You discovered Underhill's name scribbled on a pad in Bill Davis's bookbag. You went to Underhill Wednesday evening, panicked when he reached for an antique gun which proved to be decorative rather than functional, and killed him . . . Learning nothing. And even if they don't know it already, the police will soon know that the same gun killed the boy and poor old Underhill. Everywhere you go, you leave little bits and pieces of yourselves . . . Chandler's house is probably full of your fingerprints—looking at you I can't help but have that feeling." He pulled his muffler tighter, looked at his watch. "So far as I can tell, we still have only two leads, namely Chandler, wherever he is, and Underhill's secretary, Nora Thompson. If Bill Davis left the package with Underhill, then she may know where it is or what happened to it. If Chandler has somehow gotten hold of it, we've got to find him and watch him. You grasp these possibilities, gentlemen?"

Thorny grunted.

"Would you please check on Chandler's house? Can you handle that?" He sighed resonantly. "And seek an interview with Nora Thompson . . . the district attorney approach should work with her, use your credentials, and for God's sake, don't kill her. Don't pull her fingernails out. Remember, we are all God's creatures. Even you two." He stood up. "Now go away. You know how to reach me." He walked to the huge window, turning his back on them, listened while they puffed and groaned and wheezed and scuttled off into the elevator.

The old man waited quietly by himself in the eerie

104

darkness, his mind roving back and forth over the events of the past few days and just how everything had begun to go wrong. Perhaps his mind simply wasn't as agile as it had once been; leaping back and forth from one set of agents to another wasn't as much pure fun as it once had been . . . At one time he'd looked forward to growing old gracefully. What a joke. So many things worked out rather differently than one planned.

He watched the sky lighten over the Atlantic, turn the darkened city a musty, wet gray. Rain continued to spot the enormous pane of glass. He knocked his pipe out on the cement and stuffed it into his raincoat pocket. Before leaving he went to the telescope which would eventually serve tourists when the observation deck was completed. He sighted through it, saw Boston leap into distinct detail before him. Somewhere out there in the drenched city, Chandler was waiting, hiding, perhaps in shock from the unexpected confrontation with what must have been a positively horrifying kind of violence. Somewhere, wet and tired, wandering around in his bathrobe, Chandler must be feeling the squeeze. So what would he do? Where would he go?

The telescope picked out the white towers of Harvard up the Charles, the town houses of Commonwealth Avenue, the huge equestrian statue of George Washington by the Frog Pond in the Public Garden below him. He swept on, turned to Beacon Hill and the golden dome dulled by the rain and dim light of morning. Somewhere, Chandler was out there . . . Did he know where the goddamn package was? Did he know how to find it?

He let the telescope swing down and pushed the elevator button. He packed his pipe with his thumb, from a suede pouch, while he waited. Chandler must be the key. The package hadn't just disappeared: with Davis and Underhill dead, there was nowhere else to turn . . . Chandler would have to lead them to it. But what if Chandler had had enough? The elevator came and he stepped in. Was there any way to encourage the man, get him moving? If Chandler found the package, well, their problems would be over . . . And balancing

105

Andrew and Liam with one hand, Thorny and Ozzie with the other! Goodness, but it was a great deal for a tired old man! In the Rolls, he lit the pipe and reflected that tough as it was, he'd always bounced back. Just maybe he wasn't done yet.

Chandler awoke with Ezzard noncommittally sitting on his chest, licking his paw and styling his whiskers. It was seven-thirty and raining. He heard the breakfast sounds coming from the kitchen. He smelled coffee. "Come on, Ezzard," he moaned, immediately aware of his stiffness, the pains in his nose and ear. Unable to breathe through his nose he'd slept with his mouth open. His tongue felt and tasted like Ezzard's box.

Polly was eating an English muffin and reading the *Globe* when he staggered into the kitchen. She nodded, over the rim of her coffee cup. She was wearing a heavy blue sweater and jeans poked out from beneath the table.

"Make a list of the clothing you need," she said. "I'm going to stop by your house first—"

"Are you kidding? They might be watching—"

"Don't worry. I'll check—if anybody is watching I'll call you and pick up some things at the Coop. Trust me, I can handle it. God, you look ghastly . . . eat. Toast a muffin, fry an egg, get your strength back." She put the newspaper aside and began making a list on scratch paper. "How do you feel?"

"Wonderful. For a man my age who's been beaten to a pulp and chased halfway across Boston in the middle of the night. English muffins should make me good as new . . ." He split a muffin and dropped the two halves into the toaster.

"Okay, first I go to your place and get the clothes. What do you need?"

"Raincoat, shirts, a sweater, there's a pair of gray slacks, a pair of cordovan shoes, socks, a brown tweed coat, that's about it."

"Professor—"

"Colin."

"Colin, aren't you forgetting something?"

106

"I don't believe so."

"Hmmm. Aren't you the sexy little thing."

"I fail—"

"No underwear. Very provocative." She batted her eyes at him, smiled dazzlingly.

"Yes, yes, bring underwear. And a duffel bag. Who knows when I'll be back." He told her where to find the clothing.

"Right. Two, I'm going to stop at your office and dig out the bug. Do I need a key?"

"Pocket of the brown jacket. Why?"

"Evidence. And I want to have it checked. Place of manufacture. You never know what you might find out. Three, I'm going to check on McGonigle and Fennerty—"

"Look, I'm telling you, they're real, I saw their papers . . ."

"Right, well, I'm going to check." She stood up and left him buttering his muffin. Munching, he followed her back into the living room. "Would you pour a saucer of cream for Ezzard, please? And put half a can of cat food in his dish . . . I've got a lot to do." She looked at her Cartier tank watch with the sapphire on the stem. "I'll be back by ten. That'll give us time to get out to Lexington by eleven." She slipped into a sheepskin jacket and pulled on the tight brown gloves. "Why don't you get all cleaned up so you're ready when I get back. I hate to wait."

He watched from the window as she went to her car. Water was coursing in the gutters, dripping steadily from her soaked awning. She looked up and waved. Her car was a dark green Jaguar XKE, maybe five years old. Naturally.

By a quarter past ten they were crammed into the Jaguar's front buckets and Chandler felt like himself again, showered and out of his ratty old bathrobe. The three synchronized wiper blades swept furiously across the narrow expanse of rain-spattered windshield as Polly maneuvered through traffic toward Lexington. He sighed, trying to accustom his long legs to being

107

stretched almost full length before him. He watched her in profile, concentrating on driving, both hands in the tight gloves wrapped around the wheel. She was devastatingly good-looking, there was no getting around that, and he found himself growing curious about her. For instance, he'd found complete masculine shaving gear in her bathroom medicine chest, along with a variety of prescription pills, cosmetics, cough syrup, Tampons, dental floss, several toothbrushes in various colors. When he'd told her he'd used the razor, shaving cream, and the lime aftershave, he'd expressed the hope that their owner wouldn't object. He'd given the speech some premeditation, knew he was prying, and couldn't help himself.

"Don't trouble yourself, I'm the owner," she'd replied archly. "You can never be too prepared for—well, the unexpected guest."

He'd let it drop, curiosity growing but too inhibited to pursue the inquiry. Now, watching her, he imagined the energy with which she must continually be courted by the men in her life. That was the trouble with women: you always got to sex and jealousy and the touchy business of your masculinity, simple and straightforward, and their blasted feminine game-playing. Of course, he'd been the one playing the curiosity tango, not Polly. Well, the hell with it. She was nothing to him; it was all an accident. She was after a story and that was all there was to it. He had to keep that clear in his mind.

"So what happened in Cambridge?" he asked.

"Well," she pursed her lips, preparing, as if the video was about to roll. "I drove past your house on Acacia, everything seemed calm and deserted, but I went on around the corner and parked on Ash—"

"Call it Windmill Lane—a bit of history, prettier—"

"Then I went through a couple of backyards, sneaked up your back steps—you know, you really shouldn't leave your back door unlocked—and went in, got your stuff—"

"I wasn't home to lock up, sorry."

"Right. Then I came back downstairs, took a look

108

at the mess, peeked outside to make sure the coast was clear and guess what I saw?"

"Please—"

"A red Pinto parked across the street, a little way toward Hawthorn, full of two guys who looked a lot like the goons you did it to last night . . . big one with bandages all over his face and a little one with that porkpie hat. They were getting out and heading toward the house." She looked at him expectantly, made a wide-eyed scared face.

"What did you do? God, it makes me sick to my stomach."

"Me, too. Involuntary. And the fact is I'm rather a brave person. But," she said, sliding in front of a truck and stepping on the gas in the straightaway, "I got out the back door as I heard them clumping around on the porch. I don't think they saw me. I was skulking away through the backyards carrying your raincoat wrapped around your clothes, Queen of the Hoboes."

"They aren't giving up," he mused, pulling his lip. "They took the chance that I wouldn't have had the cops there—"

"I was surprised, too, when I wasn't busy being scared. Anyway, I went to your office, dug the bug out of the window box, no problems there. Nobody paid any attention to me. Then I went right down to Boston Homicide and left the bug with Lascalle and no, I didn't tell him where it came from. He's a pal, he'll check it out and let me know whatever they can learn from it—God knows how long it'll take, though."

The rain continued its tattoo, turning to sleet in the chill. The muck spattered up from the pavement. The Jaguar was so close to the ground, driving at high speed was like burrowing through a wet, gray tunnel.

"And the leprechauns?"

"Lascalle ran a check for me. No such men as Fennerty or McGonigle exist among the members of any metropolitan Boston police department, D.A.'s office, or special branch." She slid the car toward the Lexington off ramp, the signal light blinking.

"Watch out for the Cadillac—"

"Oh, really, Colin . . ." She braked at the ramp, handling the rack-and-pinion like an extension of herself, and exited like butter sliding off a hot knife.

"Well, we never thought they were real, did we . . . but the question is, who the hell are they?"

"We haven't got a clue."

"Not a theory."

"Oh, and the other two, the walking wounded, I rang the D.A.'s office and they haven't sent anyone to see you, they haven't got anybody working on the Davis/Underhill thing at all." She stopped at a light, got her bearings.

"And these four guys are watching each other as well as raising hell with me, like competitors." He made a disgusted face and rolled down his window, took a deep breath. They drove on into Lexington, down the wide main drag. It was vaguely familiar to Chandler: he'd once taken a date to an Italian restaurant which he glimpsed through the downpour.

"Maybe Nora's got all the answers," Polly said. "And maybe not."

"There's Kennedy's Drugstore." He checked his Rolex. "Right on time."

She nodded, smiling: "Trust me, Professor. Old dependable."

Old Dependable was the sort of name that would have suited Nora Thompson from her tightly wound gray bun to the low heels of her sensible shoes. She met them among the high-piled aisles of the drugstore with a thin smile and a firm handshake. She wore a tweed suit and a hardy raincoat. Introductions complete they found a booth in the fountain section and ordered coffee. "Now, Miss Thompson," Chandler said, feeling oddly comfortable for the moment in the warmth with the rain slamming against the window, "what can I do for you?"

Nora Thompson grew younger as she spoke, face coming to life, eyes shining, the years falling away. She was frightened, she mistrusted authority, and she was angry as much as sorrowful when it came to Nat

110

Underhill. And, as it turned out, she was an attentive, observant individual. Quickly she took them back to Monday, ages ago before things had begun coming undone.

"It was Monday, late in the afternoon with the sky looking like a storm was coming. Bill Davis came to see Mr. Underhill—he was carrying one of those green Harvard bookbags—they'd known each other for several months, since last autumn. That's all I know about Monday—Mr. Underhill told me to close up the shop and go home before the storm hit . . ." She paused for a moment, eyes cast down at the cup of steaming coffee, as if remembering her dead employer's small kindnesses.

"But Tuesday morning, right after I'd gotten there to do some book work, earlier than usual, about nine-thirty, Nat came in and I could see right away that he wasn't himself, face all red and blotchy . . . he had high blood pressure that kicked up when he was upset . . . and he told me to come into his office. He was slumped in his chair and I began fussing with the tea things and he cleared his throat and told me that he'd just heard on the radio that Bill Davis was dead, murdered in the street." Her dark blue eyes searched Chandler's face as if he might have an explanation for the enormity of the crime: you were his professor, she seemed to say, you must have an idea . . . Chandler shook his head.

"Nat was very distraught. And then was when your name came into it, Professor. He told me that Bill had left a very valuable package with him the previous day, that he—Nat—wanted to discuss it with Professor Chandler at Harvard . . . he called the item a 'document' and he sort of rambled on, half talking to himself about it and then he threw a scare into me—he said he had an intuition, a hunch about this document, that it was involved in Bill's murder!" Caught up in the memory, she almost gasped.

"Did he say anything about the document?" Chandler asked. "Any clue to what it actually was?"

111

She shook her head: "No, he was very close-mouthed about it right from the beginning—"

"And when was that?" Polly interjected.

"Well, Nat had known about it since the autumn, as I was saying, when Bill first came to see him. He was very excited the first time he ever saw it, he told me that much. He even took it with him to a convention of antiquarians in Bucharest during the winter—yes, he was very, very proud of it. I think it might have been what convinced him to go." She thought a moment: "At least I *think* he took it with him. If he didn't he was certainly planning to tell some of his old friends about it. Anyway, when he got back from Bucharest I knew he strongly suggested to Bill Davis that the document should be officially authenticated—that's where you came in, Professor Chandler . . . But you know college kids, they're going to live forever, he put it off . . . and now they're both dead . . ." For a moment she looked as if her composure would crack but she was made of stern New England stock, Chandler observed thankfully, and kept herself under control.

The drugstore bustled with noisy activity: Chandler had never seen anything like it. It seemed to be Lexington's equivalent of a general store. You had the feeling that everyone could hear your conversation until you realized they were making too much noise themselves and were far too immersed in their own business. He realized Nora Thompson was talking again.

"When Nat heard of the murder he didn't want to keep the package anymore, he didn't want to just give it to Bill's parents, try to make them understand about it in the middle of their grief. Then he decided that he was going to mail it—he had me get all the mailing and wrapping supplies but then he shut himself up in his office, then took it out for mailing himself. He took it out to the post office and I never saw it again. That was Tuesday afternoon . . .

"On Wednesday he was uncommunicative, even more distracted . . . I went home that night—" She swallowed against her emotions and looked out the window at the street blurred beyond the rain. "I never saw him alive again . . . I found his body at noon the next day, Thursday . . ."

Polly nodded consolingly, patted her hand.

Nora spoke again: "What I want to know," tapping her finger on the tabletop in a no-nonsense manner, "where did he send the document, whatever it is? His murder convinces me that the document is behind it . . . it's his connection with Bill Davis—I thought that he might have sent it to you. I knew he wanted you to see it." She looked expectantly at Chandler. She wasn't at all the mouselike spinster he'd expected, but rather a woman who struck him as a formidable adversary were you to find yourself on the wrong side of her intentions.

"No," he said. "At least I didn't get it yesterday. I'm sorry."

"But you're the only person I can think of," she said. "I was so sure . . . Where else would he send it? Yours is the only name he mentioned—"

"But look," Polly said, "at the mail service we get these days. I've had a first-class letter take a week to get across town, so why not a package? It could just as easily get there today, either at your office or your home—it's worth a hope, Nora—"

"Of course," Chandler said. "We can check. I'll call Hugh . . . you see, I've got to stay out of sight for a few days . . ." Quickly he recounted the events which had followed Nora's telephone call. He was surprised at the resolve he saw building in her face.

"Well," she announced, "that pretty well does it, wouldn't you agree? These hooligans think you've got it, too. And I'd bet they killed Nat . . . You were lucky last night, Professor . . . There's something really fiendish going on here." She swallowed some cold coffee. "Words sound so silly . . . *Fiendish*."

"There's an inconsistency, though," Polly said, clearly taking Nora into their confidence. "There are two other men who knew about Nat's death *before* you found the body." In another five minutes Nora knew most of the story. When it was all out the three sat staring at one another trying to make sense of it.

113

"It's like a puzzle with too many pieces," Chandler said. "Where do they all fit?"

Polly pushed onward: "You said Nat went to Bucharest. Romania. If he took the thing with him, or even if it was uppermost in his mind, he would surely have shown it to someone, or talked about it . . . So, who would have been there? Old cronies, men in the same field. We need names—would they be in his diary? Correspondence? Maybe an appointment book at the office . . ." Nora was nodding. "Is there any way you can check? Any files he kept?"

"Nat handled his own correspondence," Nora said slowly. "But he was quite methodical, kept carbons . . . Yes, by gosh, I believe I can check on it." She pushed her coffee away. "No time like the present!" She slid out from the booth, stood up, buttoned her coat.

"We'll go with you," Polly said matter-of-factly, urging Chandler out of the booth.

"I'll take my own car if you'll just take me by my house."

They all three piled into the Jaguar, obscuring Chandler's view and cutting off the circulation in his right leg. It was thus pinned blindly to the seat that he missed what came next. Polly had followed Nora's directions through side streets leading into a homey residential area, white frame houses with evergreens and tall naked trees glimpsed from the corner of his eye past Nora's shoulder. "Now, just past the middle of the block on the left," Nora said with her quiet efficient tone, and it was then that Polly delivered herself of a cry of surprise Chandler had never heard before outside of a certain kind of British comedy film.

"Oh, crikey! Look at that!"

Chandler felt the power surge back in the Jaguar's innards, felt the tires slide for a moment on the pavement, then take hold.

"What is it, dear?" Nora said. "You've gone by the house—"

"Red Pinto," Polly said a trifle breathlessly. "Look inside!"

The warning registered in Chandler's mind but he was helpless to take a look for himself.

"The bandaged man!" Nora exclaimed. "I don't believe it—"

"What the hell," Chandler cried. He craned his head but it was no use. *"My* bandaged man? He's here?" He felt his stomach give way. Polly turned at the corner and gave the Jag some gas. "Ladies," he bellowed, "tell me what's going on!"

"Yes, Colin," Polly said deliberately, keeping her voice calm. "It was the red Pinto, the one I saw at your house this morning . . . no question, a man with a white bandage on his head sitting in the passenger seat of a red Pinto, I've got to believe it's the same." She took another corner without braking and, oddly, without sending the car into a fiery, exploding roll.

"My God, are they following us?"

"No, no, they were watching Nora's house—"

"Well, then, slow down!"

"You needn't scream, Colin," she replied primly, slowing down. "It was a reflexive adrenalin rush. Fright . . . I could swear I heard sound-track music!" She laughed weakly.

"This is simply outrageous," Nora said. "How dare they come to my home? Really, how dare these ruffians approach my home?" There was a silence filled by the sound of the three windshield wipers. "How dare they do any of these things . . . " She spoke with a dying fall.

"You'd better stay with us," Polly said. "We'll go down to Nat's office."

The police had finished with it. But the chill of the tragedy was not so easily whisked away. He felt it as they entered the darkened storefront, the almost palpable aftermath of violence. Nora turned on the lamps, hesitated, then pulled up her socks and led the way into Nat's private office. Chandler knew it couldn't have been easy for her. To his considerable surprise, he realized that Polly had at some point taken his hand: he caught her eye, she smiled faintly.

With Nora doing most of the work they found enough

115

correspondence to build a picture of the men the old man had been looking forward to seeing. A Belgian, two Frenchmen, a German, two Englishmen—they were all written to, urged to set aside the final evening of the conference for an old-times dinner. He promised them a surprise, something well worth the journey to Bucharest even if nothing else developed.

There was no doubt about it: these six men would surely know the contents of the document . . .

"Let's leave this end of it up to you, Miss Thompson," Chandler said. The list of six names lay on the polished antique desk behind which Nat Underhill had been murdered.

"I'll use the telephone," she said. "I'll work right here, at Nat's desk. There's a poetic justice in that, don't you think?"

"Indeed, there is," he said, smiling down at her. "Miss Thompson, may I say that you have been a wonderful surprise? Because you have been—"

"Times of crisis have a tendency," she said, "to bring out the best in one. We're going to find out what's going on here . . . and why."

They were putting their coats back on when Polly stopped: "One thing, Nora. You cannot go home tonight, not with the red Pinto on the loose. They were looking for you then, they'll be looking for you now, and until they find you . . . We know how they treated Colin. I see no reason to think they'll be any gentler with you—"

"Hear, hear," Colin echoed. "It's the dear old Parker House for you . . . and since Channel Three is obviously benefiting from your researches I think I speak for Miss Bishop when I say they'll be glad to pick up your expenses." He beamed at Polly.

"It goes without saying," Polly beamed back.

"I won't hear of it," Nora began.

"Let's not argue," Polly interrupted. "We're getting along so well. I insist and I'll hear no more of it. You just attend to your trans-Atlantic calls. Do whatever shopping you need to do for the weekend and hold onto the receipts." She smiled fondly at gray-haired

Nora, suddenly looking properly sixtyish and spinsterish behind her spectacles. Sixtyish, but full of determination and ready to raise some discreet hell.

It was past three o'clock when they left Nora to pursue her inquiries and returned to Polly's apartment on Chestnut Street. The rain had finally slackened to a bitter cold mist with heavy dark clouds blotting the light out early. She turned on the lights in the kitchen and living room and knelt before the fireplace, threw a couple of logs onto last night's ashes. Chandler felt tired and comfortable as he dropped into the deep sofa. He watched her, the Levis tight across her thighs.

"This feels like home," he said as the crumpled newspapers caught fire, flickered up through the logs. "I feel like I've been dropping in for years."

"Well, you may as well get settled, relaxed." She stood up. "I've got to go to work, I'm co-anchoring tonight on the first shift . . . just a talking head, not a reporter, not today. If they need me for the late show I'll probably just stay on at the station, grab a bite—"

"Give me a call if you're staying," he said, surprised by a reflexive pang of concern. "I mean . . ."

"Yes?" She smiled sideways at him.

"Well, with that damned red Pinto on the loose, I just don't want to sit here worrying about your getting kidnapped and beaten up, while you're gorging yourself and cutting capers at the station . . ."

"Cutting capers?"

"Someone who cries 'Crikey!' in times of stress shouldn't mind anything—"

"I'm going to take a shower," she said laughing, leaving the room, "and get into some TV clothes. Take a nap . . ."

He knew he had to call Brennan but before he got to the telephone he was asleep. When he came to it was five o'clock and dark and she was gone. He went to the bathroom, brushed his teeth, pondered who might be the user, or users, of the shaving lotion, and went to the telephone in the kitchen. Brennan was out of breath.

"Where the hell have you been?" Brennan panted.

"I've been looking all over Cambridge for you—I even walked over to your house expecting to find you dead of a heart attack in the tub—"

"Hugh, wait a minute—"

"And what the hell happened to your house? George is broken, the TV set blew up, probably from old age, your Chemex is broken, there's coffee stains all over everything . . . Jesus, I didn't know what the hell to do—"

"So what did you do?"

"Nothing. I thought I'd give you twenty-four hours. I mean, what the hell should I do?" He sighed heavily, put upon. "There were reporters poking around the office today looking for you . . . and, get this, *somebody stole the bug from the window box!* Yeah, stole it. I wanted to look at it again and damned if it wasn't gone! Now what the hell's going on?"

Chandler took the better part of fifteen minutes telling him what had been happening, each new adventure eliciting a satisfying gasp.

"Now," Chandler said at the end of it all, "answer me one question: did I get a package in the mail today, at the office or at home, since you were there?"

He could almost hear Brennan's shrug: "I don't know, Colin. Hell, I wasn't looking for anything in your mail . . . I don't remember anything on your desk and if it had come through the department they'd have, you know—"

"You were at the house—"

"It would have been left on the porch, right? Since you weren't there? Well, it wasn't, I'd have noticed it, I waited on the porch until it was obvious the rain wasn't going to stop."

"It was a long shot. So we still don't know what Nat did with it—the package is the key, Hugh."

"What are you going to do? You know what I think—"

"What?"

"Get Prosser in on this. I don't mean to harp, but this has gone too far. Prosser *should* be told, as department head he's your boss, and he's also a representative of the college—honest to God, Colin, you ought to get his thinking on this whole thing. Everybody at Harvard knows he was into the rough stuff, the OSS, spies, cloak-and-dagger crap during the war . . ." Brennan sneezed after his day in the rain.

"I know, I know—I'll think about it. But Prosser's not the type to leap in with both hands and start bailing, if you see what I mean. It'd just make him think I was somehow untrustworthy . . . he doesn't particularly fancy coddling his staff."

"Well, keep it in mind, damnit. He knows about crazy stuff . . . Now what?"

"I honestly don't know . . . wait for Nora Thompson to turn up something. It looks like the only way we're going to find out what the hell Nat and Bill Davis were onto . . . wait until I work up the guts to go home."

"So you're shacked up with Polly Bishop," Brennan said wonderingly.

"Hardly—"

"If you ask me, that's worth an evening with the pliers man and Rasputin the Mad Monk working in shifts. Polly Bishop . . . what's she really like?"

"Don't be disgusting, Hugh. She's just a charming young woman."

Brennan cackled wildly: "Charming! Yesterday she was a monster, Eva Braun of the lampshades or some damned thing—oh, Colin, base fellow! Feet of clay . . . a smile, a tender ministering to your wounds . . ."

"Shut up, Hugh."

"How can I get hold of you?"

Chandler gave him the telephone number and Polly's address.

"Hugh," he said. "Just a word—keep a lookout for a red Pinto, okay?"

He watched Polly's news show which informed the populace that there were no new developments in the murders of Bill Davis and Nat Underhill. For once the name of Colin Chandler was left out of the story. Realizing he'd had no lunch he foraged in her refrigerator, found a frozen pizza, several frozen steaks, a bowl of chicken stock, a six-pack of Carlsberg beer, about ten varieties of cheese, and some liverwurst. He ate a little of almost everything. Damn it, he'd forgotten to press Hugh about the reporters poking around his office . . . What next?

The telephone rang.

"Did you watch me? Or sleep through me?"

"My dear woman, I would never sleep through one of your performances." It surprised him, how glad he was to hear her voice.

"If I didn't know you hated me, I'd say that was a cheap, leering double-entendre—"

"Harvard men never leer. They do occasionally need refueling, however, and I unfortunately experienced just such a moment while in your kitchen—"

"Oh-oh," she said. "I *am* sorry. All frozen, I suppose."

"Not the liverwurst," he said bleakly.

"Poor thing."

"I made do. Barely."

"Well, look at it this way. The price was right."

"A wonderful consolation. My empty, growling stomach and I await your return."

"They need me for the late show." She waited. "I am sorry, really. And I hate going on with apologies— why don't you go to bed on your little couch. You've got to be exhausted."

"I may. By way of business, Brennan tells me I didn't get a package at home or at the office. We draw a blank."

"Have you heard from Nora?"

"No," he said, having let her completely slip his mind.

"You might give her a buzz."

"Right. When will you be back here?"

"Midnight. Really, Colin, get some sleep, there's no need to wait up."

"Polly, old chum, old pal, I hate to say this . . . I miss you."

"I'll see you later," she said after a moment's hesitation.

Chandler was musing on that, not quite sure why he'd

told her he missed her, when the telephone rang again and scared him half to death. It was Brennan.

"Colin," he said soberly, "you have gotten yourself into the goddamnedest thing. I'm not kidding. The weirdest . . ."

Chandler offered a hollow laugh: "You have further developments, I take it?"

"Damn right." He took a deep breath that shuddered along the telephone lines. "I got to thinking about the package thing, thought it might have been delivered to the office after I left. So I went back up to the Yard and checked the office—spooky place, dark on a Friday night, rain, wind, perfect place for a murder. While I'm poking around and not finding anything the phone rings—it could be important, says I to myself, so I answer it. Naturally it's for you . . . it's this old guy calling from Maine, from Kennebunkport, says his name is Percy Davis and he sounds like he should be doing Pepperidge Farm commercials. Well, the name Davis rings a bell, but the old guy is canny as hell, he won't respond to the pump. All he'll say is that it's urgent that you call him as soon as possible at a hotel, the Seafoam Inn—he gave me the number. I asked him if I could give you a message and it's no dice. The only message is to call him . . . What do you make of that?" He was puffing again now, excited, nose stopped up with his cold.

"I'd better call him. Must be something to Bill Davis, some kind of relative, if there's any logic to this thing. And I'm convinced there is—some kind of logic. But I can't quite see it and that scares me." He felt a tingling on his neck as he spoke: everything scared him these days. "Look, Hugh, you said something about reporters—what were they doing?"

"It was this morning and then again in the afternoon. Newspaper guys. They were looking for you this morning at the office, then they went away to check your house, came back in the afternoon and by then they'd decided there was something really funny going on. They didn't say but I'd bet they'd gone inside the house and seen the mess and started figuring you just might be dead or on the lam."

"So what did they do?"

"Well, they pressed me pretty hard, said they'd been told you and I hang around together and where the hell were you—what could I say? I told them I didn't know. *I didn't!* They persisted until I picked up that blackthorn walking stick and started tapping it on the desk and eyeing their pitiful wee skulls and giving them my blood-on-the moon Irishman look . . . So, they got the hell out but I damn well didn't fool them. They're onto something. One guy from the *Globe* said that as far as he was concerned you were a missing person. He also pointed out that they couldn't find Nora Thompson either and if that didn't look like a conspiracy then he wasn't sure what did—"

"Did they act like real reporters?"

"They acted like assholes. Which qualifies—"

"As opposed to Fennerty and McGonigle who seemed phony to begin with?"

"Well, they didn't have press cards and funny feathers in their hatbands and they didn't have a lot of wisecracks and they weren't doing Lee Tracy impressions, if that's what you need as proof. They were young and bearded and were acting like Woodward and Bernstein. I'd say they were definitely reporters."

"Okay, okay." He heard Brennan sneezing. "You haven't got a joke, I suppose—"

"You're that desperate?"

"I guess."

"You remember my continuing character, Sir Redvers Redvers, of course?"

"Of course."

"Well, one evening at his country place, Sir Redvers was reclining in a pleasantly tepid tub being attended by his faithful valet and gentleman's gentleman, Hotchkiss. After the old gaffer had finished playing with his boats and his duck, remnants of a childhood to which he kept threatening to return straightaway, both he and Hotchkiss noticed with considerable excitement that Sir Redvers's male member was protruding with a fine

122

determination, like a ship's mast, from amid the soap-suds. 'I say, sir,' Hotchkiss ventured, 'shall I summon her ladyship?' 'I think not, Hotchkiss,' the old fellow explained, continuing, 'in fact, fetch me my baggy tweeds . . . we'll smuggle this one into the village!"

Thank God for Brennan.

"One last thing," Hugh said after repeating the Kennebunkport number. "A red Pinto followed me home, just kept on going when I got to my place. Then I looked out the front window—it was cruising by again, going in the other direction. Bright red Pinto. Thought you'd like to know. May be just a coincidence . . ."

Chandler felt the chill: it was no coincidence.

"Be careful, for God's sake."

"They'll be bloody sorry if they mess with me. I'm carrying me stick now. It's a patented Irish skull buster, m'boy. Don't you worry about Brennan. Remember the song *Brennan on the Moor?* We're a tough bunch. I'll put some blood on the moon, you can count on it . . ." He meant it: Chandler had seen him in a barroom altercation once, a long time ago, when there had been a place called Scollay Square.

Chandler went to the bay window and surveyed the visible length of Chestnut Street, deserted in the damp darkness, each parked automobile taking on an unrealistic coloration beneath the streetlamps. A Pinto thirty yards down the slope caught his eye but it was, he believed, yellow, a light color anyway. He let the drapery fall back and went to the telephone, dialed the Kennebunkport number. He let it ring twenty times: nobody home. Any inn on the Kennebunkport coastline with its freezing winds and Atlantic storms wouldn't be open for business at this time of year. Consequently, Percy Davis must be the proprietor.

He was watching the old Dana Andrews-Gene Tierney film *Laura* when he heard Polly on the stairs. She called his name as she opened the kitchen door: "Don't shoot, Colin, it's me!" He was irrationally glad to see her standing there in her pants suit and sheepskin coat. She smiled and winked: "It's rotten out there." She

123

stripped off her gloves and coat and put a pot of coffee
on. "So what's new?"

Telling her, he felt the foreboding return: the reporters after Brennan, the Pinto following him, the
message from Percy Davis . . . She rolled her eyes and
made a face. The coffee was ready when he'd finished
and she brought it in by the fire, along with a clunky
bottle of Boggs cranberry liqueur. "Maybe I should
heat the pizza—fear makes me hungry." She laughed
and went back to the kitchen. He lit a fire, poking at the
log and the banked heap of ashes.

Plopping down on the couch, she warmed her hands
on the cup and sighed: "Well, you're a part of history
now, Professor. This, whatever it is we're stuck in, is
history . . . it comes down to that. An old piece of
something, an item in your line, floats to the surface
and suddenly people are getting killed—who knows how
many years later?"

"Listen," he said, "history is my thing, not yours.
You come riding out of a journalism school, you're in
the business of making snap judgments. Every little
detail you people treat as history . . . hell, they're not
even footnotes. History has dignity, depth, meaning."
Dana Andrews was alone in Laura Hunt's apartment
late at night, the rain coursing down the windowpane,
and he was falling in love with her portrait. "What we've
got here is random violence, not history. Don't dignify
it." But the inner, thus far undiscovered, logic nagged at
him.

She gave him a look of incredulity across the vase of
dried flowers: "You seriously call this nightmare random violence? There's a point to it, Colin, a pattern,
and you know it—and whatever it is, it's linked to that
document which you, the famous historian, were supposed to pedigree."

She was right, of course, so far as that went: he heard
all the echoes from his conversation with Brennan.

For the record he was about to continue the argument
when Ezzard appeared from the bedroom, stared tiredly
at them from the hallway, as if to say that he found
abstract arguments carried on with intensity in the

middle of the night just a trifle off the mark. He bared his teeth and licked his lips.

"By the way, Colin," she said, "I didn't come out of journalism school. It was Wellesley and history was my major." She stood up and started for the bedroom: "I'm going to get into a robe. Would you drag that pizza out of the oven and hack it up? Pretend it's me?"

When he brought the pizza and beer back in, cringing at the thought of what was accumulating in his stomach, Gene Tierney wasn't quite sure if she should throw herself away on Vincent Price or not and Clifton Webb was advising her against it. It was good advice: aside from his other faults, Vincent's southern accent would have been intolerable to live with. Polly was back on the couch smelling quite exceptionally good. She snatched a wedge of pizza and blew on it.

"Sure," she picked up her previous thought, "I was going to be an historian. But then I got caught up in reality, as opposed to the fantasy I'd been studying. I found I enjoyed living in the chaos of history rather than studying, observing it after all the life has gone out of it—that decision changed my life. Look at this." She bounded up and took a small framed object from the wall. "Look at it—it's a handwritten bill and receipt for a thimble and a cream pot, made and sold and written down by Paul Revere. That piece of paper cost more than two thousand dollars and it's worth every penny . . . to me. Paul Revere handled it in the course of his daily life . . ." She paused to wonder at the thought, then swept her arm around the room. "Just like my Hezekiah Stoddard house. That's why I've never taken a network job. Boston is in my blood, I live in the midst of American history—today's history is my work, the past all around me." She looked down at him. "It's a lovely thing, isn't it? Knowing that Revere held it in his hand, wrote down the sums . . . You see, that is the American Revolution to me . . . That's what I mean when I say I live in history, you observe it. Washington's grand strategy and the principles of revolution—they interest me less, somehow, than the evidence, the details . . ."

"It is a fine piece, anyway," he said gently. Her enthusiasm moved him in an unexpected way.

She smiled, licking pizza from her lips. She was having so much fun: the thought occurred to him that it was like a college bull session when he'd sat up all night at Hayes Bickford in the Square, drinking endless coffees and wrestling with the first large concepts he'd ever confronted. There was usually a Radcliffe girl with a scarf, a runny nose, and a crumpled handkerchief across the table and the weather outside was always frightful. Twenty-five years later he was watching this clever woman whose mind ran swiftly on its own tracks, who wasn't afraid to argue and laugh at the same time, and he wondered how much he himself had changed. Had he learned anything in the twenty-five years? Or had the time simply passed, warmly, sheltered, the embrace of Harvard always there to comfort him and give him the safety of certainty?

"Well, I'll never agree with your theories on an orderly form of history," she said cheerfully. It was well past midnight and Clifton Webb was waiting in the shadows outside Gene Tierney's apartment while Dana Andrews left her alone, vulnerable, exquisite.

"I'm convinced it's all random, I'm afraid," she said, shaking her head, running slender fingers through the thick mass of her hair. "The men running things have as much grasp on the nobility of man's fate, the inevitability of his progress, as a regiment of Hubbard squash."

"That may be true," he said, "but, of course, there are other engines driving history, too. Political realities, spheres of influence, the twentieth-century journey. I can't help myself. I think there's a grandness to our story. The direction of mankind is good, because man's instincts are toward reason, harmony, peace regardless of the detours along the way."

He felt the warmth of the argument, the debate: it was akin to touching the pulse of life. Argument about issues close to you was something very like an intimate experience, was in fact intensely intimate. She looked him in the eye and he felt the flush. He felt almost as if they'd made love.

126

"And I say history is a joke on all of us," she said. She stood up and moved across to him. "But don't take it too hard, Professor." She took his hand, stroked it with her thumb. "I like you very much for making the best of it, for making the best of a bad joke . . . And I hope you're right. I'd rather have you teaching the young people than me—maybe they are the last best hope. If they swallow what you tell them, and reason asserts itself, yours may be a self-fulfilling prophecy and then, thank God, the joke will be on me—"

She knelt before him for an instant and kissed him, neither perfunctorily or passionately. It was the kind of kiss that comes when the lovemaking is over. That was just how Chandler felt as he watched her go to her bedroom. Curious business . . .

Saturday

The next morning Chandler woke to find Polly was sitting beside him on the couch, tapping the table with a rolled-up newspaper, repeating his name.

"Oh, God," he moaned. "Be quiet."

"I couldn't wait for you to wake up," she apologized. She looked fine and rested in her robe, hair brushed back, eyes shining. He felt like an old tennis sock. "I thought you might like to see this." She held up the morning newspaper, open to page three.

HARVARD PROFESSOR MISSING?
SOUGHT FOR QUESTIONING IN
DOUBLE MURDER INVESTIGATION

From beside the headline his own face peered superciliously out at him, rather fuzzy, cribbed from the faculty section of a Harvard yearbook. She handed him his glasses and he struggled to sit up, pulling his blanket up with him.

"Who the hell is seeking me? Makes me sound like a suspect—the Polly Bishop Effect, I suppose." But he couldn't quite hide the grin.

"It's rather misleading. It's the reporters who are doing the seeking, not the police—"

"Damned misleading, I'd say." There was nothing unexpected in the story: speculation, the inability to locate Professor Chandler, a reference to Hugh Brennan. "My God, they even went to Prosser," he muttered, remembering Brennan's efforts to get him to call the venerable

128

department head. Prosser had told the reporter: "Professor Chandler is a grown man who may well have gone off for the weekend to avoid precisely this sort of intrusion into his private life. So far as I can tell, Professor Chandler's involvement in this entire unsavory business is wholly the result of irresponsible media speculation. I heartily endorse his inaccessibility." It was pure vintage Prosser.

Polly followed him to the bathroom, stood in the doorway talking and watching him as he shaved. Finally he pushed her out and closed the door, preparatory to taking a shower. Damn. She was growing on him.

The voice at the other end of the line was dry, like the rustling of dry autumn leaves, and brittle, like chalk. And businesslike. Percy Davis was a Maine man who got to the point. Chandler identified himself and said that he'd called the previous night returning Davis's call; what could he do for him?

"I am Bill Davis's grandfather," the autumnal voice cracked, painting a quick picture of the old man in Chandler's eyes. "No need to console me, Professor, none. Bill's dead and I'm sure you're sorry about it. What I'm calling about is a parcel that arrived here at the Inn, sent by a man called Underhill. He's dead now, too. Pretty damned unsatisfactory, I'd call it. I haven't opened the package but there was a letter with it. I propose to read it to you."

"Go ahead," Chandler said. They were getting closer to the secret and his stomach turned uneasily. Polly sat at the kitchen table, staring at him.

" 'I believe that your grandson Bill, a friend of mine and a fine young man,' Underhill writes, 'was murdered because he had in his possession a document so curious and valuable that a human life was only a temporary obstacle to those bent on acquiring it. It seems best to me at this point to remove this document from the scene because it is simply too hot to have at hand. Be assured that no one other than I myself knows that I am sending it to you. Inevitably those who want it and are prepared to kill to get it will be confused, perplexed, and increas-

129

ingly dangerous as they discover their quarry has disappeared. But I am a desperate man and I cannot send it directly to the one party who must see it sooner or later —Professor Colin Chandler at Harvard. I cannot send it directly to this gentleman out of respect for his safety: he is too obviously the logical recipient. His evaluation of the document's authenticity is essential. I will contact you shortly as to the disposition of the parcel. Please do nothing until you hear from me again. But in case of misfortune befalling me, please take it upon yourself to contact Chandler as discreetly as possible.' "

Percy Davis waited a moment: "Odd, ain't it? Dead man's words coming like this . . . it's like the reading of a will, don't you see. Well, that's it. You may consider yourself discreetly contacted, Professor."

"Where is the parcel now?"

"The middle of the kitchen table. I'm looking it right in the eye."

"Well, I'd better take a look at it, Mr. Davis."

"You'd better take care, young man. Misfortune damned well befell Nat Underhill. Like he expected it. The way I read it, I reckon you can take this as a warning. Leastways, I would—"

"Yes, I'm well aware of that. I've already been, ah, interviewed by the men I believe killed Bill . . . and possibly Nat Underhill."

"You don't say," Percy Davis remarked laconically. "And you're alive to tell the story. No moss on you eh?"

"I've gone to ground," Chandler said, "as they used to say in John Buchan's day."

"Well, don't tell me where you are. This parcel on my table is enough to occupy my mind." He laughed, rustling the leaves again. It was the kind of laugh that made clear the notion that nothing funny was happening. "I understand your reference to Buchan, by the way. *The Thirty-Nine Steps* . . . never forget Mr. Memory. Saw an act like that once up north in Nova Scotia, in Halifax, man who remembered everything . . . well, then, what do you propose?"

"We'll have to get to Kennebunkport—"

130

"We?"

"A friend of mine, we'll be traveling up together." He looked at Polly. She was nodding, giving him a deep triangle of smile, as if to congratulate a slow student on having finally caught the drift.

"The sooner the better," Percy Davis remarked laconically. "You don't want to get yourself killed down there in the city, do you? Seems to me it could happen . . ."

"We'll try to get there this evening. As soon as I take care of a few odds and ends—"

The line went dead.

"Well, what, what, what?" Polly leaped up, began pacing a circle around the table, hands on hips.

Chandler told her about Nat's letter to Percy Davis.

"That's fabulous!" She grabbed his arm, hugged it. "We're almost there—my goodness, tonight we'll know what the damned thing is . . ." She looked up apprehensively. "Come here," she said, pulling him toward the living room. "I've a bit of bad news, I'm afraid. I was saving it, didn't want to ruin your breakfast . . ." She carefully tweezed back the draperies: "I saw them when you were in the shower . . ."

In the street, toward the top end, was a red Pinto.

He felt a peculiar jellification begin working somewhere beneath his diaphragm: "Look, we can't get totally paranoid about little red cars—there must be thousands of red Pintos in Boston—"

"But only one with that license plate," she said.

"You actually checked? You had the presence enough of mind—"

"Whatever I had or didn't have," she said impatiently, "take my word, okay? It's the same number."

"My God," he muttered, waving his arms like a man directing traffic or summoning applause, "we'd never even heard of the damnable Pinto until yesterday morning when you went back to the house . . . That's it!" he yelped suddenly, "that's got to be it—"

"What are you talking about?"

"How they found us here, of course! That does strike you as a little amazing, doesn't it? Finding us so

131

quickly?" By God, he was catching on to this kind of thing, cloak-and-dagger stuff or didn't they call it that anymore? Anyway, he was learning.

"Why, yes, I suppose it did," she said. "And do stop twirling about like that—"

"Because they spotted you yesterday morning at my place! It's your famous face, my darling. They must have seen you go in whether you saw them or not, recognized you—after all, they've probably been watching your nightly commentaries on their handiwork . . ."

"My, my," she observed, "the penalty of high ratings —what a bore, mobbed wherever I go."

"I'm serious, you moron," he said. He went back to the window and took another peek. It was gray outside with patches of blue sky hurrying away as quickly as they broke through the clouds. The street had a quiet air to it, no movement, a sleeping-late morning. It looked cold and fit weather to stay inside by the fire. There was no one in the Pinto, so far as he could tell, but he had a lousy angle: the windshield reflected the plane trees along the curb, the brick housefronts, a bit of gray sky. "Now they know you're involved, which puts you as deep in the mire as I am. Death by association, if you see my point—I could be telling you where it is, or even giving it to you somehow. You've been spotted as my accomplice . . . Damn, I don't know whether I'm glad or sorry. You bloody well deserve it for dragging me into it, but—well, I don't like putting anyone in the way of danger—"

"Man with pliers—"

"Precisely."

"Even if the person deserves it and is a rotten shit. More or less."

"Stop laughing at me and get dressed. If the goons aren't in their car, then where the hell are they? On their way here? Think of that . . ."

But she was already gone into the bedroom.

What now? He started back to the window, stopped. You can look at a little red car only so many times. The point was, what next? They had to get out and there was no hope of getting away in the Jaguar without being seen. And they couldn't make a run for it and run the risk of leading the red Pinto to Percy Davis in Kennebunkport.

When she came back, fully clothed in French patchwork jeans and a navy blue sweater with a v-neck and maroon piping, he took a lengthy, appraising look at her and whistled.

"You just do that to make me angry," she said, heading for the kitchen. "And I refuse to notice—"

"You have got one great rear end, though." He followed her, admiring. "Yes, sir, that's what we say at Harvard when we wish we could leer like the simple folk do."

"Well, you're absolutely right about my ass," she said. "It's common knowledge." She took a watering can from the cupboard, filled it, and began watering her plants.

"Now we've got to figure out how to get out of here," he said. "And then to Kennebunkport. The Jaguar is useless . . . too obvious, too easy to follow, and we can't just walk out the door."

He followed her back to the kitchen. She put the watering can away in the cupboard with the blue door, removing at the same time a squat glass atomizer which she filled from the tap.

"Since they know where we are," he went on, "but still haven't burst in and tommy-gunned us, I suppose we can assume they have chosen to keep us under observation—"

"Maybe they're waiting for me to leave so they can come in and tommy-gun you." She spoke with a lilting brightness, pumping the atomizer and misting the fern. "It's possible," she continued, "though with their various injuries they'd probably prefer to torture you a bit first—"

"I knew I could count on you to see the situation for what it really is. However, since you're coming with me to Maine, your scenario is purely academic. Do stop all this wetting and spraying. They are obviously intent on following us in the hope that I'll lead them to the thing, the whazzio . . ."

133

"The macguffin," she said.

"The macguffin," he repeated. "Do you know why Hitchcock called his plot devices macguffins?"

"No, Professor, but I have the feeling I'm going to find out—"

"Not with that kind of attitude you're not, not from me."

She put the atomizer down on the television set, said: "Please?"

"Not a chance."

She grabbed the atomizer and sprayed Ezzard out of sheer contrariness. Ezzard gave her a withering stare and sneezed. She went on past Chandler and sprayed him as well.

"Shit!" he cried. "All over my glasses—God, I hate that!"

"Good." She put the atomizer away and leaned against the blue door and told him how they could escape from the apartment unseen.

Late in the afternoon after he'd called Brennan and made certain arrangements he found himself bundling up in his Burberry, wrapping one of her mufflers around his throat, carrying her canvas overnight duffel bag, and following her down a narrow dark stairway at the rear of the downstairs entryway where he'd been dropped off by the cabdriver. They had left lights burning in the kitchen and living room, the radio on at normal volume, and now they fumbled in the gloom of the hallway. There was a doorway cut into the underside of the stairs which creaked on seldom-used, never-oiled hinges. "The light burned out years ago and no one ever replaced it," she said, producing a flashlight from her pocket, playing the beam across bare brick walls caked deep with dust, cobwebs, the sifting centuries of settling. The stairs were narrow and stone, solid but built it seemed for some tiny race no longer surviving. The steps ended not in a basement but in a small room, low-ceilinged and smelling of earth and musty growths which left the walls disconcertingly fuzzy when brushed against.

"What the hell is this?" he muttered, growling against his own impulse to claustrophobia. He swept at a dangling thread of cobweb which floated back in his wake, caressed his face.

"It is," she called back over her shoulder, a loud whisper, "nothing less than a secret passageway. I discovered it on my own one day looking for a place to put trash cans. It's not easily noticed, the door fits very flush and the latch is recessed into the wood and the hinges are on the inside . . ." She stopped: "Do you hear a squeaking noise? Like a rat?"

"Not really but then I've been busy with the hanging creepers—"

"Well, I'll pretend I didn't hear it, then." She pointed the cone of light ahead into the darkness. "We're underneath and between the buildings on Chestnut, which is to our right, and Beacon Street to our left. We're going downhill . . . just before we get to the cross street there are some steps which go up into a brick courtyard behind some tall town houses, sort of hidden in behind a couple of garages—it's all most unorthodox but I really don't think anyone ever uses the passageway for anything." She turned and pushed on in the wake of the torch. "It may have been a way servants and tradesmen moved from one dwelling to another a long time ago, or it may have been something else altogether, something quite ulterior . . . Anyway, it's getting us out of trouble."

They came out into the mossy brick cul-de-sac blinking, glad for the fresh cold air. The wind swirled in the trees above, carried a constant, clinging damp. The narrow street was quiet, traffic moving sluggishly on Beacon Street. They quickly headed off toward the Common, crossed Beacon and began the grassy descent. Out of breath they stopped at the bottom of the hill. The huge wading pool lay empty and gray like a concrete trap on a green, hilly golf course. Sheltering under a giant tree they looked nervously back up the hill: the red Pinto was, of course, nowhere in sight.

"Okay," he panted. "You go to see Nora at the Parker House. I'll go meet Hugh and pick you up at the Faneuil Hall flower stall . . . on the corner—"

"I know, I know." She touched his arm: "Now be careful . . . Those guys are everywhere." The irises of her eyes were large and almost black in the gray glow of afternoon. She gave him a squeeze and a tight smile.

"Don't worry. And stay in crowds getting to the hotel. And have the doorman at the hotel get you a cab to Faneuil Hall and don't take any bullshit from the cabbie. Give him five bucks, a buck a block—"

She was nodding: "I have been out on my own before. I'll be fine."

He watched her go, convinced she was safe: in less than ten minutes she'd be in Nora's room. He turned, tightened his grip on the duffel bag and struck off toward the Ritz-Carlton far across the Public Garden. Crossing the arched bridge over the Frog Pond he thought briefly of the swan boats which would be gliding on the still glassy waters a few weeks from now. It had been a long time since he'd ridden a swan boat, watched the couples sprawling on the grass verges, enjoyed the ducks and the explosions of color in the flowerbeds. The innocence of such an afternoon's occupation struck him as distressingly distant from the moment at hand. But Polly, he bet himself, would enjoy it.

The imposing equestrian statue of George Washington loomed gigantically ahead of him.

"George," he said, "what's your country coming to, baby?" He looked up into the noble, determined visage, farsighted, but sightless forever now. The statue was waterstained from the rain. He seemed to be the only one noticing George, surely the only pedestrian talking to him. His Rolex said three-fifty. He was meeting Hugh in forty minutes. "George," he said, "I'm doing my best."

He crossed Arlington, decided against waiting in line for a taxi at the Ritz-Carlton, and leaned into the wind, made his way across Newberry to the Boylston Street corner. No luck. He walked up Boylston, crossed at Trinity Church and damned near buckled in the gale whistling down from the open expanse of Copley Square. He waited beneath the icy upward thrust of the

136

John Hancock Building; finally, at four-oh-seven he flagged down a taxi going in the right direction and settled back, sweating and cold and getting vaguely accustomed to the gnawing mixture of fear and anticipation which had come to live in his stomach. Polly would be with Nora by now.

The huge Indian, arms outspread, greeted him silently at the Boston Museum of Fine Arts. The taxi pulled away in a cloud of noxious fumes. A streetcar wheezed into view. "Hi," he said to the Indian, wondering if there was a one-day record for speaking to equestrian statuary. "George says hi from the Public Garden . . ."

He paid and went through the turnstile and on up the long clicking stairway and on to the Egyptian collection.

Hugh was nowhere to be seen. Chandler moved on in the rooms he had almost to himself. A guard yawned, smiled wearily. The end of a slow Saturday. Chandler waited by Lady Sennuwy, the most beautiful woman in the world. Four thousand years and still the most beautiful . . .

It was fifteen minutes before Brennan lumbered through the door.

"Christ," he puffed, wiping his nose. "I'm sorry I'm late. Foul-up at Avis. Fucking wizard blew a fuse, I don't know . . . How the hell are you?"

"I'm fine. The car's downstairs?"

"Ah, yeah. Look, Colin, were you talking to this?" He jerked a thumb at Lady Sennuwy.

"Don't be ridiculous," Chandler said.

"I'm a nervous goddamn wreck," Brennan announced with a stifled sneeze. "But it's also fun in a sick sort of way. I got you a brown car, just a brown, dumb-looking car. I don't even know what kind it is . . . Look, are you doing anything really stupid? I mean, dangerous?"

"What can I say?" Chandler shrugged: "I somehow found myself in this thing—I'm not looking for trouble, if that's what you mean. But I can't ignore Percy Davis, can I? It's a legacy . . .two men have died and this is what they've left me, this thingummy on the kitchen table in Kennebunkport. I can't just ignore it."

Brennan nodded, glumly, apparently unconvinced.

137

"You haven't noticed the guys in the red Pinto, have you?"

"Not since they passed my house—hell, it may have been another red Pinto—"

"If you believe that, you'll believe anything . . . Right now they're parked outside Polly's place, waiting for God only knows what."

Brennan fumbled for a veteran Kleenex, rubbed his reddening nose: "It's hard to believe . . ."

"Well, we've shaken them now, thanks to you and the Wizard of Avis. Come on, let's get out of here."

They went out the main entrance. The darkness had fallen fast and there was a faint mist. Brennan produced the keys and led the way to the brown car. The parking lot was almost deserted, a curiously wet and dispiriting place. Water stood in puddles.

"Good luck," Brennan said, coughing. His trilby was pulled down tight against the tops of his ears. His sinuses were clogged. He looked miserable. "Be careful."

"Cheer up," Chandler said, chucking the duffel bag into the back seat. "Go home and take something for your cold. I'll be in touch." They shook hands. "I'll get this all straightened out and everything will be fine."

As he eased the brown car out of the lot and into the street, he caught sight of the bulky, raincoated figure standing at the trolley stop. The headlights picked him out and he looked up like an enormous primitive boar, his eyes reflecting red. Then Chandler turned and waved as he drove back toward downtown Boston, the stout figure of his friend fading quickly into the night's gloom.

"Jeez, my face is fuckin' killing me," Ozzie whined, his chins wobbling, his fingers hooked and raking across the bandages covering the left side of his face. "Feels like my skin is all bubbled up." He moaned softly, sucked on the last cherry-flavored Tiparillo which was doing his adenoidal condition no good at all. "Not that you give a shit."

"I do give a shit," Thorny wheezed, "but it's hard for

me to talk, you know that. So get offa me, okay? Besides, under the bandage your skin *is* all bubbled up . . . and your hair's gonna fall out. So, fuck it." He lay his battered, grease-stained copy of *The Final Days* on the dashboard and stared up at the light in the bay window of Polly Bishop's apartment.

The gray day had wizened into a dark, wet evening and Thorny suspected that his chest and ribs were at least as painful as his partner's burn. The cramped little car had become their torture chamber: it had been a long day. Worse: he was afraid Ozzie was going crazy . . .

"Fuck it yourself," Ozzie muttered deep in his chest.

"Funny thing," Thorny said. "I haven't seen a shadow up there for the past couple hours."

"Maybe they're in the sack," Ozzie groaned, shifting his huge bulk. The seat creaked. "Jeez, I'd like a crack at that broad . . . Wham." His fingers crawled upwards yet again. His pale eyes flickered like trapped maddened things.

"But the Jag's still there," Thorny continued along his own track. "Now how the hell else could they get out? Why would they bother to sneak out anyway? They don't know we're here . . ." His fingers tapped on the steering wheel. He was doing his utmost to think it through without breathing. Breathing hurt like hell.

"I wouldn't put nothing past that bastard," Ozzie said. His face and scalp felt as if the bubbles were bursting, itching, peeling away. He took a final drag on the tiny cigar and dropped it out the window. "Maybe they spotted us. Why not? I'm so hungry I could puke." He took a plastic bottle from his coat pocket and swallowed a pain-killer.

"If we lose them, the old man will have our nuts." Thorny's fingers drummed on. "If we confront them, he'll have our ass." He looked at the pained pudding of a face next to him, a few blisters bulging beyond the white bandage. He didn't know which was worse, the smell of the cherry cigar or the grease applied to the coffee burns. The odors he'd spent the day inhaling forced his decision. He opened the car door and inhaled deeply. "Let's go up and have a look."

Ozzie lumbered up the stairway after Thorny picked the outside door lock. Thorny's labored wheezing rasped like a mechanical device in the narrow hallway. They were pursuing action in an attempt to get their minds off the pain. Ozzie stood puffing at the top, staring dumbly down at Thorny's crablike progress, his hand clutching his chest.

"What the hell do we do now? Knock?"

"Sure, knock," Thorny gasped.

"What should I say if somebody answers?"

"Just knock for Chrissake! I'll do the talking—"

But the sudden hammering produced no audible result.

Thorny picked the lock and eased the door open: he had no idea what he'd say if Polly came airily around the corner demanding to know what was going on. And he wasn't at all sure he could control Ozzie, given his gigantic colleague's present state of mind. Oh, to be clear and away and safe with nobody mad at them . . .

They stepped into the apartment's vestibule, moved cautiously on into the sitting room. The music played, the lights cast a cheery, warm glow. Tiptoeing Thorny peered into the kitchen, then the bedroom, which was when he heard Ozzie's strangled scream. Returning to the sitting room he found Ozzie squared off facing a cat which had reared up, back arched like a curved handle, on the back of a chair.

"I'm gonna kill this fuckin' cat," Ozzie moaned deep in his throat. "Little bastard scared me . . . I'm gonna wring its neck . . ."

"And the old man will wring yours, meathead!" He put his hand on Ozzie's arm: "Forget the cat." Ozzie yanked away.

"I wanna do some damage, goddamn it!" He still eyed the cat which had begun to stretch, ignoring the bandaged man as merely a large sputtering, harmless creature.

"Not here. Not anyplace." Thorny spoke in gasps. "Use your head."

Ozzie turned away from the cat and kicked viciously at the couch.

"The question is, where the hell are they?"

"And how did they get out . . ."

"Everybody's disappearing," Thorny said, heading for the kitchen where he took a glass from the cupboard and filled it with tap water. "Underhill's secretary . . ." He sipped water, swallowed carefully, grimacing. "Now these two. And we're still in the dark." He sipped again. "Who's left? We need a lead. You want a drink?"

"Shove your drink," Ozzie said.

"Let's go back to Cambridge," Thorny said at last. With his handkerchief he wiped the glass clean, the cold water tap, and, as they left, the doorknobs.

At Kenmore Square Chandler nosed the brown car through the mist, straining to watch the traffic in the penumbra of his headlamps, blurring in the mist. Down Commonwealth to Arlington, then right with George Washington still on horseback, watching him. Around to Boylston, left on Charles Street, right up Beacon, irresistibly into Chestnut . . . The red Pinto was gone. The yellow glow still shone in the bay window of Polly's apartment. The wipers beat past his gaze. The red Pinto was gone! He turned back onto Beacon Street, crested at the State House, cast a glance down toward Nat Underhill's shop, and pointed into the perpetual traffic clog where School Street intersected Tremont. Past the Parker House with the doorman in breeches and tricornered hat sheltering beneath a black, glistening umbrella, he took a left and jogged through the area of pale, futuristic, massively antiseptic government buildings.

As always there was activity on Union Street and behind the glassed-in Faneuil Hall flower market. Crowds were heading toward Durgin Park and the Union Oyster House, swirling damply through Faneuil Hall and emerging with packages and paper cones full of bright bouquets. He stopped at the curb, waiting. He couldn't see her and, of course, she wouldn't recognize

141

the car. Finally he got out, leaving the motor running and went inside among the flowers and ferns and trees.

"Hey, mister—over here."

She was peering from among what seemed to be a pot full of swaying, dyed ostrich plumes. She winked as he stared.

"Get out of there," he said. "This is no game—"

"But we must retain our senses of humor when those around us are losing theirs," she said, taking his arm as they went back to the car. "What kind of car is this, anyway?" He held the door for her.

"Brown," he said. "Hurry up."

"Nora's safe at the Parker House," she offered as he pulled away. "But not having any great deal of luck. The time is all wrong to be calling Europe. It'll be better for her Monday . . . but she's all right, settled in for the duration."

"The red Pinto was gone. I just checked."

They drove northwards in silence, pushing slowly through the seemingly endless trails of brightly lit restaurants, furniture stores, shopping centers, the Bunker Hill monument to the left, on and on through the steady drip of the rain and the smack of the wiper blades. Slowly, traffic began to thin out and the night began to grip them.

She took his arm. A peculiar sense of exhilaration overcame him, simultaneously, as if they were children: the funny, off-guard sort of moment when a sense of well-being and inevitable happiness swells, fills your chest. It had a good deal to do with her and something to do with the snug, warm interior of the brown car, and the sense of adventure which finally struck Chandler as lacking in danger. They were free of the men in the red Pinto. No one knew where they were going. The macguffin was waiting at the other end and, once they had established what was actually going on, things would just naturally sort themselves out. And he'd have the time to do something about this unusual creature holding his arm.

* * *

It was five o'clock on a Sunday morning when Maxim Petrov was wakened at his *dacha* outside Moscow. He was routed from bed by the ringing of the telephone; then he'd had to wait for Krasnovski to arrive with a briefing on the problem which was to Petrov's way of thinking—at least in the beginnings of the day's events—typically trivial, unclear, and desperately boring. Two hours later, he'd begun feeling as if he'd somehow stuck his foot in it, though he wasn't quite sure how.

"If you'll excuse my saying so, sir," Krasnovski had said, crossing his legs and brushing nonexistent lint from his perfectly pressed slacks, "it's your sense of humor that's done it." The word *again* was implied in his young associate's tone of voice.

"Shut up, will you?" he said testily. The white kitchen reminded him of an operating room, modern and spotless with a bluish tinge to the light. "You sound like a wife—my wife. My sense of humor is all that keeps me sane. It may well be my best quality." He watched impatiently as the last of the coffee dripped into the pot. Outside, much to his amazement, there seemed to be a swatch of lightness across the horizon where for weeks there had been only a dull, dark gray. A touch of spring was enough to pull him back from a severe slackness of mind, even a depression, at just such a time as this. He poured coffee and cream, added sugar, and motioned to Krasnovski to pour his own.

Pulling his heavy terrycloth robe tight around his lean, well-muscled body, he left the kitchen for the heated sun porch which presented the view of a broad field, still snow-covered, leading down to a gentle stream where in the summer, beneath the vast oaks, he sailed toy boats with his grandchildren. He was still watching the horizon when he heard Krasnovski padding up behind him. He wondered if this young man looked at him as he in his time had looked at Beria? With the yearning to break his neck? But, of course, that was ridiculous. Beria had had no sense of humor whatsoever.

"You are going to have to do something, you know." Krasnovski sipped his coffee noisily.

"Don't lecture me," he said.

The younger man shrugged: "It's a matter of mutual trust. We can't have our people killing innocent civilians . . . It's bad for Sanger's people, it's bad for us, and we certainly don't want the police getting too curious. A wave of murders—"

"Two is not a wave," Petrov said wearily. But there was no point in quibbling. "There's no doubt that they're our people?"

"None. They have no idea who they're working for, that goes without saying—"

"Then don't say it."

"CANTAB hired them—"

Petrov glowered at his reflection in the window: "They couldn't possibly be working for somebody else, too?"

"It doesn't make any difference, does it? We're getting the blame."

"A point, I grant you." He swallowed a shot of coffee and noticed that his hands were shaking when he replaced the cup in the saucer. He turned to Krasnovski, smiled: "It did start out as a joke, you know."

"I know."

"A joke on Sanger." He made a wry face and moved slowly along the windowpane, poking a finger into the dry, dusty earth in the flowerpots. Everything was dead, crackled like flames licking at parchment. "And now we're littering Boston with bodies. That's the trouble with this business. You come up with a clever little idea, a joke even, and the incompetents in the field fail to grasp the subtleties, get their guns loaded and go running amok . . . Look at this plant, whatever the hell it was—you can't even trust people to water your plants." He held up a dusty finger. "Well, it's a joke no more. We've got to keep them from killing anybody else. Get word to CANTAB and have him put the lid on these guys immediately. Did all this come to us through CANTAB?"

"I believe so. I was led to believe he was worried."

Krasnovski was bored by his superior's houseplants, dead or alive.

"Did he suggest any plan of action?"

"I got the impression that he wouldn't have objected too strenuously to a termination."

"Bloodthirsty. First he hires them, then he wants to kill them . . ." He went back to the living room and put a Frank Sinatra recording on his Bang and Olufsen turntable. The room filled gently with the words of *In the Wee Small Hours of the Morning*. "Has anyone ever mentioned the whereabouts of the document we're in pursuit of? I don't mean to harp . . . but there was a point to this unhappy exercise which ought not be entirely lost. Aside from my vaunted sense of humor, there was the question of a public relations coup which would not merely discomfit Arden Sanger but the United States as a whole—"

"If I may interrupt, sir—"

Petrov nodded. Sinatra's melancholy flowed around him as the sun fully cleared the horizon. Drawn to the sunrise, he stood at the living room window to watch its cleanliness fall across the snowcrust.

"No one knows exactly where the document is, but apparently there's a Harvard professor who may have it—indeed, CANTAB feels this man either has it or knows where it is—"

"Well, why not simply take it from him? Or follow him?"

"Because he seems to have disappeared."

"Disappeared?" This was becoming increasingly troublesome: it had begun as such a lark.

"Disappeared. But not before badly beating up our two operatives—"

"A Harvard professor? What are you telling me?"

"He did them rather a lot of injury."

"Incredible. Proves my point, though. Impossible to get decent help these days. In a way, it's too bad he didn't kill them . . ."

"Yes, sir, it is."

"But since they are still alive, I suppose the professor must be found. Does he have a name, Krasnovski?"

"I suppose he does, unless they've beaten us to the numbering system, sir." Krasnovski bit off a short smirk.

"Do you know the man's name?"

"We did not receive that information, sir."

"Then, go, Krasnovski. Stop this killing and find the stupid bloody document, get the word to CANTAB. For the time being, we'll sit tight and hope that Arden doesn't get worked up." He saw Krasnovski to the door. "Arden has an unfortunate tendency to believe everything out of the ordinary is a prelude to World War Three."

While Chandler and Polly Bishop were heading northward from Boston through the rain, and while Maxim Petrov was being awakened at his *dacha* outside Moscow with the bad news, Arden Sanger, director of the CIA, was entertaining a few friends at his heavily guarded estate in Virginia, ten minutes by helicopter from his office at Langley. He also had two offices in Washington and a town house in Georgetown. He was a rich man. He'd been born that way, sixty-five years ago in Orange City, Iowa, the son of a man whose every touch seemed to produce money. Farming, insurance, land, mining, oil. It was all that money that had enabled young Arden to pursue a career as a lawyer who devoted himself to public service. Franklin Roosevelt spotted him in the late thirties, brought him to Washington, and that had pretty much settled Arden Sanger's fate.

He'd always been an amiable young fellow, well over six feet tall, given to overweight which had been curbed by a football career at the University of Iowa where he'd been an All-American fullback in the years before Nile Kinnick eclipsed his fame. As he grew larger in the years after football, people kidded him about being a big, dumb football player, and when *The Male Animal* was turned into a movie it was widely believed that the character played by Jack Carson was based on the old All-American Arden Sanger. His striking resemblance to Jack Carson did little to quell the rumor but he was never particularly bothered by it. For all he knew or cared, the character *was* based on him. Big deal. Nile Kinnick and Jack Carson were both dead and Arden Sanger was head of the goddamned CIA.

All this personal history was in his mind because an attractive young woman, the daughter of an old friend, had been flattering him with her attention all evening. He rather enjoyed talking about himself; he was skilled at never saying anything that he shouldn't concerning his professional life. All in all, it was a pleasant evening, sufficiently springlike to open the French door onto the broad flagstone patio with the pool and tennis courts beyond, the tree line beyond that, and the patrolled, electrified, and television-monitored fence beyond further still. It was, in fact, the sort of evening which found him forgetting for the moment just who and what he was. His guests had dined well and were conversing happily in his sunken party room as he and the pretty little blonde returned from a stroll around the tennis court.

"Let me tell you, Elise," he said, watching her nibble at the rim of her champagne glass, "if I'd met someone like you forty years ago I'd never have turned into a bachelor."

"Look at it this way," she replied confidently, "as a bachelor you've been able to spend forty years playing the field. Very successfully, I'm sure." She took his hand in hers in a gesture which just conceivably could have been interpreted as an invitation. His mind was flickering through the range of possible responses and consequences when he heard his aide, Dennis Herman, clearing his throat, touching his arm.

"Yes, Dennis?" It had taken Sanger almost a year to get it clear in his mind that the fellow's name was not Herman Dennis which somehow struck him as more appropriate.

"There's a messenger in the library, sir."

"I see. Elise, you must excuse me for a moment. Dennis will see to your glass, my dear." He retired quickly to the dark-toned library where Harry Stevenson himself, his most immediate associate at the company, was waiting for him, smoking a pipe and reading the current *Playboy* which featured an interview with a radical terrorist they'd seriously considered having assassinated.

"Arden," he said, blowing smoke and without looking up, "we should have snuffed this little shit when we had the chance. Now he's a media hero, wants to be a senator for God's sake." He threw the magazine at a chair and missed, tearing the cover.

"I only look at the pictures," Sanger said. He lowered his broad rear end into a cracked leather club chair and watched Stevenson from deep-set eyes, well padded with pouches of fat. In two weeks he was going in for a face-lift that would make his vision considerably clearer. But he could see Stevenson's bony, sharp-edged face well enough. It was a mathematician's face. Stevenson had come to the company fifteen years before from M.I.T. "So, what can I do for you?"

"Something funny is going on in Boston," Stevenson said cryptically.

"Boston *is* funny. Tell me something I don't know."

"I've had a call·from CRUSTACEAN."

"Indeed?"

"He's worried. He says Petrov's got two gunsels up there killing people. He doesn't much like it."

"Gunsels? I should hope not. Does he know why?"

"No, not really. It's over a document of some kind . . . well, I ran a check and much to my surprise we're not missing any plans for a sneak attack, nerve gas, germ warfare, flooding the market with unsalted popcorn. But our friend doesn't bring us in on these things without good reason. Two innocent citizens shot dead strike him as good reasons, I guess."

"I think you'd better go through this by the numbers, Harry."

It took the better part of an hour. They sat quietly for a few minutes when the story, so far as Stevenson knew it, was finished.

"Nobody knows where the damn thing is, I take it," Sanger said. "Or what the hell it is . . ."

"Check. Not a clue. Just dead people—"

"And a disappearing Harvard professor."

148

"Check."

"I suppose we'd better try to find out why the devil Petrov is so interested—"

"You know how it works, if he's interested, we're interested." Stevenson cuffed his pipe against the side of a heavy glass ashtray, blew noisily through the stem.

"Well, find Chandler—that's it, so far as I can tell."

"Not quite all. CRUSTACEAN wants a go-ahead on terminating Petrov's lads. On his own discretion."

"If it seems the thing to do, you mean."

Stevenson nodded.

"Oh, God," Sanger sighed. "Only if they hurt somebody else."

"I'll try it on, I'm not sure he won't just go ahead and do as he chooses. Old fart."

Sanger laughed. "The question is, why would Max set his boys loose and run the risk of pissing me off?"

"Maybe it's important . . ."

"Then why use a couple of garbagemen? Makes no sense."

"We shall see what we shall see," Stevenson said.

"As always."

Stevenson had reached the double doors and was about to leave when Sanger had a thought.

"The trouble with Max is his goddamn sense of humor. He makes a joke in Moscow and I start hurting in Virginia."

"This is no joke now," Stevenson said bleakly, "if it ever was. Which I doubt." But he went away knowing that if it wasn't a joke, it was surely a game. Always was, always would be.

A purist at heart, a perfectionist even when faced with the impossible, the old man listened to the young pianist turn what should have been the wrist octaves of the "Waldstein" into a sliding, rakish glissando. Just because a thing was accepted didn't make it right and the old man had a feeling that if Beethoven had wanted a glissando he'd have noted the fact as he'd done in the First Concerto. The fire in the grate at the far end of the Gardner Museum's tapestry room, long and dark and low, cast a warm glow which reached him in the fourth row. The wind outside swept off the Back Bay Fens and rattled the glass in the French windows which overlooked the garden and the murky, inclement darkness beyond. Draughts crept along the floor and nipped at his ankles.

The concert provided a respite after having spent most of the Saturday's late afternoon poking around his favorite corners of the Boston Museum of Fine Arts. Long ago he and his wife had enjoyed whiling away free hours at the museums, though they both actually preferred the Italianate Gardner with its courtyard of dripping, fragrant flowers, and the whimsical, capricious placement of the paintings. Each visit was still full of surprises for the old man who now came alone but almost as frequently.

His mother had been a friend of Isabella Gardner's and as a boy he'd met the extraordinary woman whose creation this fifteenth-century Venetian palace was. Her only son had died, an infant of two, and by the same time he'd met her she was past seventy and had taken a liking to him, a serious, knobby-kneed Beacon Hill boy of ten. Lately the old man had been thinking about Isabella Gardner because she was the first person he'd ever known who had died. What in God's name would she have thought of him if she'd known what he'd gone on to do with his life?

The mind reeled at the prospect.

Well, he had music, too. Did he have young friends? It depended, so to speak, on the precision of your definitions. He looked at his watch as the music ended and the applause swelled hastily and chairs were scraped back. Did Liam and Andrew qualify as friends? On the whole, though he rather liked them, he thought not. The other two cretins he wanted killed.

Liam and Andrew were waiting for him in the North Cloister, a forlorn, wetted-down pair matching rather well the two fish fountains on the wall across the garden. Yellow and lavender flowers bloomed regardless of the weather outside and vines dangled from above.

"Good evening," the old man said, being sure to stand clear of the wet raincoats. "I'll be brief. The evening concludes with the 'Moonlight' which I do not intend to miss." He paused long enough to fix them each, eye to eye. "I'm disappointed in your progress. You've gained no ground and you're going to have to start doing so. I have learned who the homicidal maniacs are who have killed Bill Davis and Mr. Underhill." He described them in detail, including their various bandages and infirmities and how they acquired them. "I also know that they have not yet achieved their goal— Chandler is at large and the document in question remains out of their reach, as well as ours. I want you to find them, check the Harvard Motor Lodge, check Brennan . . . but please do find them. Remember, you are at an advantage—you know about them, they are ignorant of your existence. Find them and they may lead you to Chandler and the document . . . they are working for the Russians, incidentally, and whatever it is they want, we obviously want it, too."

He could see them grappling with the information and for a moment he felt a twinge of pity. Any complex situation was so much clearer when you knew both sides, or rather two sides of however many there might be. Andrew pried his wire-rimmed spectacles from behind his ears and began wiping off rainspots with a crumpled white handkerchief. Liam was hugging his arms across his chest, rocking back on his heels, watching the crowd out of habit.

"What the hell do you think it is?" Liam asked.

"It doesn't make any difference. We can't have them killing people. If we show that kind of weakness, well, who knows where it will lead?"

"What do we do when we find them and they find this document?"

"I'm not altogether certain. We will decide then. You *must* stay in touch with me. You know how."

The crowd was eddying away, back toward the tapestry room. When Thorny and Ozzie found the damn thing and told him what the devil it was, then he'd decide whether or not to have them killed.

"I suggest you hop it to Cambridge. I realize that Brennan may have something less than full confidence in you following your music hall turn the other morning, but still . . . what else have we got? And you may run across Lum and Abner, don't you see?"

The old man nodded and walked back toward the tapestry room. He didn't look back and therefore missed Liam furtively sticking his tongue out at him.

Together, wearily, Liam and Andrew set off into the rain once again.

Getting home from the Museum was a major undertaking for Brennan. He had developed a nasty late winter-early spring cold with a fever, raspy throat, and fits of nasty chills. Of course, Chandler had to go pick up Polly right away, which left Brennan to cope with public transport. It never occurred to him to take a taxi: instead he waited in the cold and wet for a streetcar, switched at Kenmore Square and Park Street and an hour later emerged like a sick rat from the subway in Harvard Square. He loaded up on cold remedies and magazines and paperbacks at a drugstore, bought a six-pack of Tuborg, and waddled, dispiritedly toward his house.

Colin was on his own now. Nothing more Hugh Brennan could do. He was anticipating an evening of total exhaustion, quaffing cold medicine, getting smashed on Tuborg, lusting for Mary Tyler Moore. Now that was a thought: Mary Tyler Moore . . .

He soaked in a steaming tub for half an hour, rubbed Vicks on his hairy chest in memory of his mother, tore open a new box of Kleenex, and with his beer and magazines and paperbacks got settled under a blanket on his couch. He was mixing beer and Excedrin and seeing two Mary Tyler Moores, when the doorbell rang. He didn't recognize it for what it was at first, the bell taking some few seconds to penetrate the furriness all around him. It kept ringing. Eventually, swearing, tripping on the robe and blanket he wrapped around himself, he excused himself to Bob Newhart and his television family and went to the door.

He didn't recognize them, didn't make any connections which might have alerted him, cleared his brain. A small man in a flat, black-and-white checked hat and a large man with a white bandage partially obscuring his broad, swollen face.

He was farther gone than he'd thought possible, the beer and the Excedrin and the cold stuff whirring like tiny engines of destruction in his bloodstream and brain. Everything he saw, he saw twice, two outlines, and every sound was two sounds slightly out of sync. There was, he remembered vaguely, something he should know about these two men who had somehow gotten through the doorway, something . . . something . . .

Then, through the open doorway, under the streetlamp, he saw the little red car.

But by then it was too late. Strong hands had forced him back inside and he heard the door slam, the noise echoing in his head as if an echo were visible. The red car . . . He struggled to get out of his chair. No good, no strength. Bob Newhart said something and the idiotic pilot who lived down the hall said something and the audience roared and when he focused on the large man kneeling in front of him something bright and shining caught his eye.

"Professor," the smaller one said, "calm down, just sit there . . . we have a question or two . . ."

It was—oh my God, it was the pliers . . .

And it all came back to him and he began to scream. Too late, goddamn it, too late, too late . . .

"We don't want to hurt you, Professor, but we need some help . . . Don't make us hurt you . . ."

Halfway to Kennebunkport, taking the weatherswept coastal road, Chandler realized that Polly had fallen asleep, still holding his arm, her head of thick brown hair resting lightly against his shoulder. Watching her, his contentment was complete. His body was losing the

153

aches and pains which had sprouted in the most peculiar places subsequent to the attack by the two goons. His mind felt clear now that he was on the track with Percy Davis the next stop: his curiosity was, of course, unabated, but he was full of anticipation rather than anxiety. He couldn't have explained why he felt so buoyant but he hoped that he didn't lose it.

He remembered Percy Davis's voice reading Underhill's letter.

> . . . *a document so curious and valuable that a human life was only a temporary obstacle to those bent on acquiring it . . . inevitably those who want it and are prepared to kill to get it will be confused, perplexed, and increasingly dangerous as they discover their quarry has disappeared. But I am a desperate man and I cannot send it directly to the one party who must see it sooner or later— Professor Colin Chandler at Harvard. I cannot send it directly to this gentleman out of respect for his safety . . .*

Well, the point was, nobody knew where he'd gone. So he and Polly were safe.

Except, of course, Brennan. He wasn't sure if he'd even actually told Hugh in so many words. But it had been obvious: Brennan surely would have known that Kennebunkport was his destination . . .

The thought crossed his mind like a cloud, threatening his euphoria, but he brushed it away. Hugh was safe, curled up with a good book and a stiff drink and a box of Kleenex.

The rain increased, the wind hurling itself against the side of the brown car, and Polly stirred, awoke. His stomach growled. They stopped for a hamburger in a lonely, invitingly lit diner, swilled the fries and the cole slaw down with hot coffee, and he watched her smoke a cigarette. He enjoyed watching her hands with the well-defined sinews and veins and bones, like fine translucent china. Her lips closed softly on the cigarette, delicately, as if it might break. She brushed her hair back over her ears, smiled at him with the parentheses curling at the corners of her mouth and the lines at the corners of her eyes radiating outward like the rays of a rising sun.

Kennebunkport was huddled dark and close to the ground in the lashing cold rain. They crossed the bridge that led into the small main square, the leatherworkers' shop on the left alternately illuminated and darkened in shadow by a windblown streetlamp. The drugstore was closed. The café-and-grocery store sharing the same premises was closed. They turned their way through the square, following Percy Davis's directions until they found the road that ran seaward with the harbor's docks and antique shops and restaurants on the right. He watched for and saw, picked out by the car's lights, the vivid blue sign for the Arundel Restaurant, swinging in the gale. Beyond and to the sides there was a pitchy darkness pricked only by the old, blurred light of a boat or a house or a backroom. Rain washed across the windshield. They were on the right road.

Listening intently they heard the crash of the surf, the hiss of the tires on the wet road, the groan of a foghorn somewhere offshore. The headlamps picked out sandy hillocks, gorse-covered, beaten down brown and hard by the winter and the spring storms. When the road threatened to lead them into the Atlantic it swung to the left, rounding a point of land's end with rocks spraying down toward the beach and water to the right, large summer houses looming vaguely, dimly to the landward side.

A shielded bare lightbulb shone upwards against the weather-beaten sign announcing at the roadside, with an arrow pointing up the driveway, The Seafoam Inn. The gravel crunched underneath as he turned off the deserted highway.

She looked at him: "Well, we're here . . ." She leaned forward to get a better view up the hill at the inn itself. Two windows shone, blurred yellow through the rain,

155

like blind eyes, cataracts. A white porch stretched the length of the green-shingled building and turned the corner along the side with large windows behind the spokes and spindly gingerbread columns. It was clearly intended for summer habitation: like all the surrounding houses it was built on a shelf of rock that made underground pipes and whatnot impossible. "It reminds me of *Psycho*," she said softly. "If Anthony Perkins answers the door . . ."

Chandler sucked in a deep breath and drove on up the driveway, puling the car flush against a shelter of evergreens near the stairs to the porch. "Let's go," he said, and they bounded through the rain, up onto the porch with the rain drumming on the shingles overhead. The light over the door went on and the door opened, presenting a tall, white-haired, slender, and slightly stooped man wearing a beige cardigan over a plaid shirt.

"Professor Chandler, I presume," he said. "I'm Percy Davis. You folks come on in, I'm mighty pleased to see you got here all right." He gestured them inside, took their coats. "Heck of a night, heck of a night." They found themselves in a warm lobby area with a desk backed by a switchboard that had a distinctly antique look, a bulletin board with notices from the previous summer, and a calendar from a local auto repair shop. There were some overstuffed chairs, a horsehair sofa, two glass-fronted bookcases, a set of stairs disappearing upwards, and the darkened restaurant which faced outward across the porch toward the ocean.

Chandler introduced Polly.

Percy Davis nodded laconically: "I recognized you right off, miss. You're not exactly anonymous up this way." He gave the observation a sad inflection as if anonymity was anyone's most valuable possession. "You're not workin', are you?" His voice carried the autumnal rustle, the dryness Chandler remembered from the telephone. "I don't want you comin' in here with cameras, gettin' me mixed up in all this . . ." He waggled a forefinger at Polly, shook his head. "A person's got his privacy, that's the law—"

156

"Never fear, Mr. Davis," Polly said. "I'm here strictly as a friend."

Percy Davis regarded her with squint-eyed doubt, hooked a thumb in the pocket of his sweater. He was expensively dressed but he hadn't lost, or forsaken, what in Maine is usually referred to as flintiness.

"Well, maybe not just as a friend," Polly clarified, retreating under the squint. "But there's not a camera in sight, no microphones—"

"Well, young lady, see that none of them come poppin' up from nowheres. Now let's get to business, Professor. Come on out to the kitchen."

They followed him through the dark restaurant with its bare tables and upturned wooden chairs, through a swing door past a pantry into a large, well-lighted, old-fashioned kitchen, vast and clean with real patterned linoleum on the floor and a wooden rack for dish towels and a rubber drying rack. It smelled of soap and coffee and one look told you that Percy Davis kept it spotless.

"You can't live here year round," Chandler said.

"Could, could if I was a mind to," Percy said, rummaging in a cupboard. "But I've got more sense. I come out for a week at a time, use space heaters, keep the place spic and span. Ah, here it is, back behind the pots and pans . . ." Slowly and with nerve-racking care he slid the parcel out of the cupboard.

Chandler nodded at the parcel: "Thus, the macguffin."

"Don't be a smartass at a time like this," she said under her breath. "This is it, for God's sake . . . people have died for this, Colin . . ."

"Here it is, all right," Davis said. "It was all wrapped up like this with another wrapper around it. I read you the letter from the late Mr. Underhill, here it is." He handed the piece of closely written paper to Chandler. "Now, let's adjourn to the library. I've got a nice fire going and it's more comfortable."

Realizing that Percy Davis was not a man to be hurried, Chandler fought off his impatience and followed Polly and the old codger back out through the restaurant and lobby into what must have been a sitting room

157

fifty years ago, but was now lined with a dozen un-matched bookcases obviously collected over the years from a dozen different estate sales. A coal fire blazed, crackled. Comfortable chairs were everywhere. Davis led the way to a cane-backed couch, sat down, and put the package on a low coffee table.

"It's all yours, Professor. And welcome to it."

Confronted with the moment itself, Chandler felt the fine sense of well-being slipping away. Even a blind pig, his grandfather had been fond of saying long ago, was bound occasionally to find an acorn. And here was his acorn. His fingers trembled as he began fum-bling with the knotted string which crosshatched the brown-wrapped package which measured about eight inches square. Percy reached out with a bone-handled pocket knife, blade extended, looking at Chandler for approval. He nodded and the strings fell quickly away. Kneeling beside the low table, her hands balled into little fists of excitement, Polly held her breath. The grandfather clock ticked in one corner and the waves crashed on the rocks below the road and the rain lashed at the window, hissed coming down the chimney: the moment was frozen forever in his mind. He was no longer the Harvard professor, the expert, removed from events, insulated by the protective layer of two cen-turies . . . The past had risen like an adder in the dark and taken new victims, and now he held the past in his hands.

He peeled the paper away.

Revealed, in a thickish frame of plain oak, chipped in places and with a split along the grain here and there, was a small oil portrait of a woman. It had dried out over the years and the recent shuttling about had brought on some additional flaking, but there it was, a competent piece of work which struck Chandler rather oddly, almost as if he'd seen it before.

"My God, it's just a woman's face," Polly whispered, angling toward Chandler to get a better view as he tilted it up. "Not the plans to blow up Boston or sack Harvard."

Percy Davis stroked his chin: "If that isn't the Davis mouth I miss my guess. Long time, two hundred years, but bloodlines will prevail." He paused, then harrumphed: "Well, pardon me, but I don't get it. Every two-bit museum and antique shop in New England's got stuff like this . . ."

"Why kill people over this?" Polly leaned back and looked accusingly at the portrait: "What is it with you, lady . . . what gives?"

The woman in the frame stared impassively back at them: a middle-aged woman, though people looked older then—maybe she was only thirty or so. A severe face, good bones making it oval with a becoming wideness across her cheeks, dark brown eyes which were giving away no secrets, just a hint of humor in the curvature of the eyebrows, a mouth which looked made for genteel sarcasm. Her dress so far as it could be seen was beige and white with a cornflower-blue ribbon woven in at the bodice, just above the bottom of the frame. Her hair was dark brown, matching her eyes, drawn tightly back from her face, showing off a high, rather noble forehead. Percy was right: his mouth was a replica of hers.

She had been painted against a pale blue wall with a painting within the painting on the wall behind her, partially obscured by her hair. The conceit of the period presumably was intended to provide a clue to the subject's personality: in this case, the painting within the painting depicted an all-purpose high-steepled New England church with parishioners standing about outside, horses obediently lounging by a white fence. A church-going woman, pillar of the community, well aware of right and wrong and God's place in the universe.

"What's the matter, Colin?" Polly had grown attuned to him, saw the curiosity behind his eyes.

"There's something about this portrait—"

"Well, there's an envelope here in the wrapping paper," Percy said.

"I know what it is," Chandler said softly, "I know what it is . . . and I know why it was me, only me, they

159

were trying to get the painting to . . . this painting was done by Winthrop Chandler! Not a great figure in American art history but by God he makes the textbooks, barely, but he makes them. And he's the only Chandler who made a mark in art—"

"He's not—"

"Damn right, a bona fide ancestor of mine—"

"This is what always happens in these parts," Percy said. "I'm descended from Davises up the whazoo and half the family will never let you forget it, horse thief or procurer or peddler, if he was a Davis we'll claim the poor son of a bitch—"

"Well, Winthrop is one of our family," Chandler noted a trifle testily while Polly smiled. "He was an itinerant portraitist from Woodstock in Connecticut, came to Boston to study painting . . . painted houses, too, and tradesmen's signs. Had to make a living. We figure he was in Boston all during the revolutionary war . . . And the man could paint a portrait, one of the best of his day. We've got five or six in the family, there's a honey in Brookline at the Historical Association— anyway, Underhill knew I'd have a feeling for a Winthrop Chandler and he had an idea that this was one . . ."

"Is it?" Polly asked.

"I'd say it is, it's got the style, even the colors he liked best. And I'm sure Underhill's thinking went this way, if it's a Chandler, Chandler's the best man to authenticate it . . ."

"The letter," Percy Davis said.

Chandler opened the envelope and unfolded the sheet of plain white typing paper, glanced at it for a moment. "It's not a letter," he said. "It seems to be more of an explanation of how he found the painting. Here, we can all read it." He flattened it on the table and they all leaned forward.

I found this old portrait in a trunk in the attic of my parents' summer place in Chatham. I doubt if anyone had even opened the trunk in a hundred years, let alone gone through the not very interest-

ing contents as I did. And never had anyone paid much attention to this old portrait of "Grandma," as I call her—I think it's easier just to call her that since no one seemed to have any idea who she was. When I found it I had been doing some outside reading for one of Professor Chandler's courses and had somehow gotten into the art of the revolutionary period.

I handled the painting so much that one day I saw that the cloth backing had begun to come loose. So I finished the job. And that's how I found what I've decided to call "The Glendower Legacy" which no doubt comes from reading too many thrillers. I'm not sure what it all means since it is open to so many possible interpretations, but I know damned well how important it could be.

When I've finished my own research I suppose Chandler and Nat Underhill will have to do some authentication and probably take over making my findings known. Chandler's stature is such that any doubters will be disarmed before they begin. If what I've found is the real thing. And then, of course, it will no longer be my own little secret. I shall miss it.

"What *is* he talking about?" Polly said impatiently. "Or is this just building suspense? Is there anything besides the portrait?" She shuffled through the string and wrapping paper.

"Of course there is," Chandler said. "Inside the backing of the frame, just where he found it. Percy, your knife, if you please." Davis handed him the pocketknife and he slid the blade under the obviously new tape holding the cardboard backing against the frame. The backing was new, too, and tight against the wood. A few seconds later Polly was able to slide her hand under the felt. A tip of tongue protruding from between tight lips, she withdrew two more envelopes, new and yellow with metal clasps on the backs as if

161

they were preserving pieces of evidence. One envelope was labeled in block capitals WM. DAVIS'S LETTER.

The paper on which William Davis had written his letter two centuries before was thick and wrinkled and showed its age, but less so than it might have had it not been tucked safely behind the portrait. No one had ever seen it because no one had ever looked; the writing was somewhat faded but far less so than on many documents of the period. This one had never had to survive the light of day. It was dated *14 January 1778 Valley Forge . . .*

To Whom It May Concern

I am desperate afraid and stricken with the awfullest terror. Last night I have seen the impossible here at Godforsaken Valley Forge and if I Die, as all my friends seem to be Dying, I cannot take what I have seen with my own eyes to my Grave. My belongings are few and this portrait of my dear Mother is all I have of value. It is, therefore, the most likely possession of mine to survive this terrible trial.

Yesternight I accidentally witnessed treachery the likes of which I could never have imagined in my worst Nightmares. We are Betrayed to the Redcoats, plain and simple. I do not rely on the evidence of my Eyes, which are not too reliable given our diet here and the rampaging Disease in this Hellhole. But I have a piece of Evidents, signed by the Traitor himself, acknowledging receipt of payment for his dastardly deeds and his new code Name, and the Evidents don't lie, though my eyes might.

I cannot bring myself to write his name, this traitor—but I saw him in a clearing in the woods with his Masters when I was posted sentry. When they were interrupted by some of my fellows a fight broke out, men were dying, and I dashed into

*the clearing and took the piece of paper. Tho it
tore in the process, as I discovered on my return
to camp, it is Enough. But what dare I do with it?
Where can I go for help? And what if I do not
live to see the Spring? If I am found out, surely
they will kill me. And Fate may carry me off anyway. I do not feel at all well as it is. I have no
answers and must trust in the Lord to see me to
Safe Harbor.*

*I will hide this is the back of the portrait of Mother
and entrust it to my Friend John Higgins.*

*God Help Our Cause! And your servant, Wm.
Davis.*

"My God," Chandler breathed. "You can feel the
terror even now. The poor kid . . . I damn well bet
he never got home." He leaned back in the cushions of
the couch.

"I'm almost scared to open the other envelope,"
Polly said. "I almost don't want to know . . ."

"Makes you wonder just what we've gotten into. My
grandson dead, an old man dead, and now this boy at
Valley Forge . . . if he'd survived the war, this thing
wouldn't have had to wait until now. He'd have done
something with it—I think he was a brave lad . . ."
Percy's voice was choked with emotion: "I can see him
going into that clearing with the guns blazing . . . Brave
lad."

It was nearly midnight as Chandler took the final
envelope and bent the clasp back, opened it. He belled
it open and let the poor, soiled remnant of the past
flutter to the table. The paper was discolored and
spotted, smelled of a dried-out, centuries-old mildew.
The top right corner was ripped jaggedly but the message, in ink, was plainly visible. The body of the written
material had been inscribed by one hand, the signature
large and bold was the work of another.

Chandler read it aloud, slowly, and finished in a

whisper. They searched each other's faces in the silence, unable to speak. As the grandfather clock chimed mid-

night Chandler placed the antique scrap of paper on the table before them. He couldn't think of a single word to say as he read it again to himself.

10 Jan. 1778
To acknowledge the following—
1. *Receipt of agreed upon payment from the representatives of the Crown in regard to services rendered these past six months, concluding with 1 January 1778.*
2. *Change of code name, effective for the twelve-month beginning with 1 January 1778, to the single word 'GLENDOWER'.*

Signed willingly by yr. hmbl. serv.

Geo. Washington

Sunday

The last chime of midnight faded into the stillness while Chandler's sense of heightened awareness tightened its grip on his psyche. He felt like Jimmy Stewart on the rooftop in *Vertigo,* unable to resist the fall, almost needing the fall to somehow square accounts. The fire crackled and spit and he heard the squeak as Percy Davis leaned back against the ancient wicker. But all he saw was the signature, seen countless times in the past, bold, undaunted: *Geo. Washington.* And the images flickered silently through his brain: withdrawing the electronic bug from the tobacco jar, his Houdon bust exploding as it was smashed to the floor, himself staring up into the omniscient eyes, the impassively heroic face of the great man on horseback in the Public Garden . . .

Polly spoke first.

"Can it be, Colin?" She had leaned back from the table and was sitting cross-legged, looking up at him. "I mean, historically. Is it possible?"

Chandler shook his head, tried to loosen the webs of shock: "Possible? God, I don't know . . . anything is *possible,* I suppose, but this is less so than practically anything I've ever heard . . . it's like saying Franklin Roosevelt was working for the Japanese in 1941, no it's even more unlikely, if you can imagine that. It's incredible in the true sense of the word, but—"

"But what?"

"But the United States was full of people wanting to make deals with the Japanese and Germans in 1941,

165

and there were probably far more during the Revolution who sympathized with England . . . You heard my lecture the other day. Loyalty was an issue of great weight, *the* issue, but loyalty to whom . . . king or country? But, this," he nodded at the paper, "this is just beyond anything . . ."

"Colin, you've got to remember that you're a man who worships George Washington—no, don't quibble, worship or whatever word you choose. It all means the same thing—"

"The fact is, he is the greatest figure in our history, not necessarily the most brilliant, nor the cleverest, maybe not even the bravest, but taken as a man the greatest—"

"Please, not a lecture," she said, half smiling. "My question is, would another historian find it so difficult to accept? That Washington was covering himself just in case?"

"Sure, you could find historians who'd love it, snot-nosed kids dying to prove the theory that there are no great men. Look at the kick they got out of Washington's expense account . . . Petty bastards are always willing to reduce anyone to their own level of pettiness—"

Polly looked heavenward: "Oh, why did it have to be Washington, God, why?" she muttered. "But you don't buy it?"

"I don't want to buy it," he said, shaking his head. "I don't see how I can . . ." He was finding it difficult to talk and he would not really have expected anyone else to fully understand. But the foundations of his adult life were grounded in his philosophy of history: he had no wife, no children, no responsibilities to divert him from the occupations of his mind. And if his view of history was wrong—if it was a joke, a boring and rather ugly story about run-of-the-mill men who happened to get written and talked about—then what was the purpose of his own life?

And now, staring at the scrap of paper reaching across two hundred years to threaten the reason for his existence, he felt a deathly chill.

166

Betrayed, he felt betrayed, by his own convictions and by history itself.

Polly took his hand and held it in both of hers: was she sympathizing? Of course she was, but behind her concern, did he see her claiming a victory in their argument? Was history—as opposed to the day-to-day living through the events—only a false pattern applied to matters so complex as not to have a pattern? Was history a joke? Did Washington wear the cap and bells? God, it was worse than opening your eyes and seeing the threat of the gleaming pliers . . .

"Now, listen here," Percy Davis said. He got slowly to his feet and hoisted another slab of coal onto the fire, prodded it into position. He took a large key from the mantelpiece and stood watching his two guests, turning it in his hand. "What's the point in jumping in without checking the depth of the water first? Underhill and my grandson Bill wanted you to authenticate this doodad, now don't that mean that they must have had their own doubts? Damn right, it does . . . The fact is, we don't know that the man who signed this receipt really was old G.W. himself. Be honest now, we don't, do we?"

"But the *sight* of him convinced William Davis. The piece of paper, the signature, that was his clincher—" Polly had shifted the paper on the table to see it better.

"And," Percy said, "it was William D. himself who said he could no longer trust his eyes because of the lousy diet and weakness and disease all around him . . . So what he saw, I reckon, was a big, broad-beamed man who wrote G.W.'s name."

"More than wrote it," Chandler said numbly. "Forged it. It looks like Washington's signature . . ."

"So what?" Percy retorted, taking the key and going to the tall clock. "Forgery ain't nothin' we invented in the twentieth century, y'know." He began winding the mechanism. "How does the rest of it look, Professor? To the trained eye. Does it strike you as the real goods?"

"Sure, it looks okay. The paper and the writing *look* old, the style of the script itself looks authentic, the painting is the right age and I know damned well it's a Winthrop Chandler, blah blah blah—sure, somebody wrote this a long time ago, a hell of a long time ago . . . But was it Washington? Or an imposter? Or an aide who had access to his papers and mastered his signature? Did the British rig the whole thing to use it as blackmail? Or was Washington actually trying to con the British?"

"Or was he working for the British?" Polly asked. "It's a possibility we've got to consider—"

"Well, he made a damned bad job of it," Percy said, "if he was trying to help the British. You may remember, he won the war—"

"He could have switched sides again," Polly said, "once the army survived the winter at Valley Forge. It may have been that he was looking at the war and finding no way to win it, the country's most influential men divided, the army dwindling . . . he may have bottomed out in seventy-seven and decided he'd better gradually extricate his army with honor, decent terms, and the least agony possible . . ."

"If only we could see them in that clearing," Chandler mused, imagining that remarkable moment in the corner of his mind. "I'd recognize George, I'd know him in an instant . . ." He came back to them with a perplexed smile: "But it's Washington, you see, that makes it all so farfetched. Anybody else. But not Washington himself . . ."

"But he was only a man, Colin," Polly said.

"No, he was far more than that," he said. "He was a great man."

"Right, right, so I've heard," she snapped back impatiently. "Oh, Colin, I'm sorry, I know what this means to you, but you've got to be ready . . . to accept the truth, if it manifestly is the truth—"

"Well, we're a long way from that point now."

"Excuse me, folks," Percy said, "I don't mean to interrupt the seminar, but history aside, how does this piece of paper fit in with the deaths of Bill and Underhill? How could it cause them?"

"Well, let's see some possibilities," Chandler said,

having forgotten for the moment the concerns of the present. It was the same old story, the past was more real, more involving than the present. "It could be a collector who's gone crazy, or a demented historian . . . it's all nuts, utterly nuts . . ."

"A collector, or historian, who hires the goon squad to kill and maim?" The doubt in Polly's voice was hard to ignore. "I can't accept that one. We're dealing with a lot of people, you know. The guys who came to your office, Fennerty and McGonigle, whoever they really are, and the guys who came to your house . . . they're all after this piece of paper, this signature and the incrimination that goes with it—Colin, I really don't think we're dealing with an academic scandal—"

"I don't know," he sighed. "I suppose you're right— I'm baffled . . ."

"Well, how could anybody use this? Murder aside, how could anyone use it regardless of how they got it? What do you do with a thing like this once you've got it?"

Percy spoke up: "Be a hell of a blot on the old copybook, don't you think? Make us all look mighty silly if the Russians, say, or the Chinese, or you-name-it, got hold of this and let the world know . . . sort of a Bicentennial present—"

"A PR gesture," Polly said, nodding, lower lip jutting, "an embarrassment."

"Come on, that's crazy." Chandler stood up and stretched, hearing his joints crack and snap. "Foreign powers—how could they know it even existed?"

Polly swiveled on the floor, slowly, and pointed a finger deliberately up at Chandler towering over her.

"Turn the coin over," she said. "Say our side knew of its existence, knew there was evidence to show that George Washington was a traitor to his country—what would our side want to do?"

"Keep it damned well hidden, down the well for good and all, eh?" Percy rubbed his dry hands together, rising to the peculiarity of the situation. "It could be our own johnnies chasing about the countryside, killing and doing bodily harm . . . my God, one thing recent history's taught me, anything is possible, *anything*."

"Yes," Polly murmured, almost purring, "and the business of foreign powers isn't such a problem when you remember one thing."

"What, what?" Chandler asked impatiently.

"Nat visited Bucharest recently," Polly said. "As simple as that."

They proceeded to turn over the possibilities for the better part of two hours, adding nothing of great value and reaching no conclusions worthy of the name. Chandler felt his eyes tearing up from tiredness. His neck ached and he was tired from the stiffness brought on by the events of his recent night at the hands of the goons and the evening damp. But it was his brain that was weariest of all, his brain and his spirit. He yawned finally and nearly fell off the couch. He was only barely aware that the conversation had stopped. Both Polly and Percy Davis were staring numbly into the fire.

"Well, I for one can't take any more," he said. "My mind's gone all furry—can't think of anything that makes sense. I've got to get some sleep. Maybe in the morning I'll know what the hell to do . . ." He stood up and Polly stood up with him.

"Good idea," Percy said. "Things bound to perk up in the morning light. I've got a room ready—twin beds suit you? All the other beds are stripped, I'm afraid."

"Fine," Polly said, covering her own yawn.

Alone, in the large room with the glass rattling in the window frame, they collapsed on the beds. Chandler was almost asleep when he heard her voice above him. He cranked an eyelid open and saw her shape in the night's faint glow.

"What?" he asked. "What did you say?"

"Nothing." She leaned down and he felt her mouth brush his. "Just a good-night kiss." He reached for her, pulled her down and kissed her hard, holding her body against him. But he hadn't the energy to go on. "Go to sleep," she whispered, getting up. She pulled a blanket up and covered him.

"This room smells like a cedar chest," he muttered.

"About George Washington," she said from the other bed. "I really am sorry . . . maybe it's all a mistake, Colin."

"Maybe," he said, "maybe not." He intended to say more but anything else seemed just beyond him. He thought he could smell her against him, or taste her mouth on his, but he wasn't even sure about that.

He'd be damned if he'd tell them about Kennebunkport . . . but the questions kept coming, the same thing over and over again, and the pain . . .

It had been going on quite a long time and for most of that time Hugh Brennan had wished he could simply pass out. But somehow oblivion just kept eluding him: he continued aware of his surroundings, the smell of the Vicks from his hairy chest, the burning sensation in his stomach from the beer and Excedrin . . .

No. That was wrong, there was nothing left in his stomach, but it was hard to keep his mind on the track anymore. The cold sweats, the vomiting that almost choked him to death as it hit the towel stuffed in his mouth and cascaded back down his throat into his lungs, the involuntary urination, the horror when he'd bit through the towel and into the soft meat of his cheek and the rubbery gristle of his tongue and tasted his mouth filling with blood.

Before they'd gotten the towel, when he still thought he had a chance, he'd begun a story. "Look, you guys, let's lighten this up, whattaya say? Did you hear the one about the two Polacks and their pal the Swede? No? Okay, don't talk to me—hey, what are you doing there? Look, the three of them been hanging out in this same bar for years, see, always together, the three of them . . . and, hey, Jesus, what are you doing there? Oh, no, come on, don't be so serious . . . Ohhh, Jesus . . ." That was how they'd begun, ages ago.

The television had worked its way on into the second movie which meant it must be two o'clock Sunday morning, a calculation which proved to him that he still had his wits about him. He smelled the sweat pouring from

171

his torturers, watched it collect above and then drip from the one exposed eyebrow of the huge man with the pliers, watched the bandage on the man's face slip during his exertions, slip and pull away taking decomposing dead flesh and salve and hair with it. The man's eyes shone and he licked his lips as he hunched over his work. The small man asked endless questions, the same ones over and over again, and no one paid any attention. Every so often the small man went out on the porch for fresh air. Sometimes he asked the big man to cut it out, lay off, but it never did any good . . . he was afraid of the big man . . . Brennan could see why.

The force of his vomiting, the desperation to keep from suffocating, had worked the soaked towel loose and he pushed it out of his mouth with his tongue. It fell down onto his chest and no one pushed it back into his mouth. He couldn't scream: he could barely croak. "So one day," he went on, not quite able to hear himself but going on against the pain, "the two Polacks came into the bar without the Swede . . . nobody had seen the Swede for days, see . . . he was a missing person, the Swede was, see. Well, the cops came to talk to the Polacks, asking about the Swede . . . oh, God, why don't you stop?"

The first time Brennan threw up was when he looked down at his right hand and saw the bloody, frayed stubs of his fingers, where the nails had been, looking like they'd been chewed down to the bone . . . There was blood all over the chair and on his bathrobe and on the huge man's raincoat, blood and strings of flesh, and the man's hands and the pliers were smeared with blood, slippery: he had to keep wiping the pliers on his coat to get it dry enough to hold tightly . . . It was after they had finished with the one hand, before they'd begun on the other, that Brennan realized they were making a terrible mistake: they weren't going to kill him.

They kept asking him where Chandler was and they were a long time accepting the fact that he wasn't going to tell them where anybody was. After the right hand

172

was done they stayed at it just for the hell of it, but he'd gone that far, he wasn't going to tell now . . . The small man was having a lot of trouble talking and was losing interest, but the other one worked like a demon, exorcising his own frustrations, grunting, straining, pulling the nails loose by the roots . . .

"So the cops kept asking for a description," he said, trying to form the words distinctly, not knowing if he was succeeding. "And the Polacks told them what the Swede looked like and the cops wanted to know if the Swede had any peculiar identifying marks. Well, the Polacks remembered that he did—the Swede had two assholes. Two assholes! the cops say, amazed. Two assholes—how the hell did the two Polacks know that? Well, the Polacks laugh, it was easy . . . every time we went into the bar, us and the Swede, the bartender always said the same thing—'Hey, here comes the Swede with the two assholes!'" Nobody laughed but Brennan didn't care: he smiled by himself, thought about Mary Tyler Moore in a haze of fantasy and pain. Then the little man stuffed the towel back in his mouth.

Brennan wondered if his heart could hold out. Christ, what a time to die of a heart attack! The big man just kept groaning, the bandage dangling by a piece of tape from one ear, the hideous gray and pink rawness of the side of his face turning into view now and then. The hands hardly hurt anymore and Brennan waited patiently, trying to retain some control . . . Finally the huge man sank back and sat staring at the wall, as if overdosed on the infliction of pain. Brennan watched him, then dared another look at his own hands and felt the vomit turning again in his stomach. The dry heaves beginning. Like a puppet master he raised his right arm, as if it were controlled by strings and had no life of its own, and began to try to loosen the towel from between his split, aching lips. The ends of his fingers didn't so much hurt as feel mushy . . . mushy and warm. Not a sharp pain. But a constant throbbing fire. Pushing with his tongue he helped work the towel out, gagging as blood was forced out of the wet cloth. He made a faint

173

rasping sound in his throat: there was no voice left, his throat felt like the results of an hour's work with pitchfork and sandpaper. He sneezed and knew what it was like to die and come back to life. He touched his face. He was dripping with sweat, his robe was soaked through. He didn't know what to do.

The smaller man called to the big one from the kitchen, asked the other to come out and hurry up. The big man struggled over onto all fours and staggered upright like an apparition from an *abattoir,* smeared with blood and his face running, melting on the side. He rumbled out of the room and Brennan sank onto the floor himself and crossed on his knees to the sideboard, reached out with the remains of his hands, and picked up the heavy blackthorn shillelagh. He felt nothing but had to wipe the palms of his hands to get a good grip. They should have killed me, he thought, the dumb bastards.

He levered himself into a standing position, passed a mirror on the way to his post in the shadow beside the archway. What looked back frightened him, bloodstained, godawful hands wrapped around the stick, robe lank and wet and hanging open, mouth a black hole. He waited with the patience of the damned until he heard them coming back.

They were walking quickly, talking urgently, but Brennan did not give a damn what they were saying.

He timed his swing perfectly as they came through the archway. He heard himself give a hideous banshee wail, saw the deathly expression of fear on the short one's face, and felt the fat of the knobbed, gnarled stick catch the big one square in the middle of the face. One second the man was there, the next he wasn't, and Brennan's momentum carried him through the archway. As he went, robe half off, he collided with the falling body which was going down limp, the nose and eyes smashed together, the face collapsed inward. The body hit the floor and Brennan collapsed just past it with a red fog across his eyes, the cries of the small man's terror in his ears.

Then he was gone, hearing nothing . . . feeling only an instantaneous stab of lightning in his chest . . .

The old man's fluttering heart made sleep effectively impossible: at times, like tonight, he felt as if a couple of mice were scampering around his innards like happy, scuttling, anthropomorphic creatures by Walt Disney. He had enjoyed the concert, though the conversation with Liam and Andrew had been far from encouraging, and he had retired early with a Kenneth Roberts novel, *Arundel,* which had been signed for him years ago by the author and was growing tattered from rereadings. His sherry beside his bed, the thick novel in his lap, and *Die Fledermaus* on the FM band, the old man sat propped against several pillows trying to ignore the irritating commotion in his chest.

He had managed to shut out his international communications of recent days, had put flaps over the interchange with Sanger; he was losing himself in Roberts's story of Benedict Arnold. His eyes grew heavy: the inevitable thought followed—go to sleep and you might not awake in the morning. He was so accustomed to it by now that he feared if the notion failed to cross his mind that would be the night without end. Fears. The fears of the old, the infirm . . . He drifted off but the fluttering woke him and, heavy-lidded, he fought his lonely way through the night.

It was just past three-thirty Sunday morning when the green telephone rang. He winced: those goddamned butchers from out of town! He licked sherry from his lower lip, set the glass down, and picked up the offending object.

"Yes," he said coldly, his white moustache quivering as he clenched his jaw.

What followed pushed his credence to the limit. He listened earnestly: if his face had held any color in the first place it would have drained away as the recital continued.

"*Shut* up," he suggested forcefully. "Whom have you killed? Make it clear because I want to get it absolutely straight. It *matters* . . . now, pull yourself together."

175

In his mind he had already signed the death warrant for these two bunglers, just as he'd promised Sanger. His white eyebrows knitted as he waited for the second telling: "I see," he said slowly. *"You* haven't killed anyone . . . Ozzie is dead? What do you mean, dead? How?" He reached for a bottle of tiny white pills which, he was convinced, were placebos, though he took them anyway. They never seemed to have the slightest effect. "Professor Brennan killed him . . . with a *stick?"* He placed the tiny tablet under his tongue, letting it dissolve. "I don't mean to seem unkind, you understand, but we must agree that Ozzie certainly ran afoul of higher education this week . . . No, of course, it's not funny. But I'd have thought he'd have been able to hold his own with a pair of out-of-shape Harvard professors . . . Never mind, never mind . . . You ran, yes I appreciate your situation . . . You don't know whether Brennan is alive or dead . . . This was Ozzie's idea of an interview, I take it, a few hours of intense torture. I see . . . Let me say that he deserved killing, Mr. Thornhill. I only wish I could have had a hand in it . . ." He sipped sherry. "Calm yourself, for heaven's sake. I know he was your partner but that doesn't make him any less the homicidal maniac, if you see my point . . . Now, I want you to get to the safe house, do you understand? What? You know where Chandler's gotten to? . . . All right, do nothing, I say, *do nothing* . . . no, do not go to Kennebunkport . . . Thornhill? Thornhill? . . ."

He replaced the telephone and shut his eyes, stroking the white moustache. "God damn you, Thornhill," he whispered, wondering what in the name of God he was supposed to do now. He wished he knew how many bodies were cluttering up Brennan's house in Cambridge. He supposed he would have to find out . . . And what about the elusive Chandler?

Andrew Fennerty's tight little mouth had drooped open slightly and a small tobacco-stained chip of tooth showed through between his lips. Behind his round glasses his lids were closed; behind his lids his eyes were flickering rapidly as he slept. He had developed deep purple pouches which made him look like a sick man. He lay fully clothed but for his heavy brogans on his bed at the Ritz-Carlton; he had drawn a blanket up as far as his belt. On the other bed Liam McGonigle lay on his side with his back to Fennerty. His snores were hearty and rasping and may have been the cause for Fennerty's rapid eye movement.

The telephone brought him awake like a kick in the ribs. The little ferret's eyes clicked open like a doll's and he struggled to sit up, further entangling himself in the blanket. An attacker would already have killed him by that time and Fennerty was well aware of it, proving to himself once again what he already knew: he was too old for this crap and belonged at his desk where they had put him until CRUSTACEAN had gotten the wind up and called for him.

He knew perfectly well that it would be the old man himself on the telephone.

"Andrew," the distant voice said, free of emotion and sounding tired, "I want you to check Brennan's house . . . I thought I had made that utterly clear."

"But we've been there," Fennerty said. His mouth was dry and he reached for the warm, dust-laden tooth glass full of water on the stand between the beds. "We used that miserable shotgun mike and believe me, Brennan was watching television and sneezing. Nothing else."

"Don't try me, Andrew. Do as I say. You will find that a somewhat different situation obtains. Don't argue, just do as I say, and let me know precisely what you find. Do you understand? Precisely."

"Yes, I understand." Fennerty sensed a spasm or two of adrenalin; it wasn't the quick business it once had been, though.

"Point two, then. I've discovered that Chandler may be holed up at a resort hostelry on the Kennebunk coast, the Seafoam Inn." The old man sounded—what was it?—*nervous*. Fennerty couldn't recall such an instance in the past. They were all getting older. "Lum and Abner may know—"

"Lum and Abner?"

"Wake up, Andrew. The two gentlemen we've been observing, or trying to observe. They may know where Chandler is and I think they've contracted bloodlust, like sharks, I sense a pink thrashing about . . . So, you'd better get a move on. Andrew?"

"Yes . . ."

"I'm not quite sure but I believe what I'm saying is this—if Chandler gets killed it will be your asses. Chandler and the TV woman, Polly Bishop, he's got with him—I want them kept alive . . . and do what you can to relieve him of his package . . ."

"Which is more important at this point," Fennerty said peevishly, "the people or the package? If I have to make a choice, that is?"

But he received no answer. The line was dead.

Fennerty lay rumpled and confused for several moments, wondering what the hell it was all about, what he was seriously supposed to do. It was so jumbled, chaotic, and in the field you never saw it all, but only the little funny-shaped pieces that gave no clue as to the whole. In the field you knew what you were working on, the rest was all a blur, and he supposed it had always been that way. Of course it had. And that was why he wanted to get the hell out of the field forever and into an office where you could feel like a grown-up. It was about time.

He had once known a man who played football for the Washington Redskins, an elderly man for a football player, nearly forty with a face that looked closer to fifty, particularly around and behind the large, vulnerable, hurt brown eyes. And the man had once told him what it was like out there on the field.

"Andy," he'd said softly, peaceably, as they sat on the player's town house patio in Georgetown, "you're just a fan and you believe all that shit you read about football . . . the six hundred plays in the old playbook, the infinite variations, the blocking styles, the fine timing, the incredible finesse and skill, all the human chess game crap. Well, that's all a load, Andy, the intellectualization of football, making it all respectable, so that

178

assholes like Nixon can turn football slang into the words used to describe foreign policy . . ." He'd made a disgusted face but he never raised his voice, just kept the slow jock's drawl coming, slippery with Wild Turkey. "Football is about one thing and only one thing, Andy. It's about kicking ass." He had chuckled softly to himself. It had been spring and he'd probably already known he was through, going to retire. "Nothing fancy. Just blood and pain and half of the guys foaming at the mouth from some kind of dope, eyes like pinheads . . . fuckin' jungle, Andy, total chaos, and while we're up there grubbing around in the dirt and piss with bloody crap dripping out of noses, we don't know what the hell is going on in the game as you see it. And if we make sure they hurt more than we do, well, hell, about four o'clock on Sunday afternoon we wipe the shit out of our eyes and look up and people are standing and cheering and that means we won . . ."

Fennerty had often thought of that speech, treasured it in his memory, wished he'd had a recording of it, because it could have been him talking about his own job. It could have been Andrew Fennerty telling somebody what it was like to work for The Company. But you could never do that. Never. And nobody ever stood and cheered for The Company.

In any case, that was how he felt lying there at the Ritz in the dark with the light from the bathroom glowing softly. Grown man who always slept with a nightlight. What would happen if he had to go up against one of the really good ones? One of the Russians' number one boys? Or, God forbid, one of the Nazis' lads from Texas or South America or South Africa? He sighed doggedly and swung his legs over the side of the bed. His mind was wandering and he'd have to get a grip on himself. He and Liam had their hands full with these two jerks, Lum and Abner, and a Harvard professor and a woman . . .

"Liam," he said, "Liam, old sock, time to get up . . ."

Chandler woke up slowly hearing the surf and Polly breathing through her mouth on the other bed, not quite snoring. The rest had done him good: his mind felt sharp again, he knew exactly where he was and why and what he had to do. It was just past eight o'clock. He got out of bed gingerly, happily aware that the stiffness wasn't half bad and the boxed ear felt better. He went to the window, looked out into the gray light filtering through the clouds hanging low over the steely Atlantic. The surf threw itself halfheartedly at the rocky-layered shingle dropping away below the roadway. Lonely gulls dipped and swooped against the cold opaque gray sky. It was quite the loneliest, emptiest vista imaginable.

"It's obviously a hoax," he whispered in the stillness. "The British were trying to set him up. Maybe black-mail him . . . or maybe it wasn't a hoax, maybe they were already blackmailing him and he had to go along with it, feed them useless information." He nodded, agreeing with himself. "Maybe he could even pick up helpful bits and pieces for his own cause . . ." Polly moved and turned onto her back, covering her eyes with a hand. Still asleep. No point in waking her yet. He tip-toed across the small room, picked up his bag, and beetled off down the hall to the cold comforts of the unheated bathroom.

In the calm reflections of morning the certainty of the document's validity seemed to fade, though his memory of the shock at the first sight of the signature remained clear, like the memory of jagged lightning crackling across the innocent summer nights of boyhood. It was quite impossible for him to cope with the *fact* of George Washington's treachery: how could it be? He had no more of an answer in the morning than he'd had at night.

He returned to the bedroom, gathered up the docu-ments and the Winthrop Chandler portrait, all of which Polly had brought up and carefully arranged on the chest of drawers. The woman's face was arresting even across two centuries: it was as if she were watching him. His subconscious was, he knew, addressing itself to the historical problems raised by the documents, while he consciously turned over the more immediate diffi-culties of his and Polly's situation.

Downstairs he found Percy Davis in the kitchen banging a couple of black cast-iron frying pans about on the stove. The smell of bacon frying hung tantalizingly in the large room and Percy Davis waved a good morning with a spatula. "I've already breakfasted and had a stroll down by the water," he said with a wintry smile. "I'll run you up some bacon and eggs, soon as you give me the word." He drained a cup of tea and jiggled a teakettle on the back burner. "Sleep well? Behave yourself?" His watery eyes danced an instant.

"Too damned tired not to, sir," Chandler said.

"Mustn't let Harvard down," Davis said, straightfaced.

"No need to make this a matter of that import. I do need a telephone."

"Use the one at the desk. No charge, either." The dry voice rustled with pleasure. "Excitement does me good. Feel damned fine this morning—takes me back, all this business. Sorry Bill had to die . . . Ah well, use the phone at the desk. I'll get some bacon over a low heat."

"Colin Chandler, as I live and breathe!" Prosser's ripe sarcasm flooded across the telephone line, fruity and intensely welcome. So worldly, so peculiarly reassuring. "You've been a rather naughty boy of late, you know. Harvard doesn't mind its name in the papers but not as part of this *grand guignol* farce . . . bodies all about, the last act of *Hamlet*. How are you, my boy? And where are you? Well and in a safe, comfy nook, I hope . . ."

"Well enough and safe enough for the moment," Chandler began, smiling eagerly as he spoke. Prosser in all his remote, well-heeled elegant trappings still had something about him of the father Chandler had had to do without most of his life. It was to Bert Prosser that he had brought the trophies of his accomplishments, his scholarly successes, his popular books and articles, and it was Prosser who had sat him down and poured the brandy and shared the congratulatory cigar. It wasn't that he was close to Prosser: the great man was too much the confidant of heads of state to allow

181

easy access, but Chandler was as close to him as anyone from without the real corridors of power. "But as you've been reading, I've gotten mixed up in something pretty damned sticky. Frankly, I need your advice . . . I'm at the end of my string."

"Nonsense, it only feels that way. But take it from me, there's always more string than you think—however, I'm at your service, Colin. What's the story? I'll help if I can."

Twenty minutes later Colin's recital ended leaving him breathless and doubting if he'd made any sense. "God help me, it's all true," he said.

"Indeed, I'm sure it is. Most importantly, you and Miss Bishop are safe. Secondly, you have the document everyone seems to want—I think perhaps I can help you there. And there seem to be several people searching for you and it . . . Delicate situation, on the whole." Chandler heard him sipping coffee, heard the rustle of papers. "Always a way out, always a way out. As to this piece of paper, well, I hardly know what to think—is it real, or isn't it? I'll have to have a looksee and I still won't know, I expect. As to what you should do, let me tell you I think speed is of the essence . . . you must get away from this Seafoam place at once. These birds on your tail, don't be too sure you've left them behind—in my experience, that's often more easily said than done. They have their means, ways you've never dreamed of, connections you'd hardly countenance. Take my advice without so much as a moment's quibble, dear boy. I've got a summer home up north of you, way up there . . . Johnston, Maine, on the far side of town." He described the house: "You can't miss it. It's empty now—I always leave a key under the stack of wood closest to the door outside of the woodshed itself. You'll find it, just feel around for it. Then get inside, get settled, get a fire going, open a bottle of wine . . . both of you, of course, make yourselves at home . . . I'll be there as soon as I can, just hang on and wait for me. Have you got all that, Colin?"

"Yes, Bert, and I don't know what to say—I knew you'd have the answer . . ."

"Hardly the answer, dear boy. But at least we'll have some time to think and see what we're about. Now, get going."

Half an hour later Polly and Chandler were tucking into scrambled eggs with mushrooms and onions, the better part of a pound of extra-thick bacon, English muffins running with melted butter and strawberry jam, and New England coffee served "reg'lar" as Percy Davis called it, meaning with lots of cream and sugar. Percy was quizzing Polly about her job and Chandler was thinking ahead, wanting to get back on the road. Bert Prosser knew about these things; God only knew what kind of inside jobs he'd done for the government back during the forties, and if Bert said not to be too sure the bastards had lost you, then he was right, it was time to get a move on.

Percy walked outside with them: "Now take care of yourselves," he said. "You remember what I said about getting to Johnston? You didn't leave anything behind, did you? Well, I'm going to miss you two—now you let me know how this all turns out, Professor. Call me. Or come up here for a weekend . . . Don't make me get my news on the television, y'understand?" He finally rapped on the top of the bedraggled brown car, the signal to pull out. "Take care, young lady." He waved as Chandler swung the car in a tight circle and headed down the driveway. "Take care . . ." Chandler nodded, giving him thumbs up, and they were back on the road.

They clung to the slower, less traveled highway which skirted the coastline and wound through one town after another. It was tedious going but he figured that the crucial thing was simply to get away from their last stopping place; once they'd gotten clear, it struck him that any follower would assume they'd head for the quicker freeway route—though how they'd recognize the brown car wherever it was was beyond him.

The sky stayed gray over a gray knifeblade ocean. The ground was still spotted with sadly discolored snow, or with the dirty brown earth and matted-down grass that sprouted through rather grimly. What would have

183

been a lovely drive in June or October was now something mainly to be gotten through.

The conversation came in patches too.

"Well," she said, "what do you think after a good night's sleep?" There was no hint of the justified adversary in her voice, a fact which proved to be a considerable relief. "Is it real or a fake?"

"I've been at work on that in the back of what passes for my mind." He glanced over at her: "And I took your advice, I pulled up my socks and looked at it from the standpoint of a dispassionate historian, not a guy grinding an ax for George Washington."

"And?"

"I keep trying to fit him into the situation, put myself in his shoes. England was such a reality to those people and by all odds they should have won the war . . . And the Americans were so English themselves. In June of 1775 Congress appointed a dozen generals besides Washington, a dozen—and Nathanael Greene of Rhode Island was the only one who hadn't held a commission under the crown! And of the twelve, Richard Montgomery and Charles Lee and Horatio Gates had all been born in England and had served in the British Army.

"Now Washington was an American through and through, but that was more a matter of the specific circumstances of his life. He could very easily have been on the other side. For instance, there was the case of Beverley Robinson—he grew up with George in Virginia, his dad was acting governor of Virginia under the crown. Beverley raised troops for the expedition against Canada in 1746 and while passing through New York he met and married Susanna Philipse . . . After Braddock's defeat, on the way back, George met Susanna's sister Mary who was a very prominent heiress to the family's holdings in Westchester and Dutchess counties. Washington courted her but for one reason or other, it came to nothing—*but,* if he'd married her he would almost certainly have become a loyalist officer under the crown. Which was precisely what Beverley Robinson did."

184

He stopped for a light in a buttoned-down village where nothing stirred. The trees were bare and snow melted, stained the gray sidewalk. Polly was listening intently. He moved through the quiet village, past an early gardener scratching at his wet, muddy lawn with a spindly rake.

"Beverley couldn't bring himself to side with the rebels," Chandler went on, as if he'd known the man, as if it had all happened only yesterday. "So he hung on quietly at his estate in Dutchess county until 1777 when John Jay put it to him, one gentleman to another, that he simply had to choose which side he was on. Well, Beverley said no, he couldn't take the oath of allegiance as required, so he was obliged to pack up and move his entire family within the British lines in New York—his decision was made.

"But later in the war, when the colonists seemed to be winning, Beverley became the perfect emissary to try and arrange a peace stating that it was time to call a halt and end the fighting with a fair share of honor and safety and leniency."

"And you think this was the sort of thing Washington was faced with?" Polly chewed a fingernail, stared ahead at the cramped countryside between towns. Clouds seemed to be pushing down on them. A dog watched as they sped past. He was turning, walking away before the brown car was fully by him. No bark, no flicker of interest. "It was that common?"

"Oh my, yes," Chandler said, "it was that common. People were always making dippy little overtures to Washington—he always gave 'em the gate, but he was so goddamned important, so visible, that there were always rumors, innuendos, smears."

"Has there ever been any documentary evidence that Washington was ready to join the British?"

He shook his head: "Not a trace, not a shred."

She tapped a finger on the package in her lap. "Are there *any* pieces of paper, anywhere, like the one we've got?"

"It all depends on what it is we've actually got. If I knew what exactly this thing is, then I could tell you—"

"Don't be infuriating and obscure," she said. "You must know what I mean."

"Yes, I know what you mean, all right. Let's have some lunch."

He pulled across the highway to a Howard Johnson. They were surprisingly hungry, ordered fried clams to start and then a couple of steaks. They poured copious amounts of coffee into their stomachs, and they kept talking in low voices. It was Chandler who did most of the talking while Polly finished her steak and began to nibble at his.

"Look," he said, "the point is this—George Washington was not a traitor, not a British spy. Any other conclusion is outright absurd. No, there has never been any valid evidence indicating that Washington was anything but utterly, absolutely, indisputably *incorruptible . . .*" He raised a palm to stop her: "Don't talk with your mouth full, please. No *valid* evidence, that's what I said . . . which is not to say that there hasn't been *invalid* evidence. Because there hasn't been a lack of that—"

"Never taught me that in school," she said primly.

"Some history major!"

"It wasn't American history. It was English history . . . I came late to George Washington. Late and just on the surface." She made a face. "The Plantagenets I know. Can I finish your baked potato, my dear?"

"Well, there were all kinds of plots and dirty tricks—they weren't invented by Nixon, you may be sure—back then. I mean, you wouldn't believe some of them . . . everybody had a plot, in Paris, in London, in Philadelphia, in Boston, in New York, on the goddamned high seas . . . King George got a crazy letter to Franklin in Paris, for example, told him to go to the choir at Notre Dame on July sixth, a Monday it was, and meet a man who would be drawing pictures on a pad and wearing a rose in the buttonhole of his waistcoat . . . Franklin was requested to come in person . . . well, he never went, the little man was seen to come, wait, and go . . . and nobody could ever prove he was from the king, this

186

little man, Jennings was his name. Maybe nobody cared, there were so damned many plots . . ."

The brown car was back on the road, nosing through the beginnings of a fog blowing in off the Atlantic. The cold clean smell filled the car. He pushed back against the seat, straightening his arms against the steering wheel, feeling it bow slightly. He was seeing things the right way now, it was all making sense . . . thank God, he had to have his head on straight for Prosser. Bert could be a son of a bitch if you didn't have your head on straight, no matter what you'd been through. He'd probably learned that from all those presidents he'd told what to do at times of crisis . . . Truman, Ike, Kennedy, Johnson, Nixon, Ford . . . Well, Chandler was ready.

Polly sat next to him still fingering the package, trying to sort out its real value in her mind.

"I suppose every large man would have looked like Washington to Davis after his experience in the woods, once he'd seen the signature. . . . And how are we going to figure it out now?"

"That's the trick this magician can't do," Chandler sighed.

"You mean, what it may come down to is—you either believe the signature is a forgery or you don't . . . is that what you're saying?"

"Maybe. Unless Prosser can come up with something."

"So, we've got a thing people are getting killed over but, one it doesn't really prove anything, and, two it doesn't really mean anything . . ."

"Well, it means something to somebody," Chandler said.

"It's a macguffin," she said.

"That's right," he said.

"I'm going to take a nap," she said. "It makes my brain tired."

"You wanted to come along."

She slid across the seat toward him and curled up

against him, leaning her head on his shoulder. "Does this bother you?" she murmured.

"Not at all. I could get used to it."

Thorny woke with a groggy, moist feeling as if he'd been on fire and someone had doused him with a pail of water. He opened his eyes slowly, stared at the beige ceiling, the gray clouds over the bus and subway terminal next door, heard the grinding and clanging as an MTA car struggled up the incline and into daylight like a gargantuan, mechanical, clockwork mole. A bottle which had once contained a quart of indifferent gin lay empty on the nightstand, pointing its accusing neck at him like the barrel of a cannon. His head ached unbearably. There was nothing quite like a gin headache. And then he remembered about Ozzie, got a flash, an afterimage, of the huge body, open-mouthed with the gold tooth glittering going down without a whimper, lying there looking like a blood-stained raincoat ready for the dry cleaners.

Thorny took a certain pride in his insensitivity to death. Mostly, his involvement with death had centered on inflicting it. He'd inflicted it for the mob in Chicago as a boy, then for the mob in San Diego and New Orleans, then as a free lance in Texas and Mexico and Nicaragua and Paraguay, then some contracts for people he didn't know and had no desire to identify. A man built a career, made something of his life, protected his reputation, and he was bound to get good referrals. That's what this whole Boston thing had been, a referral to this old man. And now Ozzie was dead: fucking Harvard professors! He still had trouble getting his breath from the first one, and he was on his own as a result of dealing with the second one . . . Shit. He'd known Ozzie for better than ten years and they'd worked together ever since 1970: not too heavy on the brains, Ozzie wasn't, but a good piece of muscle, good to have on your side in a fight. Or he had been up until the last fight.

Yes, he was insensitive when it came to inflicting death here and there in the name of duty, but Ozzie's

188

death had upset him. Oz may have been cracking up, but that could happen to anyone. He sighed. They were the same age—forty-four—and it made Thornhill realize just how fragile a thing life was, or could be, once somebody was sufficiently pissed off.

Oz had been pissed off, particularly about the burns and pain Chandler had given him in such full measure, and as a result, Oz, who was not too awfully high on the evolutionary ladder though he was one hell of a diligent worker, would have been glad to kill Brennan once he'd gotten all the fingernails extracted. It was like therapy for Oz, like basket weaving or needlepoint, the business of removing fingernails. It was easy for the old man to sit back and blow a fuse about things getting out of hand, but you had to be in the field, you had to be getting your nose rubbed in it to know what the hell was going on . . .

Thornhill recognized the trouble spots in his own personality and he knew he was facing one of the worst. The more he thought about what Chandler and Brennan had done to Ozzie and him, the more he began to shake with anger, quite an irrational anger: or was it irrational, really? The victims had risen up, struck back at the predators, and in Thorny's experience that was unheard of when you were dealing with civilians. Soldiers in another army were expected to fight back, but civilians were expected to crack with a tap, like delicate translucent eggshells found in a robin's nest.

So what the fuck was going on with Brennan and Chandler?

Maybe Brennan was dead, he didn't really know. He'd left too damned fast to check on the state of Brennan's health. He couldn't quite understand why he'd been so frightened, but there, out of nowhere, had come the gory spectre of Brennan who should have been passed out cold in the other room . . . swinging the club and grunting with blood flying and that wet, solid sound from inside Ozzie's head . . . he hadn't had such a fright since he'd seen *Psycho* and the old lady with the butcher knife had run out on the stairway landing.

With the image of Brennan killing Oz corroding his brain, Thornhill got out of bed and staggered, head splitting, into the bathroom. Half an hour later he had eaten a breakfast of doughnuts and coffee in the glass-enclosed lobby and gotten the red Pinto filled at the gas station across the street. He also picked up a road map of New England and plotted the course northward to Kennebunkport.

Impatiently he fought it out with Sunday's family, pleasure-driving traffic. Interminably he pushed at the bonds of the Boston area, but it was useless to try to force the issue. It took just so long to get free of Boston and that was that. The turnpike signs confused him. Natives honked angrily as he switched lanes. He wondered if the old man had gone to Brennan's house: he wondered if anyone had even found the human refuse . . . he wondered how many fingerprints he'd left scattered around the apartment.

He was having a very bad day. He tugged the black-and-white checked porkpie hat down tight on his head and swore at the Pinto's lack of acceleration. It was a rotten day and somebody would have to pay. The anger and frustration kept building and he finally gave up trying to cope with it. Fuck the old man. Fuck Brennan and that goddamn Chandler and the TV bitch . . . Arnold Thornhill had had enough.

He was back to being a competent killing machine by the time he got to Kennebunkport and asked at the Rexall drugstore where the Seafoam Inn might be.

"Well, he wasn't kidding when he said we couldn't miss it." Polly was watching as he negotiated the turn off the highway into Prosser's driveway which rose, steadily toward a huge shape, a mansion that seemed to glower down on them from the top of the hill as the light faded behind the blackish clouds on the western horizon. They had slid through Johnston, a village with not more than ten standing structures, just as the grocery store connected with the filling station was being locked up. Polly had managed to buy a few scraps for dinner and Chandler had gassed the car. Then in the growing gloom they had passed on through and seen Prosser's summer home in its remote baronial splendor.

The headlights cut through the darkness and it became clear that the house was built mainly of immense gray stones with a slate roof, a dark-green wooden turret with a pointed steeple at the right, and a similarly colored wing spreading off to the left. He drove the car under a mammoth stone portcullis and stopped. Wide stone steps led up to the entryway. Chimneys protruded from the roof at irregular intervals, like fingers thrust out of a grate, stretching for freedom. Orson Welles as Harry Lime, at the end of *The Third Man,* about to die.

Chandler got out and hurriedly jogged alongside the house in the glare of the headlights, toward the woodpile by the shed Prosser had described. On his knees he ran his hand under the bottom row of logs, touched something that moved, a spider, and found the keys. Breathing hard he ran back to the car, dangling the keys before him. He grabbed the bags from the back seat while Polly took the groceries and, dropping the key only once, swung the heavy oak door open.

"Colder in here than outside," Polly said, sniffling. The front hall was stuffy, smelled of being locked up for the winter, and Chandler saw Polly's breath as she spoke. He tried the switch and the hallway was dimly illuminated by a gray light. *"Seven Keys to Baldpate,"* she said. "Come on, let's get our bearings." And she headed off toward what turned out to be the vast, cold, echoing kitchen. All the light bulbs seemed to be forty watts. The shadows held monsters, quite possibly. Ghosts, at the very least. "Cheery, fun place," she said. "Prosser must be a cheery, fun fellow—what do you do if he invites you for a weekend?"

"It's a summer house, priceless—"

"I wish it were summer." She unpacked the groceries and tested the stove. No gas. The refrigerator was unplugged. But a coffeepot responded to being plugged into a wall socket and she quickly found a can opener and got the coffee perking. "Thank God the water is running. He must have a man who comes in, keeps an eye on the place."

A quarter of an hour later, fortified with mugs of hot coffee and a plate of Twinkies, they were seated on the floor in the room at the bottom of the round turret which turned out to be a comfortable old-fashioned library with books lining the walls, flat expanses of tabletops, and overstuffed chairs. Chandler brought in logs and the fire thawed them through, made them tired and safe. Chandler felt quite safe for the first time in days. He looked up from the curling flames, feeling her gaze. She'd taken off the heavy sweater and rolled up the sleeves of her checked shirt. She smiled lazily, shaking her head.

"Well," she said, "now would seem to be the time, wouldn't it? Unless you still hate me, my profession, and my theory of history . . ." She brushed the thick hair back over her ears, grinned a trifle dangerously, just a bit of incisor showing. A forefinger tweaked a button on the front of her shirt.

"I could probably put aside my prejudices for a moment or two," he said, "if pressed."

"And precisely where would you have to be pressed, Professor?"

"That's dirty," he said. "Did you make that up? Just now?"

"I'm a grown-up. I've been around. I've said dirtier stuff than that . . ." Her voice had slowed, lost its clipped, precise enunciation. It sounded as if she'd had just one drink too many, but it was sex that was talking. And she was also laughing at them, gently.

"Don't keep reminding me of your past, please."

"Don't be sensitive, silly." She shifted back against the pillows she'd dragged onto the floor from the couch. Matter-of-factly she unbuttoned her shirt and pulled it out of her Levis, opened it wide. "I'm not sensitive about these tiny little things—you'll find they perform admirably, whatever that means."

"My expectations are up," he said, leaning across, covering a large, tight nipple with his mouth. He whispered against her flesh. She began to hum softly. He heard her unzip her Levis, wiggle them down past her hips. Behind his closed eyes he saw it all, the swell of flesh, the deep darkness between her thighs as he explored her, the clenching of her jaw as he kissed her and she pushed herself against him.

"That's nice, isn't it?" she said. "Making new friends."

"Making a new friend, singular . . ."

It took an hour and when they lay back they were both pleasantly aware that the job had been done well, indeed. He watched the fire burning down in the grate. She punched his arm lightly, grinned in the flickering shadows.

"Happy? I am. Everything is nice and natural now, we've been together so much . . . now it all makes sense." She slid her hand down his arm, touched his hand.

"So who does all the shaving gear in your bathroom belong to?"

"Would you believe my brother?"

"I guess I don't really care."

"Thatta boy, I'm proud of you." She giggled.

He suspected that he was rather proud of himself, too, but only time would tell about that. For the moment he put his arm around Polly Bishop and pulled her close and figured that worrying about somebody else's shaving cream was kid stuff.

The old man was a creature of discipline and when the going got a little, well, dicey, that was when you drew on the extra store of discipline. After his conversations with Thornhill and Fennerty, he'd taken several pills with Perrier water and forced himself to sit at the dining table while Mrs. Grasse prepared his breakfast. He read the New York *Times* and the Washington *Post* and the Boston papers. He wondered what the hell was happening at Brennan's and then Fennerty called him and told him what had happened at Brennan's and the old man told him what to do about it and took an altogether different pill, a "mood elevator," and ate three strips of crisp bacon, two poached eggs on wheat toast, and two cups of Twining's. Not until all this was gotten through did he consult the waferlike face of his Piaget wristwatch.

"Mrs. Grasse," he said softly as his cook-maid cleared the dishes, "would you please send Ogden to me? Thank you."

He sat quietly at the table, sipping his tea, until Ogden arrived, with his tightly knotted narrow tie, black suit, and pale lined eyes.

"Ogden," he said, "would you prepare the Rolls? I'll be away overnight."

Ogden nodded, resisted what appeared to be an atavistic urge to genuflect, and hastened away.

The old man took off his robe in the bathroom adjoining his bedroom, weighed himself, showered, shaved, trimmed his snowy moustache, and put on country clothes: a brown hacking jacket with leather patches at the elbows, doeskin slacks that dated from the forties, a turtleneck cashmere sweater, brown suede boots. Pills, he reflected, were what kept him going.

The question was, how far out of control was Thorny? And how dangerous? And how far could the old man go in stopping him without revealing his own involvement with both idiotic sides?

He'd asked himself those questions, in one form or another, so many times over the years . . . It was like wanting to know if there was a God and going into a cathedral, sitting down, waiting, and never getting an answer.

But the Rolls' purr put his problems out of his mind for the moment. Why, oh why couldn't everything run like his lovely black Rolls?

Thorny never knew, in the normal course of things, for whom he was working on any given free-lance assignment. Sometimes it was an advantage, not knowing who it was, because you just concentrated on the task at hand, got it done, and collected your money. But other times being in the dark was dispiriting: you had difficulty getting involved in the job, staying interested. Sometimes it was a help to have some idea of the big picture, or would have been. He knew, however, that he was only a soldier, not a decision-maker. Right now he was particularly pleased because he knew he was working for himself: the old man didn't matter anymore, it was Ozzie that mattered—he was going to raise a little hell for Ozzie and he couldn't remember when he'd last felt quite so industrious, quite so determined.

He parked the Pinto at the foot of the driveway and glanced up at the old summer house that was playing out its hand as a resort inn. It was quiet looking but a light burned in the afternoon gloom. The water crashing behind him, the cold moist wind, the lonely old building—it all frightened him. He was a city boy and the open spaces, the lifeless feel of the coastline bothered him. Getting out of the Pinto he knocked his porkpie hat off, watched as it fell with its crown down into a puddle of muddy water. He stared at it, bent to pick it up, then swore and kicked at it. It rolled partway under the car. He had no hair on the top of his head, only a dark fringe over his ears and around the base of his skull. Shoulders hunched, hands jammed in his raincoat pockets, he trudged up the rutted driveway. His momentary flood of optimism had ebbed. But he still had a job to do.

"Mr. Davis?" he said. "Percy Davis?"

The elderly gent nodded, standing in the doorway.

"Well, thank God you're here—is the professor still with you?"

"The professor?" Davis said, squinting from beneath white eyebrows.

"Aha, very good, very good, Mr. Davis," he chuckled. "Can't be too careful. I expect the professor filled you in on what it's been like these past few days in Boston —rough, very rough." He shook his head, wishing to God the old man wasn't making him wait outside in the wind. "My name is Terwilliger, Claude Terwilliger. I'm sure he must have mentioned me . . ."

"Nope, Mr. Terwilliger, can't say as he did."

"Well, I have papers here, Mr. Davis, identification." He took a leather folder from his jacket pocket and flipped it open. "CIA," he said softly as Davis scrutinized the document. The beauty of it was that it was in fact a genuine Central Intelligence Agency identification card.

"Mr. Davis, I'm freezing my ass out here. Do you suppose I could just step inside?. And you can call that telephone number, it's toll-free, twenty-four hours, and check on me . . . I'm Professor Chandler's protection, believe me." He watched the old man respectfully.

"All right," Davis said at last, "come on in."

"I don't know how much he may have told you," Thorny began quickly, hoping to divert Davis's attention from the telephone, "but he's behaved admirably through this whole thing. The man's got guts to burn— funny when you think about it, a Harvard professor, but he's all heart, I'll tell you. Could you spare a cup of coffee, by the way? I've been up all night . . ." He followed the old fellow inside, past the lobby desk, and into the kitchen where a television set was blaring on the countertop and the coffee was ready. Percy Davis pointed toward a row of cups and leaned against the sink, arms across his chest. He looked down at Thorny who poured and talked. "Right now, Mr. Davis, and I'm going to rely on your discretion in this—" He glanced up, stirring cream into the thick brew. "Right now, there are two men lying dead in a house in Cambridge . . . *They were after Chandler!*" He sipped, his tiny dark eyes watching Davis. "That's the kind of thing we're trying to guard Chandler from . . . I don't mind telling you, the way he keeps slipping away from us—he's so resourceful, but damn it, these guys are playing hardball, y'know?—we're spread pretty thin just trying to keep track of him. Why, my God, the only way I found out he came here was from Hugh Brennan . . . yeah, Hugh's a great guy, a great *friend,* he'll do anything to help Chandler . . ."

"Is there something I can do for you?" Percy Davis regarded the small man calmly, trying to remember what Chandler had told him during the long, densely packed night. There had been so much . . . George Washington clouded his specific memory.

"There's something you've just *got* to do for me, Mr. Davis—" He spread his arms, the abject supplicant.

"You've got to tell me where the heck he went from here . . ." He scowled, rubbed his eyes. "The guys who did the dirty work in Cambridge last night, they're after him . . . and the sources of information they've got, well, you wouldn't believe them—Mr. Davis, I've got to get to Chandler before those bastards do." He sighed beneath the weight of the world: he felt the solid heft of the gun in his pocket and wondered if he was going to have to do something ugly to this scrawny old fart. "Did he tell you, Mr. Davis? Do you know where he is?"

Percy Davis thought it over.

"Yes, Mr. Terwilliger," he said at last. "I know where he is." He started back out toward the front lobby. "I can show you best on a road map."

Back in the Pinto Thorny pulled a bottle of gin out of the glove compartment. He was whistling "Hello Dolly" which he interrupted once the bottlecap was unscrewed. Things were going right for a change. Too damned bad Oz was missing it. He started the car and backed up, grinding the porkpie hat into the mud. He took another hit on the bottle as he passed on through Kennebunkport. He turned on the lights. It was getting dark outside and he felt alone, but secure, with the fingers of light prying at the gathering gloom.

Chandler was sitting with his arm around Polly, half awake, watching the fire burn down to embers, not wanting to move, or come fully to life, when he saw the darkness speared by the automobile's lights. He shook his head, whispered into her ear: "He's here, Prosser is here, honey . . . rise and shine. The old man is upon us."

He went outside onto the stone balustrade and waved.

The black Rolls-Royce purred up in front of him, the side window slid down, and the old man leaned across the front seat, smiling. Chandler felt better just seeing him.

"Bert," he called, going to the window, using the

197

slightly unfamiliar first name. "Bert, I'm so damned glad to see you . . ."

The old man nodded. "It's going to be all right, son, we're going to make sure of everything . . . I'm just going to put this venerable Rolls-Royce to bed and then we'll get down to the bottom of things. Just give me a moment, Colin." The window slid back up and the Rolls moved slowly back beneath the stone archway toward the garage. Chandler heard the electrically controlled garage door open. He stood alone on the balustrade, breathing in the night air. He didn't know who to think about, Polly or Bert Prosser . . . For a man in the middle, he was unreasonably happy.

Chandler watched Prosser at his worldly, charming best with Polly. He'd been rumored for years to be in precarious health and now, holding Polly's hand, he looked his age, seemed to bear out the rumors. The pouches under his eyes were fuller, darker, and he seemed thinner than ever in his country clothes. The turtleneck couldn't hide the lined, loose flesh of his throat; while he lit his Dunhill the blue-veined hands trembled with the tobacco pouch and the wooden kitchen match. But his voice was still strong, retained the metallic harshness when he had a point to make, could soften, loosen into a plumminess when he chose.

The charm having been sufficiently dispensed, he cupped a palm over the bowl of the pipe, drawing deeply until the gray smoke wreathed his small, eggshell head. "Now my boy," he said in his resonant, plummy voice, "let's see Exhibit A and start getting to the heart of the matter. I'm a disciplined man, I think, but what you told me this morning—well, let's get on with it . . ." He sat down at the library table and tilted the shade on the old brass-based lamp so that he might have the document in the best light.

"Here goes, then," Chandler said. "First, the portrait by Chandler."

The old man inspected the frame, the backing, the canvas itself. "If you say it's a Winthrop Chandler, I'm willing to go along with you. It's more your field

198

than mine." Methodically he read carefully through Underhill's letter to Percy Davis, then Bill Davis's account of how he found the portrait and the contents thereof, then William Davis's letter which he handled with great delicacy and read with solemn concern, his eyes never flickering away from the papers. Then he considered the scrap bearing the signature. Chandler's eyes met Polly's; she winked.

"Well," Prosser said, placing the papers flat before him, "I'm rather at a loss." His mind seemed to be working behind the pale eyes, sifting, distilling, deciding precisely which of his thoughts to reveal. "We have several murders on the one hand, these bits of paper on the other. There can be no reasonable doubt that the murders and the papers—especially the signature of Washington—are related causally. But we don't seem to know why or how . . ." He looked up and smiled faintly at Polly, tamping down the ash in his pipe with the small figure of Mr. Pickwick. "My dear, what do you make of it?"

Polly shook her head: "We've theorized ourselves into a corner, we're lost, I'm afraid. We don't know if the document is genuine in the first place . . . and we don't know why it's worth killing people for." She shrugged, sat down on the tabletop, ran a finger along the edge of the portrait.

"Bert, why would anyone want this piece of paper so desperately?"

"A thousand reasons," Prosser said. "Money, for one. It would be worth a fortune to a collector, a museum . . . an institution like Harvard . . . aside from a well-preserved signature, there's the historical implications which are potentially highly explosive . . . my goodness, I detest being so wretchedly obvious!" He pushed back from the table, sucked a match flame down into the bowl. "But there are moments when there is nothing for it, but to be obvious."

"Do you call it real?" Chandler asked.

"Impossible to say so quickly, Colin," he said. "You know that as well as I do, you know the tests . . . No, what we need is time. Time and not being interrupted by the incompetents following you. I've got to put out some feelers. In Washington, I mean. Among my old chums . . . and their successors. Ah, mostly successors, wouldn't you know."

Chandler watched the old man sink into a somber silence, sucking the black stem, clicking it against his narrow stained teeth. He looked very old just then, and not at all well: there was a sallowness to his once-pink face, the cheeks were sunken, giving his face something of the look you associated with headhunting peddlers of the Amazon, skulls strung on a rope. Polly propped her elbows on the table and rubbed her huge brown eyes. Chandler would never look at her now without thinking of kissing those eyes, making love with her the first time. Watching her from across the table, he could feel the texture of her flesh on his fingertips.

Prosser shook his head as if yanking himself up from the bottom of a stupor. He blinked, looked around him with a quirky grin as if admiring a very private secret, ran the tip of his tongue along the fringe of his white moustache. His wandering eyes struck Chandler as too cloudy, his sudden loss of attention as disconcerting: in the instant, Chandler thought he saw the shadow of a dead man.

"The only safe thing to do," Prosser said slowly, "is to get you two a bit further out of the way until we get this settled. I have the most awful premonition that this is going to go off with a great clang and clatter and I'd like you two well away from the blast." He turned the pipe down in the heavy ashtray and tapped it carefully, building a mound of flaky ash. "Can you possibly manage that? If I can find the hiding place for you?"

Polly nodded; Chandler said: "I mainly want to keep us alive, Bert. If you think we should hide a little deeper, a little longer, that's good enough for me . . ."

"And there's the matter of all this," Prosser said, frowning at the goods on the table. "I think it will be safest with you two—I don't need it for the moment, my word is good with the people I'll be speaking to . . .
200

once we come down on the desperadoes, then we'll decide if old George was a British spy." He smiled crookedly. "Now, as to where you're going . . . I want you to get going straightaway, drive to Bar Harbor, sleep in the car because I'm afraid you won't find any hostelry open, and then pay a call on one Howard Kendrick in Bar Harbor . . . Howard is an associate of mine from the old days, a man who can be trusted to keep his shirttail tucked in and his mouth closed. He's got a sporting goods store down on the harbor, runs some boats, and he's got a seaplane, and it's the seaplane that's going to get you well away from all this carnage." He rubbed his chin and looked from one face to the other. "Just give him the word— *code green*—and he'll do the rest."

"Where is Howard Kendrick going to take us?" Polly asked hesitantly.

"He'll tell you when you see him. The less you know at this point the better, do you understand? Please take my word for it . . . tell Howard that you've come from me. He'll know where to take you." He covered Polly's hand with his own, closed his fingers around hers. "Forgive the hocus-pocus, Miss Bishop, but as Colin may have told you, I have from time to time done some work for various branches of our government. The place you're going is a very private accommodation which I've had occasion to use before . . . but security considerations preclude my naming it while there is still even the slightest possibility that you might fall into the hands of our enemies—please, I know you're going to be perfectly fine, but there's nothing like being on the safe side." He rubbed his hands briskly together, forcing some energy into the situation. "Miss Bishop, let me suggest you fill a thermos with some of that hot coffee and whatever else you've got among the groceries you were wise enough to buy . . . and Colin, go get a map from the desk in the hallway. A map of Maine. I don't want you getting lost between here and Bar Harbor. Have you got bags? Good, pack up—take a bottle of brandy with you." He stood up, urging the~

on. "Make an adventure of it, a game . . ." Polly nodded, headed for the kitchen.

Chandler got up, too, but the old man's hand clamped down on his arm: "Wait, there's something I wanted to spare Miss Bishop." He spoke in a throaty whisper. "Your friend Brennan . . . well, they got to him last night in Cambridge—"

"What do you mean, Bert, got to him?" The cold pliers glittered in his mind, chilling him.

"They went to work on him. At his home, torture, beat him up . . ."

"Shit! He went home right after he brought me the car at the museum—how is he? Is he going to be all right?"

"Don't know." Prosser shook his tiny, fragile head. A vein pulsed in his temple, blue beneath the translucent white hair. "Pretty badly beaten up . . . they just don't know if he's going to make it or not. I had to leave town before there was much information. There's one other thing, Colin . . . ah, Hugh killed one of them."

"*Killed* . . ." Chandler exclaimed under his breath. "And I thought I did some damage—which one did he kill?"

"A great big man, presumably the one you poured coffee all over. Brennan brained him with a shillelagh . . ." He laughed quietly into a cupped fist. "Whoever these men are, I'll wager they wish they'd never come to Boston."

"What about the other one?"

"The one you say wore a porkpie hat?"

"That's the one."

"Gone. Frankly, Colin . . . he's like a rogue, he may be out for blood. Revenge." He pressed his fingertips to his temples.

"Are you all right, Bert?"

"No, I'm not, Colin." He smiled dourly. "I'm too old for this kind of horseplay, it's like being back with Wild Bill Donovan, but I'm not the fellow I was then . . . at my age, you're dying. You're just plain dying . . . but, cheer up, I'm not dying today. Later. Today I'm worried about you and Miss Bishop and George Washington. Ach, it's all *his* fault, you know! Now get ready to make your escape."

Chandler went about his preparations, cramming the groceries into the duffel bag, tightening up the lid on the large thermos. Polly nibbled on a Twinkie. "He's worried, isn't he?" she said. "Really worried."

"I guess he is."

"But what has got him worried? Sure, sure, I know the obvious part, but there's something else going on, I swear it. I've interviewed so many men with more on their minds than anyone knew at the time—Colin, I got so I can recognize it. Something's eating at Prosser and it scares hell out of me . . . he gives me the impression of a hard man to scare who's scared half to death."

He put his arm around her shoulders and took the coffee cup with his other hand. He took a mighty swallow. "No flies on you, as we say at Harvard. *But . . .* I repeat but, don't underestimate the old coot."

"What, may I ask, is all this rusticity? Bertram Prosser a coot?"

"Shows you how calm I am, always able to make light of the deadly situation . . . remind you of David Niven? No? Not even a little? Well, it's not important. Just remember that Prosser, coot or not, is a cool cucumber . . . and the stuff we know all about is scary enough." He pressed his mouth to her soft downy cheek. "There doesn't have to be something else."

"And you are no newshound, my friend."

When they got back to the library the old man was turning a pill bottle in his hand. He was watching his hand as it shook. He didn't look up. "I've rewrapped the parcel," he said. "Oilskin pouch, very tight. Waterproof."

"In case the plane crashes," Polly said, making a face.

Prosser laughed, tore his eyes away from his own trembling hands. "Something like that, my dear. Are you all ready to go?" He looked at his wristwatch. "Time, ladies and gentlemen, time."

Chandler didn't recognize the sound of the explosion for what it was. It wasn't a bang: more of a muffled, roaring swirl of sound, unlike anything he'd ever heard. Polly flinched at the noise. It was Bert Prosser who leaped up, spinning the chair to the floor, snapping off the light switch and pitching the library into darkness. Chandler found himself frozen in place, confused. He couldn't quite believe he'd seen the frail old man move with such decisiveness. He next saw Prosser silhouetted against the window, moving across the rectangle of . . . *light*. Where the hell was the light, a brilliant, pale yellow glow, coming from?

At the window he saw it.

The brown car was shimmering amid licking flames, fire leaping like cracking whips from the windows, curling from beneath the chassis . . . while he watched, the front windshield exploded, spraying glass in a glittering shower into the darkness. There was no movement, only the burning, blistering remains of the anonymous brown car.

"He's here," Prosser said at his elbow. "I waited too long, a garrulous old man. He's out there . . . the survivor, the one Brennan didn't kill."

"Where is he?" Chandler strained his eyes at the darkness.

"Watching . . ."

"I see him. I saw him move." Polly had joined them at the window. "He's standing by the big tree, right where the driveway curves."

"He's come for you, Colin," Prosser said. "He's more than likely alone."

"So, what the hell—" Chandler felt the tightening in his stomach: God, he'd forgotten, he'd thought the nightmare was over. He felt Polly's hand on his shoulder.

"You've still got to get away. Minus the car." Chandler heard the old man's ghostly, dry clucking. "Can you handle that, Colin?"

"I'll take care of him," Polly said. "Don't worry. We'll get to Bar Harbor."

Suddenly a short, compact figure stepped away from

the tree, and paused: the window shattered and Chandler heard the slug smack into the books against the wall behind them.

"Enough," Prosser said. "He's going to pay attention to the front of the house. That's the problem when you work alone. You can only be in one place at a time . . . Off with you. Get to the tree line behind the garage, that'll provide cover, then it's up to you . . . you've got the map." Prosser was pushing them toward the hallway.

"What about you?"

"Colin, don't worry about me. It's obvious I can't hike across country. I'll take my chances with this stupid little sod. Blowing up cars! I'll deal with him. You get a good start . . . just get to Kendrick. I'll know how to contact you. There'll be good news, too, never fear."

Prosser pecked Polly's cheek and shook hands with Chandler.

"Remember," he said. "What does not destroy me makes me stronger."

Then he was gone.

Polly turned to Chandler in the pitch-darkness of the back hallway, by the door.

"Are you afraid?" she asked.

"Aside from wanting to throw up and faint, I'm fine."

"Do you have the bag?"

"Indeed I do, and our raincoats, the works. The oilskin pouch . . . It's going to get heavy."

"When I open the door," she said, "let me go out first. I'll give you the sign if it's clear. All we've got to do is get to the tree line."

"Even I grasped that."

"Just follow orders," she said, patting him reassuringly, "and you'll be fine." Then she was through the door. He waited, watching her slowly make her way across the lawn. She stopped by the shed where he'd found the key. He yawned, heard his jawbone crack, as usual. The canvas bag already felt heavy. What in God's name was he doing here? How had Hugh come to killing someone? He shut his eyes: all a dreadful, bizarre mistake, a case of hideously mistaken identity. When he opened his eyes he saw Polly beckoning. Well, what the hell else could he do? He left the house . . .

Prosser waited in the darkness, nourishing his malice, calculating the various possibilities, trusting his weary heart to see him through. Thorny had not been seen since the one fleeting shadow by the tree, but Prosser knew he was there, that he hadn't risked moving, circling the house. Though he believed Chandler to be alone in the huge house, or at worst accompanied by a woman, Thorny was no fool: he knew the damage Chandler and Brennan were, unexpectedly, capable of inflicting. Prosser could almost sense the fear that was settling on Thorny: out of anger, or frustration, he had risked the luxury of a symbol, a gesture, the incinerating automobile. Very pretty. But now he was thinking: Chandler knew he was here, Chandler had been warned . . .

Prosser packed his pipe in the dark, poking the tobacco down with a blunt, much-used forefinger, cupped the flaring match with both hands. There was nothing for it but to let him wait a bit, the fear growing, the sweat soaking his clothes out there in the cold night. Chandler and Polly must have made it to cover by now; there was nothing to worry about there. She had a good head, together they'd win through. At least they had a decent chance, better than most. Unless, of course, Petrov decided not to leave well enough alone . . .

What could possibly be going through the Russian's mind? Prosser tried to imprint his own deviousness on Petrov's, tried to squeeze himself into the man's mind, but it was heavy going. Although he'd served the Russians both as allies and enemies of the United States, he'd never flattered himself about understanding the Russian mind: for him it had remained a tantalizing blend of Oriental and European, always shifting and unpredictable. So often they ignored what seemed important to press on the trivial; yet, when you counted on that, they would brutally adhere to the obvious and mistrust the mildest sophistication. So Petrov puzzled him, as all the others had. His American masters, on the other hand, had never struck him as particularly complex, devious. It was a matter of national character perhaps . . . or the fact that he was an American himself . . .

Waiting, listening to the odd crackle from the burning car, Prosser smoked and pondered, turned his own situation before him, analyzing. How, he wondered, had it come to this? Sitting in the dark, in the middle of nowhere, counting out his life, mourning the confusion inherent in it all. What in his own character had led him to this private place of skulls? Why had he chosen to serve in both camps simultaneously? What twist was part of him, not of others who'd had the same opportunity? Was it simple greed? He smiled in the dark, wishing it were all that simple . . . Or was it the need to control others? Or the lure of the game, the competition? Well, he was tired of it. Maybe it was one project too many: that's the way it always ended, so went the rule of thumb, one job too many and you never came out the other side: like drifting helplessly into a black hole, finally giving it up. So remarkable, to end this way, with such a simpleminded number—so harebrained. Why did bloody Petrov want the damned piece of paper: what the hell did he think he was going to do with it? Could it really have been just a whim, a caprice on Petrov's part? With so much death? It made no sense, except perhaps to a Russian . . . What a finale! What a way out!

In the end he had to go get Thorny.

From the window he called to him: "Thorny, listen to me. This is your control—do you understand, your control. Chandler has been here and gone. I got here too late myself. Chandler is *gone*." Having conveyed the substance of his message, he became peremptory: "I'm not going to show myself until you're out in the open. You could have gone off your nut and be after me—now get your wretched self in here! We've got planning to do."

There was a slight wait, then the figure came away

from the tree and started toward the house. As he came more clearly into view Prosser saw the gun, dangling from his right hand: Christ, the man was walking like a zombie. He went to the front door and stepped outside, onto the stone balustrade. "Get in here," he snapped. "What's the matter with you?" By the time Thorny had mounted the steps and was even with the old man the problem was obvious. "You're stinking, you frightful imbecile! Give me that gun before you hurt yourself . . ." He held out his trembling old hand and Thorny numbly placed it in the palm. "So help me God," Prosser muttered, "you're a poor excuse, you really are a poor excuse."

He pushed the drunken, foul-smelling Thornhill ahead into the house, herded him into the library. He clicked on the table lamp. "Sit down." Thornhill sat down, eyes staring, nose running, tongue flicking again and again across his lips.

"Water," he whispered.

"Shut up," Prosser snapped, staring hard at the bedraggled specimen, head in hands at the table. "What's your excuse? Ignoring my instructions, hanging up while I'm talking to you—where's your sense of discipline, man? You disgust me . . . drunk." He fumed, banged his pipe on the facing of the fireplace as he paced. "Drunk! What did you intend to accomplish here? Kill Chandler, I suppose? Ha! You're damned lucky he didn't get you alone, the record you've got this past week . . ." He marched back to the table and yanked Thornhill's head up by the fringe of hair. Thornhill screeched and Prosser slapped his face, stood watching the man moan, thinking, *don't bring on a heart attack*. He fought the anger that was building. "Look at me when I speak to you. Vermin, you're vermin." He felt his chest tightening and stalked away to the window which had been smashed by Thornhill's single shot.

"Do you know who you're working for? Do you know who you're trifling with? Do you? Answer!"

"No, no," Thornhill said, pale, a red splotch on his cheek where the old man had struck him. "Just a job . . ."

208

"The Russians, you pathetic cretin." Prosser peered at the man. "The KGB . . . you're fouling up a KGB operation!" Thornhill showed no reaction, stared off into space. "You've been killing people, bringing attention to this entire operation . . . a simple operation. A Watergate plumber could have managed it without the least difficulty. But not you. No, no, you were up against a Harvard student, an eighty-year-old man, a couple of Harvard professors—couldn't just do your job . . . Ach, a sad commentary . . ." He came back to the table like a vulture, unable to resist the carrion. "It's not too much to say that I am disgruntled. And what do you think our KGB friends are going to say? Think about that."

"I don't know anything about Russians," he said, trying to stifle hiccups.

"Well, pray to God you don't find out."

"You, will you tell?"

"Stand up. Come outside with me. I want to show you something."

Thornhill struggled upright and clumped dejectedly back outside with the old man's hand firmly in his back.

"Do you ever think about life?" Prosser spoke softly, conversationally.

Thornhill eyed him sideways: "What do you mean? Life . . . I don't have much time to think about—"

"Well, it would have been time well spent. You lead a violent life. It ought to have occurred to you to give some thought to what it has meant, this life of yours." They were walking toward the big tree. The shape of the red Pinto loomed suddenly, close at hand. Beyond the tree, a storybook well had long ago been sunk, a tiny shingled roof built over the top, a large winding crank. "Do you think you can drive, old man?" Prosser's voice had softened, as if they'd known each other for years. "Feeling punk, eh? Weak in the knees? All right, all right. You can stay here. Give me the keys to this toy car . . . I'll put it in the garage."

"God, thanks," Thornhill muttered, fumbled the keys into Prosser's hand. "I think I'm going to puke . . ."

"Ah, well, no better place . . . Here, just fire away into the well."

When Thornhill leaned forward, retching into the mouth of the well, Prosser gently placed the muzzle of the large gun against the back of his skull and pulled the trigger. The more or less headless corpse collapsed over the rim of the well. Prosser eased him upward and dropped him down the wet, clammy darkness, heard a damp crunching sound at the bottom.

Prosser took a deep breath and leaned against the tree. The night winds had blown the clouds away, leaving a sprinkling of stars. He felt much better. Tomorrow he'd kick over whatever traces might remain. For now he'd run the stupid little Pinto in beside the Rolls and get his poor old body tucked into bed.

Christ. What a very long day . . .

Liam McGonigle sat in the leatherette booth, staring out the window at the pancake house's parking lot, the grotesque sign shining in the darkness, beckoning the Sunday night family homeward bound and unwary. Andrew Fennerty picked at the remains of a mound of syrup-soaked blueberry pancakes, chewed absentmindedly, expressionlessly. The restaurant was noisy with bawling children and weary, snappish parents. Unasked, Liam extracted a packet from his jacket pocket and slid it across the table: Alka-Seltzer. Andrew nodded and pushed his plate away. He dropped the two white disks into a glass of water, watched them foam.

"Not one of our better days," Andrew allowed, lifting his glass in a bleak toast. "I can't remember the last really acceptable day I had in the field, no, I really can't." The bubbles were dying down. "But Kennedy was President . . ." He took a deep, slow draught and waited for the requisite, soothing little belch. When it had come and gone he finished the glass and wiped the white scum from his lips.

"Not very hard to figure out," Liam murmured. "We're too damned old for this sort of thing . . . But the old man had to have us, I can hear him now . . . he's

210

worked with us before, he needed our fine touch, all the old crappola—well, it worked, he got us." He stroked the stubble on his chin with the short freckled fingers. A yawn burst through uncontrollably. "Anyway, we don't belong here . . ."

"You know," Andrew said, narrowing his eyes, "I hate to say it but I think the old boy is past it. He's held on for a long time, he's done a lot of very sharp work, but there comes a time, there just comes a time . . ." He reached back to his plate and forked up another layer of pancake. "He never should have asked for us, he should have known better and used younger men, but he knew he could handle us." He chewed solemnly, watching the parking lot. A stern wind shook the evergreens below the glass. "He's past it, he just doesn't have the touch anymore." He lapsed into silence, lit a cigarette and motioned to the waitress for a coffee refill.

It had been a drastically bad day. First, the call had come in from the old man, rousting them out of bed, tired and middle-aged and bedraggled. Then the mess at Brennan's house: the corpse of the large, bandaged Russian agent was not particularly refreshing, even as corpses usually go—dead and smelling awful from every orifice, blood filling his eyes, clotting his nostrils . . . And Brennan: they'd thought he was dead for a moment, but he'd turned out to be comatose but alive. They'd called Mass General and the police. Then they went away. They called the old man but he was gone, no answer on the number they'd been given. Exasperation.

They had then piled into the car and driven the agonizing distance through heavy traffic to Kennebunkport. But the Seafoam Inn had been locked up tight. In the driveway smashed flat in mud and gravel, they found the depressingly familiar porkpie hat.

"Well," Liam sighed, "well, well." He drummed his fingertips on the tabletop. Unfortunately he stuck two fingers into a puddle of maple syrup. "Shit, Andrew, shit, shit . . ." He never raised his voice: Liam was never quite interested enough to raise his voice. He

211

stuck his fingers into his water glass and rubbed them against one another, withdrew them, and wiped them on his napkin. "What do you think we should do?"

"Kill ourselves."

"The easy way out. Coward."

"We can't find the old man. We can't find anybody at the Seafoam Inn. The little bastard in the funny hat has come and gone, we know not where." Andrew blew smoke at his own reflection, turned his eyes back to see Liam's sorrowful face. "Look at our eyes, Liam. Between us, we've got enough bags to pack the Red Sox for a road trip . . ."

"Let's get a motel room, get some sleep—"

"But we've got to have a plan," Andrew insisted lamely. Like all fieldmen, they hated the feeling of being alone out there, uninstructed, unprovided for, unsure of what to do.

"Let's figure we'll get hold of Langley in the morning. Maybe they'll scrub the whole stupid business."

"What do you think it is that we're after?"

"Look, it's just a stupid job, more stupid than usual, that we should never have been asked to do. I don't give a goddamn what it is. I just want to get back to civilization, see my desk again, cook some steaks in the backyard, hear my wife yelling at me . . ."

The fog clung to the ground, hung in the trees, beaded on their faces like rain. They had walked for an hour, making slow headway, with nothing by which to reckon their course. The idea had been to move parallel to the tree line itself until they were well away from Prosser's summer home. For a while they had been able to make out the glow of the burning automobile but the fire faded and they seemed to be moving deeper into the woods. They were breathing hard and sweating when Chandler suggested they stop. It was then that they thought they heard something like a gunshot, but it could have been something else, it might have been nothing at all.

They rested in the darkness. The fog came and went but fortunately there was a hint of a moon somewhere above, among the clouds, throwing off enough light to give them a slight, functional visibility. They kept going after a brief rest, Chandler hauling the bag, following Polly who moved carefully, purposefully among the trees and damp grasses, slipping occasionally on bits of ice and snow. They seemed to be moving uphill but it was hard to tell, until Polly called back: "Do you smell it? I can smell the ocean—get up here." He was afraid to put the suitcase down in case he couldn't find it again so he struggled up the increasingly abrupt incline.

"Are you in danger of having any kind of attack?" She clutched at him as he drew level with her, grunting and swearing.

"Don't be ridiculous," he said. "I'm fit as I ever was—"

"Big deal. Smell it, smell the ocean . . . seaweed or kelp and sand and all that—"

"Yeah," he said sniffing. "I guess so."

"Well, we know where we are then."

"I don't know where I am."

"We will in the morning when we can see the map. We're near that water and not very far from Prosser's house." She took a deep breath. "Tomorrow we'll get to the highway—"

"And get picked up by the homicidal maniacs we're trying to avoid."

"Do you want to walk to Bar Harbor, then?"

"I want to be very careful."

They moved along the crest of the ridge. Chandler felt sand underfoot. The wind was picking up, snapping at them. He heard something move down in the scrub, felt the back of his neck prickle.

"We can't walk all night," he said. "We've got to get some sleep." He took her arm, pulled her down on the inland side of the ridge. "Come on, come on, mustn't hang back."

He found a sheltered area in the protection of several fragrant, low trees or shrubs, he neither knew nor cared what the hell they were, only that they cut the wind. He took off his Burberry, leaving his heavy oiled sweater over his shirt, and spread it on the ground. "Take off the sheepskin," he said. "Now scrunch down on my raincoat. Good." Listening to her as she settled in, he opened the bag and felt around: sport coat, another sweater, nothing really helpful. Polly was wearing a heavy sweater. He gave her the sport coat and told her to use it as a first blanket. He knelt and put the bag down as a pillow: he felt like a character from a Geoffrey Household novel; they always seemed to be out in the woods living by their wits and eating roots and berries. He flared the sheepskin coat out across them.

"Now we come down to the question of body warmth," he said. "For maximum effectiveness we lie on our sides, you see, your back to my front. Right. In this manner, we become as narrow an area as possible and your coat just about does the job. I put my left arm around you, you rest your little woolly head upon your mammy's breast . . . See, not so helpless after all. I can survive anywhere . . . Comfy?"

She groaned: "Asleep. I can sleep anywhere."

"Well, goodnight, then."

"Oh, God, don't get huffy at a time like this."

"I am not huffy. But you could show a bit of appreciation—"

She began to giggle: "Colin, I *am* appreciative. Now, go to sleep."

"Well, don't snore. I'm a very light sleeper."

There was no response and he settled down, his head on his right arm. He felt surprisingly snug, even rather comfortable in a way you wouldn't necessarily want to feel comfortable every day. But it was reminiscent of sleeping in the backyard as a child. As such, it was rather soothing. But he couldn't quite get to sleep . . . he couldn't even get near sleep. He heard Polly's breathing grow deeper, regular, as she went completely under.

He was worried about Prosser, alone in the house with the bad guy wandering around outside. What could the old man do in such an uneven contest? But, then, he hadn't seemed particularly worried at the prospect. But he had been unlike his usual self, bereft of the acerbic tongue, the elegance and the antagonism and the malice

214

which were central to his personality. Worried, under unaccustomed pressure: surely, that was the reason for the change. The old boy was in just a little over his head, regardless of his colorful, terribly important past, and he was showing the strain.

But Brennan, that was something else. How to find out what condition he was in . . . He'd killed a man, the big man with the gold tooth, what a hell of a job that must have been—but what had they done to Hugh, what had happened to him?

He finally sat up and dug his pipe and tobacco out of his raincoat pocket and got a smoke going. He was beginning to feel like a character in a novel, but it all fell apart when he was supposed to actually do something. He was simply too innocent to regard his position critically and draw clever, predictive conclusions.

Particularly he didn't know what he had done to land himself in the middle of the Maine nowhere with a beautiful woman he'd just made love with . . . A beautiful woman who had in fact dragged him into the whole ghastly business in the beginning.

By God, it was true. He'd forgotten that it was all somehow her fault.

And then he went to sleep, the bowl of his briar warming his hand . . .

Monday

Polly woke first, stirred her hips against his belly and thighs, and said: "What I'm worried about is Ezzard . . . God, how could I have forgotten?" She scrunched around on her back. "Wake up, boy scout."

"I am awake. I have a sore throat." He kept his eyes closed, tried burrowing his nose against her sweater. He snuffled in his throat, coughed, feeling vividly unattractive.

"It's just the wet, cold air. It'll go away." She braced an arm on his shoulder and sat up. "Good God, I'm stiff. Getting old, I guess."

"It's just the wet, cold air," he said. "You're just entering your prime, my dear."

"I suppose after one go-round on the floor before the fire, you're some kind of big expert on Polly Bishop." She poked his chest. "Beware of overconfidence. One swallow does not a summer make, for instance. I've got a million little sayings I've been saving for you . . . Either I start on a million examples of pith or you get up."

"All right, all right, I'll get up." When he cranked an eye open she was standing over him, stretching, reaching as high as she could. Fetching, quite fetching. He opened the other eye. "Saucey Worcester," he said.

"What?"

He shook his head: "Nothing." He blinked at the beauty of a quiet spring morning. The sun was glowing gold behind the light fog bank and it was warmer than he'd prepared himself for: he had a flash of that carefree feeling that had come and gone erratically since he'd met Polly Bishop. "Well, what do you think?"

"I don't know about you," she said, "but I'm on my way to use a bush for a bathroom. I'm only human, you know." She set off and he lay quietly on his back, her coat over him, the sheepskin up tight to his chin. It smelled like spring and the scent of the damp earth and grass and trees sent his mind going, racing off across the past. He remembered his boyhood in the little town of Oregon, Illinois, the melting of the snow and the wafers of ice coating the puddles like sugar frosting, and the cocker spaniel who'd romped madly at the season's changing as they'd climbed Liberty Hill . . . It was so long ago and he couldn't really remember the boy with the dog but there was the spiral of memory that got into the brain and waited. You could never really summon it up: it just came when the button was pushed or the right string pulled.

"The highway can't be very far," she said as they pushed out of the stand of pines and firs, into soggy grasses that sucked swamplike at their feet. She veered off toward a hump of path, sandy and wet. Highway One was an unprepossessing, narrow gray ribbon of concrete but it would take them as far as Ellsworth, according to the map, and that was all that was required. They both knew that someone was looking for them— and they were afraid of what might have happened to Prosser. But there was no going back: they had their orders. They pushed on in silence, the new day increasing in seriousness with each step. An hour after breaking camp, they found the highway stretching emptily away on either side, the golden glow of the rising sun giving it just a swipe of the alchemist's wand.

"Pray for no red Pintos," he said, plopping the bag down at the roadside. "We're really sitting ducks out here . . ."

How far are we from Ellsworth?" She'd combed her hair back with her fingers and her cheeks were flushed. He'd kissed her once and he wanted to kiss her again.

"Let's say, too far to walk."

"Are we just going to wait?"

217

"Might as well *start* walking . . ." He picked up the bag. "Listen to the birds. In the spring, a young man's fancy . . . you know."

She put her arm through his and they started off along the shoulder trying to avoid the mud.

After two cars and a panel truck had passed, he said: "Wouldn't this be a good time to tell me the history of the macguffin? I mean, if they find us, I wouldn't want to die without knowing . . ."

"Come on—"

"And what about the brown car? It's not exactly fit to return . . ."

"Good God, I hadn't thought of that—"

"So tell me about the macguffin."

"No, you'll get spoiled."

"Ha!" She kicked a stone across the quiet road. The golden glow was fading as the overcast thickened. "I am *really* hungry."

By midmorning they reached Rockland where they stopped at a gas station and diner where a couple of trucks were gassing up. Fog was gusting across the highway. "Food," she said, "food."

While Chandler picked at a plate of scrambled eggs, Polly ate the ranch breakfast, the thought of which turned his stomach. It was the fear. It was back, a dark unreasoning thing he couldn't ignore. They sat in the booth furthest from the door: he watched the highway for a first glimpse of the red Pinto, wondered what exactly he would do if he saw it. A police car pulled in and parked. Two cops got out and stretched, clumped into the diner where they were well known. Banter, laughter, a thermos being filled with hot coffee. It would have been such a pleasant, remote place, such a fine place to be with Polly . . . it would have been. "Oh Christ," he whispered. "A red car . . ." Polly shook her head: "A Toyota," she said. "Relax." He leaned back: "Be still, my heart." He wasn't kidding and knew his smile was a poor, sickly thing.

The cops finished the snappy comedy routine and left. The locals subsided into their regular laconic conversation. Chandler got up and went to the counter where a

218

well-thumbed copy of the morning's Boston paper lay unattended. He brought it back and slid into the booth. Polly was still eating. "I'm worried about Ezzard," she said.

"You said that."

"I know but I'm going to have to do something about it. I'm going to call my next-door neighbor and get him to do something."

"How will he get in?" He was unfolding the paper in search of the front page.

"He has a key."

Chandler's eyes snapped up: "He does, does he?"

"He's a very sweet boy. *Very . . .*" She smiled. "He's gay, if that makes you feel any better."

"I'm sorry . . ." He folded the paper on the table and felt his stomach do something unpleasant. It was in the lower right-hand corner of the first page.

TV NEWSWOMAN MISSING:
WAS INVOLVED IN MURDER QUERY

Polly's picture was particularly attractive: mouth open, teeth flashing, her head caught turning toward the camera, eyes bright.

"How the hell—"

"Listen," he said. "Presumably you missed a show Sunday night . . . no, they called you, or you were supposed to call in . . ." He shook his head, ran his finger through the article. Polly watched, nibbling a fingertip. "Oh, here it is—" He was out of breath. "Ralph Stratton—the station manager—spent Sunday trying to get hold of you—"

"Damned busybody!"

"And when he couldn't find you he went to your apartment and found the door unlocked and evidence of a search through the apartment by persons other than Ms. Bishop—some of our little friends, no doubt . . ."

"Does it say anything about Ezzard?"

"Polly, somebody has gone through your apartment! It doesn't say anything about the cat, no, but look at it

219

this way, if they'd killed the cat it would have been in the headline. But who did the going through?"

"McGonigle and Fennerty? Porkpie and Company? I guess it doesn't really make much difference. What do you think they wanted? Oh, hell, that doesn't make any difference either, does it?"

"No, I guess it doesn't. Says here you've played the key media role in the Harvard murders—" He gave her a sour look.

"Colin, you missed something at the top of the page."

HARVARD PROFESSOR TORTURED
KILLS ATTACKER, NEAR DEATH HIMSELF

The story was little different from what Prosser had told him but it was all new to Polly who read it with growing amazement. She finally looked up, wide-eyed. "Prosser told you about this?"

"He didn't want to worry you."

She rolled her eyes: "Brennan was conscious, told the police the story. The police got an anonymous tip . . . I don't see where Prosser fits in. It's pretty weird."

"He has lots of connections," Chandler said. "Who knows . . ."

"Well, it doesn't all hang together, not in my book." She turned to page three. "Here *you* are, my dear . . .

WHERE IS PROF. CHANDLER?

Says here that Department Chairman Bertram Prosser was unavailable for comment. Next they'll be wondering if Harvard can stand the brain drain—Chandler, Prosser, and Brennan." She finished her coffee and looked brightly around. "A few days ago this would have been amazing—"

"It's still amazing. People are still trying to kill me, Prosser may be dead . . . Hugh could die at any moment, according to the stupid newspaper—and we're wandering around the coast of Maine absolutely defenseless trying to get to Bar Harbor . . . believe me, it's amazing. And the most amazing thing about it is the fact that I haven't had a nervous breakdown." He jabbed the paper with his forefinger: "Both of our pictures are in the papers—why, hell's bells, we could be recognized at any moment!"

"Colin," she said calmly, "so what? We're not wanted for anything. It's not Cary Grant in *North by Northwest*. We're just running away. Somebody spots us, they say, hey, I know you two . . . and what are they supposed to do? That's the really scary part—the only people who want us, want the document, and would probably rather kill us than not. Walk into a police station and they wouldn't even know what to do with us . . ." She smiled.

"Okay. Let's get going."

"First, I've got to call about Ezzard. Go powder your nose and I'll be done." She went to the pay telephone hanging on the wall and took a credit card from a billfold in her coat pocket.

He went outside and asked a man with a station wagon bearing the words Down East TV Repair if he knew how they might get to Ellsworth.

"Well, you might get your thumb out," he said, winking a blue eye buried beneath a reddish brow. "You might wait for the taxi. Quite a wait, though." He turned and saw Polly coming out, her sheepskin coat open and spread back in the breeze. "Or, since I'm heading up Ellsworth way myself, you could come with me." He smiled, looking at Polly, then back at Chandler.

They all crowded into the front seat and made small talk: what are you folks doing up here without a car, got business in Ellsworth? Damn, but you look familiar, miss, you sure we haven't met somewhere? Positive? Well, I'd of bet on it . . . TV business, repairing them, that is, pretty interesting, some folks still have you come right into their homes, expensive as hell, but say you got your big console style TV, decorator cabinet, damn things weigh a ton, how the hell they gonna get 'em to the shop? That's the problem with a console . . . that's where I'm going right now, just like a doctor, doncha see, making a house call . . .

He prattled on, sneaking glances at Polly's thighs and profile, while his passengers sat in silence. It was almost an hour later that he pulled over saying, "Well, folks, it's been mighty interesting talking to you, but this is the end of the line—showplace of Ellsworth, the Holiday Inn." Chandler hopped out, grabbed the bag out of the back seat, and pulled Polly after him. "Much obliged," she cried over her shoulder. Chandler waved, muttered a cheerful obscenity, and headed across the parking lot into the motel. The clerk at the desk called a cab and they waited outside under the marquee. "He wasn't that bad," Polly said.

"He damned near drove off the road every time he sneaked a look at your thighs. Could have killed us and then where would we be, right? Rustic sex fiend."

"You picked him, darling." The cab arrived and, Chandler told him to head for Bar Harbor.

"Bah Habah? Bah Habah is closed up tight as a drum, tighter."

"Just go to Bar Harbor. Please . . . just go."

Shaking his head the driver overcame his own better, judgment, took a right leaving the Holiday Inn and drove to Bar Harbor without another word.

Kendrick's Sporting Goods sat with its rear door hung out over the water of the gray, flat bay. The surface of the water merged indistinguishably with the fog, the golden sun now totally obscured. The smell of the water surrounded them as they stood alone in the deserted street. A couple of skinny-masted boats clung nervously to the weathered, heavy-timbered dock. A man in a plaid mackinaw jacket knelt at the end of the dock peering down into the water, a cap pulled low over his ears.

Bar Harbor, for all its fabled social history, appeared to be a damp-stained, weather-beaten, echoing ghost town. Chandler went to the front door of the sporting goods store and tried the knob which refused to give. A light glowed dimly in the very rear of the dark interior. It was past noon. The wind off the water licked at the moist wood. The large window was stacked high and deep with fishing and boating gear that was quite meaningless to Chandler. Dust lay undisturbed on what might once have been a display but had become, over what looked like decades, nothing other than a weary, dull jumble. A tennis racquet from Bill Tilden's era leaned against an outboard motor: a broken string had curled up, died long ago. The archaeology of sport.

Chandler rapped on the door's split, rotted wooden frame.

"Well, it figures," he said. "Nobody home. Brother Kendrick is no doubt basking in the Florida sun. I knew I was going to regret this—"

"That's not true," Polly interrupted his wail. "You said that whatever Bert Prosser said was good enough for you. Now be honest with yourself." She cupped her hands and peered into the store. "You're just tired and sick of carrying the duffel bag. Here, kitty, kitty . . ." She tapped on the glass. "Kitty, kitty, kitty."

Chandler dropped the bag, walked to the corner of the building, and looked out across a vacant lot overrun by dark brown, matted weeds. Sand filled the cracks in the broken sidewalk. Nothing moved. The man who had been crouching at the end of the dock appeared now on the beach, emerging from among the warped black pilings, walking with hands in mackinaw pockets, cigar jutting from beneath a hooked beak. Chandler watched him turn abruptly, felt the eyes seeking his own, felt the stare. The man began walking toward him, reached some ramshackle wooden stairs which rose from the beach to the sidewalk where Chandler stood.

He was a large, square-shouldered, square-jawed, deeply wind-burned man of sixty or so, red veins crisscrossing his face with its day-old gray stubble. The cap was a battered yachtsman's that looked like it belonged in the window display. His eyes were deep-set and light gray and his voice had a strength Chandler had heard before in men who were used to solving their own problems in their own way. He had the steady gaze of a comic book hero, the same strong, obvious features.

"How are you?" he said, reaching the sidewalk. "Gloomy morning, gloomy day. Always puts me in a good mood. You looking for somebody?"

"Kendrick."

"Ah, Kendrick." He moved toward the store. "Old Kendrick . . . what could you want with an old duffer like him?"

"I'd better tell Kendrick about that."

"A close-mouthed man," he chuckled. "I like a close-mouthed man." At the window he stopped: "You like the little kittens, miss? They're such defenseless little mites." Four kittens had appeared in the window, stumbling and falling and earnestly getting back up, nosing onward. "You care to say good-afternoon to these two fellows?" He withdrew huge hands from his jacket pockets: each fist held a kitten.

"Why, they're just darling! Babies . . ."

"Ah, I always had a weakness for cats, everywhere I've gone, all over the world—a cat's a cat."

"Are those your cats, then?"

"Aye, seems I've got twenty or so." He looked at Chandler. "I'm Kendrick, and who would you folks be?"

"Bert Prosser sent us here, to see you." Chandler frowned, wondering why Kendrick had bothered with the charade over his name. "My name's Chandler and this is Miss Bishop."

Kendrick nodded, squint-eyed. Polly stroked the noses of the two kittens. "I've read about you two in the papers," he said enigmatically, put the kittens back in his pockets, and opened the door with a key. "Let's go have a sit-down and a touch of something to warm the bones." For a moment his breath filled the doorway, then he headed back among the dark stacks and mounds toward the single light. The room smelled of engine oil and rope and cold draughts. "Not much trade this time of year," he said without turning around. The kittens had wormed their way out of the front window: Chandler heard the soft patter of their feet and hoped to God he could avoid stepping on any of them. Polly stooped and scooped up a couple of small, furry black creatures. Cat box! He smelled the cat box, too. Deliver me, he moaned to himself, deliver me . . .

The office was large and cramped at the same time, smelled of endless cigars. Kendrick took a puff and carefully laid his cigar on the wide rim of a heavy glass ashtray which was set in a rubber tire. Chandler hadn't seen such an ashtray in years, since his childhood when his grandfather had had one exactly like it on his desk. Kendrick hung his coat on a tall rack: he wore suspenders over a plaid flannel shirt, heavy corduroy trousers. A space heater made the room dry, stuffy, and cats slept here and there, even among the papers on the rolltop desk. He pushed a cat off the rickety wooden swivel chair and pulled out a couple of scarred metal office chairs. "Sit, folks," he said. "Now, a nip for what ails you."

He took a bottle of bourbon out of the top drawer, lined up three glasses from a tray on top of the desk, and poured two fingers in each without seeking his guests' approval.

"Mud in your eye," he said and threw his into the back of his throat. Polly and Chandler sipped gingerly. "Wild Turkey. A man has to know where to spend his money . . . now, Bert Prosser, old Bert. Papers say you're a historian, sir. Tell me, are you intimate with Bert Prosser, do you know *his* history? Well, I do, I know his history, all the way from India during WW Two—that was where I first ran across Bert Prosser. Clever, slippery little devil. Just the man we needed. Intelligence officer. I was a pilot . . . hauled Bert here and there, here and there. Why did he send you to old Kendrick?"

"He said I was simply to tell you it was a matter for Code Green. Very cloak and dagger." Chandler shrugged self-consciously. "Does that mean anything to you?"

Kendrick lit up the stump of blackish cigar, blew out the wooden match, shook the bottle by his ear. He was running low. "Sure, it means something to me. It means plenty to me." He exhaled a vast amount of smoke and scratched the gray whiskers along the line of his straight prominent jaw. "Plenty. Code Green." He nodded.

"Is this something that happens every so often?" Polly asked. She had two tiny kittens tumbling about in her lap.

"Last time about five years ago . . ."

"What does it mean?"

"Sorry, miss, that's part of Code Green, dates from our Indian days . . . part of Code Green is that I can't tell you. Well," he said, standing up. "It means secrecy and hurry-up." He grunted and flung the filthy window open. The damp filled the dried-out room. Kendrick pointed out the window with his cigar. "Foggy out there. We're going to have to wait until it lifts or thins out. My apologies to Bert Prosser, but hurry chop-chop just won't work today." He turned around, hooked his thumbs in his suspenders, and chewed his cigar from one corner of his mouth to the other.

"Does Bert really expect us to just put ourselves in your hands?" Polly looked up curiously from the kittens.

"You'd know best about that, miss. You're certainly free to leave, with my blessings. If you stay, well, you're in my hands all right. But I wouldn't try to talk you into anything . . ." He sat down and poured another couple of fingers in his cheese glass, contemplated the fine amber bourbon.

"No, we're in your hands," Chandler said. "But I might as well tell you, I'm pretty near the end of my tether—"

"I'm used to that, people at the ends of their tethers. Don't worry about that, sir. But we do have to make some preparations, you see. Code Green is not just a spur-of-the-moment thing . . . so, if you're ready?"

Polly nodded.

"All right, then. We'll take my car." He took two tins of catfood from the splotched refrigerator in the corner and opened them with a red-handled device that didn't want to stay attached to the can. "Now, my little beauties, you won't have to eat each other." He summoned up a rather ghastly, rattling laugh, placed the tins on the floor beside a large saucer of cream, and slipped back into his mackinaw.

They drove along a narrow, slippery dirt road which swung down from the paved road toward the water, but circuitously so. The tires slid, fog blew treacherously across their path, wet grasses slapped at the sides of the

226

car. Kendrick obviously knew the road, but faith in Kendrick was hardly sufficient to keep Chandler from clutching at the dashboard.

"What the hell's the hurry?"

Kendrick laughed harshly: "No particular hurry. I just don't dawdle, that's all. Know the road in the pitch dark, coming or going."

The dirt had gone to sand and the trees had given way to nothing but beach grass. A small weathered gray house sat starkly, alone, in the sand of the beach, about fifty feet back from the road, precariously near the water. The house sat on stacks of cement blocks at each corner and at midpoints, as if expecting a half-hearted floodtide.

"No place like home, eh," Kendrick said, pulling off into softer sand. Kendrick's own dock projected out into the little protected bay and by the end of the dock an elderly seaplane bobbed softly on its fat pontoons. The outlines of the plane, only a hundred yards from where they stood, were badly smudged by the fog.

The interior of the house was comfortable and spare: a couple shelves of paperbacks, a large shortwave radio on the kitchen table, an old wicker couch in what must have once been a breakfast nook, stove and refrigerator, a rubber rack with dishes neatly dripped dry. The other room contained a bed, a dresser, and several rifles mounted in a rack on the wall.

"Travel light, that's my motto," Kendrick said by way of conversation. "Don't own anything you don't need." He moved quickly around the kitchen turning on lights, putting water in a tin coffeepot, switching on a gas space heater. There was no sign of cats. "Miss, if you're hungry you can raid the icebox. Coffee's perking. It'll warm up right quick . . ." He rubbed his hands briskly, looked around him. "Well, I've got work to do. You make yourselves comfortable and we'll proceed with Code Green as soon as we get a little weather going our way." He left the kitchen, disappeared into a small toolshed out back.

Watching him go, Polly said: "I rather resent all this,

Colin. Just who or what does Prosser think he is? This is little more than kidnapping—"

"Voluntary. We could have left . . ."

"Oh sure, wander off into the wilderness! Colin, I'm scared, too, every time I look up I think I'm going to see that damned red Pinto . . . he's out there, he wants us." She shook her head forcefully. Kendrick emerged from the toolshed carrying a metal case, trundled off head down toward his dock. "No, Prosser got us into this and now we're stuck with it. I simply don't see the point of all this Code Green nonsense—what would have been wrong with simply telling us where we were headed? It's childish . . ." She paused, struck by a thought: "Childish or governmental! Code Green sounds like something the idiots in Washington would come up with—"

"Look, he's been involved with the government in the past, off and on, advisory capacity, consultant, kitchen cabinet. He probably uses terminology out of habit. Stop worrying."

"Stop worrying," she said, making a face, pouting. "That's wonderful."

He put his arm around her, tilted her face up: "Now, look. I realize fully that I am not exactly a movie hero. But I do know Bert Prosser and if there's one thing in this world you can depend on, it's Bert Prosser and Bert Prosser's brain. When the man has a plan, it is a plan to count on. You can bet on it." He cued up what he hoped was a reassuring smile.

Polly pulled away, her face serious: "If we knew where we were going, then if they caught us, and started pulling out our fingernails, we might tell them where it was—that's right, isn't it?"

"The thought never crossed my mind—"

"Well, it's right—"

"I admit there's a sort of nineteen-forties Gestapo-movie logic to it."

"So, he didn't tell us," she said emphatically. "And now he's probably dead . . ."

"Morbidity will get us nowhere."

"Oh, don't be a Pollyanna!"

"Another archaism! You're giving away your age, my dear. "What's your favorite song—'Bringing in the Sheaves' . . . ?"

" 'You came to me from out of nowhere,' " she sang softly. "It's from a forties' movie, *You Came Along . . .* I wanted to be exactly like Lizabeth Scott, I even practiced a little lisp. She had those great, deep eyebrows, and that's the only part of her I wound up with. That movie, it was like *Love Story,* Robert Cummings was a flier dying of a funny wound and Lizabeth loved him. I cried and cried, she'd have to go on living without him. And then I grew up. And why the hell are we talking about this?"

"Archaisms . . ."

Polly nibbled at a fingernail, went to the kitchen window.

"What is he doing out there?"

Kendrick was climbing down onto the pontoon, carrying the metal toolbox.

"Going to play with his toy," Chandler said.

"Why do you suppose we're waiting for the fog to clear? Christ, he's going to fly us somewhere in that contraption . . ." She slammed her fist against the window frame.

The fog blew off in the evening after Kendrick had prepared a dinner of canned beans and toast washed down with beer. He rinsed the dishes and stacked them, dried his hands, and opened the kitchen door. "Stars are out," he said quietly. "We're in business."

Chandler carried the bag down the wooden dock, heard their footsteps sounding hollow like people walking on a drum. The water slapped softly at the pilings. The night air was wet and cold and he gulped it, trying to calm his stomach. A ladder with slippery rungs dropped down to a wooden catwalk leading away at right angles to the door. At the end of the catwalk the seaplane sat bobbing sluggishly in the dark water. Kendrick carried a flashlight. Chandler felt like Captain Midnight and the plane looked as if it were of that vintage, about 1940. The paint which appeared once to have been white was dirty, blistered in cancerous patches

229

like a scrubby garden gone to weeds, peeling and hanging like abbreviated confetti from the undersides of the fat wings.

"Don't worry," Kendrick said clairvoyantly, stepping ahead of them and fiddling with a tiny doorway. "It isn't how it looks, it's how it flies." He swung the doll's-house door open and pointed: "Up we go, miss."

Chandler heard Polly swear, watched her climb up, then followed her, pushing the bag ahead of him. He stuck momentarily, had a vision of flying off into the unknown with his ass and most of the rest of him hanging out to dry. Then he felt Kendrick's hand forcing him on into the cramped compartment, if that was what it was. Polly took his hand. He stood up with a cramp in his back and hit his head resoundingly on the top of the fuselage. If that was what it was, which he doubted. "Come on, man," Kendrick growled, "make way for the bloody pilot." Chandler settled into a tiny, inadequately upholstered seat with a metal, naked back. Kendrick joined them, kicked the bag out of his way, and pulled the door shut, slamming something metal into place with a solid click. With every step and shove and shrug the plane seemed to bob and shift in the water. Polly kept hold of his hand, squeezing hard.

"Why doesn't he get it going?" she whispered.

"Miss," Kendrick said edgily, "you read the news, I'll fly the effing plane. Deal?"

"Right, right, deal," she said.

Eventually the two engines were throbbing, rattling his teeth, then whirring smoothly and they were moving, half bouncing across the water. The instrument panel had lights of green, red, and white and the glow cast an unreal set of shadows across Kendrick's craggy, stolid face. He could have been chiseled from stone, ageless. Then they were free of the water and out ahead of them the black night sky yawned . . .

Arden Sanger was stealing an evening away from Company business, engaging in an activity that, were it known, would quite probably lead to his early demise. He was writing his autobiography and, though he had

230

only completed the section dealing with his football exploits, he was fully aware that the mere existence of such a document required the darkest secrecy. Consequently he followed no pattern in the time spent writing, altered his normal evening procedures as little as possible, and so far as his staff was concerned he was working in his locked study, just as he habitually did. But he was reliving the great Illinois game in his senior year, when Iowa City was his toy and a pair of pert little cheerleaders his post-game playmates. Jack Carson, indeed!

He had been sitting motionless at his desk for ten minutes, remembering the textures and scents of that remarkable evening, when the gentle buzzer on his desk hummed, unobtrusive but insistent, pulling him back across more than forty years.

"Yes, Dennis," he said, having capped his fountain pen and depressed a lever on the plastic box.

"Sorry to bother you, boss, but I've got Liam on the scrambler and he's very insistent on speaking directly to you . . ."

"Dennis, this is not remotely a priority matter. You realize that, don't you? I am busy, you realize that, I trust?"

"Yes, sir. But Liam suggested that you and he were friends while I was nestled at my mammy's breast . . . and he went on to imply that if I failed to put this call through to you he would personally rip my nuts off and hang them on my widow's Christmas tree—"

"Nothing to worry about, then. You're not married."

"Shall I put him through, sir?"

"For your sake, Dennis, yes, you may put him through." He stood up, picked up a pair of spring-loaded handgrips, and began squeezing them as he walked toward the French windows. Outside the spring night rested lightly on his patio, garden, pool, and tennis courts. Two men stood on the lawn, arms folded, looking up at the roof. The range of the television cameras was being given the monthly check.

"Arden, you there?" The voice came through the

231

room speakers, having made its way into and out of the scramblers.

"Liam, this had better be good—" he began.

"You sound like you're at the bottom of a well, which is funny, as you'll soon understand—"

"Don't worry how I sound, Liam. Just get on with it. I'm terribly busy. And, Liam, before I forget it, don't frighten Herman that way."

"Herman? Who the hell is Herman? Herman who?"

"Dennis Herman, the young fellow you just spoke to. What is it that you want, Liam?"

Liam McGonigle's voice grew considerably less gruff as he groped along the slippery skeleton of his story, feeling for figurative chinks into which he could anchor the unlikely narrative, keep it from dropping away into unsalvageable absurdity.

"So, the first point is," Liam broke the lancetip of his story, "we cannot actually find CRUSTACEAN . . . that is, Bert. He just snaffled, he's gone."

"I know his name, Liam. And what makes you think he's actually gone . . ."

"Because there's funny stuff going on. We're at his place in Maine right now, I'm standing in his study . . . we've been here all afternoon and, well, some pretty weird shit went on here last night—"

"How weird?" Sanger waved to the two men who had strolled over to another section of the lawn and were standing, quietly chatting. They returned his gesture. "Liam, *how* weird?"

"Well, the window here in the study is broken, glass all over, no effort made to clean it up. The slug that broke the window came from outside—Andrew found it, dug it out of the spine of a volume of Montaigne's essays. There are three sets of car tracks outside, the Rolls and a small car, a Dodge or a little Ford, I don't really know. Whatever it was, it burned up last night . . . I mean, there was one hell of an explosion and fire in the driveway last night and it was a car, no doubt about that, the smell won't go away." Liam took a deep breath; Sanger waited. "There's another set of tracks, too. Big tow truck, came and carried the wreckage away. Oh, the third set belongs to a red Pinto in the garage . . ."

"Hmmm." Sanger felt sure there was more to the story but couldn't imagine what it might be. Prosser was simply too old: he'd thought so for several years, but they shared a generation and he hadn't wanted to simply cut the old man off. As usual, sentiment was an unlucky master. Still, this operation had hardly seemed significant at the start. Simple observation, information gathering, and then it had begun to go wrong. The college kid had been killed and from then on, from Sanger's point of view, none of it had made any sense. "Go on," he said smoothly, changing his tone, not wishing to inhibit poor old Liam who, while many years Prosser's junior, was certainly not much of a field man, never had been, not even in his highly questionable prime. Liam belonged at a desk but Prosser had requested him, as well as Fennerty, and it had all seemed so harmless.

"Well," Liam hesitated, "then we found one of the opposition, that is, the remaining member of the opposition team, the little one—"

"Ah, the one with the porkpie hat . . ."

"You really amaze me, remembering that," Liam said admiringly. Sanger smiled at himself in a round, gilt-framed mirror over a bowl of yellowish flowers. "Well, we found him down the well . . . that's what I meant when I said you sounded like you were—"

"Down a well? Whatever prompted you to look down a well?"

"Just looking around—blood speckled on the side. Anyway, we took a peek down and there he was, not so deep, and most of his head was missing . . . in fact, we found a good bit of his head on the rim, once we looked a little closer."

"And what did you do about the body?"

"Left it. It's nothing to us, one of Moscow's boys, just a—"

"Moscow," Sanger said sharply. "Why Moscow?"

"I don't know, a guess . . . whoever he was working for, we can always find him if we need him."

"You think Bert killed him?"

"Well, who else?"

"Chandler. I assume you haven't found Chandler yet . . ."

"No, we haven't. You think . . ."

"Why not? They were chasing Chandler, they want Chandler, maybe they were unlucky enough to catch him. Let's say, I wouldn't put it past him."

"Chandler and Brennan," Liam mused. "What a thought."

"Am I right in saying that as of this moment you don't know where anyone is?"

"You could say that . . ."

"And we still don't know what everybody's after? That's right, isn't it? Tell me, Liam, do you know anything about Stronghold? Does the word mean anything to you?"

"No, means nothing to me."

"My God, this whole thing is the damnedest mess, no definition to it, sloppy . . . You know what it smacks of, Liam? Real life, that's what. All fouled up, unpredictable, sloppy, no order to it. I hate things like this, to be frank. Hate them . . . and this thing has been sloppy from the start . . ."

"Look, Arden, we're not that crazy about being out here . . . there's nobody left to die but us, you see what I mean? We want to come in out of the cold. Heh, heh."

"Don't talk like that. You can fly back here whenever you want. This whole blasted thing was busywork, you know that. Come in out of the cold! Nonsense!"

"Well, what do *you* want us to do? We're still hired hands. Andrew says to tell you it's a matter of—what, Andrew? Ah, self-respect, Arden. A matter of self-respect . . ."

"I see. Well, Liam, if I tell you about Stronghold, you'll have some exercise ahead of you. Are you two up to that?"

"We're not senile, for Christ's sake. You just tell us what to do . . ."

"All right. First thing, you'll need flares, red flares . . ."

Liam groaned. Arden Sanger smiled to himself. He was going to straighten this out quick. Damn quick. The autobiography would just have to wait . . .

Bert Prosser was exhausted. He knew what he looked like, there was no need to look in the Rolls-Royce mirror: face gray, eyes bloodshot, mouth terribly dry, hands shaking if he removed them from the steering wheel. He only weighed a hundred and thirty pounds and he felt as if there was no flesh on the bones: he felt like something hung in a doorway on Halloween to scare children. The fear of his own death hung about him, like the odor of old meat. Soon, he was going to die soon: everything had gone wrong, it had all blown up in his face.

Killing the drunken man—his employee, for Christ's sweet sake, a man who wisely or not had depended on him—had set him off. He'd thought, jerking awake in the middle of the night, hallucinating, that he was already dead, that he was locked in his coffin and water was seeping in at the bottom. When he woke, he'd still been able to see the man in the coffin with the water licking at him . . . but it was the man he'd killed and it wasn't a coffin, it was the damp, stinking well . . .

Then there'd been the mess of getting rid of the burned-out car, bribing a man with a tow truck, throwing his own slight weight around, making up a story. God, it was so tiring and he couldn't depend on the man to keep quiet. Too many loose ends. He had no idea where Andrew and Liam were, assumed they were befuddled, somewhere out there, and would finally work their way back to Boston and get in touch with him. Yes it was sloppy, terribly sloppy, but he was only human. Very old, very human. He would never have let things dribble off like that, not in the old days. But in the old days he didn't get the silly operations, the crazy ones: jokes, fieldmen called them. And this had been one of the worst jokes, no planning, utterly reactive, and made no sense either from Petrov's side or Sanger's. Petrov never should have gotten involved and

Prosser wondered how he had, knowing that he would never know. And Sanger had responded, taking Bert's own estimate of the situation.

Shit! He'd handled it all so badly. Indecisive. Old ...

He reached Cambridge a little after nine o'clock, put the Rolls in the garage, and went in by the outdoor entry which led to his private quarters. A light burned in the kitchen and he ignored it, sought no conversation with Ogden or Mrs. Grasse. He would call Sanger on Tuesday. For tonight, he would take some sleeping pills and blot out the worries. Chandler was safe, the woman was safe, he couldn't do anything about Brennan, and he was eventually going to have to show up at his office. What he needed was time to restore himself, his vigor, however much remained.

It was rather more than forty-eight hours since Krasnovski had visited the *dacha* and Maxim Petrov had more or less forgotten the messy result of the joke on his opposite number. In fact, once Krasnovski had departed the country house, Petrov had contemplated just how the whole ugly business might be blamed on the younger man who needed a severe lesson in humility if anyone ever had. But the means eluded him. So he'd turned his attention to somewhat more meaningful problems in Helsinki and Zurich where two of his employees had muffed the ball rather badly. As a result of trying to scour the floor after those two while keeping his own fingers clean, he had worked so late that a midnight snowstorm had caught him, made sleeping in the Kremlin preferable to going home.

Consequently he was at his desk at an altogether ungodly hour the next morning, appropriate he supposed glumly for a godless state, when Krasnovski appeared bright-eyed, pink of cheek, full of helpful suggestions. Petrov hated helpful suggestions.

"Don't speak," Petrov said. *The Sporting News,* which Krasnovski had been told was the peculiarly obscure key to a code regarding the United States which only Petrov knew, was spread flat on the desk. The Yankees had beaten Cincinnati in Florida and Petrov thought they just might possibly meet in the World Series.

"I regret to say that I must," Krasnovski said, smiling.

Petrov marked his perusal of the box score with a forefinger and stared balefully up at Krasnovski: "All right then. Speak."

"You recall the situation in Boston that we discussed Sunday morning?"

"If I must."

"Well, we seem to have stopped killing their people . . ."

"We weren't killing *their* people. We were killing plain, ordinary, innocent citizens."

"As you wish—"

"No, no, as it *is*. Or *was*. But, in any case, you say we've stopped?"

"Apparently."

"That's good news."

"Not altogether, sir."

"And why not, you irritating fellow?"

"Because now they have killed our people."

"Oh."

"Two of them. The freelances."

"Who killed them?"

"A Harvard professor, who may die from the attempt, killed one. We're not altogether sure who killed the other."

"Source?"

"CANTAB."

"He probably killed them himself," Petrov said, laughing bleakly.

"Is that humorous, sir?" Krasnovski's innocence deserved a grenade.

"It was a test, Krasnovski, and I regret to inform you that you failed. We will have no discourse whatsoever regarding my sense of humor." He returned to *The Sporting News,* moving his finger. "By the way," he said casually without looking up, "before our fellows were killed, did they happen to get what they were going after?"

"No. We are informed that the item is now out of our reach."

"Out of our reach?" Though he no longer saw the box scores, he kept his head down. His focus had shifted: he was thinking and trying to keep from screaming aloud. "*Out of our reach?*"

"So said CANTAB."

"From where did he contact us?"

"Via New York. From a roadside telephone in Maine."

"Our people are dead and the point of our efforts is out of our reach." He finally got up, went to watch the fresh snow cover, the pale light of morning, hardly light at all. It looked as if the world had been plunged back into winter. "What about the Chandler fellow? And wasn't there something about a woman who went with him?"

"Source informs us that they are missing. He cannot find them."

"Either he has rather badly lost his touch or . . . well, he may not be absolutely candid with us." Petrov impatiently folded *The Sporting News*.

"Might we not just abort the whole thing?"

"No, Krasnovski, we might not. Now go on about your business while I attend to this. Go on . . ."

Krasnovski departed reluctantly, pouting, eyes downcast.

Out of reach.

Petrov finally allowed himself a smile. *Out of reach.* That was a phrase he'd heard before from CANTAB. It had a meaning and the meaning came down to a single word: Stronghold.

He leaned back, regarded the graying sky, the snow which whitened everything he saw from his window. The question in his mind was hardly anything new: who was CANTAB actually working for? Petrov had always assumed that the old man was a mercenary, an expert who was called upon only at times when no one else would do. Did he perform the same sort of function for Sanger? But, then, why not? So long as jobs of work did not conflict: and surely this business had

238

had nothing to do with Sanger. It was only a scrap of paper, nothing Sanger could possibly have known about . . . No, it was a matter of bad luck. Bad luck that Sanger's people had gotten into it . . . *if* they were in it, if they had killed the two thugs working in Boston. He squeezed his temples between his fingertips: his days were never really less than complex, but ill-defined, long-distance problems such as this one, which found details growing more ornate rather than less so, were the things he hated most. Unimportant by themselves, acquiring importance only because they were strangely executed.

Strangely executed, indeed.

He contemplated calling Sanger on the direct line and finding out what the hell was going on. But what if Sanger wasn't in on any of it? Then his curiosity would become a wild-eyed demon, thrashing about, stirring up trouble where there had been only confusion.

He tried with considerable determination to think logically.

Did he care about the dead fieldmen?

No, not really. Bunglers. CANTAB had wanted to terminate them for the bungling alone.

Did he care about what games CANTAB might be playing?

No, not really. He was an old man who'd gotten into this business only because it seemed so simple and harmless. CANTAB would never be trusted with anything major . . . He would surely blow too easily and, anyway, his greed might long ago have made him a double agent. He just wasn't important to Petrov.

What was important, then?

The document. And the people who had it. And CANTAB had said out of reach . . . Stronghold. It had to be Stronghold.

He called Krasnovski back into the office.

"Get me the Montreal section man, please."

Not yet midnight.

Fennerty and McGonigle, awake and blinking with the aid of pills, a trunkful of red flares, headed northward on the best road. They would switch places every couple of hours to ensure the pace.

In the Atlantic a submarine floated like a dead fish, gleaming darkly beneath the moon. The officer in charge had spent an hour decoding the oddest communication he'd ever received: there was no alternative but to request a confirmation. So far as he could tell, the highly secret maneuvers which were to have been carried out against a small, uninhabited island used for practice by the Navy were now supposed to become operational—that is, *real,* for Christ's sake. So far as he could tell, there was only one possible conclusion, inescapable, but it was a tough pill to swallow . . . Behind all the bullshit and razzmatazz, it looked like the United States had gone to war!

Against *Canada* . . .

In Montreal a fat man's late evening dinner was ruined: his chief aide found him in a warm, fragrant, second-story Italian restaurant, tucking into pasta with dark sauce, a chilled bottle of Soave Bolla uncorked and waiting. Struggling into his overcoat, he hurried back to his office. He quickly had to validate an order, select the individuals to carry it out, and get word to them. It was, after all, no easy thing to carry out an offensive mission, mounted on the spur of the moment, within a sovereign nation so far from home. The instructions were long and detailed and required something akin to a miracle from the man in Montreal. He was however given considerable incentive: his career, and quite possibly his life, depended on his success. "Crazy," he thought to himself as he began preparations, "it gets crazier all the time." The telephone number in Halifax did not answer for nearly an hour . . . In the meantime he threw up twice.

Chandler was dreaming about something red and oozing, like oil sealed in a plexiglass cask, swirling and turning around and around itself. In his dream he was too close, couldn't make it out, then seemed to be dollied slowly backward so that he recognized the slippery red things as hands with shredded stumps

240

where fingers should have been. It was Brennan, mouth closed tightly, a silent scream trapped in his wide eyes, bulging . . . no, it was Prosser, an old man, hands chewed to the bone, blood smeared like warpaint across his old, sunken face. Or could it be Sir Redvers Redvers himself, not Prosser at all, but the old cad in the baggy tweeds, his man watching from a respectful distance as his master's life dripped from hoses where his fingertips had been . . . Then Chandler felt the touch of cold steel on his own hands, heard the scream strangling inside his own mouth . . .

He jerked awake, his hand asleep in a cramped position draped around Polly's shoulders, little needles stinging him. They were huddled in their few feet of space, jostling against naked, sharp-edged bits of the plane's skeleton, muscles rigid from bracing themselves in the nasty passenger seats. Chandler blinked, eased his hand out from around Polly and shook the bad dream out of his mind. Christ. He took the measure of his situation: cold, draughty, hideously stiff, duffel bag clamped between his knees, a boggish taste in his mouth, generally dispirited, rather surprised he was still alive, harboring a headache being hammered into his skull by the twin engines roaring in the night.

Kendrick was bellowing something over his shoulder, his voice cracking against the unsettling racket of the engines. The plane bounced occasionally, without any warning, and when it did Chandler closed his eyes, forced a deep breath, and prayed he wouldn't die, not this time. God, just save me this once and I'll always be good . . .

"Fog," Kendrick's voice reached him. "I'm going to drop down . . . Hold on."

Chandler heard the rain pelting the airplane, rattling what seemed like tin, and focused his eyes on the windshield in the odd glow of the instrument panel, saw the water beading up, streaking the glass as the plane slid on through the night. It was like batting your way through gray, wispy cotton: he could barely see the lights at the wingtips. With an involuntary gasp, he felt the plane sinking like a man on a funhouse slide, vapor filtering upwards, windswept past the little oval windows: each movement, whatever the direction, seemed to shake the frame of the aircraft, communicating an endless series of quivers and tremors which any sane man would assume would sooner or later result in the distintegration of the plane. Polly sagged against him, brushed at her face with a tight-gloved little fist. Chandler wondered what you'd do if you had to take a leak on this airplane . . .

He looked at his watch: they'd been flying for about two hours and he couldn't imagine where they were: "Where the hell are we?" he bellowed hoarsely.

"Well, I sincerely hope we're about a hundred and fifty feet above the water, but you never can be sure, you've got to let instinct take over on a night like this—"

"Oh," Chandler moaned. "We could get killed—"

"Definitely. But, then, I've never been killed yet, either. Look at it that way."

"Ah, where else are we?"

"We oughta be just about ten miles from the Nova Scotia coast, on the Atlantic side . . . Halifax off there to the left." He waved an arm in the general direction.

"What if we run into another plane?"

"We'd crash, probably die . . . burn up or drown, something in that line. Why?"

"Natural curiosity." Engines throbbing, head aching: why pursue the conversation? What difference did it make anyway? They'd live or die.

"Morbid, I'd call it." Kendrick shifted his weight, the leather of his chair squeaking. He drummed on the instrument panel.

"Halifax, Nova Scotia," he pondered. "Is that where we're going?"

"Can't hear you when the engines are running," he said, laughing abruptly like bursts from an automatic weapon.

"Are we going to goddamn Halifax or not?"

"Oh no, no," with much hilarity, or what passed for it in Kendrick's circle, as if no thought so amusing had cropped up in years. "No, not Halifax."

242

"Come on, Kendrick, you've got us at your stupid mercy. Be a sport, where the hell are we going?"

"Another hour or so, up around the top of the island, Cape Breton, up thataway. Can't fly over land, though. No flight plan . . . We got to just mind our own business, stay low, just get where we're going, make the drop and get out . . ."

"The drop? What the fuck are you talking about, the drop? You're not dropping anything you've got on board this crate, you can be damned sure about that, my good man."

"Don't break out in a sweat, Professor! It's a figurative expression meaning that we'll land, I'll see to your departure, and I'll then leave."

"You're going to leave us?"

"Calm down, man. Mr. Prosser's taken care of everything."

The plane dropped another seventy-five feet before Chandler could see at all and then only odd pinpoints of light flickered against the mound of the land mass, Cape Breton. He'd never been there, knew nothing about the place other than the warning of a lady traveler he knew: "It's not worth anything until mid-June when it becomes quite wonderful if you like rusticity." Well, it was a hell of a long way from mid-June, and he shivered at the temperature in the plane. Wind shrieked outside in the darkness like the hounds of hell scraping at them, trying to rip their fragile craft from the sky.

Polly woke finally, spoke thickly: "Are we dead yet?"

"A little longer. We're going to crash-dive in the raging surf where Smilin' Jack here plans to abandon us—everything's fine."

She yawned, pulled herself upright: "I want a glass of water."

"No."

"I have to go to the bathroom."

"Sorry."

"Are we there yet?"

"Shut up, little girl."

"Jesus! Is that the water down there?"

"Mmm."

"It's *right* there."

Kendrick let out another banshee cry: "Get those belts fastened! Won't be long now." He had turned on hooded yellow lamps which illuminated the fog still blowing across their path, and below them the frieze of waves strained to meet the pontoons and undercarriage, the curling water looked solid, like tortured cement ready to rip the plane to pieces at first touch. The water was a solid wall, close enough for scraping . . .

Down, they kept dropping down, his stomach lifting, the gap between plane and water tightening, thinning, fog whisking past the windows, ahead of them only water and absolute blackness where he supposed Cape Breton waited. How the hell did Kendrick know where he was? The question terrified him . . . Polly was gripping his arm, her eyes peeled wide and fixed on the oval window beside her: he saw her face in profile as he leaned forward, and put his mouth next to her ear, whispered something he couldn't hear himself, and kissed her soft, peach-fuzz cheek . . .

The seaplane smacked into the water with a shudder and a screech of metal fatigue, was hurled upwards and sideways, seemed to float dangerously away then smashed back against the flat, rockhard water, skidded, skipped again like a child's skimming stone, then it keeled forward precariously—or so it damn well seemed to Chandler—before settling back against the waves, in a kind of trough of its own making, slowing down, the metal continuing to groan and howl but quieting down as it rushed onward.

When the plane was at last dead in the water, Kendrick turned around and grinned weakly, face white in the ghastly instrument glow. "Little roughness tonight," he said apologetically. "But the important thing is, we're here, eh? Safe and sound, eh?"

"Do put a sock in it, will you?" Polly croaked, her mouth dry.

"Well, I don't blame you, miss," he said, his voice kindly, as he extricated himself from the confines of the pilot's bucket, levering himself up and out, crouching where they were. "Spot of rain out there, I'm afraid."

Kendrick dragged a package out from the rear recesses of the plane's passenger area, hugged it to him and backed wobbling past them, unlocked the hatch and opened it and pushed it all the way back against the fuselage where it clicked into a bracket. Rain blew in fine, sniping, gusting sprays through the opening, spattering their faces. Kendrick, holding tight to the packet, squeezed through the narrow doorway and climbed down the ladder, swearing at the rain and his burden until he was out of sight. Chandler hunched down and went on hands and knees to the opening. Rain lashed at him: he covered his eyes, peering down. Suddenly, with a swoosh of air, the contents of the package began to inflate, becoming a rubberized raft: when it was filled, a great awkward balloon larger then he was, Kendrick struggled with a flap which he hooked around the strut. Still swearing, he fitted the telescoping handles of the oars together, then made them fast with straps which held them secure inside the shell of the craft.

Moving slowly he began the climb back up. Chandler gave him a hand, hoisted him into the cabin.

"Miserable bloody raft," he sighed, smiling happily at his exertions: a man in his element, Chandler reflected, contrasting the pilot with himself. He sat down on a toolbox and wiped his face with an oily rag close at hand. "Now to be specific, ladies and gentlemen, let me tell you just exactly where we are and what's going to happen. We've just come in across the Cabot Straits toward the northern shore of Cape Breton; off to our right, up around the corner of the Cabot Trail is Pleasant Bay, to the left is Aspy Bay—we're head on toward Cape North . . . but I've put you down at an island, not Cape Breton itself. Got it?

"All right, then. Sorry about this rain but once you're in the raft you'll see we're only about forty yards from the beach. It's sandy all along this little inlet, rocks curving out to the sides but you won't get involved with them, not if you do as you're told. Just head straight on in, use your light . . ." He stopped and pulled a large, square, red, rubber-cased, highpowered flashlight from beneath him, patted it affectionately, like a pet. "This little baby will see you through, you'll be fine . . . there's a little weather, a little movement in the backwater, so it'll take you a few minutes to get there, but you'll be all right, just try to keep from falling out of the raft because getting back in could be a problem. Cold and dark in the sea on a night like this," he concluded, sounding as if he were quoting.

Kendrick pulled a plastic flask from his coat pocket and Polly took the first nip of brandy. Chandler followed, Kendrick gurgling happily as if it were water. "Now, then, once you reach the beach, you'll have to get to the house as soon as you can, if you want to avoid pneumonia—it's up on top of the cliffs, but there's a good path, about a hundred yards down the beach, to the left, cut out through the bracken and rock, you'll find it, just follow it up the hill—once you're on top, you'll see it, big monstrous place called Stronghold, faces out to sea with cliffs in the same direction, just like this side . . . the place is empty." He took something out of his pocket, pressed it into Chandler's hand. "Here's the key. Put it in your pocket and enjoy your stay . . ."

"Stronghold," Polly said.

"Foggy, wet place, very private, quite a nice spot, actually, if you like seabirds and storms and being alone . . ."

Chandler backed into the hatchway on his hands and knees, felt with his foot for the first rung of the ladder, then descended with considerable trepidation, making sure each foot was anchored securely before lowering the next. Everything was rapidly getting very wet: his face, glasses, hair; it was like standing in a flood. He clutched the large flashlight, clung to the handguard, slowly groping downward, refusing to look into the swirling black water. The flashlight was on and the light created a halo of spray, beyond which there was nothing but darkness, the sound of the water lapping against the pontoons. "Don't stop, man," Kendrick shouted from above. "Fuck yourself," Chandler called back, afraid to look up, afraid he might lose his concentration and slip on the oily wet metal.

At the bottom he hung from a strut and clambered into the treacherously bobbing, raking lifeboat. Kendrick lowered Polly, holding her hand as she went over the side; Chandler stretched, reached back up for her as she came closer, felt her hand grab his firmly. Then she was in the boat beside him, wiping rain from her face. Lithely, Kendrick came down carrying the duffel bag: "Stow this damn thing," he said, heaving it to Chandler. "Now get the light pointed in the right direction . . . *inland,* don't you see, there we go."

"I still can't see a damned thing," Chandler cried over the wind. The waves seemed heavier, higher with each sweeping crash.

"You keep it pointed that way, lad, and you soon will see something. Just keep paddling that way," he pointed like the ancient mariner gone to sea again, soaked, windblown. "I'll wait until you're well under way, closing on the beach, then I'm gone. Just keep paddling."

"Can you take off in this weather?"

"Don't worry about me, sport, I'll be in my own bed yet this night."

"What do we do when we get to the house?"

Kendrick laughed, his head shaking, rain flying: "Wait. You're stuck, the chief'll be in touch with you . . . Now get going." He turned away and fought against the rain and wind to climb back up into the plane. Before he pulled the hatch after him, he turned, gave them the thumb's-up signal. Then the door slammed shut and he was gone.

Tuesday

Chandler untied the raft which continued bobbing aggravatingly against the pontoon, keeping him off balance. He poked at the plane with the oar, pushing off, and the raft slowly broke away as if leaving a magnetic field. Polly grabbed the other oar and set to flailing away at the black water. Chandler began sweating under the raincoat and sweater, his body alternately hot and clammy. Quite suddenly, the raft was well clear of the aircraft. It seemed, as he struggled, spending his breath and beginning to ache, that he wasn't getting anywhere, but the plane kept getting smaller, the yellow glow of the foglights further off. Polly heaved quietly away on her own oar, steadily holding her own, while Chandler felt the kind of physical stress he associated with playing football years ago in hot weather: somehow, he wanted to avoid any explosion in his chest cavity or his brain.

"You're working too hard," Polly called, stopping, waving at him to put up the oar. "You're panicking. We're going to get there all right . . . rest a minute, Colin. Don't kill yourself." Water was collecting around their feet.

Chandler looked up again. Behind him the yellow glow hung like a ghost over the water. Polly was directing the light toward the beach, breathing hard: "Hey, I see it, I see the damned beach!" She turned smiling, her face wet, hair plastered down, looking about eighteen.

After the breather, they bent to the task of rowing,

watching the beach take grayish shape in the beam of light. Chandler was cold, wet, soaked through, water to his ankles, sneezing, but he forgot it all at the glorious sensation of the raft's bottom scraping and bouncing on the rough, sandy, rocky slope of beach . . . He sagged inside his wet clothing, feeling old and shrunken, heart pounding: it struck him that his poor heart had been overtaxed ever since the whole insane ordeal had begun . . . Well, maybe it was good for you. Maybe.

"Colin, we did it, we're here!"

He nodded, grinning.

"Darling," she said, staggering toward him bumping into the duffel bag, "you look just a little green about the gills—are you all right?"

Chandler nodded: "Fit as a fiddle, of course." He stepped out of the raft, immediately sank to his knees in a foot of water, icy water that pierced him like broken glass. Sand swirled up, settled inside his shoes. He managed to right himself, grinned against his better judgment: "Just like MacArthur . . ." Standing in the water he reached into the raft, tugged at the duffel bag which lay on its lumpy side in the water at the bottom of the raft. Thank God Prosser had wrapped the documents and the portraits in layers of oilskin. With a final heave he yanked it out of the raft, swinging it ahead of him up onto the sand. Polly, poised on the edge of the raft, fell gratefully into his arms. Together they staggered, waded up out of the surf, dragging the raft behind them, like a pair of creatures frantically speeding up the process of evolution. He dropped the raft, pushed it away from him: "I'll pick this up tomorrow."

They stood, holding each other on the beach, shivering against one another, teeth chattering, their faces ice cold, the rain spitting and blowing against them, and out on the water the yellow glow was gone, without their having noticed the departure itself.

"Thank God, we're here," she whispered, half crying tears of relief, "and you're holding me . . ."

"Well, we're safe, anyway. Are you okay?"

"Sure. I'm a tough little bastard." She laughed, wiped her nose. "Let's find the path." She picked up the flashlight and he took the duffel bag after fetching it a smart kick in the side. Damned bloody thing: it had become a grotesque extension of his right hand.

They pulled their raincoats up over their heads and leaned into the wind, trudging along the wet sand, the beam of light swinging ahead of them, pointing the way. The cliffs were laid back from the beach, a dark green blur through the rain: there was no real smell but the distinct odor of damp coldness and the wet wool of his sweater. There were slippery disks of ice in the sand and the walk toward the path was agonizingly slow, punctuated by Chandler's loud curses which replaced the quiet, awful, windblown fear of the plane and the raft.

"Good Christ!" he muttered, craning his neck as Polly tilted the lamp. "It's straight up . . ." He dropped the bag which fell over and began to roll down the beach. "Straight bloody up! I'm no mountain goat, you may have noticed—"

"Don't grouse," she said. "You only make yourself feel worse." She paused, directing the light at the path. "I admit it is rather steep . . ."

The path rose abruptly, apparently at right angles to the beach, snaking upward among the wet, harsh shrubbery, between the rock facing which glistened treacherously on either side. Chandler picked up the bag yet again and began the climb. Occasional moss-covered stones provided handholds which he used to lever himself painstakingly onward: the footing was not only slippery and muddy but dotted with patches of ice made worse by the steady rain which coursed down the path, as well as inside his collar. His feet were raw from rubbing the inside of his wet shoes. He kept finding himself on his hands and knees, trying to keep from falling ass over duffel bag back down the hill and onto the beach. How long, oh Lord, how long?

"Why did we climb it, you ask," Polly puffed from somewhere behind him. "Because it was there!"

Chandler tried to laugh but his mouth was dry and

nothing came out. Anyway, he was too tired to laugh. The angle of ascent never seemed to lessen, just went on, wet and icy and muddy and what in the name of God had he ever done to deserve this? "Shine the god-damn light up ahead," he shouted, "see where the hell we are—"

"Don't be testy and ruin everything, Colin. This is an adventure—"

"Oh, shit," he cried, slipping suddenly backward, clutching the bag, free arm flailing until he found a foothold in the rocks.

"Come on, Nimrod, we're almost there."

"Don't be cheery," he said. "I can't bear that—not cheeriness."

"You have mud all over your face."

"Ah, yes, I expect that happened when I was push-ing the bag ahead of me with my nose. In fact, my dear girl, I have mud in places where—"

"I never knew I had places, yes, yes. Very, very old."

He lay panting, clutching the duffel bag to his mud-packed raincoat: "But true, nonetheless." She sat down next to him, drew her knees up, rested her chin on them.

"Maybe we should, you know," she said, "take a little rest for a moment." She licked the rain off her upper lip and peeked over at him. "Every so often I can't quite remember how we got here . . ."

Chandler grunted: "Clark Gable and Claudette Colbert . . ."

After a while she took a deep breath, said: "Well, can you start again?"

"I'm not altogether sure."

"You take the light. I can push the bag—"

"No, my dear, I'm only out of shape, not actually dead." He stood up, balancing precariously. "Come on."

It went more quickly the second time. Ten minutes of hard slogging brought them to the top where they stood gasping, sucking deep gulps of cold air into tight, aching lungs. They were standing on a dark lawn and

251

the house itself loomed indistinctly another hundred yards away, up a gently sloping rise. Steeling themselves, they set off wordlessly, trudging across the slick grass, following the jiggling beam of light as if it were a leash and they were being wound inward.

Chandler's vision blacked out every so often, leaving him with a faint pinpoint of light and shadow, a goal, toward which he kept marching, one slogging, squishing footstep after another, shoes apparently trying to suck themselves from his feet. Polly went on, sturdy, uncomplaining, a marvel. She was slightly in the lead and he watched her, tried to absorb her determination and energy; she was the stronger at this point and it was indicative of the change he'd undergone that it never occurred to him to feel ashamed, irritated, or frustrated that she was there ahead of him, seeing him through the ordeal. He was just damned glad . . .

The house was a long red brick and gray-stone building, gabled somewhat excessively, fronted along its entire length by a porch with square brick pillars, backed at one end by leaded glass French windows like sleeping eyes, drapes drawn behind them; hooded chimney pots cluttered across the slate slabbed roof, heavy lead gutters, the architecture generally an example of the kind of 1920s brutality of weight and size, here for the purpose of withstanding the onslaughts of the Atlantic storms themselves, yet a building whose very overtness, like the presence of Marie Dressler in an old movie, finally overcomes its form and substance to achieve a variety of timeless grace. Lions with clawed feet sat at the corners of the second-floor balcony which was in fact the top of the porch. Standing in the rain, holding the light, Chandler imagined for just an instant a porch full of women in pastel frocks and men in white flannels, tennis racquets in hand, club ties waffling in the cool ocean breezes, a summer weekend fifty years before, but the images were soon gone and Polly was calling to him from the shelter of the porch. "Come on, crazy man, get out of the rain . . ."

The immense oak door, banded by black wrought-iron hinges like straps, bore a brass plate engraved with the single word in artless block capitals: STRONG-HOLD. The key worked smoothly and the huge door swung back with a creak from the massive hinges . . . It was like a replay of their arrival at the house in Maine, only on a much grander scale, as if they were stepping through a series of ever enlarging mirrors, doomed endlessly to run away, afraid, always repeating themselves.

Stronghold was in perfect running order: obviously someone on Cape Breton must have been engaged to come across the water at regular intervals and keep order, tend to maintaining the pipes and whatnot. An hour later Polly and Chandler were bathed, wrapped in huge bath towels, their clothes drying before the stove in the kitchen, a fire roaring in yet another library fireplace, more books gleaming darkly and gilt-stamped. "Hollywood must do Prosser's decorating. Polly remarked. Rain rattled like stones on the windows.

The duffel bag was unpacked upstairs where another fire was roaring. The freezer offered an array of frozen steaks, packages of vegetables, orange juice; but they settled for coffee and toast smeared with butter. They savored the steaming coffee in the library. They were grateful for the fire. They huddled close to the crackle, felt the heat full on their faces, sneezed and laughed and moaned over their exhaustion.

"You look just about done in," she sniffled. When she turned away from the fire, he could see her breath like smoke.

"In this case, looks are not deceiving." He leaned back against a chair, stretched his cold, damp feet to the fire, pulled his towel closer like a toga, yawned mightily. "Here is where we make our stand, my dear, and fight it out, get the wagons in a circle . . . I've run just about as far as I can . . ."

"You're right, of course," she said. "I think there's nothing left to do but wait it out." She made an impatient face: "I wish I understood what Prosser is up to. God, it just baffles me—everything about him sets me on edge—"

"Don't be so hard on him. I keep thinking, what if he's lying in the house back there, shot to hell by that crazy son of a bitch . . . and if he's dead, what the hell do we do then? How do we get out of here? Wait until somebody comes over to check the pipes? Just hope for the goddamned best . . . I tried the telephone, it's the one thing that doesn't work worth a damn." He frowned at the fire, sneezed.

Finally she said: "Come on, we're beat. Let's go to bed."

In the darkened bedroom they climbed into a large oak fourposter, pulled the comforters up around their chins, and watched the shadows from a newly laid fire march around the walls like sentries on guard duty. He thought back over the past few nights: the couch in Polly's living room, Percy Davis's inn on the Maine coast, the night spent outdoors . . . my God, *that* was last night. Polly whispered to him, folded sleepily within the arc of his left arm. Outside the storm cursed and hammered at the house, "I know a poem," she said softly, "from twenty years ago, from college freshman days . . . listen . . .

> *Bolt and bar the shutter*
> *For the foul winds blow:*
> *Our minds are at their best this night,*
> *And I seem to know*
> *That everything outside us is*
> *Mad as the mist and snow . . ."*

He kissed her, said: "I'm not so sure about our minds." Then he closed his eyes, hugged her, and went to sleep, as if it were all exactly as planned.

They made love in the early gray light, the room still snug from the heat of the embers in the fireplace. Pale shafts of iciness slid like knives through the thick leaded windowpanes; the carved lions on the balcony, watching the sea, cast bulky shadows. They slept awhile longer, then he got up and padded down the cold hallway, half awake but anxious to be up and about.

254

No radio, no telephone, absolutely cut off so far as he could ascertain. He took bread out of the freezer and made toast. Coffee perking: the smell of normality calmed his early morning nerves. He had climbed back into the dried-out trousers, stiff shoes, and heavy oiled sweater which had apparently flourished with the previous day's treatment. He sat munching toast, staring out into the fog, waiting for her to come down. She finally appeared in Levis and boots and a fresh heavy wool shirt nattily tailored with epaulettes and a profusion of buttoned flaps. She smelled faintly of shampoo and had a succulent moist look, freshly showered, pink-cheeked, and ready to eat a horse. He made more toast and as she ate she watched him, smiling. He felt her protection falling softly around him, felt her pleasure in it and the bond growing between them, but neither of them was tempted to comment on it. Their relationship seemed to *be,* something which already existed. It struck him as altogether pleasant, peculiarly liberating.

He broke the comfortable silence: "Well, I think we'd better look around the place, find out what we've gotten ourselves into."

Viewed from the long porch at the front of the house, the island seemed to be smoldering, a kind of smoking pile with the outlines blurred by the blowing fog which obscured the water beyond, faded the forests, and gave it all the look of hardened lava: it was an image he'd seen before, *déjà vu,* but he couldn't place it . . . He was used to the dense and blowing fog which made everything look like a battlefield with the smoke hanging all about like impending death.

Heading across the damp grass, angled away from the direction they'd come twelve hours before, they saw the character of the island take form: a huge pile of firewood soaked beyond any hope of burning, behind it a solid bank of pines and firs, dark and impenetrable, forming a wall as flat and inhospitable as a bluff of shale. They followed the tree line through the heavy fog which dampened them to their skin, heading toward the water, hearing the sound of the surf as they drew nearer, the crashing of the waves breaking through the velvety muffling effect of the fogbank.

Nearer the water the trees and the thick, grasping tangle of shrubbery clawed backwards, inland, trunks and limbs bent and twisted as if fleeing in terror from the sea. Along the top of the escarpment was yet another line of trees—hemlock, red and sugar maples, beech, and spruce—these planted deliberately by man, building a windbreak and leaving a fine view from the house which stood fully a hundred yards back and on much higher ground. They stood at the top of a long, shabby, decidedly rickety wooden stairway which zig-zagged erratically down the steep rock face, moss pasted to the cliff on either side.

At the bottom, the beach was actually a shingle of large rocks scattered across a level expanse of sand finally giving way to the sea. A dock and boathouse sat gray and wet some three hundred feet below where they stood and another fifty yards to the right. Just beyond the boathouse was an arm of slate-gray rock sloping outward, covered patchily with brown underbrush and mosses. Well out in the water, forming a natural gateway, there were six large, uneven slabs of stone projecting upward, an arc swinging across the inlet like the teeth of a hag's gummy lower jaw. The surf foamed white against the gray and purple and blue and black stones on the beach.

Even while they stood silently watching, the fog gusted in like a phantom army and swallowed the hag's teeth, leaving what seemed to be a misty, hazy expanse of uninterrupted, quiet water, moving gently toward the beach, safe and flat . . . another burst of wind and they were there again, reminding Chandler of the great stone circles he'd seen in the English countryside, left there by another race of men with their significance and their awesome silence forever enigmatic . . . this island, he reflected, and the house—they were like that, too, as if there were secrets which would never be revealed. He looked back at the house and it had now disappeared in the fog, there was nothing but the blank grayness where it had been, that and the feel of the mist on his face. Spinning back, he knew what he would see: the hag's teeth were gone, the water flat and untroubled. Polly smiled tentatively: she had seen it, too. "We're in the middle, aren't we?"

"Let's climb down," he said.

The stairway creaked but held. The beach made for tough walking and they stumbled frequently, scuffing their shoes, insult to injury which hardly made a difference anymore. Large gray boulders bore wide pink stripes. Polly found pretty little stones, scooped them up, dropped them in her pocket. The water, seen close up, had a savagery when it beat and foamed on the boulders which was not visible from above. Past the large rocks, the surf swept in across the small stones, furling and sucking at their shoes. The sky had a metallic blue-gray quality.

They walked toward the boathouse: "Doesn't look safe," Chandler said, nodding toward the catwalk leading across the foam to the boathouse and its dock. The wood was rotting, slats drooping. "Look," he went on, taking her hand, "let's skip it. We'd better get back to the house. Suppose somebody comes for us, can't find us, and leaves—"

She nodded, agreeable, squeezing his hand.

There was an idyllic quality to the moment, their breath hanging like speech balloons before them, holding hands, scuffing along the beach like a couple in a cigarette ad. They stopped once, she closed her eyes, he kissed her, wrapped his arms around her.

Yet, climbing back up the narrow stairway, reaching the tree line at the top, there was the inevitable sense of unease, the incompleteness, the waiting.

Hand in hand they walked back toward the house. A deer flickered across the lawn, white tail like a gentle flag of friendship. "Anyway," Polly said, looking up at him, "it's lovely being alone."

They were not alone, however.

A man watched from a shrubbery-covered promontory above the beach where Chandler and Polly had arrived the previous night. He watched them until they disappeared into the bank of swirling, shifting fog.

Chandler sat by himself in a window seat, feet cocked opposite himself, and watched the lawn and the water far beyond which was a darker shade of gray-blue than the fog which slid constantly across his vision. He watched but saw nothing. Alone, with Polly off puttering by herself, his mind turned anxiously back to Hugh Brennan and Bert Prosser, either one of whom could be dead: he felt desperate and helpless, trapped on the island, unable to come to the aid of either. Though what his aid was worth he wasn't quite sure. He went outside and paced the length of the porch, accusing himself of being an idiot for having gotten involved at all—then, of course, he realized he'd had no choice. If ever a man had sought to maintain his distance, his innocence, it had been sheltered, academic Colin Chandler.

In the late afternoon they grilled steaks, opened a nice claret, and lazed about the library looking through the matched sets of Thackeray and George Eliot and Jane Austen and Trollope. They snooped in desk drawers which proved to be empty and they admired the old English hunting prints. There wasn't a clue as to what normally went on at Stronghold, nothing to snap the isolation.

Polly went upstairs, leaving him alone, the fire whispering and the wind racketing outside. He might have dozed: the next thing he knew she was standing in front of him tapping his arm, holding the oilskin package Prosser had wrapped so carefully before they'd left the house in Maine.

"Let's have another look," she said. "Maybe you'll have a revelation once you see it again."

They unwrapped the package carefully. Underneath the oilskin Prosser had obviously wrapped the portrait and the documents in several thicknesses of newspaper. Polly stood watching, hands on hips, as he peeled the dry, perfectly protected pages away, came aware as he did that something was very wrong. Working feverishly,

258

panicking, Chandler threw newspapers away in a frenzy. In the end he looked up, his face pale.

"It's nothing but newspapers," he said. "It's not here, not any of it."

"He kept the whole thing," Polly breathed, a smile slowly spreading across her wide mouth.

"I just don't understand," Chandler said. He felt as if the fight had finally gone out of him.

"I knew it!" Polly gloated. "I just *knew* it . . . damn it, there's just something weird about him . . ." She kicked a piece of newspaper, beaming. "Don't you see, Colin? For once something's happened that sticks right out. Prosser told us he was giving all the stuff to us, and then he kept it—somebody whose identity is perfectly clear to us has *lied* to us. And I thought Prosser was so worried about the bad guys getting it . . ."

"I don't know," he said. "It's weird, everything is very weird . . ."

Chandler woke in the middle of the night, lay half asleep beside Polly, listening to her breathing and feeling the weight and warmth of her as she shifted, rested against him. The carefully wrapped oilskin packet of newspapers stayed resolutely in the forefront of his mind; when he closed his eyes he saw it enigmatic, mocking . . . why would Prosser have done such a thing? So far as he could tell, it made no sense: they had been under siege at the time and the logical thing had been to give it to those who were escaping: keeping it, Prosser had clearly run a greater risk of its falling into the hands of the enemy . . . Unless—unless what?

He turned on his side and watched the moon shining on the clouds. He was tired and his eyes were bleary. But why was there a pink tinge to the night sky? Decidedly pink, blurring from the left, brightening the rectangles of night through the window. Northern lights? A shooting star? More likely a fire of some kind . . .As he watched the pink glow lightened, then faded. He was groggy but he wondered what the hell made the sky do that? Polly muttered something in her sleep and tugged the covers over herself, baring him. Finally he stood up and went to the window, looked out: he saw a fogbank resting lightly on the water beyond the hag's teeth which were perfectly visible in the moonlight filtering through the lacework of clouds. The pinkness had come from the left but was almost gone now, a vague smudge that was gone as he watched. He lit a pipe of ashy, once-used tobacco and stared at the area where it had been until he was sure it was gone, that the night had returned to its normal color. He smoked, watching and thinking and worrying.

To begin with he wasn't aware of it at all, the movement below him, and then he thought it was a trick of his tired eyes, a bit of fog blowing or a shred of cloud crossing the moon, a symptom of his exhaustion and a bad case of nerves . . . then the shadows moved again, and again, and he felt his breath catching behind his breastbone, recognized the sickish feeling in his belly: it was the old fear, gnawing, turning his legs weak and his will to sweat and trembling.

The shadows were coming up from the beach where he'd stood and looked back at the yellow blur of the seaplane . . . the shadows were coming from the direction of the pink glow. He watched, immobilized, as if he'd run utterly out of responses, as they came skittishly, jerkily, like beetles picking their way across the lawn.

There were six of them, six clearly defined shadows —men—darting across the long spread of lawn toward the house. He was afraid all right, but his adrenalin was gone: how to escape? how to protect Polly? how to get help?

The shadows moved into the trees and shrubbery near the house and the lawn was empty again: had he imagined it? Christ, talk about wishful thinking! No. While the experience had had a good many of the characteristics of a bad dream, there was no doubt, he hadn't imagined it.

Forgetting the shadows for a moment, since they had stealthily concealed themselves out of his angle of vision, he found his eyes drawn upward toward a light blinking in the inlet, inside the hag's teeth, and he saw in a shaft of moonlight, what looked like a ramshackle fishing boat, a trawler, riding low in the backwater between the rocks and the shoreline. *A fishing trawler?*

Suddenly the island was a hell of a popular spot. He watched intently as the light that had seemed to blink beforehand swung nervously along the shoreline: for God's sake, it was a searchlight with a narrow, piercing beam, winking at him as it played along the sand and rocks. Perhaps Prosser had sent another Kendrick-type to stage yet another rescue? The idea flickered across his mind like the searchlight, went out. Beyond the trawler the fogbank persisted, motionless, providing a gray backdrop for the gateway of stones arcing across the bay. He smelled the sea on the wind which worked its way toward the house.

He gently shook Polly's arm, insistently, until she was awake and coherent.

"My darling, it's time to wake up. There are little men crawling all around our house and I'm not at all sure what to do." He laughed nervously.

"Try not laughing nervously and putting your pants on—"

"But that's two things at once," he said.

"Whose little men are they?"

He told her what he'd seen while they were getting into their clothes, stopping every few moments to listen and look at the window. He swung the French window open and stepped out onto the balcony, leaned over the edge, and saw them again in the shadow of the house, by the porch railing, clustered around their leader. They were whispering. They seemed to be somewhat confused.

"Well, Jesus," the leader finally said impatiently and audibly, "we can't just knock and go in the front door. You two move out along the porch and try those long windows. You two go find the back door—we'll stay here and play with the front door. Now git!"

Chandler watched from above as they scampered off, then went back into the bedroom, saw Polly standing in the doorway to the second-floor hallway, watching.

261

A dim nightlight burned outside their door, casting shadows against the stags on the wallpaper.

"They're coming in," he said. "Do you think if I ran screaming down the hallway I'd scare them off . . . no? Well, I can't think of anything else—"

"Just wait," she said. "See what they do . . ."

They heard an attempt to open the front door which was locked. An abrupt curse was followed by a throaty, muffled laugh. Footsteps moved along the porch. The silence was broken by the shattering of glass. They were coming in the French windows. The house creaked in the night wind. They heard the house filling with men, one noise after another now, coming fast: it was like floodwater rising in your own home. There was nothing to be done about it.

They were in the hall below now, voices muffled, tread heavy. Chandler heard the metallic, oiled sound of guns being handled. The hair on the back of his neck crawled. A light flared on at the top of the stairway, at the end of the long hallway. Polly suddenly shook against him.

"God," she whispered, "this is like getting raped, they've penetrated us . . ."

He heard them on the stairs and pulled her back into the room. She sat on the edge of the bed, waiting. He went back onto the balcony and looked back toward the spotlight. More shadows fanned out across the wide spread of the lawn coming from the direction of the fishing trawler, moving from the edge of the cliff with its black tree line. He counted seven moving figures and then heard a loud voice braying at him from the bedroom.

"Professor Chandler, I presume," the voice said, emanating from a large man in a dark blue sweater and trousers, with a matching stocking cap pulled down to the tops of his red ears. His face had been blackened with something greasy and his eyes shown brightly from the darkness. "Lieutenant Raines at your service, sir. My men and I are here to evacuate you from the island, sir." He glanced at Polly who had herself back in hand and was sitting on the bed, propped against pillows, ankles crossed before her, watching the lieutenant with a bemused smile. The lieutenant was carrying a gun that looked as if it would keep on firing once you pulled the trigger.

"Well, Lieutenant Raines," Chandler said, clutching his pipe, "you sure scared hell out of me."

"I'm sure, sir. Nothing to be ashamed of, sir. There's nobody on earth we can't scare hell out of, I guess." Raines appeared to be in his mid-twenties and reminded Chandler of a great many innocently pompous youths who had passed through his classes over the years. Behind him another, smaller boy, similarly dressed, appeared: "Everything as expected, sir?" His voice piped like a boy soprano.

"Sure," Raines said. "No sweat." Raines smiled: "Miss Bishop, Professor? Shall we make ready to go?" He pointed the gun barrel at the duffel bag. "Stow your gear in there." He stood watching as they did as they were told.

"Who the hell are you?" Polly asked, beginning to fume. Chandler suppressed a smile. "Did Prosser send you?"

"Special Operations Executive, Miss Bishop. I never heard of anyone called Prosser. We just do our job—"

"I know, I know," she snapped. "It's a tough job and a dirty job but somebody's got to do it—right, right. I've heard that before from people who love doing dirty jobs—"

"—and we want to get off this island as soon as possible. So let's step on it." To the smaller fellow he said: "Form everybody up in the main room we came in."

The duffel bag was soon full and Raines made sure the windows were shut and locked; he turned the light off and followed them down the hallway, down the stairway to the front hallway. The last two men were just coming through the front door. They were all identically dressed, smeared with the blacking.

Chandler whispered to Polly: "This is all right out of *The Commandos Strike at Dawn*. Brian Donlevy or Robert Montgomery is going to show up at any minute." There was no time to tell Polly about the other figures he'd seen coming across the lawn. Raines was discussing matters with his men.

"Professor," Raines said quietly, turning a level glance at Chandler, "there is a package, I believe—our instructions are not to leave without it. May I have it, please?"

Chandler laughed, shook his head: "Correction—there *was* a package. But not anymore. It's nothing but a wad of newspapers in the kitchen wastebasket . . . We were stung—"

"I don't quite understand, sir. Our orders were to bring the two of you and a small package . . . without fail. They were most insistent about that package . . ." Youth was suddenly showing through the training, the hard cutting edge. "Now I must put it to you—"

"Oh, come on, Lieutenant. Put it anywhere you like, search us, go check the wastebasket. There is no package—"

"Then we've gone to a hell of a lot of trouble for nothing, sir."

"Thanks very much. Polly, you and I are nothing in the lieutenant's eyes. Look, try to understand, we were taken—we got a dummy package, not the real thing, see, and now you're going to have to lump it. So, what are you going to do? Leave us here in a fit of pique?"

"All right," Raines said, not liking it a damn bit. "We haven't got time to search a house the size of this one. But God help you if you're lying to me." He wheeled on his expectant cadre: "Back to the beach. We're taking them out, as scheduled, minus the goddamned package. Now haul ass."

Raines made sure all the lights were out, leaving the house as they'd found it but for some broken glass on the carpet.

The first man through the door bearing the brass plate marked *Stronghold* took a brief burst of silenced automatic rifle fire, slammed backwards into the second man who fell heavily against the others. The first man was dead, died with a brutal gurgle which was intended as a scream. Everyone in the hallway was jumbled together on the floor, eyes not yet accustomed to the dark.

"What the fuck's going on here?" Raines whispered sharply, having sat down with a thud as the single file went down like dominoes. "Who's out there?"

"Christ, Lieutenant, I can smell blood, it's all over me!" A strangled cry, terror-stricken, went up from a disembodied voice. "Get him off me, shit, he's dying . . . he's dead." Groans, oaths, shouts filled the hallway, fear coloring each voice as they all lay in the tangle of arms and legs on the floor, in the pitchy darkness which somehow made it all the worse. Incredibly there was no follow-up, no pounding footsteps and racketing guns and dying. "Do any of you see anybody out there?" Raines whispered, his voice coming from the foot of the stairs. The heavy door, scarred by gunfire, stood open. "Shit no," came the answer, "and I sure as hell ain't gonna look right now . . ."

The soprano said: "What should we do, Lieutenant?"

"Shut up, for starters," the lieutenant said.

Chandler found Polly's hand, tugged at it, pulled her toward the room from which they'd just come. He scrunched up onto all fours, crawled ahead of her, hearing her behind him, going as quietly as possible. The beginnings of a plan—the response which he'd believed himself beyond—were taking shape at the edges of his mind, fragments which might be worked out as he went along. From the hallway the whispers grew in urgency. He could still smell the blood and the mess made by the dying commando, the specific smell of death, sickly sweet.

The long, heavy draperies on the French windows had been pushed back when Raines's men had broken the glass and entered: now a luminescent gray stripe of moonlight bisected the floor, streaking the carpet. Polly and Chandler crouched behind a massive desk.

"I don't know who they are," he whispered against her ear, "but I saw them coming up the lawn when I went out on the balcony . . . I think they came from a boat down by those rocks, where we were this afternoon—I saw it, too, sort of." He grabbed the desk to

265

stop his hands from shaking: cramps raced along his legs. "We've got to get out of here—I don't know who we're safer with . . ."

"We're safer by ourselves," Polly said.

A burst of gunfire came from the hallway, followed by a low moaning sound, muffled whispers. Scurrying sounds moving along the porch beyond the drapes; heavy breathing in the hall. Someone dashed up the stairs to the second floor: a door slammed above them.

"They're putting someone on the balcony," Chandler said, voice trembling, trying to hold his breath. "Raines may be down to three men . . . Come on."

He crawled slowly onward, keeping to the perimeter of the room, staying well clear of the moonlight. At last, keeping track of the odd sound, aware of the waiting game going on around them, they reached the row of French windows and huddled in the corner, melting into the draperies which felt as if they were fashioned from chain mail.

"Chandler!" Raines hissed from the hallway. "Chandler—where are you, you bastard?" Not so much in anger as in frustration. Silence: he felt Polly's fingers squeezing his.

Chandler noticed a slight movement, a flutter, in the draperies, a pushing-out from the glass side. He held his breath mightily, stilled Polly's hand: someone was coming in from the porch, moving slowly, carefully in the dark . . . There was no way to warn Raines and he was not absolutely sure he wanted to. Special Operations Executive . . . assassins, for all he knew. The drapery bulged, he felt it move against his leg, saw the shadow flitting in the moonlight not five feet from where he stood: the sense of someone struck him forcibly, the smell of a human being and the smell, incredibly unique, of oiled weaponry . . .

"Chandler?" Raines called more loudly. "You there?"

Gunfire rattled, loud and harsh, beside him, squirted across the room, deafening, like an explosion inside your head: the room lit up like a show window, for only an instant: Raines was seen in the flash, ducking back out of the doorway as it splintered and the hallway beyond filled with plaster dust from the slugs stitching their jagged way along the wall. The man firing the gun was only a black shadow ten feet in front of Chandler and Polly who wrapped themselves in drapery.

With the flash of gunfire abruptly extinguished, Chandler felt the weight and pull of the drapery moving as several more men bulled their way through the French windows: three or four had joined the original intruder in the dark room and Chandler heard them bumping into one another. Raines, he knew, could have made hamburger out of them then and there but for one consideration . . . he was afraid that Chandler and Polly might be in the way. Chandler heard them puffing, heard a click. "Grenade," someone said softly.

Chandler grabbed Polly and with his free hand found the handle of a window: they were now entirely behind the long drapery, smelling the tobacco smell trapped in the fabric for so many years. The handle wouldn't move: he felt with his fingertips for the button or lever to disengage the lock . . . finally found it, switched it, muffling any sound with the flat of his thumb, and moved the door open an inch. He wished there was a way to communicate with Polly but hand pressure had to suffice: he waited . . .

Then came a grunt followed by the sound of something heavy bouncing on the carpet, rolling: the grenade . . . he was sure that everyone else was crouching behind the desk and the heavy chairs, but nothing other than the draperies protected him and Polly from the coming blast.

Now! and he swung the door open and pulled Polly after him, onto the long porch . . .

They had taken no more than three long strides across the stones toward the railing when the room exploded, the windows all shattered and flew outward, passed over and through and around them, glittering like clockwork silver birds in the moonlight . . .

Chandler felt himself propelled forward by the blast, as if a large hand had been placed in the small of his back, slamming him against and then toppling him

267

over the porch railing. They landed in the shrubbery, sprawled half across one another, scratched and nicked but intact.

Shouts echoed in the night: the grenade had apparently not made it through the doorway into the hall, but had hit the wall and bounced back into the room ... screams of agony came from the room, a fire burned against an inside wall, the rattle of gunfire came: Chandler saw it in his mind, Raines leaping into the doorway, raking the wounded and dying with automatic rifle-fire.

He turned to Polly: "Can you make a run for it?" He felt mud clinging to the side of his face.

She brushed dirt and leaves from her own face, looked up: "Sure, boss—I think we got 'em right where we want 'em."

He craned his neck, peered up at the balcony: the man was leaning over the railing, trying to see what had happened below. Polly reached through their railing and Chandler heard the clatter of a gun being drawn across the stones. The man on the balcony heard, too, and immediately loosed a fusillade of fire at the sound, chipping the cement as they ducked.

"Can you use one of these?"

"Is the Pope a Catholic?" he said. "Does a bear— sure, all the time . . . machine guns? Don't be silly, almost never without one . . ."

He took it and was surprised by how heavy it was, began crawling along the bottom of the porch, through shrubs and mud and the odd bits of broken glass. His back stung where he knew broken glass had chewed through his heavy sweater. The gunfire from the roof was not repeated. The flames in the room were flickering higher, shadows moved erratically: looking back into the house was like peering into a woodburning stove. Intermittently a gun went off. There was just no way of telling what the hell was actually going on.

"Chandler?" a voice cried tiredly.

"Christ, if they were in there, good luck to them," came a faint reply. The voice sounded vaguely familiar, weary. But the conversation was cut short by another explosion.

At the corner of the porch and the bed of shrubbery, Chandler crouched: "Run to the shadows," he pointed, "then along the tree line toward the cliff . . . we're all right if we stay in the shadows . . ." He looked out, away from the house: "The fog's starting."

Ahead of them, the fogbank which had sat so calmly out beyond the trawler and the hag's teeth had begun seeping in: it was fifty yards away, floating toward them, thick and impenetrable, seemingly palpable in the moonlight.

The glare of the fire faded behind them as they ran for the tree line, slipping awkwardly on the wet grass, finally fetching up among the firs, gasping for breath. The house was quiet now, no sound, no movement, only the penumbra of light which mas muted by the oncoming fog as they pushed ahead, out of breath and not altogether sure where they were going. A few minutes into their flight they felt themselves wholly submerged in the welcome, protective fog, still conscious of its billowing, clammy grayness because the moon lit it from above, giving Chandler the impression he'd wandered into a crystal ball. Water beaded on his glasses. He stopped, leaned forward on his knees, a pain in his side: "We can't afford to get lost in this," he gasped. "We've got to keep the trees close on the right and that'll take us right to the cliff . . ." He looked up, smiled at her fog-blurred face: "I hope you don't think I know where I'm going . . . I haven't the foggiest, if you'll pardon the expression. My primary idea was just to get away . . ."

Polly nodded: "That's all right. I've got an idea— let's just keep on going and leave everything to me. You said there was some kind of fishing boat in the bay?"

"Or something. I don't know any more about boats than I do about machine guns." He looked hopelessly at the gun in his right hand: "Heavy little bastard."

"Keep it, though," she said. "They've all got guns, we may need it . . . God, what a thought." She sighed:

"But hold on to it." Then she set off again, every so often stopping, prowling to the right, to make sure the trees were there. He followed, relieved at having engineered the escape from the house which, glancing over his shoulder, he saw was gone, sunk like a stone in the fog, like a ghost ship with its grisly cargo.

It took twenty minutes to travel the hundred yards to the top of the cliff. Standing still, they were only just able to hear the waves slipping across the rocky shingle below in the fog. The wind had picked up off the water and blew a fine stinging spray in their faces. The rickety stairway was slippery, the handrailing rotting, and the descent went slowly: as they dropped lower down the cliff face, they came out of the fog into a heavier mist which blew in sheets off the water.

The trawler sat darkly, enigmatically, deep in the water, the needle of light picking its way along the shoreline, slowly, erratically, lingering here and there, leaping onward, as if the man controlling it was having trouble staying awake. There were no markings on the ship, at least none visible in the moonlight, no way of identifying the vessel, by name or nationality: just a black shape with the piercing Cyclopean eye.

The beam of light played well short of the rock wall as they clambered to the bottom and stood leaning on one another. Chandler felt as if he'd been out of breath since birth. "Where are you taking me?" he asked, gulping air and rain. His lungs felt hot, like bursting. The backs of his legs pained him. He was so wet. He knew his back was bleeding from the broken glass. He was going to have a hell of a cold, assuming someone didn't kill him first. Polly started off again and didn't hear his question. He slogged on, cradling the gun in the crook of his arm. At least he wasn't carrying the miserable duffel bag . . .

They reached the dock.

"Come on," she said, "where there's a boathouse there ought to be a boat."

"Oh, wait a minute—I don't know a damned thing about boats, I'm scared of boats—"

"*You* don't have to know anything about boats.

270

We're a team, y'know—now come on before the searchlight catches up with us."

He followed her, struggling up onto the rotting, soggy planks where she had nimbly leaped. The fog was coming in again, another great rolling bank: he smelled it more than saw it, and when he glanced back at the ship he saw only the vaguest outline, and the searchlight was a blur as it swung in stately fashion toward them.

"Hurry," Polly called from up ahead. "The light . . ."

In his haste, Chandler tripped over a warped, jutting plank and plunged headlong, the gun flying ahead of him as he fell heavily, skinning his knees and the palms of his outstretched hands. Looking up, panic-stricken, he found himself staring, blinded, into the searchlight, squinting as it reflected among a million particles of moisture and bounced from one to the other, from one gust of fog to another. Like an animal, hypnotized and doomed in the headlights of an oncoming truck, he lay on the wet, crumbling wood as the light swung slowly past, stopped, tracked back over him and moved slowly off down the beach.

"Come *on*, Colin," she called. "The light couldn't crack the fog, they didn't see you."

Reprieved, he struggled his seemingly endless length into an upright position, retrieved the gun, and lumbered off down the dock to the warped door of the boathouse where Polly hugged him. "Oh, God," she sighed, swallowing, "I thought . . . are you all right?"

He nodded, sweating, feeling light-headed. *God if You let me live, I'll take up squash again, jog, do anything You say* . . . The door stuck: angrily he slammed his shoulder into it, dislodged it, and they stepped into the darkness. Slowly, standing still, they let their eyes grow accustomed to the dark. The place reeked of soaked wood, gasoline, oil. Gradually the open end took gray, rectangular shape. Moonlight slid dimly through a hole in the roof . . .

Polly fumbled along the wall, finally crowed: "I knew it—a light switch! Anybody with this kind of money is going to have lights everywhere, feeding off a central generator." She flipped the switch and two bare hanging bulbs, dangling at the tips of frayed black cords, came to life, lighting the interior with a harsh glare. Knowing nothing about seagoing machinery, Chandler took stock of the device revealed before him and in his head pronounced it some sort of cabin cruiser, which sat in a trough of water, waves lapping sibilantly at the hull. Chandler took it in but understood none of it: he'd never been aboard a boat, had seen them only at a distance. Forty or fifty feet long maybe, lots of polished wood, an elegant look which made him think it had a good many years on it—he couldn't imagine anyone making such boats anymore. The back end was open but the middle third was canopied like the one Humphrey Bogart found himself on at the climax of *Key Largo*.

On the dock there were two large red gasoline cans beside a pile of rags, some carefully wrapped paintbrushes, coils of greasy rope, a scarred and dented toolbox. Polly climbed aboard, poked around mysteriously, lifted hatches, sniffed, took something from a wall bracket near the pilot's chair. She knelt down on the stairway and pushed a door open revealing a pit which he concluded had to house the bunks and galley. She closed it and came back up, stood with hands on hips, looking at him, shrugging with a smile.

"Well, we're in business. This little dandy is going to get us out of here . . ."

"Little dandy," he repeated. "Who writes your stuff?"

"No time to be brittle, my darling. In the words of the poet, they're after us even as we speak—"

"But don't you need charts, maps, that stuff?"

"There's a stack of that stuff up there." She nodded toward a shelf above the wheel. "And if that huge gunboat got into the bay, then this little—"

"Dandy."

"—can get us out."

"Are you sure you know how to—gunboat, you say?"

"It's no fishing trawler, take my word. I'd say it's

Russian, a spy ship full of electronic paraphernalia, and some armaments. They patrol the coastline all the time. Remember, this is my business—at least, knowing stuff like this."

"I never know whether to believe you when you go all worldly on me . . ."

"Believe me," she said, busying herself, presumably readying the boat for the getaway.

"I repeat, are you sure you know how—"

"Look, somebody up at the house is eventually going to win the battle and whoever it is is going to look around, discover that we are gone and the package, too, and they're going to decide that two and two make four, and we're on the spot again . . . both groups came by sea so there are two ships lurking out there in the fog . . . it's tag, and we're it. So we'd better get the hell gone and we're better off at night than by day . . . and, look, it's my neck as well as yours, right? So, of course I know how to run the damned boat . . . now hurry up and get settled."

He heard a fan going on, then they waited in quiet as Polly puttered deliberately about, then he felt and heard the engine turning over: it seemed terribly loud and whining, but then what the hell did he know? Let it be loud: just let it get them the hell out of there: "Are you sure this can work? Doesn't it seem awfully easy?" He was sitting across from her on a padded bench, his sore back angled against an edge of wood which hurt.

She nodded: "Well, I expect it to get harder fairly soon, if that makes you feel any better . . ." She settled in behind the wheel in the high swivel chair. "I don't know where we are and I'm going to have to play it more or less by—don't look at me that way—by ear . . ." He couldn't hear any more. The engine in the enclosed space was hammering at them with a considerable vengeance. She pointed with her right hand, in the manner of a tiny John Wayne, that they were moving out, and he nodded, pressing the cold, heavy weight of the gun across his knees . . .

The boat quivered mightily, edged slowly out of its

273

slip, pushed off into the fog. The two cans of gasoline rested on the floor next to his feet; he had no idea what kind of gun he was holding, nor how to use it; but Polly seemed to be giving a knowing impression of someone coping with what was going on. Suddenly, the fog was in the cockpit with them, blowing in stringy wisps between them and he couldn't see a goddamn thing . . . He stood up and crossed to his side, squinted at the windshield.

"Can't see," he said.

"Scary, isn't it?" Behind them the ghostly glow from the boathouse, filtering through the fog, looked like a flying saucer hovering curiously over the water.

"Do you remember where the rocks are? The teeth?"

"More or less."

"More or less," he repeated faintly.

"Well, what can I say? I think I know where they are . . ."

They nosed on through the fog for another minute, Polly straining to see ahead, Chandler with eyes pressed tight, offering up a prayer. When he clicked his eyes open—why at just that moment, he had no idea—he was looking to the left of their path, and he cried out involuntarily: "Jesus! Look out!"

A wall of fog had split, been shredded into flowing trailers by the mysterious ship which now loomed over them, larger than he'd have believed possible, sliding toward them like an avenger . . . He heard Polly swear and saw her spin the wheel, felt the small boat shudder and moan as it cranked sideways in the water. The engine throbbed underfoot as she opened it up.

The rocks, she's going to hit the rocks . . .

There was no way she could keep her bearings with the trawler bearing down on them, the fog swirling, the boat spinning and veering off in a new direction.

"Get the gun ready," she yelled.

"Ready? What the hell do you do to get a gun ready?"

The trawler slid past behind them and he fancied he saw the movement of men on deck. Somehow they had seen the light in the boathouse . . . or maybe they actually had seen him in the fire of the searchlight as he tripped and fell . . . or maybe someone from the attack force had radioed them from the house, had alerted them . . . or maybe they used the electronic listening device aboard the spy ship . . .

As it slithered past and beyond them, it was leaning to the left, turning, and consequently Polly was maneuvering back across its path again a few seconds later. Chandler had made his way to the back of the boat and was resting the gun on the brass handrailing, crouched, watching, and the trawler was coming at them again out of the fog.

And as it came, straight on, flame flickered at him like a match in the wind, and the fog muted the rattle of a machine gun floating like death at him as he heard, felt the slugs hit the hull of the ship beneath the railing, heard them rip away the back of a swivel chair three feet behind him. He felt as if he had somehow gotten into place at both ends of a shooting gallery, simultaneously.

All right, by God. He saw the bust of Washington floating to the floor, coming slowly apart in a million particles of dust and plaster.

He trained the machine gun at the searchlight picking its way through the fog toward them, squeezed the trigger: the weapon came alive in his hands, vibrating, chattering, as if it were fighting to get loose, free of his amateur's grasp. Miraculously, the light exploded at once and they were surrounded by the moonlit fog again. He turned in time to see Polly give him the thumb's-up sign.

Another yelp of gunfire came from the trawler which had straightened out behind them and was pursuing as Polly swung to and fro in the water, weaving her way toward the freedom of movement which lay beyond the rocks . . .

He felt the little boat take the fire briefly before Polly moved it out of range: the swivel chair near him, backless and in splinters, rotated this way and that, back and forth, as the path she steered changed, adjusted. They had to be nearing the huge hag's teeth which had seemed so close during the day . . . but where in the name of God were they? As they slowed, picking their way toward them, where they *had* to be, the trawler heaved to out of the fog again, coming briefly, riding them down . . .

Determined to get in the first barrage, having no idea in the world who the hell he was blazing away at, Chandler steadied the gun, prayed there was still some ammunition, and squeezed the trigger a second time. His fire drew a startled cry which hung in the night fog, like a banner stained bloody with the battle, then a rash of jabbering return fire which broke some glass and sent Chandler to the deck, trying to squeeze into the crawl space beneath the bench.

"I see it," Polly called. "The channel through—"

The engines throbbed wildly again and the boat leaped forward, rushing into what seemed to Chandler a blank wall of fog. Immediately the other ship was left behind and they were for the instant alone.

"Look out," she cried, "here it comes!"

And then he saw the stones.

She took the spread between them at full tilt, the waves foaming around them, driving the suddenly frail craft like a twig toward the gray stone tower on the right. Chandler knew his eyes were frozen wide, staring, and then he knew it wasn't going to work . . .

The side of their boat slammed against the stone, something ruptured and tore, gave way with a dismal tug, and they seemed to be suspended out of the water, poised, the waves on the rise holding them pinned against the great thrust of rock and he saw Polly holding firm, pulling with all of her strength and determination against the push of the waves . . . then, without warning, the boat dropped away from the hag's tooth, plummeted down the side of a wave like something cut loose in an elevator shaft, and suddenly the engines seemed to do some good again. They churned forward out into the open and miraculously they were still afloat, struggling but moving onward, piercing the sea and the fog and the cold wind.

Polly turned, grinning broadly, lower lip quivering

and he went to her, kissed her wet cheek, held her to him.

Behind them, a matter of fifteen seconds later, there was a most remarkable sound: a solid, wet smashing, like a wrecking ball smashing into soggy concrete, an enormous deadening thud followed by a series of cracks and rending noises: the trawler, or spy ship, or whatever the hell it was, had clearly run afoul of one of the teeth . . . silence, the only sound the hum and drive of their own engines . . . and then, just like in the movies, there came a rumbling explosion, darts of red and orange fire piercing the fog, reaching toward them, all of which was suddenly extinguished, leaving the silence once again and the pattering of bits of debris falling from out of the fog into the water all around them.

Wednesday/Thursday

As was the case with a great many other things in his life, Chandler was no longer quite sure as to the day of the week. But they took the plane from Halifax back to Boston on what he strongly suspected was the late morning of Thursday. The voice of the captain wafted from the speakers, seemed however to be coming from another planet, and the stewardess leaning toward him with a half-ton of gleaming teeth may well have been an earthling but she might as well have been mouthing Swahili; or not speaking at all for that matter. He felt he was smiling at her but he wasn't even sure of that: he felt like a deaf man who believed himself to be shouting at the top of his lungs but couldn't be sure, couldn't hear himself. He had gone altogether beyond tiredness, achieving what surely had to be a new state.

Next to him Polly was sipping an old-fashioned, her face glimpsed from the corner of his eye calm and cool and perfect. Though he would have enjoyed watching her for a very long time, his head kept lolling back and finally he gave it up, looked out at the ocean below, pale blue and glaring silver where the bright sunshine hit it. He knew he wouldn't quite sleep, couldn't release his grip enough to sleep, but he closed his eyes anyway and let the memories of the past couple of days blur inside his exhausted brain . . .

> A man from Cape Breton, MacBride
> Possessed a wrecked auto, his pride
> It sat in his yard
> It rained awfully hard
> Next day it went out with the tide.

Limericks, they'd made up limericks. He remembered the desolate shacks, the lawns of mud and the filthy old derelict automobiles up to their axles in the muck, as they drove . . .

> There was an old dowager from Kent
> Her last fling at Bar Harbor was spent
> She arrived there one day
> To her great dismay
> Society had got up and went.

He remembered Polly's voice as they drove the rental car from Sydney to Halifax, doing the limericks as they pushed on through the mud and snow of the early Nova Scotia spring: winter in disguise. Somehow they'd left the boat, wounded and beginning to take on water through several bullet holes and the damage from the hag's tooth, at a small fishing village on the Cabot Trail where they got a ride Wednesday morning from a lonely fisherman heading for the hospital in Sydney. Getting to the Cape Breton coast: Polly had managed that through choppy seas, smothering fog, and God only knew what else. How had she done it? The reincarnation of Bogart. He couldn't recall ever holding anyone in such awe: perhaps he'd never know how she'd done it, but the fact was that she'd gotten them safely to shore over miles and miles of inky, terrifying sea. She told him that everything he said was nonsense, that he was grossly exaggerating her accomplishment, but there was a pleased grin that went with the disclaimer. "I wasn't great," she insisted slyly, glancing backward at his theory of history, "merely heroic . . . there's a difference."

Worries danced before him like taunting, malevolent gnomes, in and out among his memories of Polly's steadfastness and the surging of the gun in his hand and the dash through the narrows with the huge cold teeth rising around them. James Bond stuff. Worries: Where was the Glendower document? Had Prosser survived? What had been happening on the island when

279

they escaped? And what of Hugh? Was he still alive, or had the ridiculous charade claimed him?

The sun's glare off the water turned the inside of his eyelids a hot, scalding red. He leaned away from the window, rested his head on Polly's shoulder.

Maxim Petrov read the decoded message, rubbed his eyes, and fought off a yawn which was in no way a reaction to the message which would have required, if anything, a fit of screaming. No. His office was over-heated and as a result he felt tired within an hour of arriving at his desk. Tell them it was too hot and you'd be frozen stiff inside of twenty-four hours and you'd stay that way until summer. There was, he re-flected numbly, no way to win.

He put the sheet of paper down, stroking it briefly with his fingertips, as if coaxing it to make sense, and looked at his list of appointments and tasks. Bureau-cratically, he faced the day. He supposed there was no avoiding giving the Intourist guides some sort of pep talk: their morale was even lower than was customary. And there was the black market in Levi's which seemed to be entering one of its peak periods: his wife had bought him two pairs and the price had been truly outrageous. And there were the informers who wanted an increase in privileges. And now, this—this utterly crazy business in Nova Scotia.

He sighed and lit a Havana and decided to see if he could smoke it all the way to the end without disturb-ing the ash.

Everything in Russia, Mother Russia, eventually landed on his desk—at least everything that went wrong. And that was very nearly goddamned every-thing. It always came back to the same thing. The KGB was too big. But from its ever-increasing size he derived his power.

The Nova Scotia affair, a perfect example. Inevi-tably the KGB's hind legs were tripping over one another while the front end wasn't in the least aware of any difficulty. Oh, it wasn't a perfect analogy, but in an imperfect world you took what was offered.

Nova Scotia . . . that involved the Canadian group, the American group, tangentially the young eager beaver in Bucharest—God, *his* career was over before it began! And now, here it was on his desk, a first class disaster involving nothing but the silliest kind of trivia . . . How had he ever let it all happen? Why did he always have to see the humorous possibilities? He felt like a boor at the party who couldn't be restrained from telling the same tedious jokes, week after week, year after year. Now, if World War III were started as a result of the Nova Scotia *contretemps,* guess who would get the blame? Madame Petrov's brightest son, Max!

His secretary, Maya, brought in his suitcase, packed. Maya was a sturdy, fetching blonde of thirty, rather far down the list of women who were cleared to serve him. He frequently fantasized about her in the washroom.

"You've heard of the American fascination with what they call Women's Liberation, Maya?"

"Yes, sir." She gazed at him levelly, expressionless.

"I was just told a new slogan of theirs. 'Support Women's Lib . . . Make him sleep on the wet spot.' "

She stared at him, expectantly.

"Do you get it, Maya?"

"I'm afraid not, Director."

"All right, then, Maya," he said sourly. "Back to work."

"Thank you, Director."

He stacked his desktop debris, glumly regarded the suitcase. No one knew where he was going, at least no one in the KGB, though Leonid had had to give a personal okay. With his approval and connivance the trip could be carried out in true secrecy, an increasingly scarce commodity in Moscow these days. The Americans thought they had problems—everybody in Moscow seemed to know everything. *Everything.*

But Leonid had been helpful. Extreme secrecy, he'd said, and what Brezhnev wanted he normally got.

And now Petrov would get away from his everyday problems and nobody would know he was gone. On the drive to the airport he had a disturbing thought. If no one knew where he was going but Leonid, what if

281

Leonid wanted him out of the way? For good? Who would there be to ask questions if he never came back?

Fennerty and McGonigle had arrived at the island by motor launch from Cape Breton, following a back-breaking automobile drive during which they kept an eye out for Chandler and the girl. They'd begun early on to forget what they knew, didn't know, and could only surmise about the entire mission. In any case, the time had come to let the old man do their thinking for them . . . not the Old Man, but Sanger, God love him.

Fennerty had watched Chandler and Miss Bishop wander the grounds of Stronghold, holding hands in the fog. McGonigle had been in charge of concealing the tent which had provided them with meager shelter indeed against the nasty wet weather. And it was McGonigle who had fired the flares to bring the submarine in with its commando landing party.

When it was over, Fennerty and McGonigle were the last to leave.

The house was full of bodies. The walls and floors were pitted and burned and blown away in places, streaked and spattered with blood. Along with the two survivors from the landing party, they had gotten back down to the beach and been picked up by the submarine.

Waiting in the wet cold Fennerty had said: "Nothing has gone right, has it? Not from the beginning."

"Like Dunkirk. It's like a bad farce, really," McGonigle said quietly, "that becomes a tragedy before you know it. And then it's too late."

The commando leader, who had been shot through the thigh, lay on the bench with his back against a slab of stone. The rain blew across his face and he whimpered in pain.

Orders were waiting on shipboard for Fennerty and McGonigle. The submarine would take them to Boston Navy Yard, from where they would be escorted to a commercial flight leaving Logan airport for Washington. They arrived at Dulles late Wednesday night—or was it Thursday morning? Time meant nothing anymore. The director himself debriefed them for several intensely uncomfortable hours.

It was enough, as McGonigle remarked to Fennerty, to make a grown man cry.

Fennerty replied that he was well short of tears, thank you, but very seriously considering getting out of The Company with a nice pension and getting into his brother's travel agency in Atlanta.

McGonigle allowed as how he suspected the director would applaud, if actually not hasten, the impulse and its result.

The sun was still shining brightly when the Halifax flight touched down at Logan. From far away Chandler had seen the crystalline glow of the John Hancock tower reflecting the warm sun of an early, false spring. He felt strangely revived, as if the brief flight had been a tonic, as if getting back to Boston alive was enough to give wing to his spirit.

But waiting for the taxi, wearing his dirty clothes which had been only partially sponged and laundered, he felt the weakness in his legs and an undeniable lag in his reflexes. His mind kept calling his body to do simple tasks but the body was on a protest strike, a slowdown. He felt as if Polly were his keeper.

The apartment on Chestnut Street was much as they had left it, but for the neatly barbered, boyishly handsome lad sitting at the kitchen table sniffing his tea while it steeped.

"Oh, hello, darling," he said with a wave. "So glad you're not dead or something. I have a cold and inhaling jasmine tea is a godsend to the sinuses."

"Peter—"

"You must be the professor. I'm Peter Shane, neighbor, confidant, dogsbody, loyal friend to Ezzard Charles, the cat." Ezzard leaped to the tabletop and Peter pushed a dish of cream his way. "Some bash you had before leaving, I must say."

"My dearest Peter, what are you talking about?" Polly threw her coat on the back of a chair. "That tea

283

smells good. Would you like some, too? Colin, I mean you—"

"Oh, sure, tea's fine. I'm going to sit down, I think."

"You'd better, old lad," Peter said, pushing a chair back from the table. "You have the look of a man who requires a chair."

Chandler sank thankfully downward. Polly was fussing at the counter, collecting cups and saucers, pushing English muffins into the broiling rack. "What's this about a bash, Peter?"

"Well, my God, what a mess this place was! Nasty . . . Ezzard was clutching the top of a door, staring like a mad thing—"

"Oh, that's just Ezzard," she said airily. "It's his mad thing stare . . . but we left the place neat as a pin."

"Our pursuers," Chandler grunted.

"Well, I tidied up," Peter said, inhaling deeply, then sipping from the cup. "God in heaven, I hate a stuffy nose."

"I'll do the same for you another time."

"Please, Polly, *I* would never allow things to get in such a state—"

"Are we still in the papers?" Chandler said. Polly placed a hot buttered English muffin and a cup of tea before him.

"You know, that's the odd thing." Peter nibbled at his thumb. "Not a word for days, all very mysterious. Your whole bizarre story has completely disappeared— I've squirreled away the papers, I've read them thoroughly, and one day you were there and the next you weren't. I'm dimly aware that fame is fleeting, but my goodness! It's weird, it's as if you'd never been written about at all . . . as if the Davis boy and the old man hadn't been murdered after all . . ." He sipped tea, watching them over the rim of his cup. Ezzard crept toward Chandler's English muffin, staring like a mad thing.

"I don't understand," Chandler said. "Which hardly comes as a surprise, I'm well aware."

"Somebody has put the lid on," Polly said. "Tight."

"And no mention on television of either of you,"

Peter said. "I called the station and they said you were on a special assignment—well, that was silly. So I asked to speak with the manager or the news director, someone in *authority*, and the bitch put me on hold for an eternity, then cut me off . . . mortifying! I wrote a letter at once—"

After a nap, Chandler showered, dressed, and listened to Polly sing *Let's Put Out the Lights and Go to Sleep* while she bathed. For a while he stood in the doorway watching her soap her breasts, then blow bubbles with the filament of soap rubbed between her hands. As the afternoon waned they squeezed into the Jaguar and headed for Cambridge.

They approached his house with considerable hesitancy: it seemed normal from the safety of the car, but he needed only to see it to think again of what had happened to him there, and all the fear that had come to him since. Standing on the porch, he peered through the window, said: "What the hell—" and unlocked the door, stormed inside.

The mess had been carefully cleaned up, a new television set installed, furniture arranged neatly, shelves dusted and contents straightened. The smell of furniture polish lingered in each room. The coffee stains were gone. The kitchen was immaculate. Not a mote of plaster dust remained of George Washington, but the pedestal had been polished and a huge, luxuriant Boston fern had replaced the bust.

"This joint has never, repeat, *never,* looked this good before," he said. "But the elves who came by night were stuck when it came to my George Washington . . . Some things can't be replaced." The thought gave him a certain self-satisfaction. They weren't infallible, whoever they were.

Polly smiled. "When they do things like this, they usually do very well. I'd say they've done well by you. Whoever they are . . ."

"You say that as if you know—do you?"

"In my business you get a feel for this kind of thing, the alias program, new identities, stories that are hushed up, murders and kidnapings and you name it . . . there

285

are people who do this kind of thing for a living. I don't know their names . . ."

Chandler gave her a long, sideways look, then figured the hell with it. Maybe he didn't really want to know.

After inspecting the entire house, which had been cleaned and polished top to bottom, they went to the study and began calling hospitals. The fourth call paid off. Sort of. Hugh Brennan was a patient.

"Please ring his room," Chandler said, thanking God.

"I'm sorry, sir, but that's impossible."

"Impossible? Is his telephone broken? Is he too ill?"

"I cannot release any information about his condition, sir."

"All right. Can I visit him?"

"No visitors, I'm sorry."

"Is he dead or alive?" Chandler fumed.

"I'm sorry. I can't give any information on his condition."

"But he is alive . . ."

"I'm sorry—"

"Why the hell did you tell me he was there?"

A pause. Then: "Look," the girl whispered, "I'm a student nurse and I only answered this phone because there was nobody on the station as I came by. I wasn't supposed to tell you, or anybody, that there is a Mr. Brennan here . . . We've all had strict orders and I'm really going to get it if you tell on me, do you understand? So, please . . ."

"Sure," Chandler sighed. "Sure, sure, sure."

He hung up and turned to Polly: "*They* have got Brennan. He's not a patient. He's a prisoner . . . a blackout."

She nodded: "I'm not surprised. They're very thorough once they start."

He called Prosser's home. No answer.

"My God, maybe he's dead. Up in Maine." Chandler had wanted Prosser to be there, had protected himself against the possibility that he could actually be dead: now the fear was no longer lip service.

They walked down to Sage's on Brattle Street in the late afternoon and bought groceries, walked back.

In the kitchen, the daylight faded, Chandler took her soft-skinned face in his hands, held her, searched her eyes. "Stay," he said.

"Yes, of course," she said.

He kissed her, held her close.

"This is scarier than anything so far," he whispered. "It's all so damned sanitized. But we *know* what's been happening—how can they make it like it never happened? What the hell ever happened to doing what's right?"

"Maybe the breed is dead," she said.

In bed that night he held her, stared at the streetlights outside, said: "I've fallen completely in love with you."

"Fallen in *like*," she said. "That's enough for now, Professor."

But he didn't dream of love. He dreamt of Prosser and Brennan and they were dead. And it dawned on him slowly that he, too, was dead.

Friday

He looked at his watch and leaped from the bed, panic-stricken by his dreams and the break in his normal routine: he was late for a ten o'clock lecture. But as he came more fully awake he realized that his world was no longer the same. Polly Bishop was asleep in his bed and no one expected him to make his lecture. He was missing and forgotten, at least for the moment. Were his students still showing up for his lectures, checking to see if he'd turned up alive and well? Or had he been replaced?

"What are you doing?" Polly shaded her eyes against the morning sun which hit the pillow and was probably what had awakened him in the first place. "Why are you staring into space like that?"

"I've got a class at ten. I'm going." He was taking off his pajama top and reaching for one of his ten blue button-down oxford-cloth shirts. "I've got to find out what's going on."

"Good idea." She threw back the covers and stood up, naked. "I'll go with you." She stretched, brushed her hair back over her ears.

"As a reporter?"

"I don't know yet. Maybe."

They made it to the Yard in five minutes. The lecture room was full, some two hundred students, the one meeting a week which was a large group because it served three interlocking but separate courses. The speaker's lectern sat at the bottom of an amphitheater pit and the staging area was empty. It was two minutes until the time the students would begin to get up and leave but there was no more restlessness than was customary: the loud babble of voices, people craning over the canted rows to chat, stragglers loping down the steep aisles. Chandler and Polly sat at the back, far to one side, melting in at the end of a row of nondescript students, none of whom Chandler recognized from his own small group.

At precisely the last moment, the lecturer arrived: the esteemed chairman of the history department, Bert Prosser. He wore a heavy tweed suit in russet brown, a red tie, clumping red brogans, came toward the lectern banging the bowl of a shiny briar into his palm. He laid the pipe down, hooked the tiny microphone around his thin, pipestem neck, and cleared his throat. Before speaking—he had no notes, as was his custom—he jammed his fists down into his jacket pockets to hide the slight palsy Chandler had been noticing the past couple of years. Chandler felt Polly's fingers tighten on his arm.

"I know that my colleague, Professor Chandler," Prosser began, signaling the room to silence by the quality of his voice, "who by the way, will be back among us come Monday—" He raised a pink palm to quiet the audience: "No cheering, no demonstrations, I beg you. I know that he has been treating many of you to his well-known and rather remunerative theories concerning the espionage aspects of the American revolutionary period.

"But since I've gotten the floor away from him for today, I thought I'd subject you to some quavery, old man's thoughts. And I know quite a lot about espionage and heroism. But if I were to live up to the legends which persist about me around this place, I would fall somewhere among J. Edgar Hoover, Allen Dulles, and the Scarlet Pimpernel, who is not a man in a Cadillac cruising Boston's combat zone . . . but, of course, the truth is somewhere else altogether and I intend only to touch on it today . . ." He paused, clicking the stem of the pipe against his front teeth.

"Like Professor Chandler, I believe in great men," he

289

went on, coolly surveying his audience, "and if you don't, it is because you are foolish and cynical, if not actually wicked, children. The Revolution produced several undeniably great men on our side—not simply because they were on the winner's side, but because they made huge commitments, risked everything . . . You may make the comparisons which leap so readily to your minds—Ho Chi Minh, of course, and Mao, of course, no sin in that, though I must say that our revolution was an even prettier example of great men and great principles.

"I'm sure that Professor Chandler has already told you that great men set our revolutionary period apart, full as it was of what one side or the other called treachery and treason . . .

"Now, what can I possibly add to Professor Chandler's thesis about these great men he's always going on about?

"Believe him!"

As Prosser droned on Chandler's mind wandered, but to no great effect. Prosser was wending his way through his often expressed contentions that we were living in an age overrun by moral pygmies . . . moral clones. The fate of the planet had been pretty well left to the technologists and their various contraptions, thereby robbing modern man of an even nodding acquaintance with greatness as it was known in the past. "A machine," Prosser said, "whether a computer or a tiny eavesdropping microphone or a heat-seeking missile, a machine cannot exceed its specific limits . . . and exceeding limits is at the heart of any kind of greatness . . . Greatness is behind us, I'm afraid . . .

"Adlai Stevenson said something to me once, summed it all up . . . 'Our Victorian ancestors felt embarrassed,' he said, 'in the presence of the base. We feel embarrassed in the presence of the noble.' " Prosser sighed and began unhooking his microphone. "I don't expect you to understand what I'm talking about . . . why should you? What could you know of greatness? We are faced with a peculiar proposition which is part of your life . . . them and us, don't you see, there's no longer any difference that matters . . ." Without saying another word, he walked slowly off the stage.

Polly tugged her scarf tight, looked up at Chandler. The sun's brilliance bathed the Yard in a kind of life-giving light but the warmth had gone. She brushed her hair back against the nippy wind, her tight brown gloves against her cheek.

"These are the same steps," he said. "We came out and you stuck your damned microphone in my face and before I knew it I was in it up to my ears . . ." He looked out across the Yard at the scurrying students. "Ah, I'm an older but wiser man today."

"Colin, what the hell was Prosser doing up there? What kind of a lecture was that?"

"Rambling off the top of his head . . . it's his style. Famous man, chatting with the boys and girls. He was just filling in . . ."

"It had the sound of a valedictory of some sort," she said.

"He was in a mood."

"Pretty damned strange—here he is, Colin."

Bert Prosser came through the door, puffing his pipe. He stopped on the top step and smiled down at them. He tamped the bowl of his pipe with Mr. Pickwick. "You two," he said. "I am so glad to see you." He came down the stairs, dapper and pencil-thin in his velvet-collared chesterfield. "My dear," he said to Polly, acknowledging her. "I must say, you've given me a good deal of concern these past few days—"

Polly laughed harshly, shook her head: "I think we're due an explanation, Professor. It's only by damned fool luck we're alive and here at all."

"Aha," Prosser nodded. "She has a point, hasn't she, Colin?"

"Offhand, I'd say she does have a point."

"Where are the Glendower documents?" Polly said. Colin felt her energy and anger.

Prosser glanced at his watch. "Are you free for a late lunch at the Harvard Club? All will be revealed, I promise you. But I do have an appointment first—"

"There's a very involved cover-up going on here," Polly said.

"Patience, my dear," Prosser said. He puffed on the pipe, produced a wintry smile.

"What about Hugh Brennan?" Chandler asked.

"Prosser smiled enigmatically: "Lunch, say one-thirty?" He nodded to them and went on past, out of the Yard, leaving the cold sunshine behind.

Beyond the window of the Harvard Club, on the grassy strip dividing Tremont Street which was just beginning to show a niggling but of green, a man and a woman knelt beside a black briefcase of the old-fashioned kind and withdrew a tiny black cat. The woman stood then, hand on hip, and smiled as the man placed the kitten on the ground. It took a few gingerly steps and looked up for comments. Chandler turned away from the window and scene which reminded him of something that had happened a long time ago and watched Prosser. Though the pinkness had returned to the old man's face there was still the sunken, less-than-healthy look about him that Chandler had noticed that night in Maine. Chandler watched him sip post-prandial sherry which was brown and translucent in the glass: the small brass Pickwick stood by the ashtray where a freshly packed Dunhill reposed, gleaming. A leather tobacco pouch completed the still life. A cold draught played across the windowsill.

"Well," Prosser said quietly. "I call that a civilized luncheon. And, Miss Bishop, I appreciated your patience as to my explanations. You've told me of your excursion to Cape Breton and you both seem to be taking all these little inconveniences with exceptionally good grace . . ."

"Not for much longer," Polly said. "Don't forget that I'm a reporter. All my professional instincts are giving me a run for my money—I've been through the kind of stuff that gets you on the *Today* show—"

"Don't underestimate me," Prosser said, smiling faintly. "Your occupation and instincts have been much in my mind lately. Let me anticipate some of your questions, if you don't mind. Is that all right with you, Colin? In the matter of the Glendower documents, arrangements have been made for them to go to Harvard where they will be buried for another two hundred years with several thousand other documents, collecting dust . . . the portrait will go to you, Colin, since it is a Chandler . . . Good. Perhaps first we should deal with your most recent hairbreadth escape, the affair at Stronghold. Oh, yes, I know all about it, the number of dead, the works . . . you were caught between CIA and KGB raiding parties—no wonder you survived! What a bunch of muttonheads!"

"But what makes you so sure?" Colin blurted. "How could—"

"Please, Colin. It will be easier if I just tell you what's been happening. No matter how queer the truth actually is. You wouldn't ask the right questions, you see. Go back to the night at my place in Maine. Before that imbecile put on his show—my plan was to salt you two away at Stronghold, give you a couple days of rest while I checked on the Glendower documents, then have Kendrick drop back in on you and bring you back. Simple, a logical plan, though I regret my little falsehood about the oilskin package of newspapers. But you wouldn't have understood my keeping them while my home was under siege from a band of homicidal maniacs—"

"I still don't," Chandler said. "You *were* under siege and you could have been killed and the documents could have been taken."

"So it would seem, Colin, but appearances are not always quite what they seem. You see, I knew who was laying siege to the house and I had no reason to fear him . . . quite the contrary, in fact. He had every reason in the world to be afraid of me. I was his boss." Prosser, enjoying the moment, lit his pipe with a wooden match, watching his two guests past the billowing smoke.

"But I thought he was one of the men following us," Polly said, "one of the bad guys—"

"Quite so, my dear. He was just that, one of the bad

guys, the one so often seen in the checkered porkpie hat. A professional killer by trade—"

"How the hell were you his boss, then?" Chandler said. He gave his head a violent shake.

"He was employed on this matter by a KGB agent, *me* . . . I have been for many years." He puffed calmly in the stillness. The wind sighed outside. "That sounds a good deal more sinister than it actually is, but I'll come to that. I was running those two cretins, the two who visited you at your home and really set this thing in motion. They overstepped the boundaries of their assignment from the beginning, by killing the Davis boy and Nat Underhill. There's an appalling decline in the quality of these fellows. Then they went after you in that uncouth manner and you gave them a good what-for . . . and they were having no luck retrieving the elusive documents, which made it all the more ridiculous. And they had completely lost you, remember. So there we were, no documents and no Professor Chandler, and you were the only lead we had." Prosser leaned forward and patted Chandler's arm: "Buck up, old fellow. You're alive and well and you'd never have found your lovely new friend if it hadn't been for Oz and Thorny, the two ruffians. Best to look on the bright side, take my word. You, too, miss. Bright side takes you further every time.

"Then these two oafs interview Professor Brennan and he slaughters one of them outright . . . and I say more power to him. Send up a cheer for Brennan—"

"You're totally crazy," Polly said matter-of-factly.

"Oh, there's much more to come," Prosser said, the soul of gentle amiability. "You see, at the same time the two KGB hirelings are looking for you and the document, as well as killing everybody they come across . . . the CIA has gotten into it. That's right, the CIA. But, as is customary, The Company hasn't the least notion what they're doing—all they know is there's some KGB action in the Boston sector. So they send a couple of their men up from Washington—"

"And they are Fennerty and McGonigle!" Polly said.

"Very good, Fennerty and McGonigle, a couple of

294

men who should never be sent into the field at all, perhaps, but good men. And, after all, this Boston thing is small . . . just a maybe. They know nothing about any documents, no names, all they have is the identity of the two KGB men. So they begin to follow them, and they discover that for some reason the KGB men are killing people and are also taking long hungry looks at Professor Colin Chandler. So they become interested in Colin Chandler, too. You know how that went—"

"But how do you know so much?" Chandler's brain was working, slowly. He heard Prosser's story but he wasn't at all sure he was making sense of it. "How do you know all this CIA stuff?"

"Because I was running Fennerty and McGonigle, too. I am a company man, as well. I thought I'd made that obvious. That's why this entire thing got started—because I could see both sides of the table." He tamped the ash, got another flurry of good smoke going. "I am paid by special arrangement dating back a long time with both parties. A double agent, you see, paid by the case, as it were. CANTAB to the KGB, CRUSTACEAN to the CIA . . . And by reporting to the CIA that there was a certain amount of KGB action here I could double my income for the duration—simple greed, I am afraid. But how else could I have the Rolls, the house, the servants?

"Obviously I had no idea how complex and violent things would become, that goes without saying. My sin is greed, not sadism. I saw it as a very limited action, relieve the college boy of his little package, run the rats around the cage in a fruitless pursuit for a few days, take my money . . . that's why I asked for Fennerty and McGonigle, hardly gung-ho types, ready to get out of the business altogether . . . but then it got so much more difficult! The boy didn't have the package, Underhill didn't have the package, and your name got into it, Colin. It was all out of control before I knew what was happening. I even grew confused, myself knowing so much . . . too much, trying to keep it all straight. Which brings us back to that night in Maine . . ."

"What happened after we left?" Polly asked.

"I killed the man in the porkpie hat. Executed him. I told Moscow it was coming and it simply had to be done. The man had come all unhinged . . ."

"All right," Chandler said, tightening his grip on the facts. "This may all be as you say. But if you were stashing us away at Stronghold for safekeeping, why did we get invaded by everybody and his brother that night?"

"The problem was—is—that I am quite plainly past it, Colin. Ready to pack it in, go die in a warm clime, don't you see? I've become so predictable, it pains me to acknowledge the fact but there it is, sitting in the corner staring at me . . . Two gentlemen, one at the top of the CIA, the other his opposite number in Moscow, took one look at the situation and reached the same conclusion—namely, Stronghold. An old dog keeps going back to the old tricks, the things he knows best. And they were right . . . thus, rehearsal for World War III goes off on my little island . . ." His face was sagging in on itself, growing plaintive, morose. "And all those young men, muttonheads though they were, had to die . . . It's been badly fouled up from the start. I take the blame, I could have kept it from happening, from going so far . . ." He pulled on the dead pipe, looked at it with an air of mournful distaste.

The couple on the grass snatched up the kitten, dropped it into the briefcase. Polly said: "That means they live in an apartment that doesn't allow animals. They have to sneak the kitten in and out. I used to live in such a place and that's what I did. Do you mean to say that you've been working both sides of the street for, what, thirty years? That's a long, long time not to get caught, Professor."

"My only advantage has been the size of my employers, so huge that they think very slowly . . . they have no idea we're having this discussion—they don't know what the hell's going on . . . but time," Prosser mused, "time is running out . . . what is it they say? The Swiss measure it, the French hoard it, the Italians squander it, the Americans say it's money, the Indians say it doesn't exist . . . I say Time is a crook. I knew a man who used to say that. He died . . . Sure, it's a long time, Miss Bishop, but I don't flatter myself on being a superspy, not by any means. I've become one of the cowardly technicians I spoke about in my lecture this morning, a greedy functionary with no eye for morality, or causes, or ideals. I've done all this for the money because I saw right after the war how it was going, one side becoming so much like the other . . . it made no difference which master you served, don't you see?

"And, of course, they may have been onto me for a long time, it's possible that they know I'm a double agent and don't really care. Maybe they look at it as my pension . . . Damnation, we know that the other side knows, we're just like button salesmen and ribbon clerks, all in the same line of work . . . we know our business, that's it. It is now and always has been, at least in my day, nothing but a game." He paused, sighed under the weight of memory. "No, I take that back, it was no game when they parachuted me into Greece and Yugoslavia during the war, there seemed to be principles involved then . . . nothing to do with democracy, of course, but I was anti-Nazi and so were the partisans, communists to a man. But that was a long time ago and didn't quite turn out as we'd planned, anyway. But since then, all the same, business as usual . . . And what would be the point of putting me in prison? Or killing me? Absolutely none . . . I've been a very useful conduit, at times. Almost a diplomatic adjunct. And if any harm befell me, well then, there would be a rash of reprisals. Pointless. So I've gone about my business, useful to both sides. That's why I am absolutely safe, always have been. Either they don't know what I am or don't care. I'm a convenience they can afford."

"But you're telling me," Polly said. "What's to keep people from listening to me tell the story . . ."

"Now, now, your heart isn't in that, my dear. You are a worldly woman. You know the kind of pursuers, discreet and not so discreet, your government can bring to bear when they are well and truly angered or humiliated. Or both. And what would you have accomplished? Frankly, I can't think of a thing . . . Détente may be given a momentary hiccup, the public would shrug because they assume *anything* since Watergate, young Davis and Underhill would still be dead and in any case the men who killed them are also dead." He smiled sympathetically: "It's a case of no story, Miss Bishop. No one would care, even if they believed you, and I could issue a very believable statement about my service to my country and some rather important people in the government would leap in to back me up . . ."

"But how the hell do you live with yourself?"

"Colin, you haven't been listening. I'm just a man, not one of your Great Men, and so are the men I've worked with and served. You're trying to make us fit your classical standard and, sadly, ours is not a classical age. Give it up, Colin. Stick to history, where you belong, where you are at home."

"I have a question," Polly said: she had grown good-humored, as if accepting what he'd said about the realities of the situation. "Once you had the Glendower documents, why didn't you avoid the whole fracas by giving them to the KGB men? That wouldn't have compromised you in the least—you'd still have been paid by both sides, your first commitment in this case was to the KGB . . . Why did you make it so difficult for yourself and everyone else?"

Prosser applied another kitchen match to his pipe and leaned back. The sun was dipping, throwing long shadows across the Back Bay. Traffic moved sluggishly on Commonwealth. Chandler had a headache.

"My first commitment," Prosser said slowly, brushing a knuckle along his white moustache. "My commitment underwent something of a change that night in Maine, a cleansing you call it, when I saw what the documents, as we thought of them, actually were . . . not some tedious figures about units of production or troop allocations or how amenable a congressman might be to selling his vote. No, we were dealing with something else here, the kind of thing I'd begun to forget.

"You will appreciate this, Colin. I was thinking of history and of the great men who had made it, history —the only record of the course man has taken, all we really have, the real legacy. How have men behaved before us? And as I studied the documents even cursorily I made certain judgments about them . . . and against these judgments I balanced the corruption and venality of my masters, the purpose to which these pygmies who employ me would put the documents . . . I saw them being twisted and reshaped and used by men who could not begin to imagine what George Washington and his men needed in their bosoms to survive that winter, and not only to survive but to prevail in the end." He straightened up abruptly and rapped on the table: "By jove, a man has his limits! And I have reached mine—I never minded about tampering with the present age of the pygmy, but to stick our poker and thongs back into the age of the giants, rearrange things from afar? Damnation, that is going too far . . . my blood was up, I tell you! Let the KGB have this information for use in some cheap joke? Never! I'd sooner die . . . and, children, I hadn't come across anything worth dying for in such a long time . . ."

"What was your final decision about the Washington letter?" Chandler asked.

"First, the Davis lad was delirious—he was living in a charnel house, his friends were dying, there was virtually no food, they'd damn near run out of hope. Who knows what he actually may have heard as he stood there half-frozen, frightened out of his wits? We'll never know. And what did he actually see? A large broad-beamed man in a cloak signing a paper . . . and then a gunfight that left him pissing in his pants. That's what this undeniably courageous lad is dealing with, under the severest kind of stress. And, second, we know of all the shoddy plots afoot at the time to undermine Washington's stature—good Lord, the man was like a God to much of the populace, they'd have gone through what they did for no one else . . . so there were rumors, innuendos, accusations and a great many forged documents purporting to show the godawful *real* George Washington . . ."

Prosser shrugged: "It's a fake. George Washington never signed that piece of paper . . . Nat Underhill should have known better, then none of this would have happened. But he wanted it to be true . . . capstone to his career. I understand, I understand . . ."

The telephone rang in Chandler's study late that evening. Polly had just put on her sheepskin coat for the drive home. The chill of winter was back in the air. They had gone over Prosser's remarks in a state of dulled amazement, not knowing whether to laugh or cry at the peculiarly meaningless absurdity of the entire business. And the telephone cut through their good-night kiss.

"Colin, for chrissakes, what's happening? I thought I was a poor dead son of a bitch there for awhile . . . then I'm not dead but I'm in some fuckin' quarantine with no goddamned fingernails and a helluva cold . . . ever try to get Kleenex out of a box with bandages all over your hands? Well, don't . . ."

"Hugh," Chandler cried.

"Old man Prosser was just in to see me—Prosser himself! Said he was bringing the message from you that all was well, and that I was getting sprung tomorrow . . . fuckin' heart attack I thought I had, but you don't know about that, do you? Anyway it was a pulled muscle . . ."

"Tomorrow?"

"You owe me a ride, too, you bastard . . ."

Saturday

Chandler's telephone rang at seven o'clock Saturday morning. He came awake as if he'd been doused with ice water. Where the hell was Polly? He didn't like sleeping alone anymore; it had taken him hours to drift off after she'd left. He'd wanted her to stay with him, brew another pot of coffee in his marvelously renewed house, sit at his kitchen table and talk about what had happened to them, but she had insisted, had said that she had a home, too, that she enjoyed being there with Ezzard, had missed it. And he had the good sense to let her go. But now the telephone was ringing and he reached for it with a burst of hope.

It was Polly and he sank back on the pillows, smiling like a schoolboy.

"Colin, I woke up with the most awful thought," she said, sounding dry and still half asleep. "I knew we'd forgotten something . . . Nora Thompson!"

"Nora Thompson," he repeated. "My God, she's still down at the Parker House, poor thing. She must think the earth opened up and swallowed us—"

"Well, we've got to take care of her, do something—"

"She has had a nice vacation, though. Expenses paid, if you recall . . ."

"Pick me up in an hour. I've got to spend at least forty-five minutes in a steamy tub. I've never been so stiff in my entire life. It's just hitting me now."

"Me too. See you in an hour."

The morning was bright, clean, cold, with a sweet-smelling ground fog hanging over the Cambridge Common as he drove past. Polly was waiting at the curbside, doing deep breathing. She wore a navy peacoat, gray slacks, penny loafers. She kissed him. Her mouth was cold and fresh.

Over breakfast an astonished Nora Thompson heard

301

a carefully edited version of their story, accepted their assurances that it was over. That somehow the world had been made safe for Nora Thompson to go home again.

"You know," she said, "I've known for several days what the package contained—"

"You have! How?" Colin felt his eyes widening.

"A professor at Oxford returned my call, he'd been on one of poor Mr. Underhill's lists, and he said a Belgian who'd been at dinner with Mr. Underhill that last night in Bucharest told him about the document." She nodded, agreeing with herself, sipping her coffee. "That's right, can you believe it? Told me all about George Washington's signature and his being an English spy . . . I asked him what he thought about it, did it seem like the truth. 'I've no doubt your Mr. Underhill had a document,' he said, all huffy and pompous, 'but the document's rubbish! Poppycock! Should have known better, I'd say.' His exact words."

Polly glanced at Chandler, said: "That seems to be the general opinion. Professor Prosser, Colin's departmental chairman, said much the same thing, didn't he Colin?"

"Most certainly. Said it was all nonsense."

"Then these people have died for nothing," Nora Thompson said wistfully.

In the afternoon they collected Hugh at the hospital. He looked a trifle peaked, a state he attributed to the difficulty involved in trying to eat with large, mitten-like bandages on your hands. Otherwise, he was in good spirits, if rather confused as to what precisely had been going on.

Prosser told me I'd killed one of the bastards. That made me feel much better about the whole thing. Said there would obviously be no charges . . . and get this, he said there was some speculation that Pliers and his little wheezer of a pal were Russian agents! Well, Christ, what can you say to that? Quite a guy, Prosser . . . damn good thing you contacted him and you are very welcome for the suggestion. Now, Miss

302

Bishop—Polly, if I may—tell me how you've been fighting off this fellow these past days . . . or is it weeks? Jesus, I don't know which end is up, to be perfectly frank—"

"Hugh," Colin said as the car neared the Yard on Massachusetts Avenue.

"Yes, my lad."

"Hugh, have we got a story for you."

"You don't say . . ."

Together the three of them strolled the jumble of streets converging on Harvard Square, braced by the sunshine and the cold. The world had a brittle, newly minted air about it. Polly and Colin took turns with the telling, left out nothing. They finished at the foot of the Widener Library steps.

"So now I'm supposed to believe all this," Hugh said. The color had returned to his face and already it seemed to be filling out.

"Could we make it up?" Polly said.

"You have a point there," Hugh said. "Colin?"

"So help me God."

"It's just a game then, that's what you're telling me —what Prosser told you." He considered the contention, shrugged. "Well, why not? It makes more sense than believing that there's some big point to all the bullshitting . . . I mean, if Prosser's right, it explains a lot. Jokes—we're living in a world of bad jokes. It makes too damned much sense . . ."

"Tough on the people who die, though," Polly said. She put her arm through Colin's, then through Hugh's, walking between them.

"Hell, tough on the people who just get their fingernails pulled out."

"The rotten part," Chandler said, "is that they didn't even know it was a game."

"What about Washington, though?" Hugh asked. "The kid back there at Valley Forge . . . he said he *saw* him—"

"I choose," Colin said, "to believe that he was mistaken."

* * *

Polly decided that it would be best for Hugh to room with Chandler until his hands became somewhat more manageable. It wouldn't do, she argued, to have you survive the torture of KGB thugs only to starve to death in a kitchen full of food. Consequently they stopped at Hugh's, packed the essentials, and carted them over to Colin's house where there was an extra bedroom prepared for the guest.

They sent out for pizza and Chandler broke out a bottle of champagne. There were several toasts: to survival, to the remarkable Harvard professors, to Bert Prosser and his Rolls-Royce . . .

"And to Polly Bishop," Colin said, lifting his glass, pausing.

"Yes, man," Hugh cried, "get on with it!"

"Whom I love with all my heart!"

Polly gave it a good try but one tear escaped, hung beneath her long dark lash. Colin kissed it away.

"Hark," Hugh said. "Did I hear a sound at the door? Could it be the pizza man?" He lumbered into the hallway. Polly sniffled. Colin Chandler looked down at her fondly, feeling as if it had all somehow become a fairy tale.

"What the hell is this?" Hugh was making peculiar sounds in the hallway. Then the door slammed and presently he reappeared pushing a large cardboard packing box along the floor with his foot. "No pizza . . . just this and a car making off down the street. Well, don't just stand there—I'm in no condition to open boxes . . ."

"There's no name on it," Polly said, kneeling.

"I'll open it," Colin said. "Is it ticking?"

He pulled the packing tape off and folded back the flaps. Slowly he worked his fingers into the excelsior packing material, took hold of something smooth and cold, pulled it slowly up out of the box until it was in plain view—creamy white, noble, sightless, perfect. Dumbstruck, they could do nothing but stare.

Houdon's bust of Washington.

Epilogue

Cambridge

Odgen was holding Prosser's velvet-collared black chesterfield when the master came down the steps. He was wearing dinner clothes, bound for a formal dinner at a friend's club. It was in fact an Old Boys' dinner, an annual gathering of men who had attended the same preparatory school. Prosser rather enjoyed the chance to see so many men who had turned out to have surprisingly little in common but their adolescence. Usually it made him feel rather good about himself, a state of mind he wasn't experiencing much lately.

"I'll be driving myself tonight, Ogden," he said, slipping his arms into the narrow sleeves.

"I know, sir. Old Boys' night." Ogden nodded gravely.

"Is there something wrong with the Rolls, Ogden?"

"On the contrary, sir."

"Good, then. I saw you working away on it so diligently this afternoon, I thought there might be a problem." Ogden had been with him for nearly thirty years, ever since he'd been able to afford a good butler *cum* valet *cum* batman.

"I wasn't aware I'd been observed, sir. I was merely tuning it up a bit, making sure it was ready, since you'd be taking it out yourself this evening. Here, now, let me give the collar a quick brush."

Mrs. Grasse appeared at the end of the hall, watching.

"Ah, Mrs. Grasse, a parting thought—would you be

307

so kind as to leave me a plate of biscuits and a thermos of cocoa before you retire? The digestive biscuits?"

"Yes, Professor. I'll remember. It's Old Boys' night . . . you're a creature of habit, you are, Professor."

"Yes, well, that's as may be." He pulled on his gloves, tugged his white silk scarf into place, made sure the fly front of the coat was flat. "Well, then, good-night. Have a pleasant evening. Go to the pictures . . . something."

"A quiet evening of television," Ogden said. "Good-bye, Professor."

The moment the door closed behind the departing professor, Ogden turned and made a shooting motion at the blocky figure of Mrs. Grasse. "Hurry," he said impatiently. "The cellar stairway . . . no, no, I'll close the door after me." Ten seconds after Prosser left, the hall was empty, the door at the end which led to the cellar closed tight.

Once again, taking precautions paid off.

When, at the turning of the key in the ignition, the Rolls-Royce exploded with a consumptive roar, all the windows across the front of the house exploded inwards. The windows above and flanking the front door filled the hallway with needles of broken glass. The front of the garage disappeared as well.

Florida

The afternoon sky covered the visible world like the inside of a perfect robin's-egg blue bowl, a sort of metaphysical bell jar under which all was perpetually well. Gentle breezes blew in from the outfield, carried the shouts of the ballplayers as the sleepy game dawdled into the sixth inning. The Pirates had built a six-to-three lead over the White Sox but had just sent an untested rookie to the mound.

"It could be a good game yet," Maxim Petrov said. He was wearing a yellow waterproof windbreaker he'd picked up in Havana. The sun baked his face. "The pitcher is a mere boy . . . the White Sox just might hit him . . ." He bit off a huge piece of mustard-drenched hot dog and licked the remnants from his mouth.

"Baseball is for the birds," his friend said, taking a great swallow of cold beer. He handed the oversize cup to Petrov who washed down the rest of his hot dog. He picked up another hot dog.

"Arden, what you lack is the subtlety to appreciate the infinite complications. To you it is boring . . . to me it is a hotbed of conflict . . . damn! I love it! Do you think I should defect?"

Arden Sanger winced: "Don't say that, not even in jest."

"All right. But I love baseball." A White Sox batter doubled down the right field line. Several hundred spectators clapped perfunctorily. They were, for the most part, old, or infirm, or both.

"And don't lecture me about subtlety," Sanger said grumpily. "Not after unleashing those two imbeciles in Boston . . ."

"But I did not unleash them, as you perfectly well know. It was such a simple job—a joke, as I've told you—and we sent Prosser some low-grade merchandise. I can't accept responsibility for every mistake . . ." He frowned at the thought: "If I did, I'd have no time for anything else. I thought those two men were perfect for such an elementary task . . . I was wrong."

"You can say that again." Sanger finished the beer.

"You must admit it would have been embarrassing . . . the Father of your country nothing but a traitor . . ." He chuckled ruefully.

Sanger grunted.

"You've finished the beer," Petrov said. "I still have half a hot dog . . ."

Sanger motioned for another beer.

"Following your logic," Petrov said as another White Sox batter smashed a double, this one to left, making the score six to four, "I should say that you wiped out an entire landing party and a very costly fishing trawler—" He took the beer. Sanger paid.

"Fishing trawler," Sanger said sourly. "Is it my fault if your boys are no damn good in a shooting match? We lost some, too, you know."

"Some, yes. We lost every man." He shook his head, licked foam from the corners of his mouth. "What a mess . . ." He sipped more beer. "You know that you owe us something . . . we discussed that. We are agreed, is that correct?"

"Grudgingly. But, yes, agreed. Tit for tat."

"And what is it that you're going to give us?"

"It's already done." Sanger stared straight ahead at the game.

"Indeed?"

"The old man," Sanger said. "To show our good faith."

"I hadn't thought of that. The old man . . . We're both better off."

A White Sox batter took two quick strikes. It appeared for the moment that the kid pitcher was out of trouble. The batter hit a home run on the next pitch.

"What did I tell you?" Petrov said, wishing he weren't going back to Moscow at midnight. "The score is tied."